City of Dragons

*

Also by Kelli Stanley

*

Nox Dormienda

City of Dragons

KELLI STANLEY

Minotaur Books
A Thomas Dunne Book
New York

A THOMAS DUNNE BOOK FOR MINOTAUR BOOKS.
An imprint of St. Martin's Publishing Group.

CITY OF DRAGONS. Copyright © 2010 by Kelli Stanley. All rights reserved. Printed in the United States of America. For information, address St. Martin's Press, 175 Fifth Avenue, New York, N.Y. 10010

www.thomasdunnebooks.com
www.minotaurbooks.com
Design by Kathryn Parise

The Library of Congress has cataloged the hardcover edition as follows:

Stanley, Kelli.
    City of dragons / Kelli Stanley.—1st ed.
       p. cm.
    "A Thomas Dunne Book."
    ISBN 978-0-312-60360-1
    1. Women private investigators—California—Fiction. 2. San Francisco (Calif.)—History—20th century—Fiction. 3. Chinatown (San Francisco, Calif.)—Fiction. I. Title.
PS3619.T3657C58 2010
813'.6—dc22

2009039817

ISBN 978-0-312-66879-2 (trade paperback)

First Minotaur Books Paperback Edition: September 2011

10 9 8 7 6 5 4 3 2 1

For Mom, Dad, and Tana—
and the friends I made and the family I found
at Bouchercon 2007 (Anchorage)

Acknowledgments

I took a gentle ribbing for the lengthy acknowledgments in my first book, and so will try to be less loquacious, if not exactly terse . . . I have a lot of people to thank!

First, heartfelt gratitude to my editor, the wise and wonderful Marcia Markland, at Thomas Dunne. She is my dream editor, a soul mate, a tireless advocate, and a great teacher. My protagonist, Miranda, and I are blessed to have such a home and such a friend.

Countless thanks to my publisher and terrific publishing team: Andrew Martin of Minotaur Books, for his vision and support; the brilliant and charming Sarah Melnyk, my publicist; Courtney Fischer, stellar marketing maven; the much-missed and indefatigable Diana Szu, Marcia's former assistant, and the equally invaluable Kat Brzozowski. Special thanks to David Rotstein, Senior Art Director and cover design genius, who rendered Miranda's world so beautifully and evocatively. Great thanks to Kathryn Parise, whose beautiful and evocative interior design is a book lover's dream. And with thanks to Elizabeth Curione, my production editor, who successfully and skillfully midwifed the finished book through a short delivery time.

Thanks, too, to Sally Richardson, Thomas Dunne, and Hector DeJean, and all the amazing people at St. Martin's, who go to the Flatiron Building every day and dedicate themselves to the tough and exhausting business of publishing. You are all heroes.

And that brings me to another hero in my life . . . my amazing, supportive, and fantastic agent, Kimberley Cameron, without whom none of this would be possible. She is a shining light in the lives of her clients and all who know her, and I am blessed to have her represent my work. She is the epitome of all good things, and I can't thank her enough. Kimberley, *je t'adore!*

Big thanks, too, to my foreign rights agent, Whitney Lee, Dutch-language agent, Walter Soethoudt, French-language agent, Lora Fountain, and my film agents, Mary Alice Kier and Anna Cottle of Cine/Lit Representation. I count myself as incredibly lucky to work with you all!

My journey has been filled with helping hands. From the International Thriller Writers to Mystery Writers of America to Sisters in Crime and the Private Eye Writers of America and Mystery Readers International, the friends, colleagues, readers, bloggers, librarians, and fans of the crime fiction community have been tremendously and incredibly supportive. The best part about being a writer is the company you keep!

Special thanks to friends Rebecca Cantrell, Ken Bruen, Laura Benedict, Jordan Dane, Bill Cameron, Rhodi Hawk, Jennie Bentley (who also kindly allowed me to use her real name for one of my characters), Sophie Littlefield, CJ Lyons, Alexandra Sokoloff, Heather Graham, Margery Flax, Andrew Peterson, Julie Kramer and Robert Gregory Browne. And a huge thank-you to Kay Thomas, who helped come up with the title.

Profound thank-yous to the extraordinarily generous colleagues who took the time—the scarcest commodity in a writer's life—to read and blurb *City of Dragons*. The list includes Louise Ure, Lee Child, Linda Fairstein, Robert B. Parker, Tasha Alexander, Cornelia Read, George Pelecanos, Michael Koryta, and Otto Penzler.

Great thanks to the Latinist and all-around wonderful Wilda Williams, the amazing Janet Rudolph of *Mystery Readers International*, fabulous media gurus and stalwart supporters Jon and Ruth Jordan of *Crimespree*, Kate and Brian Skupin of *Mystery Scene*, and George Easter of *Deadly Pleasures*, and the many reviewers, readers, and bloggers who dedicate enormous amounts of time and energy to talking about books.

Immeasurable gratitude to the backbone of the industry, the libraries and bookstores. Thank you for welcoming me into your world, for recommending my books to your readers and buyers, and for making it possible for me to be a writer! Special thanks to Ed, Pam, Jen, and all the fabulous staff at M is for Mystery (my home away from home); Diane and the fantastic San Francisco Mystery Book Store, for hosting my first-ever launch; Fran, J.B., and Janine at my special "hometown" store, the Seattle Mystery Bookshop; all the terrific folks at Murder by the Book in Portland, Oregon; the indefatigably welcoming and wonderful Linda and Bobby at The Mystery Bookstore in Los Angeles; Alan and the great crew at Mysteries to Die For; and the brilliant, wise, and supportive Barbara Peters at Poisoned Pen in Phoenix.

Finally, thank you to the ultimate heroes in my life, my family. They put up with a great deal—and believed in me when I didn't. From Tana, who keeps me steering straight ahead and makes everything good; to my dad, who reminded me that Steinbeck was published during the Great Depression; to my mom, who is a one-woman book-pubbing dynamo and just the best person in the world—they've never faltered in their faith . . . and in so doing, kept mine alive. This book—and all my books—are because of you.

Part One

The Party

One

Miranda didn't hear the sound he made when his face hit the sidewalk. The firecrackers were too loud, punctuating the blaring Sousa band up Stockton. Red string snapped and danced from a corner of a chop suey house on Grant, puffs of gray smoke drifting over the crowd. No cry for help, no whimper.

Chinese New Year and the Rice Bowl Party, one big carnival, the City that Knows How to Have a Good Time choking Grant and Sacramento. Bush Street blocked, along with her way home to the apartment. Everybody not in an iron lung was drifting to Chinatown, some for the charity, most for the sideshow.

Help the Chinese fight Japan—put a dollar in the Rice Bowl, feed starving, war-torn China. Buy me a drink, sister, it's Chinese New Year. Don't remember who they're fighting, sister, they all look alike to me.

Somewhere above her a window opened, and a scratchy recording of "I Can't Give You Anything but Love" fought its way out. Miranda knelt down next to the boy.

"You OK, kid?"

She guessed eighteen or nineteen, from the cheap but flashy clothes and the way his body had fallen, trying to protect itself. No response. She dropped her cigarette, and with effort turned him over, the feet around her finally making some room.

She bent closer. Couldn't hear a goddamn thing except Billie Holiday.

"Kid—kid, can you hear me?"

Nose was broken. So was his jaw. Missing teeth, both eyes black. What looked like burn marks on his cheek.

She loosened and unknotted the flimsy green tie around his neck. Eyelids fluttering, color gone, face empty of everything except memory. Unbuttoned the shiny brown jacket, saw the hole in his chest.

Miranda shouted over the music: "We need a doctor! Anybody a doctor? Anybody?"

The feet around her moved back a little, ripple of noise running through the crowd, music bright, singing about love. Always about love.

Couldn't risk looking up. His eyes were open now, brown clutching hers.

Love and happiness. Fucking happiness.

She took a deep breath and yelled, voice straining.

"Doctor! Get a goddamn doctor!"

The cement was still damp with slop from the restaurants and tenements, and his fingers clawed it, looking for an answer.

The crowd shivered again, surged forward. His eyes asked the question and hers lied back.

"Who did this? Can you understand me? Who—"

He turned his head toward the direction he'd been thrown from. Last effort.

Then the bubble. Then the gurgle. Then the cop.

"Move, you bastards. Move!"

His boots stood next to her, staring dumbly at the boy.

"He drunk?"

The voice faded, happiness run out. The record made a clacking sound, and the needle hit the label over and over. *Clack. Clack clack.*

She stood up, tired.

"He's dead."

The record started up again.

I can't give you anything but love, baby . . .

The cop at the Hall of Justice was the hard type, but that was the new style for 1940. One too many George Raft and Jimmy Cagney movies, and they all wore their hair short and their mouths even shorter. No wink and a smile with this one. Burn at the stake, every time.

Miranda inhaled deeply on the Chesterfield and crossed her legs. It distracted him for a few seconds. She watched and counted the clock ticks as he picked up her lighter, her compact, her *Chadwick's Street Guide*, her hat, her comb, her lipstick, her keys, her address book, her cigarette case, her notepad, her pocketbook, and a few gum wrappers and matchbooks, and looked at them as though they might be hiding a .38.

"So you say you don't know this—Eddie Takahashi?"

"I said so."

He sat back in the chair. "Just because you got a license that makes it all legal . . . you're still nothing more than the girls down on Turk. I looked you up."

Her dress hitched a little higher when she leaned over his desk to rub out the cigarette in the scarred wood. His eyes fell.

"Congratulations. You can read."

Sour smile, spit at the corners. Pulled his eyes back up while he rocked on his feet, the chair squeaking in rhythm.

"I can read all right. It's some record. Spain with the Reds. Came back and worked for Dianne Laroche as an escort. Then hooked up with Charlie Burnett on divorce cases . . ." He paused, savoring it, looking her up and down. "He was never one for fresh bait. Then Burnett gets bumped off, they claim you figure out who, and you get a license and take over his business and land some cushy World's Fair job on Treasure Island, guarding Sally Rand. Takes a whore to know a whore, I guess. So . . . who was the dead Jap—a client?"

Miranda dropped her eyes from the clock on the wall to the shiny, stubbled face of Star number 598. She stared at him until he flinched, his chair shrieking one last time.

"Get on with your job or I call my attorney."

His hands clenched around the fountain pen, red and pulpy. "Your attorney. He your new pimp?"

The section gate swung open, banging against the partition. Phil stood, twirling his hat, looking at Miranda. Star number 598 flushed purple, jumped up from the desk.

"If you want to take over, Lieutenant . . ." The words trailed off in a mumble while he slid out into the hall.

Phil took off his hat, lines on his face deeper than she remembered. More gray on his chin. More paunch in his belly. Goddamn it. She wasn't up to Phil, not today. Better to deal with the Puritan.

"You do something to Collins?"

She reached across the desk and took another Chesterfield out of the gold case, not speaking until she snapped it shut and returned it to its pile.

"Objects to me on principle."

Phil's eyes followed her hand when she picked up the YELLOW CAB matchbook. After two attempts, she struck one on the desk and lit the stick, hand shaking slightly. Leaned back in the hard wooden chair and met his eyes.

"Been awhile, Miranda. You look good. It's been—how long? Since the Incubator Babies racket last year? They must be treating you right, all your Fair friends."

She shrugged. "Pays the bills. And I'm keeping busy in the off-season."

"Still with divorce cases, I hear. Well, good for you. Kept Burnett in clover." He cleared this throat, looked down at his large hands, unexpectedly helpless, folded on the desk.

"So one more year . . . guess one bankrupt World's Fair's not enough. Maybe '40'll be more magic than '39, who knows. You going back to work in May?"

She took a deep drag on the Chesterfield and blew a smoke ring. Gave him half a smile.

"Same troubles, same fair—shorter season. Bigger Gayway this year, though, more girl shows, more work for me. So yeah, I'm hitching my tent to Treasure Island again."

He cleared his throat again, studied the floor at her feet. Pressed his hands tight on the desk, fingers splayed.

"I'll be retiring soon. Chief Quinn's going home in a few days . . . the mayor's appointing Dullea. You probably heard about it. There'll be changes—always are. I'm not always going to be around to watch out for you. I'd like to see you get settled."

Miranda stared at the lipstick stain on her cigarette. A woman two rows over was sobbing into a handkerchief.

"If by 'settled' you mean married and not working, sorry, Phil. I appreciate the doting uncle routine, but I can take care of myself."

Color spread across his face, eyes dropping to her purse contents. Same story, new year. Same Phil. She readjusted herself in the hard wooden chair.

"Let's get on with it."

Hurt eyes, sad eyes, baggy, bloodshot, old. He took a piece of paper from the drawer, dipped the fountain pen.

"Name?"

"Don't you have all that down? I've been sitting with Officer League of Decency for half an—"

"I'm the lieutenant. You're the witness. Let's keep it formal."

She blew another smoke ring over her shoulder, watched it sail over the head of a uniform a few desks down.

"Miranda Corbie."

"Hair?"

"Auburn. Or red. Depends on the henna."

"Answer the questions. Eyes?"

"Brown."

He looked up. "I thought they were . . . yes. Hazel."

She tapped some ash on the cheap metal ashtray. "They're brown to me."

"Height?"

"Five feet six inches. Without heels."

"Weight?"

"130, stripped."

"Age?"

"Same as last year, except a year older. Thirty-three."

"Address?"

"640 Mason Street, apartment number 405. No phone."

He fished around the pile on the desk and pulled out a battered card. "Monadnock Building? With the Pinkertons?"

"Closet on the same floor. They sometimes throw me the small fry in return for Sally Rand tickets."

"Good for you. For getting your own office, and moving out of Burnett's."

She shrugged again. "It was never much. Neither was Burnett."

He busied himself with writing. "Phone at the office is EXbrook—"

"—3333. Easy for clients to remember. I was lucky."

The eyes came back to her. Like kids at a candy shop.

"They got your numbers memorized, Miri—at least their husbands do."

She stubbed out the cigarette in the same spot on the desk and dropped it in the tray.

"Like I said, I'm lucky. C'mon, Phil, let me go home. It'll be hell getting through—they're expecting a hundred thousand tonight."

He leaned back, scratched his neck. "So what happened?"

"I was on my way home from here. Had to ID a phony check pusher, who also happens to be a bigamist."

He frowned. "You see Riordan?"

"Unfortunately. Tried to lick my face like a dog. I took a shortcut through Chinatown, forgetting about Rice Bowl, and got stuck on Sacramento between Grant and Waverly. About five o'clock, an hour before the street carnival, but still goddamn hard for anybody trying to get anywhere else. I saw this kid facedown on the street. Thought he was drunk, flipped him over, saw the exit wound, yelled for a doctor, and The Law shoved his way through with a nightstick. That's it."

"Eddie Takahashi. Sure you don't know him?"

She shook her head. "Never seen him before. Got a record?"

His voice hesitated. "Small-time. Used to be a numbers runner for Filipino Charlie, here and down in South City. Family lived on the edge of Chinatown—until '37."

Miranda reached for her cigarette case again, opened it, grimaced, and shut it.

"You got a stick on you?"

He searched inside his coat pocket and pulled out a crumpled Old Gold package and a tarnished lighter. He lit one, his hand shaking when he took it out of his mouth and handed it to her. She inhaled, leaning back in the chair.

"Nanking changed a lot of things in this city, Phil. Suddenly every Japanese bayoneted babies."

He passed a hand through his short gray hair, sweat starting to bead along his scalp. Kept his voice low.

"That's the problem. That's why I want you to go home, and forget about this kid. Chalk him up to Nanking."

Miranda stared at the clock above his head, minute hand sweeping the time away. No use trying to make it cleaner. Not in the Hall of Justice. Not with Phil.

"You mean because he got killed during the Rice Bowl Party we fucking forget about it? Just blame it on what made Nanking in the first place?"

He found a yellowed handkerchief in his pocket and wiped his forehead.

"Watch your mouth. You talk like a sailor, not a professor's daughter."

"Keep my father the hell out of it."

Voices swirled around the room, staccato, sharp. Miranda was breathing hard, the cigarette burning between her fingers forgotten.

"You're not even going to investigate this, are you? A few feeble courtesy calls on Filipino Charlie, who'll have an alibi, and then you'll forget about it, stick it in a drawer, because a Japanese kid had the bad luck to get plugged in Chinatown on a day when the Chinese are raising money to fight the Rising Sun. Happy, happy fucking New Year, Phil. *Gon Hay Fat Choy* to you, too."

His eyes glittered, and he stood up, shoving the chair into the desk with a hard clatter.

"Save yourself for Sally and the mashers, honey, and spare me the soapbox. The Fair will reopen in a few months, and you'll get by. You always do. There are always men willing to make a pitch at you and fat wives willing to pay you to do it. Or do they pay you?"

The minute hand ticked. Somebody coughed. The clatter of typewriters started up again, the sound of bored questions and shrill answers pounding out to an eight-bar beat.

Miranda calmly rubbed out the half-finished cigarette in the wood of the desk. Phil sank back into his chair, the map of broken veins in his cheeks and nose shining purple against the white.

She started to gather her things. Unhurriedly, carefully, last time. He watched her, lit a cigarette. She was putting on her hat when he said something, voice hoarse.

"Don't do it. I'm not warning you, I'm telling you. We've got a new chief coming in, and nobody needs the trouble right now."

She made her voice sweet and mellifluous, just like Dianne had taught her.

"I'm no trouble, sugar."

She adjusted the hat, walked around to his side of the desk, slowly, as if she were at the Club Moderne and on a job. Stood in front of him, bent forward, made sure he couldn't help looking. Then she put a hand on his upper thigh, and rubbed it a little. His mouth hung open, desperation and horror etched on his face.

"You're a good Catholic boy, Phil. Even if you're sixty. Do us both a favor and go to confession. You don't want to be my uncle, and we both know it."

She left him with his face in his hands, her breath ragged and trembling by the time she got to Kearny Street.

That night she dreamed of Spain and Johnny.

The fields were golden with yellowing grain and dotted with the wings of birds, black against the cloudless sky, and they walked on dirty red roads, past one-room houses of ancient stone, and smelled the grapes in the cellar and the olives in the press. There was that moment, that one flash of truth, when she turned to him and looked in his eyes and his soul answered and everything went away and she was blind, and knew only joy, and the feeling of being whole, complete, oneself and yet more than oneself.

Then the breeze from the coast brought the smell of petrol and sulfur. And the horizon was red, it was evening, and a drone, not a bee or a locust, grew louder. She tried to hold him, to hold him tight, and he fought her, overpowering her, bruising and hurting her until she had to let go, and she screamed, and she screamed, and she screamed.

Miranda woke up, shaking, sweating. It was three in the morning.

She flung off the cover, and swung her legs around the small bed, grabbing an almost-empty package of Chesterfields off the nightstand on her way to the window. She pushed it open, inhaling the fog that pulsed downhill on its way to Market Street and south of that to the piers, the street lamps dim with cloud-wrapped cataracts, the traffic noises muffled as if by a damp wool blanket.

1937. At three in the morning it was always 1937.

She watched a couple in evening clothes stroll down Mason toward Union Square and the big hotels. She watched the man put his arm around the woman, watched as she leaned into him, their footsteps beating a sharp tattoo in the wet pavement. She lit a cigarette, and watched them until they were out of sight.

She smoked, and thought about Eddie Takahashi, and shivered a little. She'd be alone, but Miranda was used to that.

Two

Spain taught her what war could do, to living and dead and the ones in between. But Nanking . . . the old world wasn't over, Middle Ages not done. Torture not out of style, not just yet.

The reporters reported, of course; that's what they did, whether anyone was listening. Then the Japanese bombed the *Panay*, American gunboat, American refugees, and suddenly Joe and Jane Doe woke up. Not just Orientals killing Orientals anymore. The story of Nanking seeped out of China, red and running, Yangtze no longer golden.

Chinatown sobbed from every pasteboard window, every CHOP SUEY neon sign. Three hundred thousand gone, Nanking a graveyard. Cry for Mother China. Then sobs turned to speeches, weeping to war relief. Boycotts, in place since Manchuria, intensified. No Japanese trade, no shops, no merchandise. Feed China, they pleaded, help us feed the starving victims of Nippon.

Rice Bowl Parties raised money from people with money and others without, those who recognized suffering: liberals, Communists, Socialists, unions, Jews. Whoever understood this wasn't just a "European war," whatever the hell Lindbergh said.

Miranda always knew better, knew what was coming. Three o'clock in the morning around the whole goddamn world.

She watched the sunrise, eating hot cakes and bacon at an all-night diner near the St. Francis Hotel. Checked in at the office, found an envelope waiting from the bigamist's wife, a thin, spare woman of old family and older morals, who didn't believe in detectives, private or otherwise, but managed to hold her nose long enough to pay with brand new bills. Miranda rifled through and counted it twice. Seed money for Chinatown and Eddie Takahashi.

Fifteen minute walk to the southeast end of Grant, Japanese end of a Chinese city. Most of the shops and sake houses gone, dried up in the red wind of 1937, or chased out with the boycott six years before. Some still clung to the Yamamoto Hotel, largest business left. Some found room in Little Osaka, down in the Western Addition. The Takahashis lived in Chinatown, once upon a time, and they would've lived here.

Chinese? Go to Chinatown. Filipino? Head for Chinatown. Japanese? Try—yeah, Mister, I know you can't tell the fucking difference. Always Chinatown, always fused together, human chop suey, dish made in America.

A green neon light turned on at the lone sake place on the corner. She walked down to the doorway, looked up at the Japanese lantern, torn and faded above the entrance. Soot and dirt covered the door. She pushed it open, wishing for gloves.

Dark filled a long narrow space, filled it wherever the bar didn't. Rich brown wood from a richer era, Lillie Langtry flirting with her ankles while she danced on the smooth, polished top. Scarred by time, sad and lonely, except for an old man at the far end. He crouched on a stool, bathed in a dim red light from somewhere behind him.

Miranda felt her way between the bar and the small tables crowding the floor, fingers gliding along the pits and scratches in the mahogany. He watched her, his voice cracking the silence.

"Hus-band?"

A woman entered through a back door. She was lost somewhere between forty and sixty, wrapped in a tattered kimono. Red light lit up the back of her head, silver hair gleamed through the black. She wore it pulled back, bound tight.

Eyes froze Miranda's, then drifted toward the man on the stool. He groped at the bar, pulled out a battered crutch, Civil War vintage. Right leg was missing from the knee down. Propped himself up, grunting, and hobbled into the red-black darkness.

"What do you want?"

"Information about the Takahashi family. They used to live around here." Small intake of breath. Looked Miranda up and down.

Miranda pulled out a wallet. Scrutiny over.

"Why do you ask about them?"

"I'm a private detective. Eddie Takahashi was murdered yesterday afternoon in Chinatown."

Her eyes widened, trying to figure out how much there was in what she had. Miranda pulled out a couple of dollar bills, made a show of unrolling them. The woman drew her kimono together more tightly, hands older than her face.

"They lived here. Across the street. Moved about two years ago."

Miranda put a dollar on the bar. "How many, and where are they now?"

The woman was watching the paper between Miranda's fingers. "Father, mother, son, and daughter. No more children. Mr. Takahashi was a client."

Miranda didn't ask of what or whom. "Do you know where I can find them?"

She let the dollar dangle from her fingers, hovering just over the bar. She could get the information if she felt like flirting with a cop or someone in the coroner's office, but that came with a higher price tag. Especially since yesterday.

The woman's eyes met hers before falling back to the money. She turned around, her back straight and elegant through the scuffed silk, and walked toward the red light, disappearing behind the door.

Miranda reached into her purse and found a crumpled Chesterfield, rolled it between her fingers while she waited. No cops would question this woman, even if they bothered to look. No murder case, not Eddie Takahashi. He was a public relations project.

Chinese boy with an empty rice bowl, staring from newspapers, walls, and streetcar fronts, reminding bankers' wives about the Rice Bowl Party, reminding them to buy Humanity League ribbons and their maids to drop a quarter in relief jars. Rice Bowl, so fashionable this year among the social set. Dust Bowl farmers and Kentucky miners, so terribly '38.

So first a police delegation to the Six Companies, supposed ruling body of Chinatown, another one to Japanese business groups. Phil with hat and assurances in hand for the money men on the charity circuit, gentlemen who served on a Bay Area–wide Rice Bowl committee with a name as long as their bank deposits. Charity was a big investment. Nobody wanted to lose money over it.

She leaned against the stool the old man vacated, fingering the cigarette, fighting the urge to light it. Everyone would wring their hands and talk about what a shame it all was, and Filipino Charlie would be questioned and produce an iron-clad and rusty-from-use alibi that was full of holes and leaked orange water. But not Eddie Takahashi's blood. Nobody would ever be found guilty of that.

The woman came back in before the cigarette was in Miranda's mouth. She was holding a torn piece of butcher paper, with careful, small writing on it: 8 Wilmot St. Miranda dropped the other dollar and lit the Chesterfield. The woman watched her, made no move for the money.

"Thanks."

It passed by, unacknowledged. She made her way toward the door, her fingers trailing against the comfort of the pock-marked mahogany. Gave a quick glance back; both the woman and the dollar bills were gone.

Clouds smothered the sun, yesterday's warmth all spent. Fog on its way, white fingers curled in a lover's clutch. She climbed the couple of blocks back up to Sacramento and Grant, where she'd stood the day before, stuck in human traffic, trying to get back home.

Odor of firecrackers lingered, sharp, blending with sidewalk slop from chop suey joints. Acrid and sour, catching her throat when she passed the cheaper restaurants, sandwiched between nightclubs like Forbidden City and the Chinese Sky Room.

No crowd on Sacramento except for pigeons. Cigarette butts, newspapers, spit. And a barely visible chalk outline, already faded and wiped, in a hurry to be forgotten.

He had looked to his right. Last act of communion. The First Chinese Baptist Church, Romanesque brick and brimstone, guarded the corner of Waverly Alley and Sacramento. Below it clustered shops for locals—Chinese herbalist, grocer, bathhouse. Eddie fell or stumbled or was thrown from one of them.

Across the street the YMCA, large and modern, hugged the hill. It and the church gave this end of Sacramento Street a claim to respectability, let the City Fathers feel self-righteous whenever the world "slum" was mentioned.

Phonograph squawked from a window, same one as yesterday. Miranda looked up, squinting, high fog too bright for her eyes. Teddy Wilson and Billie Holiday again. Someone liked jazz.

A cigarette that bears a lipstick's traces . . .

Goddamn it. Not that song, not 1936. Miranda walked quickly toward the grocer. Boxes of tired-looking vegetables and fruit were stacked on the sidewalk, and she fingered some bok choy, trying to forget the music. A middle-aged man in a smock came out, smiled at her, swept the sidewalk, dust and ash obscuring the chalk marks a few feet away.

Eddie. Think about Eddie Takahashi.

She walked inside, hoping to drown the words, but they chased her, cornered her near the chrysanthemum tea. Goddamn it, not New York, not Johnny, not now. Not now.

The grocer gave her a curious look. Song still playing, louder, filling the street.

Breathing hard, panic. Blind. Run from the store, run from the song, don't think, don't remember. Up the pavement, inside the herbalist without planning it, quieter, breathe. Look around.

There was a man inside, an old man. Angry. He stood over another old man, probably the herbalist.

You came, you saw, you conquered me . . .

The angry one looked up at her. His fist too close to the herbalist's throat, hanging, suspended, finally falling to his side. Muttered something in Chinese. Pushed out the door past Miranda, bumping her shoulder.

These foolish things remind me of you . . .

Herbalist stared past her, eyes wide, still terrified. She backed out of the doorway, followed the other man. He walked up the hill with purpose, fury driving his legs forward, arms bent and fists again clenched. Turned down Waverly, too angry to notice her.

Miranda crossed the street and pretended to study the church façade, fingertips tracing the rough edges of bricks. No music. Song finally over.

She leaned back against the wall and lit a Chesterfield. Watched the old man walk through Waverly, past the barbershops, the gambling joints, associations, and whorehouses. Whorehouses always circled churches. Temptation and repent, cause and demand. Production for fucking use.

Tobacco hit her lungs, helping to calm her down. Temporary booths from the Rice Bowl street carnival stood silent, closed, waiting for the fortune-tellers and Chinese calligraphers to open one last time. He crossed Clay Street. She hesitated, then followed him, chasing a hunch.

Sharp right on Washington. Miranda walked faster to catch up. Too many shops that interconnected, too many honeycombs. Chinatown was built of opium, by opium, and for opium. Each little store, shop, bar, restaurant, and flophouse held a deep basement, forgotten attic, and plenty of corners no cop ever looked into.

He walked into Sam's Restaurant, one of the narrowest in Chinatown. Two floors, both small, everyone watching everyone else. He could already be half a block away, using building-to-building routes the Chinese guarded like gold. She dropped the cigarette and rubbed it out on the pavement.

Headed for a bakery across the street, elbowing her way between a man with a briefcase and a teenage boy in high-waisted trousers trying to give her the eye. Pulled out fifteen cents, plunking it down on the counter, the harried waitress flinging a cup of tea at her. Miranda wiped up the spill with a napkin.

The tea leaves couldn't tell her anything. Couldn't explain why she was sitting at a scratched Formica counter, eating a sesame ball, looking for reasons for Eddie Takahashi. One more sesame ball, and the old man emerged, carrying a cloth bag of food. She shoved the fifteen cents toward the young girl behind the counter and the teenager's hand off her knee and hurried out the door.

His walk was calmer. From Washington he turned left into Wentworth Alley. Miranda could smell it halfway up the block.

Fish scale covered the pavement. Smoked fish hung in cramped sidewalk stalls, old, crooked women haggling over price and digestibility. Not many fishmongers in Wentworth left, but it was still Salty Fish Alley to the locals.

She stepped around the worst of the fish guts, watching the old man hunch over a stripped-down apartment-house door. Younger man opened it. Handsome face. Sharp clothes, slick hair, looked like the front horn section for Tommy Dorsey. The old man barked something in Chinese, took off his hat, and pushed his way in.

She retreated across the street, taking out her notebook and another cigarette, making a note of the address: 36 Wentworth. Fuck the tea leaves.

Brick wall behind her was covered in handbills, some in Chinese, some in English, plenty of posters with the boy and the empty rice bowl next to BOY-COTT JAPAN signs. She watched the market, inhaling the Chesterfield. They lived up to their motto and satisfied, but only for fifteen minutes at a time.

A middle-aged man walked out of an acupuncture place across from number 36. He stood, hands behind his back, looking over the bargaining. Their eyes met. Miranda opened her purse and handed him a cigarette.

He smiled, surprised. Front two teeth were missing. He lit the Chesterfield with a pack of matches, took a drag, smiled again.

She gestured toward the apartment.

"Nice boy."

He shook his head, brow wrinkled. She repeated it, made the gesture a little larger. He muttered to himself, casting around for meaning.

She gestured again. "Name?"

He patted her arm and went back inside, returning with a bored-looking middle-school kid wearing glasses and reading a *Detective* comic book. The kid peered up at her, still bored.

"You want something, lady?"

"Yeah. The name of the family who lives across the street. Old man and a younger one, good-looking."

The acupuncture man looked from her to the boy. The kid translated in a monotone, barely looking up from the comic book. No sense showing him her detective license and disillusioning him.

The man was nodding again, speaking rapidly, smiling at her.

"My father says you must mean Kuan-Yin Li. His son is Fai Fen, but calls himself Frank Lee. Kuan-Yin Li owns the printing shop next door." He pointed to a run-down, redbrick storefront next to the door of 36 Wentworth.

"Frank work there?"

The kid turned to his father, whose face got darker at the question. He inhaled again, coughed, shook his head.

"Father says Frank is no good. He works in a nightclub, spends too much money. Dishonors his father."

Miranda wrote it down in the notebook. "Anyone else in the family? No mother?"

He turned to his father and she grabbed the boy's sleeve. "Ask him if the family knows Eddie Takahashi."

The Japanese name sounded harsh, invasive in the alley. The man stared at her, slower in response. Looked away, toward his right, and the wall covered in posters. The boy gave the report with an air of finality.

"Kuan-Yin Li's wife died a few years ago. Fai Fen has been seen with many girls. People say there's one he wants to marry."

The kid looked up at her, curiosity mixed with self-importance. "Dad says he doesn't know the name Eddie Takahashi. That's Japanese."

"Thanks." She rummaged around, pulling out a change purse. "Here's a quarter. Go buy yourself some more comic books."

He accepted it as no more than his due, said something to his father, and went back inside the shop. The father looked at her, curious. Not quite as friendly.

She gave him two more Chesterfields, and he took them, hesitant, still avoiding her eyes. He bowed, and melted back into the dark, somber storefront. She looked up to the second story of 36 Wentworth. No laundry, no flowerpots. No music. No answers in Salty Fish Alley.

Three

Miranda shrugged, and crushed the cigarette butt under her pump. Back to Sacramento, start again. She turned down Grant, and almost ran into one of the downtown beat cops.

"Well, well. Miranda Corbie."

Red face on a short, stout neck. Doyle always reminded her of a bordello lamp. She tried to sidestep him. He extended a beefy arm out and held it against her shoulder.

"I hear you were at the Hall yesterday. As a witness."

"Then your ears still work. Let me go."

He leaned closer, all bad breath and stale beer.

"I hear a lot. I hear you rode Phil pretty hard. The lieutenant's tryin' to protect you. It's good of him. Too good."

She shrugged her shoulders. His arm stayed in place. She reached over with her right hand and flung it off.

"He can quit being a saint any goddamn time he wants. I don't need the fucking missionary act, Doyle—from him, you, or anybody else."

Miranda started to push past him when he grabbed her arm. "You should watch your mouth, leastways for your father's sake. You talk like a tramp."

"Get your goddamn hand off my arm."

She was two paces down Grant when she heard his voice, lower, more careful.

"About this Takahashi mess."

Miranda turned around, eyes wary. "What about it?"

He rubbed the end of nose. "Forget it. Orders, Miranda, and not just from Phil."

They looked at each other. Doyle, with six kids and always one more on the way. And a Chinese girl down at the International Settlement every Friday night.

"You've done your duty. Go home to mama, tell him Miranda's going to be a good girl from now on. Go on, Doyle. Drift."

She waited until he crossed Washington, watching his fat back pulling against the dark wool coat. Strode away in the opposite direction, fast, welcoming the Chinese music and Benny Goodman that blared through various doorways. Bars and restaurants were already filling up, ready for the last party.

Her stomach growled, and she walked into Fong Fong, Chinatown's best soda fountain. Miranda sat at the counter, next to a couple of teenage girls flirting with the soda jerk, checking their reflections in the mirror behind him, tapping their fingers on the milkshake cups.

She looked around and noticed some boys next to the jukebox. Cheap, flashy clothes. Small-time air of importance. Any of them could've been Eddie Takahashi. She watched them and ordered a chop suey sundae.

One of the sharpies fed the box, and Martha Tilton crooned "And the Angels Sing." The two girls next to her looked away from the soda jerk and over to where the bad boys were. Bad boys were like that.

Then the sundae came, and she dug into the crushed fruit, ice cream, and sesame cookies. So Phil wanted to protect her. Didn't they all.

Her watch read eleven o'clock straight up. She finished the sundae, listened to the Ink Spots sing "If I Didn't Care" and Judy Garland warble "Over the Rainbow"—twice. The soda jerk had his elbows on the counter, frowning at the two girls, one white, one Chinese, making eyes at the Dead End Kids in the corner.

She drained a coffee cup, paid for the check, and bought a pack of cigarettes. Walked over to the jukebox, put in a nickel. The teenagers stared at her. Bold eyes, hunger of the young. The girls pouted and arched their backs, pushing their breasts out.

Mostly newer songs. She hit Miller's "Moonlight Serenade."

The leader of the pack crossed his arms and leaned on top of the Wurlitzer. Older than the other two, probably twenty-one or twenty-two. Wore a scar on his upper cheek like a medal, making sure his hair was combed back so it could be admired. Looked Filipino.

"Wanna dance?"

"No, thanks. I'm a little sad. That's why I'm playing this song, for an old friend."

He leaned in a little more, draping his long arms across the machine. "A tomato like you—sad—what a waste. Who is he? I'll—" He made a gesture with his finger across his throat—"For you."

"He's dead."

The kid lifted himself off the jukebox, pulled a long face. "Sorry, lady. But, you know, maybe it's time to move on. Whadda they say at the movies? 'Time—marches—on.'"

He delivered the line in an imitation baritone. The others laughed.

She shook her head. "I was reminded of it yesterday, when that boy got killed—what was his name?"

A small, skinny one piped up from her right. He looked about seventeen. "Eddie Takahashi. Nicky knew him, dincha, Nicky?"

The leader ran a finger along his thin mustache. Suddenly careful.

"Yeah, I knew him. A swell kid." The girls' eyes were as wide as the cuffs on Nicky's trousers.

"It's terrible. I hope they catch the killer. It's so hard on the survivors—the family. He had family, didn't he?"

The skinny one answered again, finding a niche of self-importance. "I seen him with his sister a lot. They used to come here, sometimes. Kinda stuck up about her, her bein' pretty an' all. Didn't let no one get too close."

Nicky snorted and took the bait. "I got plenty close. She ain't that good-lookin'. But yeah, Eddie took real good care of his family. He was a good kid. We figure it was an accident, maybe."

Miranda looked up, met his eyes. Shrewd and calculating.

"Such a tragedy. I expect it's as you say, and a terrible accident. Thank you for telling me—it does make me feel a little less lonely."

She walked away, his voice behind her soft. "You don't ever need to be lonely, lady."

She flinched, glad her back was to him. Benny Goodman and Martha Tilton followed her out the door.

We meet, and the angels sing . . .

Miranda pushed through the growing crowd already lining up for the Dragon Dance Parade, dodging strolling tourists gawking at pagoda architecture and wondering aloud how anybody ate anything with chopsticks. She reached the Far Eastern Bakery and swerved left, leaning against the Commercial Street side, pumps braced against the incline.

She took out the deck of Fatimas from Fong Fong and lit one, closing her eyes. She wasn't sure what she was doing or why. It was Sunday, her day off, and she could be watching ships dock at the piers, or feeding sourdough to seagulls, or listening to the radio and taking bets on when England would be invaded. She had so many things to do.

She took another drag on the Fatima, then dropped it on the sidewalk and stepped on it with disgust. Weak and tasteless, probably older than the kid who sold them to her.

Tea, coffee, sesame balls, sundae, and conversation. Not counting the lecture from Phil through Doyle. She wanted answers, needed answers, or at least the right questions. Before she visited the Takahashis. Grieving parents took a strong stomach, and she was fresh out of bicarbonate.

The smell of moon cake floated out of the bakery. Miranda took out her compact and checked her face, dabbing some Midnight Red on her lips.

A lot of gambling rooms in Ross Alley, tucked in basements down rickety stairs. Some of them were Filipino Charlie's. The kid at Fong Fong had known Eddie, known his sister, probably knew something he shouldn't. And he looked Filipino.

Firecrackers exploded down by Portsmouth. She jumped out of reflex. Just the New Year, Year of the White Metal Dragon, a good luck year as long as you weren't a Japanese numbers boy in Chinatown.

She closed her eyes again. There was a Filipino dive on the edges of Chinatown, somewhere on Kearny or near it. Manila something. Clip joint. Maybe Eddie downed a few there, gulping gin like he was twenty-one and would live forever.

Someone hit a car horn, kept hitting it until the others started, fucking San Francisco symphony. She opened her eyes, looked down Commercial toward Kearny and the Bay.

Dark green Olds, too large for the street, turned up off Kearny, crawling when it got close. Parked across the street in one of the few spaces left.

Miranda counted to three. No one got out. Windows dark, not just with the shadows of Chinatown. The hair on her neck stood up, and she walked into the bakery.

Instinct, he'd told her, trust your instincts. Saved her life more than once. Her instincts told her to go back to the herbalist. She could get over to Ross and around to the Filipino section in plenty of time to grab a White Front on Sutter and ride it down to 8 Wilmot Street and Little Osaka and the Takahashi family. What was left of it.

She came out of the bakery holding a moon cake. The green Olds was gone. But her skin still tingled, and she hurried up the hill on Sacramento, handing the cake to No-Legs Norris, who was begging at the north corner of Grant.

The bells on the door of the herbalist chimed, out of tune. The old man wasn't there. A younger version in Western clothes sat in the same seat. Surprise, then wariness. Then a phony smile of welcome that was worth about as much as the counterfeit jade the tourist stores pedaled on Grant.

"Good afternoon. You speak English?" She minutely changed her posture, giving the hips a slight wiggle. He didn't need to speak English to understand that.

His smile stayed in place, eyes missing nothing. "Yes, I speak English. How can I help you?"

She sat in a thronelike chair across from the cherry-wood desk and looked around. A long hallway led to a dim back area on the left. Eddie Takahashi wasn't beaten or shot in any storefront window. He'd been killed in one of the warrens, here or behind some other door on Sacramento.

"I'm—I'd like something to—to help me watch my weight."

He was thin, medium height, wiry, about thirty-five to forty, with a blue suit and black tie from Sears and a five-cent haircut from the barber on Waverly. The aftershave was even cheaper.

She'd planned on cornering the old man and waving her license at him, simple intimidation. Would never work with the son. The weight line gave him a chance to look at her, and he was taking advantage of it. Behind the glasses, his eyes lingered on her legs.

"You don't look like you need to reduce, Miss, if you'll pardon me. But if you like, I can make you a mixture."

He rose. "Are you sure that's all?"

Miranda cleared her throat. "I'm—I'm actually hoping you might have something for—for loneliness. I'm alone, you see. I don't—don't want to be. I've heard you—I've heard you Chinese have medicines that can—that can . . ."

She broke off, too delicate to explain. He sat back down, nodded his head. The smile was genuine this time.

"Have you ever been—married?"

She bowed her head and whispered. They always wanted to hear it, and they liked to hear it soft.

"No."

Face flushed, he didn't ask why he'd gotten lucky, why she'd walked in the dingy little hole on Sacramento Street. Genuine virgin, get it while you can.

"I think I know what you mean, Miss. I may—I may be able to help you."

Miranda forced herself to smile at him. She could bank on looking ten or twelve years younger, especially in dim light. Swallowed the bitter taste in her mouth and asked: "Do you—do you need to—to examine me?"

Took him by surprise. She should've waited for him to suggest it, for him to lead her to the back room. Then he'd tell her to undress so he could diagnose her sad state, and give her a homemade remedy for exactly what was wrong.

The doctor game, played by men in dirty white coats and cheap business suits in alleyway clinics. You lonely, lady? Doctor can help. You don't want a baby, lady? Doctor can help. You need some extra money to help Bobby stay in school, lady? Doctor can always help. Rape's a dirty word, lady. You asked for it.

The women never called the cops. They just went away, finding refuge in a new kind of aloneness, drowning guilt in a bottle of rye. It was their fault, after all. They asked for it.

He roamed her body up and down again, fast, his tongue involuntarily licking lips suddenly dry. Threw a glance to the back rooms.

"I'm a certified doctor of Chinese medicine. An examination will be necessary, Miss. If you don't mind, of course."

She adjusted her hat again, making her voice come out small.

"I haven't been to a . . . to one of our doctors yet. But a friend said—said to try a Chinese doctor. You can—I would appreciate—" She dropped her voice on a cue of embarrassment, looking up at him from below the hat brim. "I'm sorry—I don't know your name."

He bowed easily. "My name is Ming Chen. My American name is Mike. Mike Chen. Doctor Chen."

She held out her hand, wishing again for her gloves. Not the hands of a collegiate virgin. More like a Scotch-Irish peat picker.

"Thank you . . . Doctor Chen. Are you the only doctor here?"

He looked furtively toward the back rooms again.

"My father. My father and I own this business. He's also a doctor. Now, if you'll follow me . . ."

He put up a closed sign and locked the front door, then led her down the hallway. Shelves of small glass jars, some opaque, some dusty, lined the dark wooden cases.

Miranda pointed to the bottles.

"Are these more medicines?"

"Yes."

More like drugs. She wondered whether Mike Chen sold cocaine or heroin or still clung to opium. The hallway ended in a dingy gray room with a daybed and a rust-streaked sink. Left corner was curtained off in orange-red brocade. He picked up a pack of Lucky Strikes on the bed, lit one, and gestured to the drapes.

"Please—undress there. I'll put a robe over the curtain for you."

"Do I—do I have to? Can't you—can't you examine me like this?"

He eyes drifted toward the daybed. "It would be better—"

"But Doctor Chen—I heard—I heard there was a murder near here yesterday, and—well, I'm a little frightened."

Nervous titter. Skirt smoothed down her hips. He took a drag on the cigarette, smiled at her indulgently. Forgot to ask her name. Too busy salivating.

She raised her arms above her head and took off her hat, laying it on an upholstered chair. There were cigarette burns on the arms. Indentations that looked like rope marks. She remembered, suddenly, the burns on Eddie Takahashi's face.

Miranda was pulling her arms out of the small tweed jacket when she felt him close behind her. He put his right hand on her waist.

"You should relax. The medicine works much better when you relax. Go behind the curtain. I'll fix you up. All right?"

He was close enough for her to feel his breath on her neck and his erection pushing through the tweed of her skirt. She fought the impulse to kick. At least the tweed was thick, good for more than just the San Francisco fog. She walked quickly behind the curtain.

"Did you—did you see it?"

He was opening an ornately carved, three-legged armoire that tottered against the opposite wall.

"See what? What are you talking about?"

"The murder. I understand it happened right before the—the Rice Bowl Party yesterday."

She bent low and mimicked unrolling her stockings, watching him through a worn spot in the thin brocade. He took an old silk robe out of the armoire and stared at the curtain that separated them.

"Don't worry about that. There won't be any more killings. I'm holding a robe for you. Let me know when you need it."

She looked behind her. A small, dirty steamer trunk, lid unlocked. She opened it slowly, coughing so he wouldn't hear the creak. A couple of opium pipes, old juju sticks, empty liquor bottles. On top, a box of fresh cloth bandages, a couple of bloody ones shoved into the middle. Somebody had done some bleeding recently. She was betting it wasn't young Doctor Chen. She rolled a juju inside one of the bloody cloths and stuck it in her bra.

"I'm almost ready, Doctor. But I'm—I'm still frightened—about the murder—"

He was getting impatient, rubbed the cigarette out on the chair.

"I'm telling you—there won't be any more murders. Don't be afraid. Please, Miss. I have other patients—"

If he was telling the truth, then Eddie Takahashi wasn't a tong war killing or mob hit. They never stop with one. But the beating he took looked like a lesson, and not just for Eddie. That would be the Japanese—or so thought the cops.

The curtain flew open and Mike Chen stood in front of her. The silk robe fell to the floor.

"You—you're still dressed—"

Game over. She held her hands behind her back and didn't bother to hide the contempt.

"I changed my mind. I'm not so lonely anymore."

His hands were clenched, face red, fingers curling and uncurling. He took one step toward her. Her right hand came up holding her .22.

"Back off and sit on your bed."

He moved backwards, hands by his belt, slowly sat on the mattress. She threw her jacket around her shoulders and shoved on the hat. He watched her, his angled face tight with fury.

"This isn't a grift. I want some information—about Eddie Takahashi."

His mouth stretched to a thin, compressed line of recognition. His body tensed, hands to the side, ready. She braced herself. Then the doorbells screamed.

She gestured with her gun to the hallway. "Get up. I'll be behind you."

He rose reluctantly. Miranda pressed the barrel into his back, prodded him forward.

The old man was sitting behind the mixing desk, his back hunched, the gray hair in his beard long and unkempt.

Miranda murmured, "Give me some medicine, and keep it in English."

She lowered the gun, holding it beside her, and Chen reached for a small, dusty jar on the shelf. Fear twisted the old man's face. She wondered if he knew what went on in the back room.

The son didn't bother to hide the threat: "The lady wants something special to help her sleep at night."

His father started to speak, then glanced at Miranda and stayed quiet. She backed up toward the exit.

"Thanks, Mr. Chen. I'm sure I'll sleep just fine from now on."

He grunted, pouring about half an ounce of a greenish-yellow powder into a small paper envelope. Then he sponged the seal, wrote something on the envelope, and threw it at her.

"On the house. And you don't need to come back."

She took the envelope with her left hand. Her back was to the door, both purse and gun in her right.

"Thank you, Mr. Chen. But I'll be back. And I'll tell my friends." Worry about that one, you fucking son of a bitch.

She pivoted out of the shop and was around the corner and on Waverly and Clay before she looked at the package in her hand. Next to the Chinese letters was written, "Ground powder of Deadly Nightshade leaves. Mix with warm water and drink until dead."

Four

She tried to smile. Her breath was still a little ragged. She was standing against the shadowy side of a tailor's shop on Clay, trying to light one of the remaining Chesterfields with shaking hands. The souvenir Fair lighter kicked a spark and nothing else. She threw it back in her bag, rummaging for a pack of matches.

She found an unused pack from the Moderne, lit up and smoked under the red awning. Blew a puff out the corner of her mouth. Watched the smoke drift, disintegrate, toward one of the association doors that lined Waverly, past the barbershop and Twin Dragon nightclub with its bright chromium exterior, past the carnival booths that reminded her of the Gayway on Treasure Island.

Chinatown. Grant and Washington, Chinese Sky Room, teashops and gin joints and St. Mary's after dark. A kind of a home, one for the homeless, one for the outcasts. Nowhere else to go.

White men locked the gate, then bought the opium, bought the girls, bought the silks and the food and the jade, white men kept coming back for more. The Chinese shrugged. And made exclusion pay. You want exotic, Mister, you can have it, but you mind your city and we'll mind ours. It's where you locked us up, remember?

Smoke from her cigarette drifted back down Clay, toward the people already lining up three bodies thick on Grant. She watched it swirl, wondering if it would form a tiger or a lion. Chinatown was a city of outcasts. They'd made the most of it.

So had she.

The fog was creeping down from the Mark Hopkins and the Fairmont and the exclusive set on Nob Hill. It flowed sinuously over Stockton and Clay, past the GOLDEN STAR RADIO SIGN, drowning out the yellow neon in a sea of thick white haze, heading for the piers. A foghorn belched, the low hum filling one of the few silences in the heart of Chinatown. Real fog was an event, not just a shapeless cloud of moisture. As alive as the dragons of Chinatown and the ghosts of gold rush San Francisco.

One o'clock. Parade would start in an hour. No time for a stroll through Ross Alley or down to Manila Restaurant or over to Japantown. Miranda was out of smokable cigarettes, the day old enough already. And the bloody bandage in her bra was making her itch.

Chen's left a sour taste in her mouth. She was getting too old. Use what you have, Miranda, use it up. Charlie Burnett on detective work. Her cases were her own, now, not Burnett's setups or Dianne's Shriners, wanting a decoration on their arms and a piece of something else after the show.

The drugstore next to the Republic Hotel was out of Chesterfields. She turned down the druggist's suggestion of Lucky Strikes, and picked up copies of the *Examiner* and the *Call-Bulletin*. The pharmacy didn't carry the *News*, and Miranda knew better than to think the *Chronicle* would run anything.

Eddie was a-second-to-the-last-page item in the *Examiner*, placed a couple of pages up from that in the *Call-Bulletin*. There was a quote from Phil about Eddie's record, and assurances by a mouthpiece for the Bay Region Committee in charge of the Chinese Civilian Benefit Campaign, and still more from someone on the Chamber of Commerce. The conclusion was obvious: Eddie was a criminal, and no one really gave a fuck about who murdered him, as long as it wouldn't spill over into Rice Bowl festivities and freeze out-of-town pocketbooks. Scratch it over, boys. Chalk it up to Nanking.

Back to the Monadnock Building, a few paces ahead of the fog. Miranda enjoyed the strain on her calves, the pain immediate, simple. Market Street was already loading up, ready to get loaded, Sunday night party in Chinatown. Gaiety that much more desperate since Monday morning was at the other end.

She walked into the lobby, the girl at the newsstand counter holding her carefully curled, not-so-carefully bleached head in her hand, bored and eyeballing a Latin-lover type with wide shoulders waiting for the elevator.

"Got any Chesterfields, Gladdy?"

The crate operator whisked up Cesar Romero, and Gladys handed Miranda three packs, with a sigh.

"Been savin' 'em for you. I don't know why everyone wants a Chesterfield, suddenly."

"Haven't you heard? They satisfy."

Gladys snorted. "Who're they kiddin'? Now, him"—she jutted a thumb out to where a thin bald man with an umbrella had replaced the Latin lover in line—"he was what I call satisfaction."

Miranda quickly lit up a stick. "You got the latest *News*?"

Eddie had moved up in the world. The *News* ranked him on page two, and had the guts to point out the obvious: he was Japanese and murdered right before the Rice Bowl Party. She folded the paper and tucked it under her arm. The article meant she could expect a call from Rick.

"Say, Miri, that guy—the good-looker—he got off on the fourth floor. Maybe he's coming to see you."

She smiled at the girl's hopeful face. "If he is, sugar, I'll send him back down to you."

She left Gladys a tip, took a spot in the queue. The Monadnock, survivor of the Fire, always busy. "The Railroad Building," a good place to get a quick ticket to one of the invisible one-block Main Streets between here and Des Moines, Union Pacific or East Coast lines. A good building to get lost in.

Miranda squeezed into the middle car next to a fat lady with a feathered hat and a dead animal around her neck. She was the only person to get off at four. Started walking the big square to the small corner where her office was tucked, when the tingle came back. The green Olds on Commercial Street. She wondered if she'd noticed it outside but had been too tired to realize it.

Pinkertons was always busy, office as well groomed as a matinee idol. Low-key lighting, not too overdone, modern art not really modern, carpet thick enough to choke on. The only thing missing was a spritz of Chanel No. Five every three minutes.

New girl at the front desk. Not much on looks, but money to help what was there. They were always breaking in new ones, since the old ones were either getting married or getting experience. Too much experience at Pinkertons got you fired.

Disapproval from every pore. "Can I help you, Miss?"

Miranda lit up another Chesterfield, staring levelly at the woman. "I'm Miranda Corbie. My office is down the hall."

The receptionist's lip was itching to sneer. Miranda blew some smoke over the girl's right shoulder and watched one of her curls unhinge.

"I'm a detective, honey. Not competition, not for Pinkterton—or Pinkertons. Allen Jennings has the office closest to me. I'm wondering if he's in."

Some starch went out of her pinafore. She pushed a couple of buttons and checked, while Miranda walked back to the doorway, smoking.

"Miss—you can go in now."

She took a last inhale. Then stubbed it out in the invisible-until-you-needed-it ashtray, walking through the small gate to the inner hall and along it until she found Allen's office. His cell sported a second door that fronted the main hallway outside, offering him the bonus of seeing anyone on the way to see Miranda.

Allen was a portly man, with muscle that had run to fat but was still hard enough to matter. His head was bald and shiny, his eyes twinkled, and he was over forty. Not a casting agent's idea of a detective. Neither was she.

"What's your trouble, Miranda?" He knew it wouldn't be a social call.

"I'm not sure. Someone may be tailing me. Could be the cops."

He shook his head, leaned back in the chair until it squeaked, un-Pinkertonlike, and looked at her shrewdly.

"I thought you could always spot a tail, especially from the bulls."

"This is just a feeling. Anybody come through here and not come back? Or has that goddamn door been closed all goddamn day?"

He laughed for a while, and popped a hard candy into his mouth. "I've only been here for ten minutes myself, and it's been closed. So you'll have to go into the lion's den unprepared. Sorry, kid. That's the breaks."

Miranda reached over and took one of the lemon drops out of a cut crystal dish on his desk corner.

"My breaks, anyway. Be seein' you."

"Yeah. Safe travels, kid."

She crossed in front of him to the outer door, and stood in the frame. Footsteps on the polished floor echoed around and around the square center, impossible to trace. Voices rumbled through the ventilated air, vacationers and business travelers and those who sought advice from private investigators. There was no way to know and only one way in.

She walked into the hallway, her own pumps adding a pleasant tapping to the swirl of sound. Paused in front of her office, reading her name on the door—MIRANDA CORBIE, PRIVATE INVESTIGATOR—the black-and-gold lettering strong and purposeful. Then she took a deep breath and opened it.

No carpet in the office, no mahogany desk with a pretty girl, no art, modern or otherwise. It held an old-fashioned oak desk from Weinstein's, two file cabinets, a cathedral radio, three miscellaneous chairs, two of which were comfortable, a calendar, a portable closet, a chair for herself she'd spent a commission on, and a used safe she picked up from Wells Fargo. Also the Latin Lover from downstairs and a surly-looking Irish cop with pits for pores and teeth to match.

Miranda strode toward the desk like she didn't see them. Cesar Romero stood up. The other one ground his toothpick and sneered.

"Miss Corbie?"

She waited until she was behind the heft of the desk and nestled into the padded leather of the chair. She snuck a glance at the desk drawers. They'd been opened, and pushed back with enough carelessness to advertise the fact.

"Can I help you?" Best-bred Lady Esther voice, the one that smelled like violets and spoke of yacht clubs and opening night at the opera.

The one standing was a looker. Tall, about six one, pencil mustache, well-cut, dark clothes. Almost too well cut to belong to an honest cop. He didn't show his teeth when he smiled. Eyes large, brown, and sympathetic.

"Inspector Gonzales. This is Assistant Inspector Duggan. We'd like to talk to you."

He made himself comfortable in the chair, graceful motion. Duggan was staring at Miranda, and suddenly spat a wad of chewed toothpick on the floor.

She didn't give him the pleasure of flinching. "Mind if I smoke?"

Not waiting for an answer, she opened the top drawer of her desk and took out the nearly empty pack inside. She lit a cigarette with the heavy desk lighter, offered one to Gonzales, who shook his head politely.

"Go ahead. Talk."

Gonzales cleared his throat, and took out a pad of paper from his inner coat pocket. His shoulder-holstered .38 flashed at Miranda.

"I believe you were in Chinatown this morning, asking questions about the death of Eddie Takahashi."

She leaned back, ignoring the sudden weight of the bloodstained bandage in her bra. Blew some smoke in Duggan's direction. He was ticking, and she wanted him to go when she was ready for it. Miranda studied Gonzales's smoothly handsome face.

"Mind if I see your identification, boys?"

Gonzales smiled good-naturedly again, reached for his billfold. Duggan jumped up suddenly, and leaned on her desk, both hands hairy and flat on the surface, his veined nose about a foot away from hers.

"'Mind if I see your identification' she says." Singsong, vicious falsetto. "Can the class act. We know who you are and what you are. You fuck with this case, we haul you in for obstruction. And anything else we can find. We won't have to look far."

Gonzales's face was red, and he was still half-holding out his buzzer. Miranda gave him a brief nod. Then she stood up, slowly, and stared at Duggan, his face still jutting forward, his small eyes mean and as yellow as his teeth.

"Why don't you sit down, Inspector? I'm afraid I can't offer you a cuspidor, but you're welcome to spit on your partner there. You seem to be good at it."

His back got tense and long and arched itself, and he lifted one of his hands, letting it freeze in the air. Gonzales's voice came out quiet.

"Sit down, Gerry. Let's try to talk to Miss Corbie like we're professionals, and not some he-man cartoon cops out of *Argosy*."

Duggan's eyes turned from her and raked over Gonzales, who was now standing. He said nothing, but threw his shoulder into his partner's as he walked back to his chair. Gonzales took it stolidly, just as he did the stage-whispered "Fuckin' Mex" under Duggan's breath.

"So why are you here, Inspector? Last I checked, I was free, white, and twenty-one. That usually buys you the freedom to go to Chinatown and talk without being questioned by the police."

"This is more of a courtesy call, Miss Corbie."

She raised her eyebrow and glanced at Duggan, who was staring out the window.

"Oh. Forgive me if I couldn't tell." She extinguished the cigarette in the Treasure Island ashtray and added, "Let's get on with it. I've been warned away, and I didn't take the warning. So what are you going to do? Arrest me, as Sir Lancelot suggested?"

Duggan turned his neck slowly like the mechanical clown at Playland.

"Gloves are off, baby, and don't count on Phil. Seems like you fucked him one time too many, and the last one didn't take. A little spell for solicitation'll wipe that smile off your face. Send you right back to the whorehouse."

"Duggan—"

"This greasy bastard wants a piece of your action, honey. I'd charge him double if I was you."

Gonzales was pale. He walked calmly over to stand in front of Duggan, who sat, his legs wide apart, smirking up at him, another toothpick dangling between his lips. Gonzales reached into his coat pocket, brown eyes empty, and took out a pair of pigskin gloves. With a quick, sudden motion, he lashed Duggan across the face with them. Twice.

"Outside. I won't dirty my hands with you."

Duggan was staring open-mouthed at Gonzales, the toothpick stuck to his lower lip. His rolling, apelike shoulders and arms seemed to shrink and hang loose, like a puppet without a puppeteer. He stood up, not looking at either of them. Then he braced himself against the wall with uncertainty while he put his hat back on, his heavy footsteps scuffing the wood floor as he walked out of the office. The door swung softly and automatically closed behind him.

Gonzales turned to Miranda. "I'm sorry, Miss Corbie."

She shrugged. "Nothing I haven't heard before. I'm sorry you've got such a son of a bitch for a partner."

"Like you said, Miss Corbie. Free, white, and twenty-one. I fit two of those categories."

She dug out another Chesterfield. "Call me Miranda. I appreciate you being square with me, and I appreciate the way you conduct yourself. How can I help you?"

He took a couple of minutes to calm down, drifting over to her windowsill and staring at the Market Street traffic.

"I'll be brief. The new police chief would very much appreciate a low profile for the Takahashi case. So would District Attorney Brady. So would the mayors of San Francisco, Oakland, and Berkeley. And a lot of other people, almost as important."

"Check. I'm not with the *Chronicle*."

He smiled, a charming one. "Yes, I know. But you know newspaper men, you've worked with them, and—forgive me—you tend to generate a certain amount of publicity yourself."

She shrugged again. "I had some high-profile cases last year, yeah. But it's not like I'm in the society column every Sunday."

He stared at her earnestly. "Duggan was telling the truth. We've been assigned the Takahashi case, and we were told to call in vice if we have to. Brady is prepared to throw everything he can at you—or anyone else who doesn't let it lie. He can't afford another Atherton Report."

Miranda blew a stream of smoke toward the window. "Seems to me cleaning up the police department—such as it is—has given him enough to do in the last three years. My lawyer would have me out in thirty minutes and the case would be dismissed."

"I know. But it would do you damage. Even if you didn't lose your license, the publicity—"

She leaned forward. "Listen, Inspector. I used to work for an escort service. Everyone knows that. The Board knows it, the chief knows it, Brady knows it, even your pal Duggan knows it. I was never nailed there, and I won't be nailed here. And it so happens that I do have a few friends, a couple of them in higher places than the Hall of Justice, and I'm reasonably sure that as long as I keep my nose clean I'll be hanging on to my license. As for the publicity—why do you think I get the clients I do?"

She learned back in the chair again, shaking her head. "I won't be scared. I don't work that way. Just makes me stubborn."

The appreciation on his face had nothing physical in it. Miranda looked away and smoked and wondered if he drove a green Olds. Gonzales walked back to the chair facing her, sat down and cleared his throat.

"I wouldn't count on any state or federal contacts in this case. Rice Bowl Parties are being held in Chinatowns all across America. Ours is the largest. Over three hundred thousand people showed up for it last year, and we raised more money than all the other parties combined."

Miranda stubbed out the cigarette, grinding it slowly into the Tower of the Sun. "I saw your Humanity League badge next to your buzzer, Inspector. I've bought a few myself. And I blink the water out of my eyes when I watch the newsreels, or tsk-tsk when I open a *Life* magazine and see the pictures, and then I get out a hanky and blow my nose and send another fifty cents to the Red Cross. But no matter how many sweet little children are starving to death on the streets of Shanghai—or in the concentration camps of Germany—or even in the central valley, right here in California—no matter how unjust and cruel and evil that makes the world, and I'd say it makes it pretty goddamn bad—Eddie Takahashi was murdered yesterday. Who the fuck mourns for him?"

Her hands were clenched and red, on top of her desk. Goddamn it. She hadn't meant to lose her temper.

Gonzales reached in his coat and pulled out a billfold. It looked like Moroccan leather, and she wondered again how he got his money.

"Here's my card. Call me if you turn over something."

She frowned. "I thought the SFPD wasn't interested."

"Maybe not in prosecuting. At least not for murder. But there are other crimes."

She reached across and took it from his fingers, staring at it. "I assume this offer doesn't include your partner?"

"It includes no one but me, Miss Corbie."

She looked at him. "Fair enough. And I have a question for you. The herbalist on Sacramento near where Eddie was shot—the young one—Mike Chen. You talk to him?"

Gonzales fished for his notepad again and flipped a few pages.

"Only briefly. He has a record—served a couple of years for peddling reefers. He's been clean since."

"Maybe he just hasn't been caught."

Gonzales raised his eyebrows, and she smiled.

"It's been a long day, Inspector."

He stood up graciously, holding out his hand. She took it. His palm was warm and dry.

"Thank you, Miss Corbie. I suspect we'll be seeing you."

"Thank you, Inspector. And tell Phil he's lucky to have you."

Gonzales's cheeks blushed a light shade of red as he put on his fedora.

"I'd tell him the same thing about you, if that wouldn't be presumptuous."

Miranda turned toward the window. A trombone slide squealed from somewhere on Market, but was drowned out by a streetcar clang and the irritated horn of a car before she could figure out the song.

"It would be. Very much so."

He nodded. "Then forgive me, please."

She called him back when he turned to go. "Inspector—"

He looked at her with a question on his face, his hand on the doorknob.

"If you need cigs or a paper, buy them from the girl down in the lobby. She thinks you're a dreamboat."

He laughed at that, easily, and walked out the door, his coat billowing slightly behind him.

Five

Miranda waited two minutes before locking the office door. She walked to the window and opened it, breathing in Market Street, breathing out cops. No green Olds parked in front, just a throng headed up Kearny for the Rice Bowl Party.

Crowds poured around Lotta's Fountain, brushing fingers on the ornate metal work, one or two giving the bronze an affectionate pat. In a rare gush of sentiment, Miranda's father once told her she'd taken her first drink of water from it. Then he proceeded to quote Shakespeare and take another shot of brandy. Not his first.

She shut the window hard, displacing a morgue of dead flies. Sank into the chair behind the desk and pulled the bloody bandage out of her bra. The marijuana cigarettes were still intact, and she poked at them with a pencil, smelling them, then sealed them in an envelope. The bandage she set aside, along with the package from Mike Chen.

She was reaching for the phone when the receiver jangled, and she jumped, letting it ring three or four times. Grabbed the receiver and held it to her ear in a single motion of decision.

"Answer your damn phone, Miranda. What're you doing, playing hide-and-seek?"

Rick and his goddamn lilt. Battered felt hat pushed off his forehead, blue eyes apparently guileless while hunting for the next front-page exposé. She liked Rick, liked him a lot, and tried not to blame him because he wasn't Johnny. It was just that goddamn lilt she hated.

She held the phone with her shoulder and fished out another Chesterfield.

"I was playing hopscotch with a couple of cops. What do you want, Rick?"

Low whistle on the other end, while she reached for the desk lighter and snapped a spark.

"Hopscotch, huh? Sure it wasn't hangman? Or should I say hanglady?"

The sympathetic approach usually worked for him. Sympathy honed writing Lonely Hearts columns for some rag in New York City. She repeated, after taking a puff on the Chesterfield: "What do you want, Rick?"

"You know what I want. The *News* is the only newspaper with balls in this city, the only one that hasn't ground up and fed its liver to Old Man Hearst. This Takahashi story is dynamite—and I want to light it off."

"So?" Miranda blew a smoke ring.

"Don't bullshit me. I know you. You don't like getting the shove-off. The cops and their bosses, and the bosses of those bosses, have all told you to mind your own business and keep your legs crossed like a lady. Well, I'm betting you're not taking no for an answer. You got something and I want it."

She stubbed the cigarette, half-finished, on the tarnished Tower of the Sun ashtray. "Tell me again why I give a damn whether you need something."

His voice got deeper. "Look, Miranda, those Fair cases we worked on— not to mention what I did for you over Burnett's murder—when did I ever—"

"You got paid, Sanders. And you got a raise, if I remember correctly. Spare me the Irish singsong, and answer my question."

Through the phone she could hear the chaos and bustle of the newsroom, men shouting, the *rat-tat-tat-tat* of typewriter keys like machine guns.

"I hope you'd do it out of friendship. We've—shared some moments, Miranda. Maybe I figured wrong. Maybe I forgot that no one ever gets close enough to really know Miranda Corbie."

Somewhere a church bell rang the hour. *Dong.* Another bell. Rick was still on the line. Still waiting.

"All right. But—come through, Sanders. I'll need your help, too."

"Glad to give it. Listen, why don't we just start over? Let's go out tonight. I've got reservations at the Twin Dragon—we'd be on the spot for the Rice Bowl Party."

Dong. Three o'clock already. She didn't want to go out with Rick, didn't want to watch his eyes light up when she walked to the table, or pretend that her ankle was sore so she wouldn't have to dance, didn't want to talk about Spain or New York or Johnny or life beyond a fucking church bell.

She took a breath, fingernails tracing the indentations and scars of her desk top.

"I'll go, Sanders, but just for a drink and to tell you what I know. And what I need. Fair enough?"

"Of course. What else would I suggest? This is business, Miss Corbie, strictly business. I'll pick you up at five-thirty. You still at the Drake Hopkins?"

"Yeah. 640 Mason."

"See you tonight."

" 'Bye."

The cradle clanged when she dropped the phone. She waited until the line was clear, spent it looking through the Kardex on her desk. Picked out a card, dialed a number. The bandage and the small brown package of herbs were staring at her.

"Medico-Dental Building, please. Healy Labs . . . H-e-a-l-y. Uh-huh. Thank you."

She reached for another cigarette and caught herself, opened a side drawer.

"Healy Laboratory? This is Joan MacIntosh. I'm looking for Edith Placer. P-l-a-c-e-r. That's right. She's—let me see—she works there on Monday, Tuesday, and Friday evenings. Oh, I'm a friend of her mother's . . . down from Portland—that's right. She told me to look her up, but I don't have her current home address, just this one. Would you? Thank you so much—no, not yet. I saw the Fair last year, though . . . quite spectacular, I thought. I don't see how New York's could be any better—oh, thank you! That would be lovely. Yes, I have a pencil."

Her fingers found an ancient package of Wrigley's gum in the back of the drawer. She frowned at it, tossed it into the wastebasket under the desk, and wrote on the bent, gray card.

"Edith Placer, Garfield 9645, Braeburn Apartments, 861 Sutter—oh, I think I can find it. Yes, yes, I will. Thank you so much! 'Bye."

She was surprised not to have the address. Edith was a friend—as much as anyone. Miranda hesitated with her hand over the receiver, then picked it up and dialed the number. No answer, Madame. Please hang up the phone, Madame. She lowered it back into the cradle. Sat, unblinking, unfocused. The phone rang again.

She waited until the noise became insistent.

"Is this the Miranda Corbie Detective Agency? Miss Miranda Corbie?"

It was a voice usually smoother, more modulated. The harshness that crackled beyond the edges was a recent development.

"This is she. How can I help you?"

The woman paused. Miranda could hear thoughts being gathered and a story being put together on the other end.

"My—my husband. He was murdered."

Miranda sat back. "Madame, that's for the police depart—"

"They're doing nothing. Nothing! They said it was a heart attack, that he'd been in the hotel with—with a woman. Lester would never—"

"Ma'am, the police know—"

"They know nothing, they do nothing!" The woman wanted someone to hear her, to listen to her. There were a lot of women like that, not all of them with dead husbands.

"All right, start from the beginning. Your husband was in a hotel—"

"The Pickwick. In San Francisco. We live in Alameda. He works as an engineer for a shipping company. He didn't come home Thursday night, and I called the police. Then—then Friday morning they called me and said the maid at the Pickwick had—had found . . ."

"They said it was a heart attack?"

"Yes."

Miranda was silent until she heard the woman's breathing come back under control.

"Why are you so sure it was murder?"

"I—I just am. Lester would never—"

"You'd be surprised how frequently 'never' happens. I'm sorry for your loss, but I can't help you."

"I'm not without funds, Miss Corbie."

Miranda reached for the cigarettes again and this time gave in.

"It's not that." Deep drag, savored the Chesterfield. "Though it helps. I need to know why you're so certain. I need you to be honest with me, even if you're not with the cops. There's no point, otherwise."

The woman wrestled with herself some more while Miranda blew a smoke ring.

"It's a family matter, Miss Corbie. Not something I want to discuss without meeting you in person. I'll be in San Francisco tomorrow to see our attorney—settle Lester's . . . Lester's affairs. Can you meet me around one, at the Owl Drug Store lunch counter on Powell and Market? I'll pay your fee or whatever it is for the day. Is that all right?"

Miranda leaned back against the heft of the chair. She didn't have much room left over for anything other than Eddie Takahashi. But the lady was a paying customer. Her favorite kind.

"That's fine. What's your name?"

"Helen Winters. I know what you look like—I've seen your picture in the paper. I'll find you."

"Mrs. Winters—there are a number of private investigators in San Francisco. Why did you choose me?"

The woman paused again, choosing her words with deliberation. "For reasons which I will discuss tomorrow. Twenty dollars a day is your rate, is it not?"

"Normally, yes."

"Until tomorrow at one, then."

"Good-bye, Mrs. Winters."

She didn't realize the phone was off the hook until it made an irritated buzzing sound, and the whiny voice of a switchboard operator came on to scold her. She hung up, staring again at the bloodied bandage and poisonous powder from the herbalist. Then she reached for the trash can under her desk, looking for the morning paper. Saturday morning, before Eddie Takahashi died.

She found a *Chronicle* neatly folded, pulled it out and turned to the shipping news. On the bottom was a brief notice: "Believed to have died of a heart attack, marine engineer Lester Winters was found dead in his bed in the Pickwick Hotel on Fifth and Mission, San Francisco, on Friday. He is survived by his wife Helen Winters, of Alameda, and daughter Phyllis. Police suspect no foul play."

The church bell tolled the half-hour. Miranda locked up the poison and marijuana cigarettes in her safe. Grimacing, she retucked the bandage inside her bra, shoved on her hat, and headed for home.

"How's the Sling?"

"What?"

"I said, 'How's the drink?'"

The swirling gleam of the Twin Dragon's famous circular bar was dull

with excited clamor, peanuts, spilled booze, and the bad breath of the sales-
man on Miranda's left, most of him and his Rob Roy spilling on Miranda.
She shrugged her left shoulder hard, but he was beyond feeling anything. It
was Sunday night, the last night to tie one on for China.

She leaned into Rick. He was standing in between her and the blonde determined to jiggle what she had before the market dried up.

"What happened to that goddamned reservation?"

Rick smiled, shook his head, and gestured to his ear. Spilled his own
scotch-and-water when the blonde fell on him, guffawing over a thigh-slapper
from the gent two stools down. Rick helped prop up the dime-store Mae West,
while Miranda wiped her shoulder in disgust. So much for her Persian lamb
coat.

She downed the rest of the Singapore Sling, leaving a washed-out cherry
at the bottom of the martini glass, pushed it across the bar, and slid herself off
the stool. He nodded, and they squeezed through the bar crowd. They emerged
in a Waverly Place nearly as thick and almost as drunk.

Miranda and Rick turned right and followed a deer trail against the side
of walls and doors, past the Rice Bowl benefit auction for a new electric Frigi-
daire, past the Chinese band, past the firecrackers, finally reaching the corner of Waverly and Clay, home to the street carnival.

A fat lady was drawing betting money on a guess-your-weight machine,
the smell of popcorn, hot dogs, peanuts, and cotton candy masking the more
aromatic odors of Chinatown. Miranda leaned against a slab of old brick
wall, watching the wheel of fortune go around two booths down.

"What the hell are we doing here?"

Rick shook out a Lucky Strike, offered her one; she shook her head, he lit
it and finally answered.

"We'll find a place to talk. That's not the problem—"

"It isn't?"

"The problem is you need to relax. You had a shock yesterday, the cops are
riding you, and you need to lighten up and relax. For God's sake, Miranda—"

"You think I'm the problem? Listen, bright eyes, I agreed to meet you so
we can discuss this case you want to blow wide open—remember? And if I
need to relax so goddamn much, then why the hell did you bring me back to
Chinatown? You said it was business—remember?"

"Shhh. Shut up." He pulled her back toward the wall, and she angrily
threw his hands off.

"You cocky Irish bast—"

His mouth was on hers, suddenly, his body pressing her against the brick. On reflex, she opened her mouth, let herself be handled, let herself be used, before jolting back to the present. Rick wasn't using his tongue, the kiss not motivated by lust. Her hands unclenched and she held them gingerly against his back.

He whispered: "Good girl. Doyle and other cops, walking."

He tilted his head to the left, his hat obscuring any view of her face. His mouth was on her right ear.

"Gone yet?"

"Talking at a booth." She could feel his lips brush her hair. "What's the perfume?"

"Vol de Nuit."

"Not your old stuff. In New York."

His body was warm, and she squirmed. She stopped wearing Je Reviens the same year she stopped remembering.

"Too old-fashioned. They gone?"

"Wait. Turn your head."

She faced Clay, watching the roving bands of partygoers laughing under the neon signs.

"S'OK now."

Miranda took a deep breath, fixed her hat, met Rick's eyes. They crinkled at the edges, which irritated her.

"Thanks. I think. So what do you suggest now, Sir Galahad?"

He took her elbow. "Let's go get something to eat."

"In this mess?"

He shrugged. "We'll find a couple of seats. Universal Café, Shanghai Low, we'll find something."

They threaded through the games of chance with no chance at all, pop the balloon mister, throw a dart, do it for China. Men with sweaty necks tried to arm-wrestle the Chinese acrobat and win a dollar.

End of the alley, Sacramento Street. Drunks wavered by, unhindered by cars, all traffic except human closed off until tomorrow. Rick pulled Miranda toward a tawdry black tent, propped against an association wall. The sign outside read MADAME PENGO—PAST—PRESENT—FUTURE."

"Where the hell are you going?"

He pushed his hat up, eyed the long line of Madame Pengo's customers, mostly women, mostly older, mouths gnawed by petty tyrannies and dimly felt loss. A petite, pretty brunette in silver sable waited too, drinking it in, electric despair, excitement of struggle. Escaping the ennui of plenty.

"Madame Pengo—I remember that name . . ."

"Sanders, goddamn it, we either talk or I go home."

He shrugged, and led her to the corner. Miranda hesitated, not wanting to pass the herbalist, not wanting to see where Eddie fell. Not with the crowd, the girls in strapless dresses, hair perfumed, boyfriend tight.

Something hard brushed against her, and a little girl darted by them, rag-tag blur, maybe seven, maybe eight. Blindly running. She tripped and Rick caught her. Bloody, scraped knee. Dirty dress, dirty face. Deep circles under eyes too old for childhood.

Noise from the fortune teller's tent. A woman dressed in gaudy rags parted the waiting line of customers.

"Is she all right?"

The child backed against Rick's legs. Miranda put a hand on her shoulder.

"You're not her mother."

She didn't know why she said it and knew it to be true.

The woman's face faded against the cheap shiny jewelry.

"Come inside. Bring Anna."

They followed, Rick lifting the little girl into his arms. Her customers stood silent, curious, watching, a fat woman in gingham reaching out to touch Madame Pengo.

They stooped into the darkness. A table took up most of the space, covered in a stained white cloth and a cloudy crystal ball. The fortune-teller gestured to a couple of chairs. Walked to a crate behind the table, pulling out a ragged scarf and a bottle of rye. Wetted the fabric, and knelt in front of the little girl, dabbing the torn knee.

"Anna's not a relation, exactly. I'm watching her for her mother."

"Maybe you're spending a little too much time in the past and the future."

Not a flicker. "Lady, I'd be a rich woman if I had a nickel every time a child goes missing at a carnival. I'm not from Chinatown, and she knows it— figures she can run out on me. But she knows where she lives, she knows me, and I would've found her eventually, though I appreciate you getting her out of the street."

Her face was strong, hardened like only the once vulnerable can be. Elegance clung to her, faded and almost invisible, lingering behind the gauzy gypsy rags and imitation jewels. A woman who'd lived well when times were good, and times hadn't been good for a while.

Rick stared at her. The little girl remained expressionless, almost somnambulant, the energy that sent her running all gone away.

"Didn't you make a big ruckus in New York, about fifteen years ago? It was before the Crash . . . you played the hotel circuit, didn't you? Made quite a name—the Eurasian medium sensation, or something. No one could prove anything against you, but you disappeared. I guess fashions come and go, even in the crystal-ball circuit."

Eurasian. Explained the child's haunting beauty, explained her worn dress. Explained, most likely, where and what her mother was. One of the whores in one of the Chinatown bordellos, charging by exclusivity of service. Whites only, Chinese only, Orientals only. No such restrictions for the poorest, the most desperate.

Miranda said: "I know all the acts in this city. When did you get here?"

Madame Pengo smiled at Anna, ignoring the question. The little girl twisted out of Rick's grip, running to hug the fortune-teller.

"You see? Anna knows me. Her mother's a friend of mine."

Miranda fished in her purse, pulled out a Chesterfield. "You mind if I smoke?"

The gypsy shook her head. Rick lit the cigarette with a lighter. Miranda took a long drag on the Chesterfield, looking at the older woman.

"I think I know where her mother works. Does she get enough to eat? Does she go to school?"

Madame Pengo whispered something to Anna Miranda couldn't hear. Together they walked behind the table, the little girl standing, leaning against the woman while she sat.

"She's taken care of, lady. Her mother puts something by, when she can. I do, too. She gets fed, more than some people. You think it's easy? We're Eurasian. Chinese don't want us, whites don't want us. We're treated like mongrel dogs. But I've got enough money put by, in case—I've got enough money put by."

The fortune-teller stroked the girl's hair, and Anna pressed against her, eyes closed. Miranda thought of the other children she'd seen seven years ago in the Central Valley. The land of plenty, the land of hope, the land of racial purity. Aryans and Daughters of the American Revolution, all the rest cotton-pickers, hayseeds, stoop labor. No poor, no Okies, no coloreds, no mongrels allowed, not in agricultural towns. Not much of a new deal for them. No fucking deal at all.

Rick nudged Miranda. She squeezed the cigarette out, put the rest of it back in her purse. Madame Pengo looked up at them. Her voice was quiet.

"Thanks for helping Anna. If you sit down, I'll give you a free reading. I think maybe you could use some advice."

Miranda stared at her and the little girl, sat down in one of the wobbling chairs.

"What makes you say so?"

The fortune-teller studied her for a few seconds. "I know who you are. You're in a dangerous business. Word travels fast in Chinatown."

She was still stroking Anna's hair. The little girl watched Rick and Miranda, eyes unfocused, clutching the older woman's side.

Miranda said slowly: "General advice . . . or do you have something specific in mind?"

Madame Pengo shrugged. "Both. If you've got a good man, hold him." She nodded at Rick, who took the other seat.

"He's not my—"

"The Chinese say whoever learns without thought is lost. But whoever thinks without learning is in great danger."

"Am I in danger?"

Madame Pengo paused, looked at the floor for a minute. "And read your Bible. It's been a great comfort to me, lady, I can tell you. Let me see. I think Acts . . . Acts 27, 10 or 11, my memory isn't what it used to be."

No one spoke. The band music was still blaring from Stockton, the shouting and laughing outside getting louder. Madame Pengo's head sunk further on her chest, her hands resting on the table. Anna leaned against her. Her eyes were closed.

Motionless, the woman and the little girl, statue-still, carnival Pietà. Miranda stood up. She opened her purse and took out three dollars, most of the cash she had. She left it on the table, looked over at Rick.

He nodded, dug in his pockets, contributed a five. They walked toward the tent flap.

"She will be all right." The voice was deep, sonorous.

Miranda pivoted. No one else in the tent. The voice came from Madame Pengo. Flickering light, shadows on the thin high ceiling of the tent playing tricks, the woman's rags gleaming like silk and velvet, cheap trinkets like

Spanish gold. Little girl suddenly old, unnaturally still, face like a Madonna.

Madame Pengo opened her mouth, still motionless, and Miranda saw the words come out, foreign voice, clear and rich over the band, the shouts from the alley.

"She will be all right. There is much evil when child turns against father, but also salvation. She will be all right."

Miranda looked up and around the tent, unnerved, trying to spot a wire. Voice was too loud. Rick stared at the fortune-teller, mouth open, as if reading to himself.

"He loves you. Unlock the box. She will be all right."

Too loud, the voice, like cannon fire, like bombs in Madrid, church bells tolling the dead, sound pulsing through her body. Sweat trickled down Miranda's neck, her breath short, shallow, staccato.

"Paths cross. Find the way. He is lost. Find your way. Unlock. Open. Live. She. Will. Be. All. Right."

Miranda stumbled backward, hands pressed to her ears, face wrenched, agony. Rick was standing dumbly, staring at her. Before the gypsy could say anything else, Miranda turned and ran out of the tent.

Six

Rick found her across the street on Sacramento, leaning against the wall of a small rooming house wedged in between the commercial storefronts.

She was smoking, staring at the herbalist shop through the massed bodies of partygoers crawling up the street.

"Are you OK, Miranda?"

She looked at him, blew smoke out the side of her mouth. A percussive banging was crawling up from the cement and into their spines, chased by chanting, cheering, and crashing cymbals. The parade was finally arriving on Grant Street, four hours late, timing their entrance with the final rays of sunlight sinking behind Ocean Beach.

"Weren't they supposed to march in the afternoon?"

"They did. Got stuck on Market—too many people throwing money. You know the city."

"Yeah. We give 'til it hurts."

Darkness crept out from basements and swept up from Market Street and the piers, the Chinatown neon glittering with brittle pink and blue hues. Miranda shivered in spite of her coat, in spite of the Chesterfield. She dropped the cigarette and ground it with her pump.

"Where are we going?"

He took her arm, leading her down the hill to Grant. Worry framed his face. "I owe you dinner, but I don't have much left for anything more than a quick bite at the Universal. At least it'll be away from the parade."

"How in the hell are they going to fit any more people in here?"

He shrugged, pulling her aside. Four couples from the smart dinner set tinkled by, glissading up the Sacramento grade.

"Miranda . . . are you sure you're all right?"

She jerked her elbow out from his hand, and walked faster. "Quit goddamn asking me. Why wouldn't I be?"

Firecrackers popped behind them, the noise carried aloft on the drums of the parade and the horns from the band up the street.

"Don't pull that crap with me. You were damn rattled back there. I was, too."

"She's a carny. Like the rest of them. Hustling people out of dimes and nickels, preying on desperation, smelling fear. I've seen it a thousand times on Treasure Island, and in every two-bit flea circus between here and the end of the road. Except this is the end of the road."

"But the kid—"

"Listen, Sanders . . ."

She stopped in the middle of Grant, while a family of five wove around them, the parents calling the oldest son back to watch his little sister.

". . . I don't want to talk about it. I don't like getting rooked. The kid wasn't starving. Maybe the whole thing was a setup, who knows? The kid'll be fine. She'll be—"

"—all right?" He looked into her eyes. "You know, once in a while it's OK to show some vulnerability, Miranda."

She held his gaze and then broke it, staring ahead at the corner of Washington and Grant, the *pound-pound-pound* of the parade a couple of blocks behind them echoing her heart beat.

"The streets are littered with vulnerable women."

She strode ahead, not looking back to see if he was following.

The band warbled and wailed, trying its best to ride a Cole Porter number before getting bucked off. Rick was clutching her bare back, pretending he knew how to dance. Every step proved he didn't.

Miranda repressed a belch, brought up by the ham and cheese she'd eaten too fast, standing up, at the Universal Café. So much for dinner. They'd drifted toward the YWCA building, still searching for a place to talk. She agreed to dance. She didn't want to think about why.

"So record on this Mike or Ming Chen, record on Filipino Charlie. Your friend will get the blood type on Eddie Takahashi. And the green Olds . . . are you sure it was an Olds?"

"Yes."

He shook his head. "Maybe you don't know your models as well as you think you do. If it was a newer Dodge, it could be the hit-runner on Seventeenth Street everyone's looking for. That was a green coupe. I can look up the poor bastard that got killed—see if there's any connection. All I know is he was an old man. And I'll keep my ear to the ground for rumbles about Gonzales and the other cop—what was his name?"

She winced, as his left foot crushed the top of her pumps. "Duggan."

He drew her closer, looking down into her face.

"What about Phil, Miranda? I thought you and Phil—"

The song was over, and she pulled away, the crowd clapping without enthusiasm.

"I see a place we can stand."

Rick followed her to a spot on the wall behind a palm frond. "Are you cold?"

"No."

"You look cold, why don't I—"

"No, Sanders. Quit worrying about me, for God's sake."

He shrugged, taking out a cigarette, his voice flinty.

"You're no good to me in the hospital with pneumonia. Don't you own a whole dress?"

"Look around, Adrian. It's the style. My evening clothes are working clothes."

He struck a match on his thumb and lit the Lucky Strike. "Doesn't look much like a uniform to me. You never answered about Phil."

She drew in her breath, trying to control the impulse to run away.

"Phil's got nothing to do with this."

"He put the kibosh on the case. He's sending goons like Duggan to harass you. What do you mean, he's got nothing to do—"

"He's retiring, goddamn it. He's old, he's giving it a rest, he doesn't want me around to fuck it up for him with his new boss. OK? Lay off, Rick."

He shrugged again, took a drag, and tried to sound nonchalant.

"Just wondered why he was treating you like a golden girl last year and now he's hung you out to dry. I know he's the fatherly type. Though frankly, that's not how the boys in the newsroom described it."

A boy singer stepped up to the stage in an ill-fitting white dinner jacket and handled the microphone like it was his first date. His voice cracked before he hit the high note in "If I Didn't Care."

Miranda turned to Rick. "You know what, Sanders? Fuck the boys in the newsroom."

"Miranda . . ."

"As a matter of fact . . . fuck you, too."

He jerked the cigarette out of his mouth, let it fall to the ground, and crushed it with his shoe.

"You're lucky I know you. Although maybe I should say knew you."

She was watching the sweat trickle down the singer's forehead. Rick stared at her.

The song warbled on, the boy singing about something he didn't know, didn't understand, never had, never felt.

"You've gotten really good at locking people out, Miranda. A college degree in three years. But you weren't the only one who lost Johnny. And one of these times you're gonna find yourself in an empty room with no furniture. And nothing to keep you warm."

She turned to watch him leave, his shoulders square and tight at the hat check counter. She watched him pick up his battered coat, covered in ash and food stains, and the old brown fedora that matched, the brim slightly too wide for his face.

She watched him dig around for his last quarter to leave a tip, and watched him, without a backward glance to the dance floor or her, stride through the door, the Chinese doorman smiling broadly and tipping his hat.

. . . if I didn't care . . . for . . . you?

The song set was over, the singer retiring with relief and the audience clapping with it. Miranda collected her wrap, her coat, and her hat—she never danced in a hat—put a quarter in the tip tray and headed out.

Noise hit her on Clay, the kind you couldn't dance to. Rice Bowl Party in full swing, the drunks in charge. High-class drinkers flitting out of the nightclubs, bees from a hive, honey for China, spiked by a dry martini and the promise of a hand job after the fireworks. Lower-class drinkers wandering, looking for a trash can or a gutter to empty their guts in, a quick blow in the alley if the B-girl could get it up.

She stood in a doorway, planning the shortest route back to the apartment. Saw a young woman, shoulders hunched in the damp cold, hurrying down Clay Street, a dress in her hands.

Chinese, beautiful, not as young as she looked. Hell, thought Miranda, none of us are anymore. She ran across the street, narrowly missing some screaming Stanford fraternity boys getting carted up the hill in a rickshaw.

"Betty—Betty Chow!"

Recognition. Then something else, something Miranda didn't expect. Fear.

"I'm sorry, I don't know who—"

"Yeah, you do. It's Miranda. We worked at Dianne's together a couple of years ago."

Betty laughed nervously, clutching the silk and brocade gown she was holding. She wasn't wearing a coat.

"Oh—of course. Miranda Corbie, wasn't it?"

Miranda stared at her. "Still is. What's wrong, Betty? Dianne treating you badly, or aren't you with her anymore?"

"Nothing's wrong. I'm just late for the fashion show. I ran out without my coat on." Voice evasive, stockings too shabby.

"Something's wrong. Is it Dianne?"

Betty looked at her wristwatch, glanced up at Miranda's face, then looked around at the street full of people. None of them seemed to be paying any attention to the two women standing on the north corner of Clay. She bit her lip, rubbing some of the Tangee off. Miranda noticed her nails were chewed, too.

The Chinese girl seemed to reach a decision, and lowered her voice.

"I can't talk here, and I'm late. I'm not—not with Dianne's anymore."

Miranda raised her eyebrows. Dianne and her illusions protected the women, the cloaked respectability of the tearoom and gathering place for escorts. It was usually their choice on how much of an escort they were willing to be. Away from Dianne there were no choices at all.

"Betty—call me. I'm in the Monadnock. Maybe I can help."

Betty clutched the embroidered red and gold dress tighter, her body halfway gone already. Something was holding her back. She licked her lips again, her voice even lower than Miranda's.

"You're gonna need some help yourself. Don't—don't track the Takahashi case."

She was already half turned toward Stockton when Miranda put a hand on her arm. "Betty—what's—"

The girl shook herself, pulling away from Miranda's arm, and scuttled down the hill. Her head was down, but from the angle of her neck, Miranda could tell she was scanning both sides of Clay Street.

The Memory Box was shut and dusty. The only way to open it was with some scotch. Or rye. This time it was rye, neat, a little ice, the moisture beading on the glass, the cubes making that oh so pleasant clink of conviviality. Good times. Memories.

She was sitting by the window, her usual seat when she couldn't sleep. She'd gone to the fashion show, noticed the dresses were getting shorter, didn't notice Betty. Betty was gone. Rick was gone. Miranda was alone, but again, she was used to it. She even liked it that way, most of the time.

Just her and the Memory Box. And the scotch. Or was it rye?

The fireworks were all the *Chronicle* said they'd be. She'd stood up in Portsmouth Square, next to a young couple who didn't know any better than to be happy. She'd watched them, watched them watching the sky, her red lips gasping, making an O of delight while he held her, held her close and whispered. When the firework that showed refugees from the U.S.S. Panay lit them up, lit the sky, and the crowd gasped, not sure whether to applaud or stay silent, the girl with the red lips got teary and he held her tighter and then they went away. Miranda was alone.

She came back to the apartment, tried some music, but it was all Someone to Watch Over Me and Just the Way You Look Tonight and I've Got You Under My Fucking Skin. So she figured what the hell. If the radio was going to do that to her, she'd play along. She took out the Memory Box.

She kept them in there so they wouldn't spill over and make an hour or a minute suddenly messy and sodden. The pain she hid well and buried deep, mixed and swirling, rye on ice, indissoluble from memory, and locked in the same box.

She tried to throw away the key, but it always came back.

1937.

They made love in a small clay house, in a bed that was a straw mattress and too small for one of them and so just big enough for both. He insisted on going to "where the action is." They argued. She lost. They made love some more, eating some dry cheese and bread they'd stored in the wardrobe and drinking from a jug that fit under the bed.

The taste of his skin filled her mouth. His lips on her body. Inside her. Johnny.

"Go back to New York."

"Not when you're here."

"Randy—I've got to go. You know that."

"I know the paper is paying you to cover the war, not fight it."

"Same thing."

"No it isn't. You don't need to go to the front."

"I won't argue with you."

The sun would rise soon. They could feel the light coming, and their bodies responded with urgency, blending together as if the force would stop the earth, stop the sun, stop the time. More wine. Not enough.

"I mean it, Rand—go back to New York."

"I trained to be a nurse."

"How can I do my job if you're there? At least go back to the capital. Wounded men are everywhere in this poor goddamned country."

"I want to be close to you."

He couldn't answer her, just held her close. She felt his lungs expand, his heart beating. She felt him warm and strong next to her. She was happy.

Another building. Gray Spanish hospital, the sleepy decay of a few hundred years crawling on the walls like ivy.

There were men in there. Old men, young men, but always poor men. The Americans and Europeans sometimes had money, but never the Spanish.

She looked at them, the harrowed, lined faces, the dust-dried skin, the corroded bodies, twisted like barbed wire. The pain. It was everywhere. If you were blind you could smell it. If you were deaf you could taste it.

There were women, too. Separate ward, until they ran out of space. Mothers, daughters, wives. Defined by the dying men next to them. They all belonged to somebody. They usually went without complaint, without notice, staring through the ceiling, looking for the God that had forsaken them, taking his hand. Father. Son. Husband.

No matadors in Spain that year. No robust country boys daring the bull from his fence. No Cava for the old men. No pity for the young. Not Hemingway's Spain. She never saw Hemingway.

She found him there. But it wasn't him. It was someone who looked like him, but already didn't smell like him. Someone who had been too close to a shell. Too close. To the front. Too close. To the cause. Too close. To her.

Johnny.

There were always couples walking down Mason. The Curran was down the street on Geary, the hotels were around the corner. Couples liked places like that, places that danced and swung to a gentle rhythm, his hips against hers, her lips brushing his neck.

The ice was melting, diluting the amber brown of the rye. She eyed it critically, looking for something, forgetting what it was. Eddie Takahashi, maybe. Or Betty. Or Mrs. Whatsit's husband's killer, if he was killed, which who the hell knew. Or Rick.

Last year she'd told him "No expectations." He didn't listen to her. They never did.

There'd never been any, and never would be any. She made sure of that. But hope . . . hope died slowly and painfully, one gasp—one call, one drink, one look—at a time. She saw it on his face.

She didn't want to hurt anybody. She just wanted to be left alone. With the Memory Box.

Phil found her at Dianne's once, and she'd known he wanted her, wanted her bad. It was one of the social hours, when the young men with old faces came in, sweat on their eyelids, looking. Phil smelled like a cop, like cough drops and tobacco and carbon paper. They never smell like guns . . . only in the pulps. They never look like Spencer Tracy or Gary Cooper, either.

Dianne called it teatime, and her girls were always on the menu.

Before Burnett's.

She'd felt him tense, felt him wish his hair wasn't gray and his stomach muscles were what they were back in '17. She felt him want her, but she didn't let him have her.

He was a decent man. And he wanted her too much.

So they played like they were uncle and niece. Phil the protector. Phil, the man who helped her nail Burnett's killer. And the Incubator Babies racket. Phil. Who wanted her too much.

A party of six was walking down the hill now, loud, wearing the white badges of humanity and playing with chopsticks that one of the men was throwing in the air. Their looks said: I care about China, and incidentally, I like a damn good time.

She was fair. She'd stayed a friend. She didn't fade, didn't disappear, didn't melt into the city and forget their names. No, she remembered. She locked them in the Memory Box. Separate compartment.

She didn't need Phil. Or Rick. Or her washed-up, drowned-out father. Didn't need anyone. Would never need anyone again. Once in a while, she liked to be around people, people eating and drinking and making noise, and she reached in and pulled out the name of someone still around, someone who was still talking to her. She called them friends. Sometimes they called her back. If they didn't, she moved on.

Miranda Corbie. Private Investigator. That was who she was. She liked the sound of it. She took another drink.

Her name meant "things to be wondered at." In Latin. She'd heard him recite "Oh, brave new world, that has such people in it" too many times to give a shit anymore. She figured he named her so he could repeat the line.

She'd been conceived the third day of the Quake and Fire. His father, when sober, was meticulous in his reporting of the incident, as he called it.

Her mother was a girl, barely sixteen. She worked in a bar. When it hit, she thought she was going to die. She and another boarder, an educated man, a teacher of English literature and a very minor poet, escaped together, ran from the tremors and the fire and found solace in a tent in Golden Gate Park.

It was an act of desperation for both of them. Probably the last time her father ever thought with anything other than his frontal lobes or a whiskey bottle. He was such a pissy bastard when he didn't drink.

She was born on a cold, crisp January Sunday, nine months to the day. She never knew her mother. Her father made sure of it. He had a career to think of, and he made it clear to the world that he was caring for a relative's infant who'd been recently and tragically orphaned. He'd adopt her later. Like that made a difference.

Miranda Corbie, Private Investigator. She liked that. Her mother's name was Corbie. She'd never been able to trace her, figured she was dead, and took her last name. It meant "raven" in Scottish. She liked that, too.

The Chesterfield tasted good with the rye. She leaned her head back, staring across at the brick apartment building she faced, watching.

Once in a while she saw someone who danced like him. Someone who walked or smoked or flirted like him. And she'd unwrap the Memory Box and take it out, drink too much. Like Madame Pengo, she'd look through the highball glass and see her past.

She didn't really give a damn about the future.

Miranda got up from the window, tumbler in her hand. She flipped on the radio, but all they were playing that night was "Someone to Watch Over Me."

Part Two

The Parade

Seven

San Francisco yawned and stretched, waking to Monday morning with a hangover. Chinatown shutters squealed open on rusty hinges, the streets shut off now, self-contained, the cotton-candy smell evaporated, the carnival gone on a dilapidated coach car to smaller, more simple places.

Old women swept chicken bones and popcorn and cigarette butts from foyers. Incense burned, sending curling waves of smoke drifting down to the Bay, to tickle the noses of businessmen on the ferry to Oakland.

Filipino and Japanese businesses huddled around the outskirts, lumped into the district by default, hanging on to what warmth they could find. Walls outside, walls inside. Hemming them in. Driving them out. Nowhere to go but back to Chinatown.

San Francisco watched, blind. Any holes in the wall were filled with money, Rice Bowl Parties, parades. As the drunk at Vanessi's was fond of saying, they all looked alike.

Light streamed through the gap in the curtains. Miranda opened an eye, watched the dust motes dance. The other side of the bed was cold. She reminded herself to get a smaller one.

The satin sleeves of her tailored nightshirt soothed her skin, and she padded to the window, across the wooden floor with its scattered rugs and faded polish. The weather was bright, and it was later than she wanted. She peered out on the Mason Street traffic.

There was a green Olds across the street.

She cursed her slowed reflexes, jerked her head behind the curtains. Her tongue was thick, didn't belong to her. Goddamn it. Wake the hell up, Miranda.

She stumbled toward the kitchenette, her hands shaking while she poured the Hills Brothers. A victory in not dropping the glass ball. She splashed some water on her face, rubbing it with her hands. The deep brown liquid bubbled to the top, the aroma of hot coffee filling the small apartment. Her own version of incense.

She walked to the window. Olds still there. Dark windows. She couldn't make out the plates.

She found a couple of dollars crumpled up in the purse she'd used last night, threw on her robe and pressed the buzzer for the doorman downstairs, waiting for the sound of footsteps before she opened the door.

"Miss Corbie? You needed something?"

Roy stood in front of her, hat in his hands, his uniform hanging loosely on his thin frame. Thirty-five and overeager, he cruised the piers for an occasional sailor, but never brought him home to Mother.

"Can you leave the building for a minute, go up the hill to the market on Bush, come back down with some cigarettes?"

"Don't you worry, Miss Corbie, I've got some Chesterfields if you—"

"I need you to walk out of the building. Check something for me but not get noticed. Can you do it?"

His blue eyes, always on the vague side, darted back and forth, from her to the dollar she was holding.

"Can you do it?" she repeated, fighting the urge to scream at him.

He whispered: "It's a case, isn't it? I'll be happy to help, Miss Corbie. Anything you want. You know I—"

"Take this. Walk up to Bush, go to the corner market. Buy me some Chesterfields and a pint of Tom Moore. Across Mason, you'll see a green Olds with dark windows. Don't look at it too much."

Roy shrank further back into his uniform. His voice rose into a stage whisper. "Are they criminals?"

Miranda rubbed her forehead. "I don't know. Just memorize the plates—the license plate numbers. As soon as you get to the market, write them on a card."

She fished around in her purse. "Here's one of mine. Walk back down the hill, don't look at the car, come straight up here. If I'm in the shower, slide the card under the door and bring the bag back later. Got it?"

He nodded. His Adam's apple bobbed beneath the uniform tie.

She handed him two dollars. "Pack of Chesterfields and a pint of Tom. Or any bourbon, if they don't have it. Keep the change for yourself."

He raced down the stairs, not waiting for the elevator. She didn't dare look out the window again. Ran a finger through her hair, feeling her cheeks and throat. Goddamn rye. Bourbon never made her feel like this.

The pipes whined when she turned up the hot water. The heat felt like ice running down her thighs and hips, washing away the stains of the night before.

Miranda stretched a long leg out on the toilet, rubbing the latest cream to promise eternal youth into her calves and ankles. Legs, breasts, and face. Her meal ticket, along with the carefully folded license in her pocketbook.

She examined her skin. Bent and stretched again, knees straight, feeling the backs of her calves pulling her as her fingers dangled above the ground, enjoying the tension in her muscles, the pain of the exercise. She slowly lifted herself up, faced the mirror.

Cupping her breasts in each hand, Miranda judged them with the dispassionate interest of an artist. Still firm. Cleavage good. Nipples not too big. They'd last a few more years. If she stayed away from the rye. She massaged the cream into them, adding more to her elbows, her upper arms.

Calistoga, after this. After the Takahashi case. Cases, she reminded herself. There was Mrs. What's-her-name this afternoon, the one who thinks her husband was knocked off. Eddie Takahashi and Mr. Whithers or Whatsit or something. Winters. That was it—Winters.

She slapped under her chin, making faces to keep her skin taut. Layered on more cream, taking extra precautions around her eyes, not looking in them. They were a little too red. She'd need some drops.

She stood back, hands at her side, facing the mirror. A few more years. After that, maybe they'd all be dead.

Miranda threw on her long, thick robe, tucked her feet into slippers, and walked to the foyer, making a skidding noise on the slippery wooden floor. Time to find out who the hell was following her around.

She frowned. No card, no Roy. Her hand froze halfway through her wet hair. She'd forgotten to lock the door chain. And on the entry table was a card she'd never seen before.

The gun was in her purse . . . or was it? She fought the urge to run, forced herself to stay still. She could still smell the coffee, and now . . . a trace of something else. Cigarette. And men's cologne.

The knock at the door made her spin, her robe gaping. She backed up against the wall by the door, trying to control her breathing. Another knock.

"Miss Corbie?" Roy's voice sounded tremulous, apologetic.

Miranda leaned against the cold stucco, tightening her robe. No one else was in the apartment. Not now. But while she'd been in the shower, while she'd been taking care of her body, someone violated her home.

She opened the door. Roy held out a small paper bag. "I had to walk three blocks to find the Chesterfields, Miss Corbie."

"Did you get the plates?"

He stuttered, plucking at an eyebrow. "I-I couldn't remember it all—I had to w-walk farther, trying to remember, and b-by the time I came back down the hill they were gone. I c-could only remember part of it."

Miranda grabbed the card and bag out of his hands, and started to shut the door. "Thanks."

"I'm r-really sorry, Miss Corbie—"

"Don't worry about it."

She finally got the door shut, and leaned against it, her hands behind her, staring at the foreign object on her entry table. There wouldn't be prints on it. If they could get into her apartment silently, on a Monday morning, they were too good to leave prints.

She picked it up. Joe Gillio's, an Italian café out of the Olympic Hotel. A gathering hole for retired bootleggers. Except bootleggers never retired, they just changed cargo.

Miranda flipped it over. There were two words scrawled in pencil: "nice legs."

Roy was wringing his hands when she left the Drake Hopkins. She gave him a pat on the shoulder. Fear, then anger hit her in a wave, making her legs shake.

No green Oldsmobiles clutched the grade or merged into the apathetic traffic. She gathered herself, feeling the city swirl and surge around her like the merry-go-round at Playland. Looking up and down the hill, she pulled sunglasses from her purse. Just another sunny day in San Francisco.

She headed for the hotel bustle of the St. Francis. Her feet, sheathed in navy pumps that eased the strain on her legs, walked down Mason toward a more expensive breakfast than usual. This morning she didn't really give a damn about saving a quarter.

The St. Francis. One of the oldest hotels in the city and one of the stateliest, overlooking Union Square and the grand department stores with the presumptive authority of a floor walker. It had survived the Quake and Fire, and like the other buildings that lived, scattered throughout the city, the experience graced it with an air of stability, even arrogance. Build your steel and glass and chrome, the St. Francis said. I'll be here forever.

Miranda crossed the street at Union Square, staring up at the flags that stretched and snapped against the red-brown brick above the doors and awning. She needed that attitude, that sense of permanence. For fifty cents, it came with pancakes.

The Braeburn was one of those nondescript brick apartment houses that faded against the sun and damp. Eventually it would disappear. Some of its tenants already had.

It squatted on Sutter between Leavenworth and Jones like an apple lady on a park bench. Young couples with too many kids, spinster matrons, and men who worked the nightshift called it home. The building reeked of barely-there respectability.

Miranda stood outside, the blueberry pancakes and four cups of coffee from the St. Francis filling her stomach with more than food. Ten o'clock. Time for work.

She buzzed number 343. The little tag that read PLACER was almost indecipherable. No answer on the first ring, except for a large man in overalls who stumped down the front steps, giving her a look and forgetting about her immediately afterward. He spat a wad of tobacco into the gutter, and whistled as he walked down Sutter toward Leavenworth.

She rang again, this time keeping her finger on the buzzer. A baby started crying somewhere inside, and a window in the front yanked open. A baggy-eyed face with hair that looked like it washed floors stared down at her, and the window shut again. Finally, the opening buzzer rattled the door, and she pushed her way into the foyer, taking off her sunglasses. Edith was home.

The fourth stair creaked and the pale orange carpet was stringy along the sides, the smell of antiseptic smugly masking any tenant's second thoughts. Rooms were hard to come by in San Francisco. Clean usually cost extra.

When she reached the third floor, she heard a small gasp from the quiet darkness of the landing.

"Miranda? I haven't seen you in months. Haven't heard from you, either. I kind of thought you'd moved east."

The voice was whispered, not too reproachful. Miranda turned right, smiling, toward the middle-aged woman with her head out the door.

Edith was dishwater blond and dumpy, a woman who wore cheer on her face by default. She was perched on the edge of forty but hadn't fallen over yet.

"I'm sorry, Edith. You know I'm lousy at staying in touch, particularly with all the work at the Fair."

Miranda led with her trump card. Edith's face brightened immediately, though she still didn't open the door, and kept her voice a whisper.

"Oh, yeah—I remember reading about you. Those were some big cases, huh? Guess it beats nursing all to hell."

"So far it's a living. Can I come in? I'm on a case—that's what I'm here about."

Edith's cheeks flushed. "I—I've got someone . . ."

Miranda raised an eyebrow. "Say no more." She leaned closer. "Sly girl, Edith. Who is it?"

Clutching a pink robe around her neck, Edith stepped into the hallway, shutting the door carefully. The flush spread down to her neck.

"I don't want to wake him. His name is Milton. He's a clerk at Mount Zion's." Her face grew even softer, and her eyes drew back to the doorway, as if she could see through the wood to Milton snoring in bed.

"Have you set a date?"

She shook her head, and the red intensified. Miranda hurried over it without stumbling.

"Well, look, Edith, I'm very happy for you. I'm on a case right now . . . I was hoping you could help me."

"What do you need?"

Miranda squeezed her friend's shoulders, suppressing a twinge of guilt. "I can't give these things to the cops. Don't ask me why, it's better you don't know. But I need to see what you can tell me from the bloodstains . . . blood type, maybe how old they are?"

She pulled out a paper bag from her purse, and handed it to Edith, who stared dubiously at the bloodied bandages inside.

"You work at the Medico-Dental later tonight, right? Healy Labs? Can you run some tests?"

Edith was poking her finger at the bandages. "Yeah. I guess so, Miranda. I can try, anyway. When do you need to know?"

"As soon as possible. You know how it is."

"Yeah." Edith gave her an embarrassed smile. "I hope you can come by and meet Milton sometime. Maybe go to lunch. It's been a long time."

"Sure. Let's do that. Here's my card—phone's in my office, if I'm not there just leave a message with the service."

"All right. I hope we can get together. It would be nice to talk about old times, you know?"

Old times meant Spain, when they were both there as nurses. Miranda had fudged her qualifications, got in by taking a few classes and strong-arming the Red Cross. Edith was an at-home convalescent nurse, caring for elderly people, wanting excitement in her life. After Spain she'd had enough.

"Sure, Edith. And thanks for doing this for me—I don't know what I'd do without you. Ring me if you want tickets to the Fair next year."

"Oh, can I? I'd love to take Milton!"

Miranda smiled at her, putting on her sunglasses. If Milton were still around, she'd make sure they both got tickets.

She stepped into the coolness of Sutter Street. A White Front streetcar was gliding toward her, headed for the not-so-fresh air of Whitney's and Topsy's and Laughing Sal down at the beach.

Miranda climbed on, nodding to the conductor, who was arguing about whether Lefty could lead the Seals to another pennant.

The car rolled away, heading down Sutter. She leaned back against the hard seat, looked out the window. No green Olds. She clutched her large black leather purse, feeling the outline of the Smith and Wesson with her fingertips.

Ten blocks or so until she reached Webster. She took out her *Chadwick's Street Guide*, flipped to Wilmot Street. The Number Two car would continue on down the Richmond District, crawling to a stop at Sutro Baths. The hobo in front of her needed one. She opened a window to clear the air, her eyes behind the sunglasses still hunting for green.

Miranda opened her purse, taking out her wallet. She removed the card from the lining and held it to her nose. Sweat, cigarettes, and cheap aftershave. She flipped it over and looked at the writing, her stomach tightening. Block letters with a blunt pencil, deliberate and slow. Just like he'd learned it in the second grade.

She put the card away carefully, taking out a pair of gloves. They matched her dark blue tweed jacket. She was dressed to be demure today, the respectable Miss Corbie, as tame as an undertaker's secretary. Two more stops.

The conductor rang his bell at a rickety truck blocking the tracks. A squawking of chickens erupted, and Miranda stood up to look outside. The poultry man was rushing back to start Old Bessie. After four or five attempts, a rooster crowed and the ignition turned over, to the general amusement of Miranda's fellow passengers. The White Front crawled along.

She wasn't sure what she was going to say to them. What could she say? Sorry I saw your son die? Sorry I couldn't save him? Sorry no one gives a fuck about who did it?

She stepped out at the corner of Webster, walked uphill toward Bush, then half a block to Pine. Wilmot was a small residential street, hovering on the outskirts of Little Osaka. The air was quieter here, and colder, the wind from the two cemeteries of Calvary and Laurel Hill blowing a somber chill through the Western Addition.

Number 8 was a small, wood-frame rooming house, smaller and more worn than the Braeburn. It had given up the fight for respectability long ago, and now just wanted to sleep, decaying slowly, one board and one boarder at a time.

She climbed four front steps, knocked on the door and waited. Shuffling feet behind it answered her. A small, elderly Japanese woman opened the door.

"I'm looking for the Takahashis. There wasn't a number or buzzer."

The woman stared at her, drawing the edges of her kimono together. "You police?" she demanded.

The question surprised Miranda. "No. I'm not with the police. But I do want to help—"

She started to close the door. "Don't need help."

Miranda took two steps at a time, holding her hand against the wood shutting her out. "I think you do."

The woman looked at her again. "Who are you?"

"I'm the woman who found Eddie. I was with him when he died."

The woman met her eyes. This time she nodded. She opened the door, and Miranda stepped over the threshold into another small, dark foyer. It was as clean as the Braeburn but claustrophobic, with cherry-wood furniture and altar incense burning behind a lacquered screen.

"I get them."

She walked up the narrow stairway, her small feet soundless. Miranda heard a knock, and then several voices, raised in discussion, speaking Japanese.

Time to meet the Takahashis.

Eight

Gray-brown smoke curled languidly, hesitating before it drifted past the stairs. The incense suffocated her and so did the room. Add satin padding and it could've been six feet under. Miranda moved near a paint-scratched door that presumably separated the kitchen, wrapping both hands around her purse so she wouldn't reach for a cigarette.

The voices were louder now, none of them under fifty or inclined to climb down and speak with her. The sharpie at Fong Fong mentioned Eddie's sister. Miranda flipped up a corner of the worn, ornate carpet with her shoe. This wasn't much of a place for the young.

A photograph in a tarnished silver frame gleamed dully by the entrance door, perched on a mahogany hall tree more expensive than the rooming house. She ran her gloved finger across the rich red brown. No dust.

The handsome young man stared proudly and fiercely into the camera. The clothes were her father's generation. Maybe Eddie's grandfather. She searched the taut, high cheekbones for a resemblance, and though Eddie had been a good-looking kid, the pride had transformed into something less, the ferocity into something more.

She set the frame back in place and looked around. Four rooms, all in a row at the top of the stair landing. Four boarders or more, depending on how many people slept in each room. She wondered if the Takahashis paid the rent or collected it. And whether Eddie's work for Filipino Charlie had helped.

A creak signaled a settlement had been reached. She smoothed down the tweed. The old lady who let her in was climbing down the stairs. Two other people, a man in his dotage and a woman thirty years younger, hovered behind her.

Miranda's eyes accidentally met those of the younger woman, and she blinked, almost flinching. The last time she'd looked into them had been two days ago. When Eddie was dying on Sacramento Street.

Eddie's father was stooped, crooked, bald. A cane kept him propped in a semi-upright position. His rheumy-red eyes dragged from the floor to peer at Miranda. No sign of greeting or grief.

The woman behind him was a different story. Sadness. Rage. And fear—just like Eddie.

The old lady with the tatty kimono spoke first.

"Mr. Takahashi. Mrs. Takahashi. You talk, you talk down here."

No upstairs invitation then. Must've been part of the settlement.

"Thank you. I'll be brief."

She wanted to ask who the hell the lady in the robe was. She focused on Mrs. Takahashi instead. The wife kept still, behind her husband.

"My name is Miranda Corbie. I was with your son when he died."

Eddie's mother was a pretty woman, early fifties, with a few gray hairs fluttering around a soft, round placid face, worn at the edges by mourning. She wore a floppy black dress about eight years out of date and glasses that made her look dowdier than her figure suggested. Her eyes shifted around Miranda, cautious, not looking at her directly.

"Yes, Miss Corbie. The police explained who you are. We appreciate that you tried to find help for our son."

The old lady in the kimono was following Miranda like a watchdog. Miranda looked first at Mrs. Takahashi, then the old lady, flicked a glance at the husband. He was staring ahead, at nothing. Or maybe he saw something no one else did.

"I'm sorry. I'm doing everything I can to help bring your son some justice."

The old lady suddenly let loose a volume of Japanese. Mrs. Takahashi replied sharply until her husband rasped out a monosyllable. So he could hear, or at least speak. All three turned back to face Miranda.

Eddie's mother spoke slowly. "You understand we cannot pay you. We did not ask you to search—"

"Of course. There's no question of payment. This is *pro bono*—free—for the sake of your son."

Mrs. Takahashi stopped clutching her hands so tightly. The old kimono lady knew what free meant but didn't quite believe it.

"But—but why, Miss Corbie? You didn't know him."

"I don't know, to be honest. It doesn't matter, shouldn't matter to you. The point is to find out who killed Eddie. And I don't need your money, but I do need your help."

Another stream of Japanese. The father didn't say anything this time. The two women seemed to be disagreeing. Eddie's mother finally uttered one sharp syllable, and the old lady backed down.

Mrs. Takahashi offered a hesitant smile, smoothing her dress with her hands. "I'm sorry, Miss Corbie. My husband's sister doesn't speak English as well as she understands it. Would you like to come into the kitchen, please? It will be more comfortable for all of us to sit."

Miranda nodded. Out of the coffin and into the mortuary.

They formed a procession, with Mrs. Takahashi bowing to Miranda, holding the kitchen door open and gesturing toward a large, dark table, again ornate. Like the hall tree, it didn't belong at Wilmot Street.

Miranda bowed her head in return, and sat down in the middle seat, taking off her gloves. It took a few minutes for the wife to usher in Mr. Takahashi and place him at the head of the table. His shrunken shoulders looked like a child's against the high, carved mahogany chair back.

Mrs. Takahashi rapped out a few more sharp commands to her sister-in-law, and the old lady, glaring, got up and put a kettle on the stove. There was probably tension in the family before Eddie's death, exacerbated by the husband's isolation. The infirmities of age walled him in his own world, increasingly limited, increasingly distant. The women battled each other for control, even if both were careful to walk three steps behind him.

Eddie's mother gave Miranda another pained smile. "Please. You are our guest. Do you like Japanese tea? Have you tasted *matcha*?"

"Yes, Mrs. Takahashi. Thank you. I attended a tea ceremony at the Fair last year."

The woman raised her eyebrows and looked pleased. "Good, good. I'm sorry this will not be a formal ceremony. If my Emi were here . . ."

The staccato word sounded like a bark. Even the old man pivoted to look at his sister, whose face was flushed and angry.

"That would be Eddie's sister?"

Mrs. Takahashi's glasses glinted, as she bent her head down, trying to hide her embarrassment or anger. The kimono lady threw her another withering look.

"Yes, Miss Corbie. Her Japanese name is Emi. She likes to be called Emily, just as Michi preferred Edward." Behind the glasses, her eyes found a corner of the room. Miranda decided not to press her. Not yet.

She leaned forward. "Mrs. Takahashi, was Eddie in trouble?"

The whistle of the teapot made everyone except the old man jump. He seemed to be asleep in his chair, the mention of his son's name not even provoking a flicker. The sister-in-law rose, grudgingly, and stumped over to make the tea.

Mrs. Takahashi's voice trembled. "My Michi was a good boy, Miss Corbie."

Silence, except for the sister-in-law whisking and stirring the powdered tea. Miranda pressed her hands against the table.

"But not all of his friends. Did he ever mention a Filipino Charlie? Or a Ming or Mike Chen, a Chinese herbalist?"

The liquid burned, and her arm flew backward, almost hitting the old woman who sloshed it on her arm—probably on purpose. Eddie's mother was lost in memory, not noticing anything except the past. Miranda brushed off the tea, gripping the traditional bowl with both hands, while the sister-in-law glared at her and retook her seat. She wouldn't give the old bitch the satisfaction of wincing.

"He was a good boy. He was confirmed at St. Francis Xavier—I am a Catholic, my husband is a Buddhist. And he almost finished high school. He liked music, liked the bands. I—I urged him to join the Japanese Marching Band, but by then . . . it was too late."

She shook her head and seemed to make a decision, the fear and sadness dissipating like so much incense smoke. Anger replaced them, anger that made her hands shake the tea she wasn't drinking.

She met Miranda's eyes. "You know what killed my son, Miss Corbie? Chinatown." Spittle landed in flecks on the table, on her hands around the bowl.

"Chinatown killed Michi, Chinatown and all the gangs and the crime and the boys who wander the street. He met them there, his friends, Filipinos and Chinese. No time for his heritage, no time for his parents, just swing music and nightclubs and girls and money, always money. This is what Chinatown taught him."

Miranda sipped her tea, waiting. The old lady in the kimono, for once, was nodding her head in agreement.

"We all drift to Chinatown. Too difficult to find a place to live here, among our own people, unless you have money or family already in San Francisco. Those of us who came after 1913 cannot own property. I was lucky—my husband was here long before. He owned a tailor shop—and married late. I was very young, a picture bride from Matsue. No children at first. Then the babies come. So where do we go? Chinatown. They send us to Chinatown, with the Chinese, thinking we're all the same."

Mrs. Takahashi stared at the wall, her tea still untouched. Miranda spoke gently. "It must have been very difficult. Especially after—especially a couple of years ago."

Tears welled, her shrill voice cutting through the quiet darkness of the kitchen. "Do you know they spat on my Michi? Spat on him! He protected his sister, thank God, protected her from everything. And still, he was friends with Chinese, Filipinos, riffraff. Emi learned some of the language in school, but I won't let her speak it here. I don't say I agree with war, Miss Corbie—I'm an *Issei*, yes, but an American first. But the Chinese are mongrels. And the Filipinos are just as bad or worse."

Miranda's sharp intake of air shut Mrs. Takahashi off. She busied herself with the tea, bright red. The old lady in the kimono was still nodding her head and smiling for the first time.

"Of course, I don't expect you to understand." The tone was plaintive now, the resentful undertow still dangerous. "You're white. And you're not married, don't have children. Maybe you think the Chinese have a right to their parties and their parades and the filthy lies they print in their newspapers."

The sister-in-law got up to make more tea. Miranda tried to put the sympathy back in her voice, thinking of Eddie. And this woman who looked at her with Eddie's eyes.

"I'm not here to discuss the political situation, Mrs. Takahashi. I'm only interested in solving the murder of your son. Maybe your daughter would know if he mentioned these men?"

The father woke from his reverie with enough energy to raise his eyebrows. He asked his sister something. She looked at Eddie's mother. Mrs. Takahashi looked elsewhere.

"Emi is a delicate girl, Miss Corbie, and was close to her brother. She is too upset to speak with anyone right now."

"Perhaps another time, then?"

The women ignored the question by pouring for the old man. An invitation to leave. Miranda stood up and put her gloves back on.

"I'll be in touch."

Mrs. Takahashi's glasses caught the glare from the overhead lamp, and she rose, her frumpy dress wrinkled again.

"Thank you, Miss Corbie. Please do. I'm sure it's as the police suggested. If you're looking for Eddie's murderer, look no farther than Chinatown."

Miranda bowed her head and left the room. A cacophony of angry Japanese erupted from the kitchen when she shut the rooming house door.

Fog from the ocean was crawling over the Geary hill, wrapping around the few headstones remaining in the Richmond cemeteries. The dead were moving to Colma, unable to afford the rent in San Francisco. Miranda lit a Chesterfield and headed for Stockton.

Her wristwatch said eleven-thirty. An hour and a half to get to the Owl lunch counter and a meeting with Mrs. Winters, who was a paying customer and presumably expected her to be on time. The ones who paid always did.

She looked up and down the wide street. A White Front was in the distance. She could stand at the corner and arrive at the appointment early. Or she could take a stroll around Little Osaka, and try to learn more about the Takahashis. At least the younger generation. She'd had her fill of the older one.

The metal taps on the bottom of the navy pumps made a pleasant clink against the pavement. She crossed to the east side of Sutter, turning north, where a strip of businesses lined up, hands out.

First an art repair store and a dental office. Then a small, dirty storefront lined with spools of faded thread, the closed sign handwritten in English and Japanese characters. Takahashi Tailors.

She peered through the window, pretending to check their hours. None were posted. The place was shut and dry, the low wooden counter cleaned off.

Next door was Matsumara's shoe repair shop. She hoped Matsumara was a nosy neighbor. She crushed out the cigarette on the sidewalk, and walked in.

The wooden door jingled, and a cheery man about forty-five emerged from behind a dark curtain to smile at her. His counter was lined with shoes from baby size to Gary Cooper, all neat and shiny like children on a Sunday school picnic.

"Good morning, Miss. May I help you?"

She smiled back. "Do you sell shoes as well as repair them? I'm looking for a pair of brown pumps."

Matsumara's counter was as smooth as the leather on the footwear, cleaned and buffed with the long exchange of money. He angled his head to one side, his grin in place.

"What size? Seven?"

"Seven B, thank you."

"Be right back, Miss, don't go away."

By this time another customer rang the bell. A girl about eighteen, long, glossy hair upswept in one of the feathered hats from last season. She smiled nervously at Miranda, holding a pair of black shoes that looked too matronly for her.

Matsumara bustled out from the back, where Miranda caught a glimpse of another wooden counter, this one scarred, and covered in tools and leather. He was holding a pair of black and tan spectators, a small sunburst of contrasting leather highlighting the toe.

"These might be a little narrow . . . we don't get many sevens, mostly fives and some sixes. You can try them on, Miss, if you'd like. Oh, hello, Rose, how's your mother?"

Miranda moved toward one end of the counter, and the girl stepped forward shyly.

"She's fine, Mr. Matsumara. The leather on the straps is wearing out, and she'd like to see how much it will cost to fix."

Miranda slid out of her left shoe. The shoes were too small. Mr. Matsumara tilted his head to one side again, making a *tsk-tsk* noise.

"I've saved your mother enough money to buy a fur coat over the years. Tell her I said so, and tell her she knows it."

Rose held her hand to her mouth and giggled. "You're funny, Mr. Matsumara."

He sighed dramatically. "That's what they call me. The Japanese Georgie Jessel."

Miranda slid back into her navy pumps with gratitude, holding up the black and tan sunbursts. "I don't mean to interrupt—"

"Oh, not at all, Miss, please, how do you like the shoes?"

She placed them on the counter. "Very much, but they're a little tight. Any way you can stretch them for me?"

Matsumara picked up both pumps, looking them over carefully and feeling the leather. "I think so. You'd have to come back in a week, and I'd have to charge you a little more."

Miranda smiled at Rose and winked. "How much is a little?"

The shoemaker threw his hands in the air. "You see, Rose, what your mother does to my reputation? A lady not from the neighborhood walks in, and she thinks I'm going to overcharge."

Miranda laughed, shaking her head. "In my neighborhood I'm missing out. You don't get a vaudeville routine with the shoe repair."

"You from the city, Miss?"

"Yes. Downtown, near the theater district."

Rose's eyes glowed when Miranda mentioned the theater. "You must get to go to all of the new shows. I saw Benny Goodman at the Fair last year. Artie Shaw is my favorite. He's dreamy."

Miranda smiled. "I'm not able to go as much as I'd like. Quite a few good bands play in the city. I heard one the other night, at the Rice Bowl Party."

She dropped it on the counter, waiting for the thud. But the only reaction from Rose was disappointment. Matsumara's mouth turned down like a sad clown.

"I wanted to go—I was supposed to, with a friend of mine. But she couldn't." Rose lowered her voice. "Death in the family."

The shoemaker shook his head. "Poor Eddie. Poor Emi. My neighbor, Miss, the tailor next door. You may've read about it in the papers. Their son was killed during the Party on Saturday."

Miranda made a sympathetic noise. "I do remember reading about that— terrible tragedy. And that hit and run, too—I don't know what the city is coming to. Have the Takahashis lived here long?"

"Oh, no. Only the last couple of years. They used to live near Chinatown, but Hiro moved his family into his brother's house after he died. Lives there with his sister-in-law and his own family. But he's owned the tailors shop for, let's see—at least thirty years. He was able to buy before the law changed."

She turned to Rose. "And you know the sister? How is she? Such a terrible blow, to lose a brother."

Rose's hat feather trembled as she nodded her head. "I wish I knew how

Emi is. I haven't seen her. Not Saturday, not yesterday. I asked my mother to ask Mrs. Takahashi when I can visit her, but Mrs. Takahashi won't say. Just says that Emi is in her room and won't talk to anyone. But that's not like Emi. Is it, Mr. Matsumara?"

The shoemaker folded his arms together, assuming a thoughtful look. "No, I wouldn't say so. Emi's a delicate girl, but strong, too. And a talker. Though she's been more quiet in the last six months than I've ever seen her. But that may just be growing up."

He let his hand drop on the brown shoes. "So, Miss, would you like to come back in a week? Shoes plus stretching will cost you one dollar fifty cents. And they come with the Matsumara guarantee."

"And what is that?"

"It changes with the shoes and the customer. For you, that a Prince Charming will find you when you wear them."

Miranda smiled again and took out her change purse. "How can I refuse?" She put two quarters and a dollar coin on the counter.

"Do I fill out a ticket?"

He pulled a carbon-copy pad out from the counter and wrote a couple of words on it. "Just put your name and address down here, on the receipt."

While she wrote, Miranda asked carefully: "What sort of boy was Eddie Takahashi? From what I've read in the papers . . ."

"You can't believe everything in those, Miss. Look at the shoe prices." Matsumara was staring at Rose. "I wouldn't have trusted Eddie around my daughters. But he was good to his sister. You could tell whenever you saw them together, which wasn't so often anymore. He didn't stay home or in the neighborhood much, and frankly, I don't think he lived with his parents."

"He didn't, not anymore. Emi told me he moved out about a year ago. I didn't know him very well; my parents never let me see Emi when he was home." Rose blushed. Eddie had been a good-looking young man.

The shoemaker was writing out his portion of the receipt. Miranda said: "Too bad he didn't take his father's trade. The tailor shop looks lonely, doesn't it?"

Matsumara looked up, handed her the copy. "It is, Miss. It's been shut up for over a year. Hiro's too old to run it. His health's no good anymore. Started to fade about two years ago."

"Why don't they sell, or lease the space? Surely on a busy street like this . . ."

"Oh, they could sell. They could even lease it to me, I could use the room.

More new shoes." He winked at both of them. "But they won't. Eddie used to open it up sometimes in the late afternoon. I close at five, so I don't know what kind of business he was doing, and I don't want to know. There, I've said enough. Matsumara, the human talking machine. I'm worse than that phone company robot at Treasure Island."

Miranda laughed, waving good-bye to both of them. The shoes were worth a buck fifty. And so was everything else.

She wanted very much to know what Eddie was doing in his father's closed shop at night. And where the Takahashis were keeping his sister. And why.

The White Front was chugging along Sutter, and Miranda climbed on board. Mrs. Winters and her dead husband were waiting.

nine

The lady with the Owl Drug Store bag wanted to make conversation about the state of her bowels. Miranda smiled and nodded for as long as she could, finally telling her to believe her doctor and lay off the headcheese and ice cream cake.

The woman harrumphed and made a theatrical performance out of moving her polka-dotted bulk to another seat. Miranda leaned back, relishing the extra space, and lit a Chesterfield on the second try.

She should've guessed Eddie wasn't living with his parents. Not if he was working for Filipino Charlie. He was just so goddamn young.

She lowered the window, blowing smoke and watching it drift down the street. She'd have to call Gonzales. She didn't like that part of her wanted to.

Her eyes widened when she saw a green car parked on the corner of Taylor. Breathed again when an elderly party that looked like Hollywood's idea of a judge got in. Tall, gray hair, portly from too many well-cooked pot roasts served by Ma Hardy in her floral-print housedress while dispensing advice to Andy. Good old Judge Hardy. Probably a prosperous bookseller with a pornography business on the side.

A few stops to go before Powell and Sutter. She took the card out of her wallet again. The smells had faded; it was just a dirty, dingy little card, from a dirty, dingy little man.

Miranda climbed out at Powell in time to dig for seven cents and catch the cable car heading for the turnaround at Fifth and Market. She squeezed by a man in soiled dungarees and found a seat inside next to a pimply faced boy in his Sunday best, holding hands with the girl from the ice cream social. Fresh off a farm in Fresno. Homely as mother's apple pie.

The girl giggled at every lurch, and Miranda noticed a gold band on her left finger. The girl was twisting it nervously, her high-pitched titter cascading up and down the scale. Miranda turned toward the man in dirty Levis, who was busy with a wad of tobacco and using Powell Street as a spittoon.

She checked her wristwatch. Twelve-twenty. She'd still get there early enough to eat lunch and look like she'd spent all morning thinking about Mrs. Winters and her late husband.

A few shoppers stepped in at Union Square, those who didn't mind paying the two cents they'd saved on lace hankies for the luxury of the seven-cent cable car. The White Front Market Street Railway cars cost a nickel, but you paid two cents more for history and atmosphere, that peculiar, lonely little clang when the gripman found the cable and the conductor rang the bell past the St. Francis.

The ladies were fresh from the cosmetic counters at The White House and City of Paris. A blonde wearing the new "hot pink" lipstick shade leaned over Miranda, nearly suffocating her with too much Shalimar, until the homely Sir Lancelot gave up his seat. By the time they reached Market and Fifth, Miranda never wanted to smell Shalimar again.

The Owl Drug Store dwarfed the cable turnaround, a small city of departments occupying the basement and ground-floor levels of the venerable Flood Building. The store serviced nearly every human need. Those that it didn't provide you could find elsewhere in the city with little trouble. So extensive was the Owl that if you sealed yourself inside for six months, you'd reemerge five pounds heavier and with a complete stamps-of-the-world collection.

Miranda took the stairs down to the basement floor and the lunch counter. The normal assortment of wives and mothers were gathered like buffalo at a watering hole, their children occupied with ice cream sundaes, the gossip revolving around who cheated at bridge on Saturday and whether Mary Noble, Backstage Wife would ever really leave Larry.

The only open table hadn't been cleaned yet, and it was in the middle—not the best place to be discreet. She took it anyway, sitting and smiling at the waiter while he bussed it. He smiled back. Hostility from some nearby ma-trons perfumed the atmosphere, making it smell like Shalimar.

Miranda adjusted her hat, and the old cows went back to chewing cud. She checked her wristwatch. Twelve-forty. She hoped Mrs. Winters was the early type.

The waiter came back with a menu, still smiling.

"Valentine's Tuna Salad is the special today, Miss."

"I didn't know tuna was part of the holiday."

He laughed, drawing a few disapproving looks from the barnyard. "It's not, Miss, but the tomatoes are." He leaned over conspiratorially. "It's our regular stuffed tomato salad except the cook cuts the tomato to look like a heart."

"I'm sure it's beautiful. I'll take the Waldorf, rye toast, and a cherry Coke. Is that a paper on the counter? May I see it?"

"Certainly, Miss. Of course." He nodded, a thin man in his forties with a boyish, West Virginia drawl. Probably lost his job and came out to California to find it. Like everybody else.

He turned to the counter, and a fashionable woman with a fashionable figure and country club in her face approached Miranda's table, one gloved hand on the red vinyl and chromium chair back across from her.

"Miss Corbie?"

Miranda jerked her head at the waiter. "Don't worry about the paper."

The woman, an ash blonde, stood elegantly, looking nervously between the two of them as if she expected Miranda to announce their engagement. When the waiter scurried to help a young mother of two needing fresh nap-kins and a mop, the woman pulled the chair out and sat down. Miranda reached for her purse and pulled out her half-empty pack of Chesterfields.

"How do you do, Mrs. Winters. I've already ordered."

Helen Winters was wearing one of the new hats from the City of Paris window, veil down. Gloves immaculate, except for a tobacco stain on her right forefinger. Black of course, but tastefully lugubrious. One didn't want to overindulge, whether in dessert or mourning. It ruined the waistline and ran the mascara.

She looked around, the veil not concealing her worry or distaste, though it helped hide the age lines of a woman fighting to look under forty and not quite winning.

"I thought you'd find a table more . . . discreet. We're sitting in the middle."

Miranda lit a cigarette and took a long drag before responding. "The Owl

Drug Store isn't exactly known as a reservation-only rendezvous. We take what we get, Mrs. Winters, and this is what we got. You can come back to my office with me, if you'd like."

She was pulling at her gloves, a repetitive motion that made her seem almost human. "No, Miss Corbie, that's all right. If you don't think we'll be overheard—"

Miranda leaned forward. "As long as we keep our voices down, Mrs. Winters."

The matrons and few working men at the counter were either busy with their own conversations or distracted by the screaming three-year-old. Mrs. Winters's air of respectability was thick enough to choke the Owl Drug Store, but at least it kept buffalo eyes off of both of them.

The waiter emerged from his wrestling match with the mop, the children, and the harassed young mother, and addressed Mrs. Winters, slightly out-of-breath.

"Good afternoon, Madame. Would you like a menu?"

She lifted the veil, eyes pale and sharp and all business. "No, thank you. Coffee, please."

He nodded, throwing a quick glance at Miranda before he bowed and walked back to the kitchen.

The older woman was finally removing her gloves. She wore a French manicure with an accent that was strictly Emporium. Mrs. Winters's gray eyes, watery like melted ice, lifted up and stared at Miranda. Her voice was clear, cold, and quiet.

"I want you to find out who murdered Lester. I don't care how long it takes. And if you happen to find out his daughter was involved, don't let that stop you. There's a reason why certain species eat their young, Miss Corbie."

Miranda knew from the phone conversation that Helen Winters wasn't Shirley Temple. But she didn't expect Bette Davis on a bad day. The waiter bustled noisily to the table, giving them a few seconds of warning. Miranda stubbed out her cigarette in the glass ashtray next to the salt shaker.

"Your cherry Coke, Miss. Waldorf salad will be right out. And for you, Madame." He placed the thick, white cup in front of Mrs. Winters along with a small, matching creamer. "If you change your mind and would like to order—"

"I won't. Thank you."

Peremptory dismissal. He shrugged, moved off. Miranda stirred the drink with her straw, watching the cherry-flavoring swirl in patterns through the dark brown sweetness of the Coke.

"I haven't said I'd take the case."

The other woman's lip stretched slightly, her nose wrinkling as she sipped her coffee. She left it black. "You're here, aren't you? I assume you do work as an investigator, that is what the papers say . . ."

"I work for myself. It's my prerogative whether or not to accept a commission. Give me the facts of your husband's death, the particulars of your family situation, and why you suspect your daughter's involvement. And if I decide to investigate it, I'll let you know."

Mrs. Winters leaned back against the vinyl of her chair, her coffee cup wearing a red gash from the imprint of her lips. "If you're not going to work for me, then my family is none of your business. It seems we're at cross purposes, Miss Corbie. You will investigate depending on what I tell you. I will tell you what you want to know only if you agree to investigate. I'll pay you twenty dollars a day—that is your going rate?—and give you carte blanche to do whatever is necessary to solve my husband's murder."

Miranda caught the waiter's eye coming forward with the salad, and she shook her head very slightly. He nodded, setting it on the counter. She opened her bag, removed another cigarette, and lit it with a Sally Rand lighter. Mrs. Winters sipped her coffee.

"Why is it that you want to hire me in particular? You said you'd explain if we met."

"Because, without putting too much of a fine point on it, you associate with the right—or should I say wrong?—type of people."

"Most detectives do."

"Most detectives don't have your background. And that's why I want you. I could hire a man, I could hire Pinkerton, but it will take too long. I think you have a chance of quicker success."

"By background, you mean as an escort."

Helen Winters looked toward the counter. "Your salad is waiting. That's exactly what I mean, Miss Corbie."

Miranda exhaled, sending smoke toward her left. The waiter was still watching her.

"Won't doing business with me be harmful to your position?"

The lower half of Mrs. Winters's face cracked into an eggshell-thin smile.

"I married beneath myself, Miss Corbie. Lester was an ambitious man, and I helped him achieve what he wanted to achieve. My first marriage. His second."

"I'm relieved they won't throw you out of the club."

Mrs. Winters narrowed her eyes, and removed an alligator wallet from her purse. She counted out ten twenties and laid them on the table in a precisely spaced row.

"You don't have to like me, Miss Corbie. You just have to like my money. That's two hundred dollars for your retainer."

Miranda stubbed her second cigarette out, half-finished. The owl on the bottom of the ashtray was missing an eye.

"Because I'll do anything for it? No thanks, Mrs. Winters. You strike me as a woman used to getting her way. On the phone, you were a little hysterical. I felt sorry for you. Right now, I just feel sorry for your—what is she, a stepdaughter? How clichéd." Miranda waved to the waiter.

"I'm not able to be bought and sold, contrary to what you may or may not have heard. So you can drop the class act, it doesn't impress—or convince. If you married down, there wasn't much lower to go. But don't worry . . . I won't be checking."

The waiter brought the salad, placing it in front of Miranda with a flourish, and adding a basket of rolls and butter. Mrs. Winters's face drained, matching the cold ash of her hair and making her look less like the cover girl on *Town and Country*.

"Here are my terms. You tell me the truth. About your husband, your stepdaughter, whatever and whomever you suspect. You tell me why, and let me make up my own mind. If I agree and think there's enough there to buck what the police and coroner are going to say, then I'll take the case, and you'll pay me. If I don't, then I'll tell you that, too, and you're free to go hire some cheap bastard who really will do anything for money. But that's not me, Mrs. Winters. Your call."

She drained the cherry Coke, and plucked the maraschino from the bottom of the glass. The lettuce in the salad was a little brown at the edges. She started in on the apples.

Mrs. Winters's face gradually flushed into pink, then a pinched crimson, which shone through her thick face powder. Her arms hung at her sides as if she didn't know what to do with them.

"She's a drug addict. Lester was looking for her."

Miranda scraped some of the mayonnaise off the lettuce. "Your stepdaughter, I presume. Cocaine?"

The woman nodded mutely. Miranda took another bite, wiped her mouth, then reached for her purse and took out her notepad and pencil.

"Name, age, and I'll need a photo. Also a list of her closest friends, classmates—people who might know where she is. How long was your husband looking for her?"

"She's been gone with no word for three weeks. She's eighteen, just graduated from Sacred Heart. Her name's Phyllis."

"How long has she been on coke?"

Helen Winters shook her head. "I don't know. She never confided in me, never liked me. Daddy's little girl, even though she was three when we married. I do know her grades started slipping this year. She managed to graduate only because her father made a donation to the convent. Much larger than we could afford." She took another noiseless sip of coffee, as if drowning her bitterness in blacker grounds.

"She was close to her father?"

Mrs. Winters shrugged. "Lester is—was—a busy man. The shipping company wasn't paying him to nursemaid his own daughter."

"But they used to be close."

"Yes. Until she turned sixteen. Then the boys began to turn up, and we'd have row after row with her. We gave the little bitch everything she could want," she added, almost as an afterthought. "Fine way of thanking us."

Miranda looked up at her, then took another bite of salad. "So why do you think your husband was murdered?"

Urgency tugged at her lips and eyes, stretching the Max Factor. "Because Lester was looking for her. That's why he was in the Pickwick. He was supposed to be meeting someone with information."

"Did you tell this to the police? Do they know Phyllis is missing?"

"Not—not entirely. They know she's missing, but not about the drugs. Lester and I were trying to handle this ourselves. He was in line for another promotion . . . once we found her, we were planning to send her to a sanitarium. Obviously, we couldn't do any more for her."

Miranda pushed the remaining salad to the side, took a drink of water. "Obviously. What were the circumstances of Lester's death?"

"Heart attack, they said, but I've requested an autopsy. The inquest is next Friday."

"You'll need to tell them about Phyllis. If they find evidence that he was murdered, they'll also find that you've suppressed information, and you may be held as an accessory. The police aren't stupid, Mrs. Winters."

"That's precisely why I want the girl found before this goes any further."

"What about the woman he was supposed to be with?"

Her mouth curled, the dry lines on her lips deeper without the red lipstick. "A maid says she saw a prostitute come out of the room. A Chinese. Lester would never stoop to that level."

Miranda wrote on the pad, and asked without looking up: "Who's the boyfriend?"

"You mean Phyllis? I have no idea."

"Someone does. Get me a list of names and addresses of her friends from school, anyone who might know. Places she liked to go to dance, ballrooms, clubs. And a picture."

Mrs. Winters fished around in her clutch and took out a small photo. "This is Phyllis. I knew you would need it."

The girl smiling at Miranda looked younger than eighteen, a vapidly pretty blonde a little too soft around the eyes.

"Thanks. Who's *your* boyfriend?"

The coffee cup dropped out of her hand and hit the saucer hard, not enough left in it to spill. The noise drew a few eyes.

"What—what did you say?"

Miranda waited until the race results and recipe pages summoned back the interested parties. "I asked who your boyfriend is. It would be easy for me to find out, but I'd rather you told me."

The well-groomed face began to melt, its features drifting toward the middle like puddles of wax.

"I—I fail to see . . ."

"Maybe you don't, but I do. You're trying to set up your stepdaughter to take the fall for your husband's alleged murder. You wouldn't pay money to see it done unless you had a motive yourself. I figure you've got two: Lester's money and a boyfriend on the side. That's why you want Phyllis found right away, before the police look too closely at you."

Miranda sat back in her chair and crossed her legs, watching the colors play on the other woman's face.

"I'm not saying you're guilty, Mrs. Winters. I think you've figured the angles, and you've heard something that didn't make the papers. What I want to know is why they're hushing it up . . . because if there's an inquest and we're still waiting for an autopsy report, it's not just because you requested it. So you know it was murder and you play outraged wife. Jump all over the foul-play bandwagon, blowing your trumpet early, hoping to deflect suspicion. And then you time your announcement about your daughter's addiction when you can control what she says, safely under lock and key. No embarrassing questions."

Mrs. Winters's fists lay stiffly on the table, her nails digging into her palms. "What are you going to do?"

Miranda shook out another Chesterfield, lit it with a matchbook on the table.

"I'm going to take the case and take your money, but only with a few rules. Number one: you tell me everything, if not here, then by tomorrow. Number two: I'll find your stepdaughter, but not so you can frame her. Addicts aren't exactly subtle when someone gets in between them and their fix, and whatever you've got on her or whatever you think she's got on you, let it play out. Number three: You go down to the Hall of Justice now and tell them about the cocaine. Keeping her out of it because you want to control her story won't work—not with me, the cops, or the papers. In return, I'll produce her before the inquest, or you don't pay me anything. Once again—your call."

The other woman's eyes hardened, hiding nothing, glittering like quicksilver. She looked at the money on the table. She looked at Miranda.

"You think I had Lester killed?"

Miranda spoke in a level tone. "No, I don't. You were comfortable. From the sound of things, you didn't need to murder Lester. He's been unofficially dead for a long time. The only time he bucked your orders was over his daughter. And she fell in with the wrong crowd, probably out of rebellion, probably to get away from you. No, Mrs. Winters, I'm willing to find Phyllis because I'd like to see her get a chance in life. Her and the Chinese woman, if she's innocent. Because that's who they'll be looking for."

"And you're willing to take my money to—"

"I'm willing to pocket a one-hundred-dollar retainer, and fully refund it if I can't find your daughter before next Friday. Minus expenses, which will be documented."

Mrs. Winters stared at her empty coffee cup. Then she slowly picked up five of the twenty-dollar bills still on the table, folding them neatly and carefully into a billfold.

Miranda was writing something on the notepad, and pushed it across. "Read and sign it. It says you've hired me to find your daughter within fourteen days, for twenty dollars a day plus expenses. It acknowledges your one-hundred-dollar retainer, and if I can't produce her by the morning of the inquest, you owe me nothing except out-of-pocket costs."

Mrs. Winters bit her lower lip as she read it. She hesitated, then signed her name in pencil.

"I'll send it over—what you want to know."

"Right away, please. After you walk down to the Hall of Justice."

The woman stood, her chair scraping the linoleum, her fur stole drooping over her shoulders. She arched her long neck, trying to summon up the act she'd walked in with.

"You know—I don't usually do business with whores."

Miranda smiled. "Neither do I, Mrs. Winters."

She watched as her client flung herself out the side door on her way up to the toiletries department. Then she caught eyes with the waiter, who walked over to the table, his tall, lanky frame too small for the uniform. He took the plates, looking at her curiously.

"Anything else, Miss?"

"Another cherry Coke."

Miranda leaned back against the red seat cushion, studying the herd of women still gathered at the counter.

Ten

There were times when she just wanted to be left alone. Like Garbo, in *Grand Hotel*, though of course Garbo never really wanted to be left alone, she just didn't want to face an audience. Miranda listened to the chair back squeak, letting the din of clanking plates and the staccato syllables of the short-order cook set her adrift.

She'd seen the picture eight years ago. When she was twenty-five, still wearing her hair bobbed and curly, still fresh from the Mills College days and still swigging bootleg gin. She taught English to hungry children, heads too large for permanently shrunken bodies, taught them together with their leather-skinned parents, as dry and thin as the autumn leaves they burned to keep warm. Hooverville coal, they called it, when they were lucky enough to find a tree.

The children grew old at ten, working in factories or stockyards or cotton farms, their fathers and mothers sewing the clothes and cutting the machine parts and planting the corn that covered and ran and fed the cities. If they voted at all, they voted for whomever their local boss told them to vote for. Then 1929. Suddenly the bosses were gone, along with the jobs and the crops and the homes.

1932. Worst year of the Depression. Three years before New York.

No, she wanted to be alone like everyone wanted to be, in their soul of souls, bereft, empty, not feeling, nothing to feel against, nothing to provoke emotion. Emptiness.

Sometimes the swirl of the cigarette smoke took her there, sometimes she closed her eyes and felt the hollow, the comfort in solitude. Like playing solitaire on a cold night, not watching out the window, not listening to the radio, not hearing, not seeing, not caring.

It was something more than numbness, something less than what the Hindu fakir told her about nirvana. The Treasure Island Gayway was enough nirvana for some. Men and women, restless, searching, craving sex, thrills, whatever basement-sale stimulation could be had for a nickel, twenty-five cents tops. Reminding them of life while they moved aimlessly, bacteria under a heat lamp.

A midget village, babies in incubators, and thirty-five-year-old women with saggy tits and cowboy hats playing nude volleyball at Sally Rand's. Every day they'd find paper bags and handkerchiefs in dark corners where one of the nirvana seekers had jerked off, a souvenir from paradise, a memento for his achievement.

The girls got paid. That was nirvana enough. Two bridges and nudie shows kept San Francisco from drowning in the Depression, but the bridges were over, and all that was left was the Fair. The last hurrah before the storm.

Except the storm was lashing France and England, drowned Mother China three years before. The wreckage washed against America, lighting Liberty's crown with shell fire, bathing her robe in soldiers' guts. Huddled masses begging for help, begging for asylum. Liberty looked away, country-club membership still exclusive.

She turned away the SS *St. Louis* last year, sent Jews back to concentration camps in Europe. Sure, give us the wretched refuse of your teeming shore. But not your Jews, Catholics, or nonwhites. Hitler's got a plan, did you hear?

Plenty of Yankee Doodles, champions of Liberty, were screaming holy hell about the European War, how it was their problem, not ours, and by the way, the Germans really do impress, remember the Berlin Olympics? And the trains run on time. So clean, so white, so pure. Nobody likes Jews and Bolsheviks. See—Hitler's got a plan.

So if Charles A. Lindbergh, an honest-to-God (and maybe only to God) aviation hero thinks we should stay out, and let the English sink or swim (remember the War of 1812!), then by God or by the Devil, we're staying out.

All we want is Peace in Our Time.

Fuck everyone else's.

Miranda opened her eyes. The waiter was watching her, a strange expression on his face. Then the jukebox started, and it was "Oh, Johnny, Oh, Johnny, Oh." A cue to leave. She walked out of the Owl, heading for the Pickwick Hotel.

The Pickwick towered over Fifth and Market, a large middle-class hotel built fourteen years earlier, with all the macabre gothic optimism of the late, great Roaring Twenties. A venture of the Pickwick—now Greyhound—Stage Lines Corporation, the hotel was a perfect meeting place for disreputable reputable citizens, an architectural embodiment of a bus ride.

You could check your blackmail photos, pack your mistress off to Topeka at the adjoining coach station, or fuck whomever you were paying to fuck in the privacy of your own room, complete with ice water on tap and for only $1.50 per night. You could even, occasionally, get killed there. Just dial GArfield 7500.

Miranda stared up at the light henna brick. Hammett, the pulp writers' Hemingway, wrote about the Pickwick in *The Maltese Falcon*, back in '30, when the hotel was new and so was Hammett. Both looked like they'd had a few drinks over the last ten years. Hell, didn't everybody?

She read the book on a lark, a bet from a boy with a name long forgotten. And years later, when she took the job with Burnett, she remembered what a bastard Sam Spade was. But he still didn't hold a candle to her ex-boss.

She tossed the cigarette on the sidewalk, crushing it with her toe. A doorman dressed in the garish plumage of his breed stepped into her path. His shoulder tassel was loose, and he smelled like cheap whiskey.

"Any luggage, Miss? Be happy to call the bellhop."

"Thanks, but I'm not staying. I need a word with the house detective."

The beefy, red-faced Irishman raised his eyebrows. "And why would a pretty little thing like you be needing the house detective? Somebody bothering you?"

"At the moment, only you. He in today?"

The doorman paused, rubbed his fat thumb along the stubble on his chin. "He's here, been here every day. Quite a change for Finnigan. He's from one of the wrong counties."

She nodded. "And that would be whatever county isn't yours, right?"

The grin gave him deep dimples. "He's a lesser specimen, girlie. Why not stick with me?"

Miranda sighed, removed her wallet, and extracted her license. "This is business, not the goddamn blarney stone. You know anything about the man that died here on Friday? What room he was in, the skitter with the staff?"

He took a step backward, squinting at her. "I would never've figured a looker like you to be a peeper, now. What's in it for me if I talk?"

She drew him toward a spot against the brick, away from the doors. "Depends on what you've got to talk about."

He rubbed his chin again. "You'll want to see Finnigan. He was runnin' around givin' people the third degree like he was Hoover, right after the guy got knocked off. The maid who found him ran to Finnigan before she decided to pass out. Then the coppers came, and he was out in the cold."

"A bump-off?"

The Irishman shrugged his massive shoulders and they strained against his uniform, the shoulder tassel dancing. "That's what Finnigan says. But you can't believe anything he tells you. All I know is it was room . . . room 327. And the guy wasn't drilled—Estelle thought he was asleep, went to shake him. No blood, you get me? She says some Chinee girl walked out of the room when she was coming up the hall, and lammed off down the back stairs. And ever since, Estelle acts like she was holier than the Sainted Virgin. Except she ain't one."

He leaned over and leered at Miranda. "I talked, so what'll it get me, eh?"

She'd palmed out a dollar earlier, and held it out to him. "Thanks, Pat. Buy yourself another pint, and make it better than what you had for lunch."

His face showed confusion, as she pushed past him toward the door. "How'd you know my name was Pat?"

Miranda looked back briefly. "It always is."

The manager, a spectacled, nervous man in his early forties, examined her license. She thought about handing him a microscope. The lobby was slow and overly warm, decorated with a couple of the old people who reside, lodged like potted plants, in hotel lobbies. They were of indeterminate sex, their genders muted with age, though one was wearing striped trousers and the other a baggy brown dress. They sat across from one another in separate arm chairs, not speaking, not reading, but crouched, listening to footsteps and laughter and trying to remember what life felt like.

Miranda lit another cigarette while the manager called his boss. The Pickwick was part of a chain of hotels, strung together by the coach line, and if one of the girls in the chorus missed a kick, they'd all fall down.

He cleared his throat, and she turned back toward the ornate marble counter.

"Everything seems to be in order. Mr. Finnigan's office is down the hall, past the elevator banks, on your left. I've rung him. He'll be expecting you shortly."

She nodded. "Thanks."

Miranda walked toward the rear section, behind the scenes where the carpet wasn't as clean. Down a hallway that smelled like cherry pipe tobacco. A door on the left was open about a foot. She tapped on the frosted glass.

A deep voice drawled, "Come in."

She walked into a room the size of Mrs. Astor's closet. A tall, gray-haired man, lean, hard, and brown, sat behind a desk, his long legs stuck out in front of him. He wore a fedora, but a western Stetson would've suited him better. She expected to see a six-gun strapped to his hip, and a wanted poster for Billy the Kid on the wall.

"You're Finnigan?"

"No, I'm Parker. This here's Finnigan."

He nodded with his head toward a portly man in a derby with mealy skin and bright, shifty eyes.

Neither of them said anything else. Parker reached into his coat pocket, and pulled out a pipe, filled it carefully with tobacco, and lit it with a match he ran along the top of Finnigan's desk.

"Finnigan." He gave a small jump at the sound of his name. "The manager called you. I'm Miranda Corbie."

He grinned, took out a stained handkerchief out of his display pocket, and wiped his forehead. The sweat stains on the inside of his shirt collar clashed with the faded blue suit. Miranda pivoted, turned toward Parker.

"And just who the hell are you, Mr. Parker?"

He blinked at her, his eyes indifferent. "I'm with the Bureau of Marine Investigation and Navigation."

"Aren't you a long way from the Port?"

He shrugged. He wore his collar open, with a clean white t-shirt peeping out the top. Checkered shirt, pressed pants. He didn't look like a cop.

"This Lester Winters was an engineer for the NYK Line. Nippon, Yusen, Kaisha."

"I know what it stands for. He didn't die on board a ship. If he did, he'd still be the territory of the SFPD—unless he died in international waters, then the Coast Guard would have something to say."

He shrugged again. "I might ask you the same thing, Miss Corbie." With a graceful move, he rose from the desk. "Don't look like murder, anyways. Natural causes, if you ask me. Well, Finnigan—it was nice jawin' with you."

The house dick grinned, stood up from his chair and reached out to pump Parker's hand. "Sure was, Inspector. Come back any time."

Parker nodded, disengaged himself from Finnigan, and with a couple of long strides left the room, shutting the door behind him with a soft click.

Miranda said slowly: "Did he leave a business card?"

Finnigan looked confused, patted his pockets. "I—I don't think so, Miss Corbie. But the operator can call—"

"Yeah, I know. Thanks. Would you show me 327? And tell me what happened?"

Finnigan wedged behind his desk and opened a door, pulling out a flask of rye that was three-quarters empty. He uncorked it, tilted his head back for a messy swig, and then corked it again. Then he looked up at her, uncorked it again hurriedly, wiped off the top with his sleeve, and offered it to her in the spirit of brotherhood.

She accepted it only to win his confidence, closed her eyes and felt the familiar warmth bite through her intestines. "Thanks. Let's go upstairs."

The Pickwick elevator operator, a Negro in a pressed uniform with a patient smile, crated them upstairs. He looked smart and alert; a good man to talk to, particularly if he'd been working on Friday. Miranda wrote his name down—Cheval—while Finnigan chattered.

The short man wasn't one of those house peepers that kept himself to himself. He spread it around, as thick and smelly as manure. It was hard to shut him up, and harder still to figure out what was Irish bullshit.

"So like I said, Estelle—and she's a good kid, Miss Corbie, hardworking, supports her mama and four younger sisters—she's out of breath from running, see, and screams 'Murder in 327!' and just flat out—*pfffft*—like that, on the carpet, and, well, I think we've got an escape from Alcatraz the way she's carrying on—you remember what happened last year, when they shot Doc Barker—so I get my .45—I use a Colt semiautomatic, had it since the War, and I—"

"We're here, Finnigan. Mind if I take a look?"

He yanked out the handkerchief again, mopped around his hairline, and fished a key out of his pocket.

"Sure thing, Miss Corbie. Cops were here twice already, came back and dusted the second time, though I sure couldn't get much out of them, tight-lipped they was, and Estelle, she was sure it was murder, though—"

"Thanks." Miranda pushed the door open, leaving her gloves on. The room was spare, not the lap or even the elbow of luxury, but comfortable. "This is one of the cheaper rooms, isn't it?"

"Why yes, it is, Miss Corbie, smart of you to know that. This here's our dollar special room. The Pickwick is a good, moderate hotel, good business clients, a lot of out-of-town salesmen, some conventioneers. We were full up during Fair season, expect to be again when it opens in May—too bad about the shorter season, though, we could really use the—"

"Why did Estelle think it was murder?" She opened the closet. Any luggage or clothes had been cleared out by the police. Or Winters hadn't brought any.

"Well, she's a Mexican, Miss Corbie, and they can be flighty. She's been reading a lot of them magazines, and she's always talking about Alcatraz—just seeing it scares her—and when I come back to ask her, she says she'd just come on duty around five in the morning and saw a Chinese girl leave the room, kind of scurry like they do, and then run down the back stairs. The door to the stairway is only a few steps away, and Estelle said the girl just out and out ran. She's a flighty girl, Miss Corbie, but you know these Mexicans, they get feelings sometimes, and Estelle, she said she got cold all over like something bad had happened in the room, and she just knew Mr. Winters had been murdered. " He stopped momentarily, out of breath.

Miranda moved to the small desk near the bed, and started opening drawers. "Did Mr. Winters bring any luggage? And did he request this room in particular?"

He flushed, scratched his head under this derby. "You know, I don't rightly know, Miss Corbie. I didn't see any luggage, and I don't know if the cops brought any out, because they had me down in the office. I reckon Burt—he was the clerk on duty when Winters checked in, I do know that—I've questioned everyone I could think of about this, figurin' the cops could use the help, and thinkin' I don't want no Chink girl gettin' away with poisoning somebody on my watch—so Burt could probably tell you whether . . ."

The desk held a Bible with an uncracked spine and a copyright of 1911, some envelopes and paper. Miranda took them out and counted them, while Finnigan watched with his mouth open. A few ink blotches stained one sheet; she set it aside on the desk. "How many pieces of stationery and envelopes do you give the guests? And are they replaced every time the room is cleaned?"

Finnigan's mouth opened and closed again. "I—I wouldn't know, Miss Corbie. Estelle or the other maids could tell you."

Miranda nodded, and turned to the wastebasket, full of newspaper and evidently ignored by the police. She pulled out folded-up sections of the *Chronicle*, and laid them open on the desk. "When did he check in?"

"About—I think Burt said Thursday night."

"Night or evening?"

"Let me see." Finnigan pulled a black memorandum book from his inside jacket pocket, and rifled through it, making nervous humming noises.

There were three days' worth of *Chronicle* sections—front page for Wednesday and Thursday, shipping news section for Tuesday, Wednesday, and Thursday, and movie pages for Wednesday. Either Winters brought the older papers with him or the maid hadn't cleaned up after the last guest. Miranda folded them carefully and tucked them under her arm.

"Says here—I always keep detailed records, Miss Corbie, only way to work, and the Pickwick appreciates it—why just last year the general manager of the whole line stayed with us for the Fair, you know, and he told me—"

"Evening, was it? After work hours?"

His mouth shut like a clam. "Why, yes. He checked in at five-thirty Thursday night."

"You said the police dusted . . . did they look for hair samples, anything like that?"

"Can't say. I was downstairs, most of the time, linin' up the staff for interviews, and—"

"Did they find anything to suggest his death wasn't from natural causes? The paper reported it as a heart attack."

Finnigan shook his head doubtfully. "I—I don't think so. They came by twice, first time with uniforms, second time plainclothes with one of the medical examiners from the coroner's office. The plainclothesmen looked around, took a few things that belonged to Winters—mostly pocket change, I guess, I remember seeing a wallet and some change and matchbooks on the desk there, when I came in—but, like I said, they were tight-lipped, you know how coppers are. Always jealous of us ops, thinkin' we get the cushy jobs. They got more interested when Estelle told 'em about the Chinese girl, though. Figured Winters had one on the side, and went back up to look around."

"Had he stayed here before?"

His face brightened. "You know, I thought of that. I looked through the hotel registry myself, but I couldn't find any record of him stayin' here before. Don't mean nothin', though—he might've used another name."

"You didn't see anything suspicious? No sign of forced entry or violence—no one heard any noise?"

"It's a funny thing," he said slowly. "When I came up to see him, after Estelle fainted and all—I noticed the radio was on low, not enough to keep people awake. But it was some show I never figured Winters for—something for women, you know, cooking and recipes. Funny, what goes through your mind. I kept hearing this woman's voice talking on and on about a Valentine's cake, and then I went to shake Winters, thinking he'd passed out, you know, and Estelle was just excitable. Then he wouldn't wake up, and I held my fingers to his mouth, and then I tried to find a pulse and then I—well, I ran out and called the cops."

"What time did she find him?"

"I'd just got in—it was kind of late, you know, Estelle said she'd knocked earlier, but didn't want to bother him, figuring maybe he wanted some privacy. It's a hotel, we get all kinds, though the Pickwick is pretty clean, and mostly I just have to keep the parties in line when the conventioneers are in town—and sometimes watch for the bad checks, you know the type. What was I saying? Oh, yeah—it was about ten o'clock. Estelle didn't get an answer again, and figured she'd just peek in the door. Once she'd seen the Chinese, you know, she probably got a little curious."

"Did the cops give a time of death?"

"The M.E. said he'd kicked off in the middle of the night sometime, I guess after him and the Chinese got done doin' what he was payin' her for. Beggin' your pardon, Miss Corbie."

"Did anyone see the Chinese girl—or anyone else—go into Winters's room on Thursday night?"

His head shake was definitive. "No, sirree. I asked everybody that question. Nobody remembered nothing about Mr. Winters."

"Nobody took anything out of the room except the cops? No cigarettes or booze?"

Finnigan looked horrified. "Certainly not, Miss Corbie. I locked up the room until the cops arrived. I like a snort now and again—like everybody—but nobody would touch a thing. They couldn't. I remember seeing some cigarettes—Lucky Strikes, I think—on the desk, and a quart of Four Roses, about half empty, with a glass. Don't remember two, but then I was tryin' to get Estelle calmed down. I'm sure they were still there when I brought the police back up."

"All right. Thanks, Finnigan. I'd like to speak to Estelle, if she's on duty."

He checked his watch. "She gets off at three, so you've got time."

They rode back down to the lobby, Finnigan filling the air with his reasons for believing Winters was murdered. They boiled down to Estelle's Mexican superstition and the fact (well known, according to Finnigan) that poison was a Chinese weapon. Miranda opened a new pack of cigarettes.

Estelle was a thin woman with dark circles under her eyes. They darted over Finnigan's office, over Miranda, looking for an escape, full of an exultant terror.

"Can you describe how she was dressed?"

"*Sí.* She wore a bright dress and fancy. Not a nice lady clothes. Red, very much money."

"Did she wear a coat? Try to remember, Estelle, this is important."

The maid coughed in excitement, her eyelids fluttering. "I—I am not sure."

"Why don't you lean back and close your eyes? And here—have a drink."

Miranda pulled Finnigan's drawer open. He wasn't there to complain, and she'd given him five bucks already. She handed Estelle the nearly empty bottle. "Finish it."

The maid eyed it greedily, and took her time with it. Then she rested her head on the seat back as Miranda suggested, shutting her eyes tight.

"Relax. Just think about Friday morning. You'd just come to work—"

"*Sí, sí—*"

"—and you were setting up on the floor, still sleepy, and then maybe heard a door open . . ."

"Yes! Then I see her. Red dress, no lady. Chinese. Pretty, I think, but no lady. I think must be *puta*. No hat. Coat over dress, but . . . *pequeño*. Too small."

"You mean not for cold or fog?"

"*Sí*. Too small. Matching dress, like fancy lady."

"Did she carry a purse on her arm? Can you remember?"

Estelle squinched her eyes tighter, and spoke slowly. "*Sí* . . . I think so."

Miranda fished around on Finnigan's desk, found a *San Francisco News*, and tore through it until she could find a suitable ad.

"You can open your eyes, Estelle. Was her dress like this, more or less?"

The maid tilted her head to one side in thought, then nodded slowly. "*Sí*. Except more Chinese. And *puta*."

Finnigan knocked on his own door, then entered with a gangly young man about twenty-seven. "Burt just came on duty, so I brought him over, Miss Corbie. You done with Estelle?" He winked at the maid. "See, she don't bite."

"Yeah, thanks, Finnigan. And *gracias*, Estela. *Encantada*." Miranda handed her two dollars.

"*Gracias, senorita, eres muy amable*." The maid stood up, hovered with uncertainty, then pushed past Finnigan and Burt.

"Did she tell you about the stationery?" His face was eager.

Miranda shrugged. "She said they get ten sheets, and the maids are supposed to make sure they're refilled, and give them more if requested. There were five in Winters's desk. She swore she'd taken care of that room before he checked in, and there were the requisite number of sheets and envelopes. But that's what I expected her to say. Maybe the cops took them, maybe she forgot to check. You're Burt?"

She turned toward the young man with her hand out. He held it like it was made of glass. "Have a seat. Finnigan, can you line up that elevator operator for me? Cheval?"

"You mean the shine? Why do you want to talk to—"

"Just get him, Finnigan. Please."

The house detective laughed, showing off a red throat lined with yellow, tobacco-stained teeth. "Never argue with a lady, says I, and you'd be smart to follow the same advice, Burt. If'n you ever want to get to be an op, that is, and Burt says he do." He pulled the door shut with a self-important clatter.

Burt was eyeing Miranda's wallet, which she had out on Finnigan's desk.

She came around to the front, pulled herself up so she could sit on top. Burt cleared his throat nervously, looking anywhere but at the wallet, the desk, or her legs.

Miranda lit a smoke, and stared at Burt. "Do you remember Mr. Winters checking in, Burt?"

He swallowed. "I do, Ma'am. I mean, Miss. He came in around five-thirty. Seemed preoccupied, I thought. A nice gentleman, nothing seedy about him. You can usually tell."

She nodded. "That's right. That's why I wanted to talk to you. You develop an instinct for people. You have to—you need to know who might be trouble, who might try to skip. It's like being a detective."

Burt blushed up to his hairline, which was glistening with pomade and sweat. An odor of bay rum drifted from his collar. "That's what I tell Finnigan, but he don't believe me."

"I do, Burt. So talk to me. What was he like?"

"The cops didn't ask me nothing like this, Miss—they just wanted to know when he checked in."

She blew a stream of smoke over toward the pin-up calendar of the girl bending over in a pair of silk stockings.

"They don't have time. We do. Tell me what you thought."

"Well, I figured he was a family man. Distinguished, you know, like—like William Powell. He seemed upset, maybe, sad and upset and . . . and a little angry."

"At anyone in particular?"

"No—just impatient-like. He kept tapping his foot when I explained the hotel rules, signed the register in a real hurry."

"Did he use his real name?"

Burt nodded. "I showed the police. You can make out the L and the W and not much else. You're supposed to sign it so's you can read it, but I didn't want to make him do it over or nothing."

"Did he have any luggage?"

"No luggage. I told the police the same thing. He had a briefcase, though. He kept hold of it the whole time, like he didn't want to let go."

She leaned forward. "What did it look like?"

Burt thought for a minute. "It was brown leather, kind of heavy-looking, bulged in the middle. Worn out, some."

"Did he mention anything about why he was staying at the Pickwick?"

"He said something about business. I figured that's what the case was for. He listed an address in Alameda, and I thought maybe he had to work late on something and couldn't get a ferry back."

"Good deduction." He blushed again, and loosened his collar with a finger. "Did he request any type of room? You know, by price, or amenity, or location . . ."

Burt stared at her, forgetting about her legs in the camaraderie of detective work. "It's funny you ask that, Miss Corbie—he said he wanted the cheapest room we had that was nearest to the stairs. That's what made me think he was going to go back to work at night, maybe, after checking in."

Miranda took a deep drag on her cigarette, not saying anything for a few seconds. "Thank you, Burt. Is there anything else you can remember, something you thought, maybe, while you were checking him in?"

He struggled for a moment, then gave up. "No, Miss, I think that's all."

She smiled, opened her wallet and handed him two dollars and her business card. "Thank you. You've been a big help. If you do remember anything, would you call my office?"

He turned as red as if she'd asked him to dance. "S-sure thing, Miss. Thank you."

"'Bye, Burt."

As soon as he opened the door, Finnigan stuck his foot inside. He was smoking a cigar. "All done with Burt, are you?"

"Where's Cheval?"

"In the elevator. I'll not have him in my office."

Miranda slid off the top of the desk. "It stinks like sweat and cheap rye in here, Finnigan. And you should brush your goddamn teeth."

He backed away from his office door in surprise. Miranda stuffed her wallet back into her purse along with the deck of Chesterfields, and slammed the door on her way out. The noise made Finnigan drop his cigar.

She cleared a break for Cheval with the manager, who was shaking with nerves, probably figuring he'd be out of a job by tomorrow. Her watch showed twenty to four. She'd been at the Pickwick for longer than the police.

He agreed to accompany her to the York Café, a place he suggested would serve them both. That meant it was a colored café; they usually didn't have a problem serving whites.

It was about three blocks from the hotel, on Sixth, and on the way she stopped at a liquor store. He waited outside; they didn't talk. Safer not to, especially for him. A drunk crawled out of one of the alleys, tried to spit but his throat was dry. Contented himself with "goddamn niggers" before diving for a cigarette butt in the gutter.

The place was quiet, a screen-door hash house with a tired, heavy colored man behind the yellow Formica counter, holding a swatter. A fly buzzed around the cash register.

"What're you doin' off work, Cheval? This ain't your day off."

He asked the question, but stared at Miranda. There were two other people in the place, sitting in separate booths along the left side, an old lady dressed like she'd just come from church, and another young man in railroad uniform. They all stared at Miranda.

Cheval took a seat at the counter, and Miranda sat next to him. "Gotta talk to this lady, Reece. Serve us up some of that gumbo you got back in the kitchen."

"You know I been savin' it for dinnertime. I got catfish and okra . . ."

"Gumbo, Reece. And hurry it up. I ain't got all day."

Reece grumbled his way back to the kitchen, looking back every few seconds at Cheval and Miranda.

She pulled out a pint of Old Sport Kentucky bourbon out of the paper bag, and set it on the counter.

"And bring us two glasses, Reece."

Miranda said: "Three. There's enough for all of us."

When the cook glanced back and saw the whiskey, he waddled back with three glasses, wiping them first with the towel draped from his apron. Miranda poured a shot into each. They were waiting for her, so she drained it.

Reece followed, smacked his lips, went back to the kitchen for the gumbo. Cheval studied Miranda while she poured another. Fear creased his face.

"Miss, I appreciate what you doin'. But I need my job."

The church lady was looking at them with all the disapproval she could muster. The railroad porter was just looking at the bourbon.

She met his eyes. "You think talking to me will get you fired?"

He shook his head. "No, Miss. But maybe not talkin' to you will."

Miranda watched Reece ladle gumbo onto heavy plates. She knew better than to try money, not with Cheval. Finnigan would dig up his own mother for two bits, spit on the corpse for a five-spot. But not the colored man. He was scared, confused. A white woman treating him like a human being was too much of a fucking rarity.

"It's between us, Cheval. Nobody else. And it's your choice. I think you saw something, noticed something . . . something that could help me. Maybe help somebody else, too."

Reece set two thick Buffalo China plates full of hot New Orleans–style gumbo in front of Miranda and Cheval. Hot sausage, ham, and Bay shrimp peppered the okra and corn file, all spooned over rice.

The fat man lost no time in downing his second shot. Miranda drank, too, as did Cheval. She poured more. The bottle was a little more than half-empty. She took up the fork, spread the paper napkin on her lap, and started to eat. Cheval joined her. There was silence in the small diner, except for the sound of the two of them eating and one or two flies drifting close enough to buzz hungrily. The smell of the gumbo filled the narrow diner with a warm and drowsy peace.

After a suitable interval, Miranda paused, wiped her mouth. Looked at Reece.

"Thank you." She raised her glass as if in a toast, and the other two men didn't wait this time, but joined her, the whiskey flowing down their throats together.

Reece smacked his lips. "You want some sweet potato pie?" Cheval nodded, as did Miranda. He went back to the kitchen. She poured another round. One more to go.

Cheval looked down at the plate, at the glass with a brown line of Old Sport near the bottom. Turned to her and lowered his voice.

"My pastor say we need to help people. My wife say keep your head down and mouth shut. I'll do what I can for you, Miss. What you want to know?"

"You were on duty when Winters checked in on Thursday night."

"Yes, Miss. I work from five until three in the morning. I go to day classes at a school couple of days a week, so 'sometimes I get real sleepy, but not on that Thursday, because I weren't in class on Wednesday."

"So you remember Winters. Did he go straight to his floor?"

"Straight to the third, and in a hurry. Can't seem to get the elevator there fast enough for him."

"Did you see him leave?"

"No. Never saw him no more. I was off work when they found him."

"Do you remember—do you remember anyone who went up to the third floor that night who—well, who didn't seem right to you? It would've been late at night, probably after midnight."

Cheval stared again at the whiskey in the glass he held. Reece bustled over, whistling a Cab Calloway tune, and slid two pie plates covered in huge pieces of sweet potato pie à la mode. Miranda picked up her whiskey, and as one, they drained each of their glasses, this time more slowly, lingering on the taste of the Kentucky bourbon.

Reece wiped his mouth. "That is fine liquor. Fine liquor is good for a man."

Miranda said: "So is fine gumbo, and sweet potato pie."

He looked at her, then Cheval. "I'll be in the kitchen, if y'all want anything else." She got out her wallet, left two dollars on the counter. He protested.

"That's too much, Miss."

"It's too little for fine cooking, Mr. Reece."

He laid a large hand over the money, let it stay there for a second. "Thank you, Miss."

She poured the last of the bourbon, giving Reece and Cheval the larger portions. They drank it quickly this time, not lingering over good-bye. Reece slapped the swatter down without catching anything, and waddled back to the kitchen, hand on his stomach. She and Cheval ate the pie and ice cream in silence.

When they finished, Cheval was still looking at his glass dreamily.

"I didn't tell no one this, Miss. Coppers didn't ask me, and I didn't plan on tellin' no one. Two men came up to the third floor about one in the mornin'. One small, carryin' a bag like a doctor. He didn't say nothin', just stood there lookin' at the floor. The other one, now, he worried me. He wore one of them big-brimmed hats, like somethin' out of one of them movies. Big nose, dark for a white man. Ay-talian, I think he was. He stood in the corner of the crate, and I'd been tryin' to keep my eyes open. One in the morning sure is a hard time for a man to work, even if he can sleep during the day. But when they came in, I got gooseflesh all over. Got awake after that. He smiled, an' it just made my blood run cold. Wore a dressy coat, camel hair looked like, big buttons to match the hat, shiny shoes. Leaned in the corner of the crate, just said, 'Three.' That's all he said, but I hurried that old elevator up like it was built yesterday."

He shook his head. "I ain't seen them men come down after that, and I looked, Miss. The big one weren't right. I seen boys packin', and I swore he was carrying something under his arm, even through that coat I could tell.

But the funny thing is Mr. Winters weren't shot or nothin', so I stays quiet. I figure I'm safer that way." He smiled at her, a little sadly.

Miranda picked at a piece of crust on her plate. "Would you be able to recognize them, Cheval? From a photo?"

He thought about it. "I would say so, Miss. But I wouldn't like to do it, unless I knew my family was safe. I got me a wife with a baby on the way, and I'm tryin' to get more education so's I can get them something better. I want to help, Miss Corbie, but I can't go puttin' my family in no danger like that."

She surprised him by putting her hand over his on the counter. "I understand, Cheval. I wouldn't ask you to. And thanks for telling me."

He pulled his hand out from under hers and smiled at her with embarrassment.

Eleven

She spread the newspapers out on her desk. Wheels screeched, and some-one on Market Street laid on his horn. The office was cool, almost cold, though the fog hadn't shimmied its way downtown yet.

Miranda studied the sheets, where they were wrinkled, what it was that Lester Winters read and cared about. Maybe died for. But detail work took concentration, and the day had already been too long.

She folded them and put them in the bottom drawer of her desk. Lit a cigarette. And unlocked the left-hand side drawer, drawing out the gun she kept in the office.

The long, sleek black line of it calmed her. She checked the cartridge, set the pistol down on top of the desk, and lifted the phone receiver.

"Operator? Can you connect me to someone about getting residential phone service? Yes, as far as I know. I'm calling from my office. The Drake Hopkins, in San Francisco. 640 Mason. Uh-huh. All right, I'll be here until five-thirty or so."

She hung up, staring at the phone with a dissatisfied expression. Then she picked it up again.

"This is Miss Corbie. Any messages?" Laying the cigarette in the ashtray, she opened the front drawer of the desk, taking out a pencil and a scratch pad. "Uh-huh. Uh-huh. She leave a number, a time? All right. Thanks."

Miranda set the phone receiver down carefully, slowly. Picking up the cigarette, she stood up and walked to the file cabinet. The old cathedral radio on top reminded her of the Pickwick. She twisted the knob, and pulled the antenna line out from behind the cabinet, letting it dangle off the side. She turned the volume down low, but enough to recognize human voices once the tubes warmed up.

She moved by the window, leaning out the sill, staring at the city, searching for a green Olds. A shrill whine and some static startled her. She flicked the tuner, managed to find a station with a voice, a rube on a banjo.

She sat down again, the chair comforting her as it always did. The chair and the gun.

She dropped the cigarette stub in the ashtray and opened the pack of Chesterfields in the desk drawer. Pulled out another one, used the desk lighter. One spark this time. Picking up the phone, she dialed, waited a few seconds.

"It's Miranda." Her voice was cold, hard as iron. "How long ago did Betty leave?"

Her foot tapped the floor in the near-silence, the twang of an instrument drifting toward her occasionally from the radio.

"I don't care, Dianne. I really don't. She called me, I wasn't in. She's in trouble about something . . . last night, at the Rice Bowl Party. On her way to the fashion show. Uh-huh. Uh-huh. That's what I thought. Well, if she's in trouble . . . no, not that. If you find out anything, let me know. Yeah, I'll do the same. 'Bye."

She leaned back in the chair, still tapping her foot. Betty hadn't left a phone number, just a message that she'd called, that she needed to talk to Miranda as soon as possible. With no number listed, the only choice was to hit the clubs Betty worked, in order. But she'd left Dianne's six months ago, so the club angle was a crap shoot. Still, Miranda would have to try.

A search in the desk produced a nearly full pint of apricot brandy, a gift from a client. She twisted it open with difficulty, took a swig from the bottle. It was sweet and fruity, and she appreciated the heat, though she would've preferred something more bitter to wash away the conversation with Dianne.

A church chimed the half-hour. Four-thirty. She pawed through the Kardex, and after two passes, found the business card. Lifted the receiver.

"Bente? It's Miranda. I know, I know. In May. Yeah, I'm going back. No, I've been busy. Once you're in the papers . . . yeah, I read about that. So no strike this year, you think? Well, it's only a matter of time before we're in it, and then—yeah. Yeah, I know. Listen, I'm on a case about a marine engineer . . . I don't know yet, they're doing an autopsy. Maybe. His name is Lester Winters, worked for NYK. Can you get me the skinny? Also on a Marine cop called Parker? Tall, thin guy, looks like he climbed out of a saddle. Bureau of Marine Investigation and Navigation. No, he was at the scene, talking to the house peeper . . . yeah, I know, that's what I thought."

Miranda sucked down the cigarette, making it glow brightly, before she set it back in the ashtray, stubbing out the end.

"Money, for one thing. Contribution to your fund. And I'm trying to find his daughter—maybe a frame job. She's a snowbird. There's a Chinese girl involved, probably a prossy . . . uh-huh. I figured you would. I might be able to use you for a nightclub job. No, they know me . . . Well, someone got in my apartment . . . yeah. This morning. I'm fine, they just left a warning card. Takahashi case. Yeah, that one. Nothing, except they drive a green Olds and eat at Joe Gillio's. I'm working on it. OK, call me with anything you find. I'll let you know. 'Bye."

Bente Gallagher. An improbably named and improbable looking Communist and union organizer who worked the waterfront, trying to prevent another 1934. Bente's brother lost his job in the strike, figured he lost everything. Killed himself a year later. Bente tried to follow him in Spain, but lived to fight another war at home.

She was a couple of years younger than Miranda, with rich red hair inherited from her father's Irish side, and the imposing figure of a Scandinavian goddess, the gift of her mother's Norwegian heritage. She liked helping Miranda, especially when she could make a few extra dollars for her various causes. Most of them huddled around campfires and cardboard shanties, out by the waterfront Hooverville. It still squatted near the early-numbered piers, not part of the San Francisco–Treasure Island–See the West tour package.

Miranda yawned, staring at last year's Pinkerton calendar on the opposite wall, letting the velveteen voice of a radio host drone about laundry soap. The chair creaked when she shifted suddenly, bending forward to open the center drawer. She removed two sheets of paper and the blotter.

Dipping the pen in the inkwell, she started to write, not slowing down or hesitating except to rewet the pen. She wrote "Eddie Takahashi," and underneath a column of words: *sister, mother, bloodstains, store, address, money, Betty, Madame Pengo, green Olds, license plate, Joe Gillio's, Mike (Ming) Chen, Filipino Charlie.* She blotted the paper, and set it aside, pulling the second sheet closer to her.

She'd written "Lester Winters," followed by *Pickwick, Phyllis, coke supply, newspaper, poison, wife, money, other man,* and *stationery,* then paused, her mind drifting over the day, her ears tuned to the band music playing on the radio.

The voice was deep, and it said: "You should lock your door."

She was on her feet and had the pistol in her hands and aimed, her finger on the trigger, when she recognized the lightly accented English. Gonzales stood in front of her, minus Duggan, smiling. She didn't lower the gun.

"You should know better." Miranda was breathing hard.

"Evidently." His manner was easier than yesterday, almost familiar. He took off his hat and sat down in the chair across from her, crossing his long legs, and lighting a cigarette with a match he struck on his shoe.

"The pistol is a beauty. Spanish-made, I believe?"

"Republic of Spain. Nine millimeter. Shoots like a dream."

He eyed the barrel, still pointing at his chest, then looked up at Miranda.

"Ever kill someone with it, Miss Corbie?"

She lowered it, slowly, not relinquishing her hold on the handle. "Why are you here, Inspector? And without your pet ape?"

"Assistant Inspector Duggan has been transferred to Vice. It's where he began, breaking the heads of bootleggers. He was a good cop in his day, Miss Corbie."

"I feel sorry for Pickles and the girls. And I suppose he'll be out for my blood."

"Not officially. But that hasn't stopped Duggan before."

Miranda pulled her chair out and sat down, keeping a distance between them. She laid the pistol on the corner, closest to her right hand, and took out the brandy, offering it first to Gonzales. He shook his head, and she didn't drink either, but kept it on the desk.

"That explains the Duggan part. What about why you're here? If you're trying to get yourself killed or frame me for it, there are easier ways to go about it."

He threw his head back and laughed, his throat muscles tight and brown against his shirt collar.

"My mistake. I won't do it again. I tried to call you earlier, but your line was busy."

She reached for a cigarette. He was leaning over the desk with a match before it was in her mouth. She met his eyes briefly, inhaled, and sat back down. He waited for her, resumed his seat.

She looked at him steadily. "As a matter of fact, I was going to call you. Eddie Takahashi's address. I need it. I also had a question about that hit-runner you're chasing. Near Seventeenth Street. Was it a green Oldsmobile?"

Gonzales raised his eyebrows. " '39 Dodge coupe. Why do you ask?"

She passed her hand over her forehead. "Who the hell knows. Maybe I can't tell the difference anymore. Any damage on the car, make it recognizable?"

He shook his head. "Not by now. We found the bumper, but by now they've replaced it, possibly repainted the car. Why? What's wrong?"

Concern crept into Gonzales's tone. Miranda wasn't sure if he was trying to keep it out or coaxing it across for her benefit.

"Nothing I can't handle. So I told you why I wanted to phone you, and I don't think you're here because you read my mind."

"I'm afraid not. I dropped by to warn you about Duggan, and to tell you I spoke to Mike Chen."

"And?"

"He claims to be an honest merchant, of course. He's got a record . . . served some time on a dope charge. I looked back further, and found reference to an attempted rape, later dropped. That was in Los Angeles, about fifteen years ago. Swears he did not know Eddie Takahashi, that Takahashi must have stumbled out of Waverly Alley."

Miranda blew smoke toward the ceiling and watched it drift toward the window. "Exactly what I'd expect him to say."

"He also mentioned that you propositioned him, and was thinking of filing charges."

Her hand hit the desk. "What the—you're fucking kidding me."

He shrugged. "That's what he said, Miss Corbie. I wanted to warn you, because if Duggan gets hold of it—"

"—yeah, I've got that much imagination, Inspector. Thanks. A dope peddler and rapist—who was on the spot and in the right location when a man was murdered—claims that I propositioned him. How nice to know the city's money will be spent trying to imprison me for my obvious nymphomania."

She stabbed the cigarette out on the Tower of the Sun ashtray with a violent twist.

"I'm just trying to—"

"Yeah, I know. Thanks. The honorable Mr. Chen must have forgotten that I've got a packet of poison he gave me, with a threat against my life—in his handwriting. Except that I don't think Mr. Chen forgot it. I think you're trying to keep me off the Takahashi case, like every other nickel-plated dick in this town. Maybe you think you're protecting me, I don't know and I don't really give a damn. I've got all the protection I need."

She picked up the pistol, took out the cartridge and reloaded it, while he watched.

"And yes—I've got a permit. I'm as legal as Mayor Rossi. Maybe more. You disappoint me, Inspector. I thought you were going to play fair."

He slowly pinched his cigarette out with his fingers. "I am not lying to you, Miss Corbie. That's what Chen said. Maybe it's his way of trying to checkmate you? You have this poison—which you might have mentioned to me, if fair play is to be dealt on both sides—he has his testimony. Perhaps he regretted writing such a threat—perhaps he is trying to nullify what he sees as your advantage."

Miranda set the long black pistol down on the desk again. "Possibly. If you're telling the truth, and I'm not entirely sure you are."

"And I'm not entirely sure you are, Miss Corbie, so we are well matched."

He leaned forward, stubbing his cigarette out on the ashtray. "But you're the one with the nine millimeter semiautomatic on the table. And I'd like to know why you're so curious about green Oldmobiles."

Church bells outside started ringing in five o'clock; shadows sprawled on the office floor through the open window. Miranda waited, letting the moment play out.

"All right, Gonzales. Give me Takahashi's address, and I'll talk about green cars and Mike Chen. And you can let the boys know I'm working another case—in fact, I'll be at the Hall tomorrow morning."

"They may not let you in."

She shrugged. "I'm an authorized investigator. Authorized by law, with a signed contract. They'll open the goddamn door."

He smiled. "I believe they will. What is the case?"

She smiled back. "None of your business, Inspector. Eddie's address, please?"

His grin broadened, and he searched his inner coat pocket for a notebook, which he looked through briefly.

"Hotel Bo-Chow. 102 South Park."

"No roommate?"

"None that we could find."

South Park made sense for Eddie. Close to the wharves and piers, it was the old Japantown, twenty years ago, now home to new immigrants from the Philippines and elsewhere. The people his mother didn't like. She wrote the information down on the sheet of paper with Eddie's name, still lying on the desk.

"All right. I found some bloody bandages in the back of Chen's shop. I'm getting them analyzed. I'll let you know when they come back, and hand them over."

Gonzales gave his voice an edge. "You know we won't be able to use the evidence. And you could be charged with theft. Or obstructing justice."

"Justice? Don't fucking kid me. You boys crossed the bastard off your list. If you'd done your job in the first place, the bandages wouldn't have been there for me to find."

He scratched his ear, visibly trying to control his temper.

"And the car?"

"Been following me around. This morning it was in front of my apartment, and when I was in the shower, someone decided to pick the lock and leave a card."

He nodded his head in the direction of the gun. "You should take that home with you. Normally, I'd suggest a tail, just for your protection, but—"

"—even if I weren't *persona non grata* with the brotherhood right now, Gonzales, that wouldn't work. I'm a private detective. I know the risks."

"So you do." He took the fedora from his lap and put it back on, then stood up. "Remember, Miss Corbie—cards, not guns, on the table."

Miranda pushed her chair back, standing up as well. "So long as you remember, Inspector—to knock."

He glanced at the pistol. "Don't worry. And watch out for Duggan."

"Thanks."

When he shut the door softly behind him, she sank back into the seat, shaking.

———

It was five forty-five, two cigarettes, and several gulps of brandy before Miranda felt like herself again. She finished the list for Winters, adding "autopsy," "NYK," "Parker," and "Italian." Her stomach growled, letting her know dinner was late.

She placed a call to Rick. He wasn't at work. She dialed home. No answer.

Miranda locked up the brandy and papers and pistol, and put the newspapers in the safe. She straightened her hat, her stockings, took her shoes off and straightened her toes. On her way out, she picked up the phone, and dialed the Club Moderne.

"Hi, Nancy, Joe around? No, just want to see him. Business. Yeah. I'll be around tonight. No, different kind of case. Listen, you see Betty anywhere? Betty Chow, used to work for Dianne . . . huh. All right. Just dinner, as soon as I get changed. Yeah. See you."

She dropped the phone in the cradle. The .22 in her purse felt heavy as she walked out the door, locking it, the Monadnock still noisy from people trying to get out of San Francisco.

Monday. The longest fucking night of the week.

Once out on Market, she decided to walk to the apartment. The financial wizards of the Stock Exchange—those that survived '29—were hailing taxis and climbing into Pierce-Arrows and heading for the peninsula or Nob Hill. Their underlings rode a streetcar or cable car to a nearby apartment house, or climbed into a Ford and drove across the bridge to Oakland.

The cold, moist air cleared her head. Clangs and rumbles and whistles. Music blaring from jukeboxes in corner bars, kids pouring out of soda fountains. Pinball kings with girls on their arms. The women holding their hats from the wind and rushing home to make dinner before their husbands arrived, the old ladies emerging from lecture hall morgues in the libraries and institutes, clucking their tongues over the rising hemlines . . . all of it surrounding and embracing her, making her body feel warmer, her mind less her own. No thought, not tonight. Oblivion. Nirvana.

She reached Chinatown, the outskirts empty but still littered with refuse, some of it moving. Miranda stood on Bush Street and stared, at San Francisco, her world, her city, the cold air biting her face and hands. She closed her eyes. Let the bastards come, she thought. Let 'em come.

They washed over her like late summer rain, but not gently, never gently.

Eddie Takahashi. And Betty and a Chinese woman who'd walked into a dead man's room. And the anemic blond girl, her nostrils red with white powder, her eyes manic and snapping with dull energy.

Phyllis was somewhere in the city, close to a supply, somewhere where men with greedy eyes calmed her down with more powder, teaching her to use it, teaching her to want it, and to do anything to get it. Use your tongue, use your lips, use your throat muscles, baby, that's it, keep going.

And she thought of Madame Pengo and the sad-eyed little girl, what she grew up seeing and hearing, and God help her, feeling, the men walking the alleys with furtive eyes, hunting for the young.

And she thought about the Italian with the staccato voice and the large hat, and Mr. Reece and Cheval's wife, with a baby on the way.

She thought about the Japanese girl who knew Emily, who liked Eddie, who still smiled with innocence and bantered with a shoemaker. And Edith, too, and she hoped Milton would marry her, because Edith was running out of time and options, and what she wanted, more than anything, was to be someone's wife.

And she thought about the men who had made her afraid, who had violated her and about all the others who'd tried, about the ones she allowed, the ones she fought off. She thought of Rick, and his sad Irish eyes and easy smile, and she thought of Gonzales, and how he aroused her physically, and how none of it mattered, none of it mattered a good goddamn, because none of them had been Johnny, none of them were Johnny, Johnny wasn't marching home again, and there were no fucking hurrahs.

She opened her eyes. Lit a cigarette. A familiar croak made her spin around.

"Miranda?"

No-Legs Norris was sitting on his chunk of plywood, staring up at her, his eyes questioning, probing. He'd come back from the War half a man, but he liked to say that people were like cigarettes and booze bottles, and half of one was better than none at all.

One of the hardware stores donated some wood and wheels, and a carpenter made him his platform. He'd lived through the Depression on it, selling information, cadging crumbs and smokes and booze, watching people, remembering what he saw. Miranda wasn't sure where he lived, but she always knew where to find him . . . somewhere near Chinatown, usually on Grant.

He pulled his platform up against the wall of a restaurant, leaning his back against it, the smell of bok choy and soy sauce drifting over them, making them both hungry. His arms were strong and muscled from propelling himself up hills and through the alleyways. Someone gave him some gloves early on, and he wore through a pair about every month.

"Hey, Ned. How's tricks?"

"Almost got run over during the parade. Glad things're normal again."

She handed him a smoke, crouched down to light it for him with one of the Treasure Island lighters. The flame sparked on the third try and reflected in his brown eyes. While she bent down, she whispered: "You got something?"

His gaze shifted both ways, up the steep hill at Grant and along Bush. Miranda never knew how Norris found out about what she was working on, but he never approached her unless he had information that was worth something.

The gravel in his voice submerged to a low rattle. "Yeah. I hear you're workin' the Takahashi killing."

She knelt by him, pulling her skirt down over her knees, one hand on her hat. "What is it?"

He stared at her, as if by staring he knew and understood. "Word on the street is the kid owed money. To people who don't loan, if you get my drift."

The breeze puffed up the navy hem, and she smoothed it again. "Names?"

He shook his head. "Just talk, Miranda. Some say tongs rubbed him out, he was stealin' from a Chinese gambling op, some say Italians up in North Beach in the International Settlement, some say Filipinos and Mexicans."

"Filipino Charlie mentioned?"

Norris shrugged. "He's a bit player, minor key."

"That it?"

He grinned, his smile missing some teeth. "That's enough."

Miranda pulled herself up, her knees creaking on the high heels. She opened her purse, looked in her wallet. Seven dollars, and eighty from Mrs. Winters. She handed Norris the seven.

"You get any more, I'll be around. You see Betty by any chance?"

"B-girl friend from your old days? No, can't say I have."

Miranda nodded. "Thanks, Ned. Be seeing you."

He pocketed the money faster than a magician with a card trick. "Be seeing you, Miranda."

She watched him pull himself up the hill on the plywood, his back and shoulder muscles quivering with effort, the smell of bok choy pursuing him up Grant.

Twelve

The Moderne was at 555 Sutter, right around the corner from her apartment, irresistibly drenched in neon and glistening with a kind of cheap Hollywood glamour. Joe Merello, a short, dapper Italian with some of the best cooks and fastest hands for a floor show number in the city, ran the operation and owned the club, but not all by himself. His profits and showgirls both fell into more hands than his own.

No one ever knew who Joe's partners were, and no one cared, so long as he fronted, because the drinks were fair and always had been—even before repeal. The club's matchbooks and menus read A DINNER FOR EPICURES, and he always made sure that the slogan fit, regardless of whether you were sober enough to taste the French-Italian specialties.

His own specialties were about five-two and nineteen, and the "Sensational!" floor show changed as frequently as his appetite: a three-month stint or when she turned twenty-one, whichever came first. The club wasn't as busy as Joe Vanessi's, but Merello managed to pull in his share of the socialite/celebrity mix, who figured the "e" in Moderne stood for "elegant" instead of "easy." Not that they would know the difference.

Miranda walked through the double chrome doors bathed in the spotlight, while a couple of women in furs and pomaded rich boys let the valet park the Duesenberg, and waited their turn on Sutter. The hat check girl raised her coiffed head from her palm, replacing the bored expression with a grin.

"Hiya, Miri, where've you been? No old ladies wantin' the goods?"

"Hi, Marie—been busy, that's all—different cases. Just dinner tonight. Joe on the floor?"

Marie rolled her eyes, her blonde eyebrows arching dramatically. "Probably on his office floor, and with the new chanteuse. Or in the room. Some high-rollers tonight—all that charity for the Rice Bowl Party—now they want it back."

She motioned with her head toward Sutter, where a line had formed. Tailored specimens waited for admittance under the critical eye of Raphael, who considered himself the reincarnation of the artist. Joe ran a high-class gambling room behind the stage, as did many of the nightclubs in the city, and continued the regular donations to the Policemen's Fund he'd started back during Prohibition.

"Marie—you see Betty Chow lately?"

"Betty . . . which Betty? Oh, the Chinese girl from Dianne's? No, can't say I have. She OK?"

Miranda frowned, checking her lipstick in the mirror behind Marie. "I wish I knew." She opened her cocktail purse, and took out the photo of Phyllis. "How about this girl? She seem familiar at all?"

Marie craned her graceful neck to get a better look, studying the picture for a few seconds, before loud, self-conscious laughter signaled another party had been admitted. She whispered to Miranda: "Can't say I have, sugar. But I'll keep the eyes peeled."

She winked at Miranda, and turned her attention to a slightly inebriated man about thirty, who was leaning on the counter and commanding her to take his hat off for him.

Miranda stepped through the faux marble columns, passed the empty, waiting tables for two, and took three steps down to the main floor. A thin, balding man in a tuxedo hurriedly approached with a smile on his face, while the band leader exhorted the trombone section to play "Wishing" just like Miller.

The thin man said: "Good evening, Miranda. Are we expecting someone?"

"Not tonight, Clark. Just dinner, though I'd like to show the boys—and you—a picture, when you've got a minute."

He clicked his heels soundlessly, bowing low enough to muss his blond comb-over. "Of course."

He snapped his fingers, and a good-looking young man about twenty-two, with a dancer's build and a dark complexion, appeared at his side, his teeth gleaming appreciatively at Miranda until Clark threw him a jealous glance.

"Table Twelve, Jorge. And hurry it up."

Jorge shrugged imperceptibly, his menu under his arm, and escorted Miranda to a small table near the stage. After he seated her, she took out the photo again.

"Look familiar? I know you like blondes, Jorge, even if Clark thinks they're the wrong sex."

The boy grinned again, smoothing down his long, slicked-back hair. He held the photo by a corner, studying it carefully, then shook his head.

"No, Miss Corbie. I have not seen this one. She is not a very good blonde— she is too pale. I would remember."

"Thanks. Would you do me a favor and when the boys working tonight take a break, ask them to come over?"

His bow was lithe, sinuous. "Of course, Miss Corbie. Have you decided on your dinner?"

"The usual. And a Blue Fog, please. Thanks, Jorge."

He nodded, and she watched his back as he retreated to the kitchen. The orchestra was still making a dirge out of "Wishing."

So if you wish long enough, wish strong enough . . .

Maybe they'd take a break and her drink would arrive.

Another waiter approached with a cocktail glass full of blue gin and a cherry. She smiled.

They were used to seeing her, usually sat her next to one of the columns or sometimes where she was now, half-hidden by a palm frond. Even when it wasn't the Moderne, most places had stopped giving her the kind looks, stopped the ever so slight big-eyed stutter when she told them she was by herself.

Musicians learned to ignore her the hard way, after she explained what "no" really meant with a string of epithets that would've made the men who built the bridges proud. Men sitting at the bar usually eyed her nervously, wondering what was wrong with her, not finding anything on the surface.

She was fair game if she was working the place, or even with another man, but on her own, her very aloneness made her off-limits. And if any of them asked the bartender about her, he'd shrug, and say, "Take your chances."

Sometimes, in between the faster numbers, the courageous ones would ask her to dance, and sometimes she'd say yes, then despise the weakness of wanting a body against hers, warm and tight.

The women ignored her, their too-thin legs shimmering in pale silk, the too-white flesh soft from too many easy answers. Summers on the Cape, winters in Switzerland until the refugee problem, but at least there was still Sun Valley, thank God. Eyes mascared, nails painted, voices modulated, bodies sullied only by the drunk of their own class, they turned away, comforted with money, wrapped up in it until that was all they could smell. Untouched, unmoved, unwarmed by the Spanish sun, voices tinkling like the ice in the cocktail glass.

Sometimes Miranda would overhear fragments, snapshots of lives lived lightly—"Will Cal beat Stanford, do you think—I just adore that Jimmy Stewart—Sally Rand's nude ranch—no, really, they only wear—New York's is going bust, at least we'll recoup this year, more rides, more girls—the bridges won't last, wait and see. Next earthquake and boom! Ferries are the only safe way to cross the Bay . . ."

Once in a while she might catch a mention of Hitler or Mussolini or Japan, a "poor England" or "poor France" whispered in a guilty exchange, as if apologizing for not talking American. And about every three months, a man or woman in last year's hat, self-conscious and with the evening's special on the table, would murmur something about Nanking or Spain, and how the world knew it was coming.

Then, if she was working, Miranda wouldn't come in for a time, move to Bal Tabarin or Vanessi's, or to a hotel restaurant, or anyplace else where her prey could be found with a drink in one hand, a girl in the other, and a band and gaiety and where people talked about the Big Game.

The girl singer had assumed the stage, and was warbling "I Get Along Without You Very Well," a sentiment Miranda agreed with. She was on her third cigarette, had finished the small appetizer plate of olives and peppers and mozzarella, the mixed salad with capers, tomatoes, and Italian dressing, and the rare-grilled steak smothered in mushrooms. Most of the pasta in red sauce was still on the table, along with two nearly empty Blue Fogs, a half-cup of coffee, and the piece of cheesecake.

No luck with four of the waitstaff and the bartender. No one saw Phyllis, or remembered her if they had. Finally Joe came out of the hidden door behind the stage, holding a blonde with one hand and a redhead with the other. He glanced over, recognized Miranda, smiled with all of his teeth in a genuinely happy grimace, whispered something to the girls, and approached her, picking up her hand out of her lap and leaving a lingeringly wet kiss on it. Joe was harmless as long as you were over twenty-five.

He was wearing his trademark white derby, a red rose in his lapel. His face shone like a cherub's, no doubt from a brisk business in blackjack.

"Ah, Miranda, *bella*, *come stai*?" He rested the hand with the diamond pinkie ring on her shoulder, smiling paternally.

"*Sto bene, grazie*, Joe." She sipped her coffee, and he slid into the seat beside her, his sharp eyes on the singer, who was still trying hard to put it over.

"The boys tell me you asking questions, want to see me. Not the usual, not looking for a man. You got something going on, something new?"

She removed the photograph. "A couple of things. This girl, for one. You recognize her?"

Joe stared at it long and hard, his tongue between his lips. She was about the right age. He handed it back regretfully. "I never see her before, Miranda. I send Vicenzo out, maybe he know. What else you got?"

She inhaled the last of the cigarette before rubbing it in the ashtray. "Have you seen Betty Chow? Chinese girl, worked at Dianne's same time as I did?"

A soft expression settled on Joe's round, creased face at the mention of Dianne's name. Rumor was they'd been lovers. Joe carried a small torch, about the size of a match, easily extinguished by the soft moan of a nineteen-year-old. Dianne had drowned hers long ago, in gin bottles and a fat bank account. Neither of them ever let a good time stand in the way of money.

Joe shook his head. "No, you know we don't get many Orientals. They stay in Chinatown."

"All right. One more thing, Joe, this is kind of tricky."

His hand gesture was expansive. "Whatever you want."

"Couple of finger men at Gillio's—Olympic Hotel—with a dark green sedan. Maybe the one they're looking for that ran over that old man near Seventeenth, I don't know. I think it's an Olds. They broke into my apartment, tried to scare me off."

Joe scratched his ear with his index finger, furry eyebrows raised. "Those boys, Gillio's—they play rough. Me, I never do business with them. No class. But they do this to my friend, to you, I keep my ears open, OK?"

"Thanks, Joe. *Grazie mille.*"

"*Ti amo, bella, hai capito?*" He pushed himself out of the chair, his hand on her shoulder again, bent down to kiss her cheek. He whispered: "*Guardati*, Miranda. I can only help so much."

He stood up, his knees creaking slightly, patted her on the shoulder, and added in a normal voice: "I send Vicenzo to see you. He remembers everything, got a memory like Caruso's voice. *Ci vediamo, bella.*"

Miranda watched as Joe walked quickly back to the gambling room, snapping his fingers at the door for the girls to each take an arm. She lit another Chesterfield, and waited.

Vicenzo closed the door softly behind him, looking nervously toward the floor. He caught Miranda's eye, but showed no sign of recognition, and took a circuitous route toward her table in case a customer was watching.

He was a tall, skinny Neapolitan with a hawklike nose that looked like it had been lifted from a Roman coin, and hands faster than his employer's—at least with cards.

He stood behind Miranda, scanning the floor. "Signorina Corbie?"

"*Buona sera*, Vicenzo. You ever see this girl?"

He stooped over to see the photo where she'd set it on the table, flattening the immaculate crease on his black trousers. His reaction was immediate.

"*Sì.* Yes, yes, I have seen her. She was here with a man, losing money fast. Very excited, *frenetica.* They spend a thousand, fifteen hundred—poof!—then she get tired, want to go home."

"When? *È molto importante.*"

He counted back on his fingers. "*Lunedì, martedì . . . sì, martedì*—Tuesday. Late, close to midnight. They stay, maybe, half an hour, no more."

"What was the man like?"

He made a motion as if to spit on the floor. "*Bastardo. Bidonista, faccia di culo.* He got dirty fingers. Slap the girl, she cry, go home."

"Italian?"

"*Sí. Siciliano.*"

"You ever see him before?"

He shook his head slowly. "*Non mi ricordo.* But I don't think so."

"Do you remember what kind of clothes they were wearing?"

"*Grandiosa*—he look like he try to be somebody, but nobody, *capito*? Tan suit, hat, light cloth, no good San Francisco clothes. From out of town, I'm thinking. Los Angeles, maybe. She was wearing nice dress, but *troppo seno*, you know?" He gestured to his chest. "Like a *puttana. Sí, sono come una puttana e il suo protettore.*"

Like a whore and a pimp. Miranda was silent for a moment, then nodded, placing a twenty on the table. Vicenzo started to protest.

"*Non è necessario—*"

"*Lo so.* It's a present. *Voglio fare un dono, prego.*"

He smiled at her imperfect, Spanish-accented Italian, bowed slightly. "*Sempre piacere, signorina. Cos' è altro?*"

"Did they mention where they were going, where they lived?"

He shook his head. "No, Signorina Corbie. But I think they go to many other places that night before they go here. He say something about more money, and she laugh and say, 'Don't worry, Sammy.' Then she get tired, sleepy like a baby, and complain, and he slap her, and then they go away, *grazie a Dio. Non mi piacevano.*"

"Not my type, either. *Grazie*, Vicenzo. For helping me."

He bowed again. "*Piacere, signorina. Lei parla bene.*"

"Italian by way of Barcelona, I'm afraid. Take it." He didn't try to protest again, but smiled with embarrassment, picking up the twenty with deft, long fingers, used to handling someone else's money.

"*Grazie*, Signorina Corbie."

He left the same way he came, winding his way around the giant palm, hugging the outskirts of the floor, until he faded into a cloud of cigarette smoke, and disappeared through the barely visible entrance of the back room. She caught a glimpse when the light stabbed the darkness behind the stage, heard a drunken laugh, the friction of fabric and money, and an exhortation to "place your bets." Then Vicenzo shut the door, and his world went with him.

Miranda picked up her cocktail glass regretfully, drained the last bit of gin from her last Blue Fog. Jorge sidled from an alcove with the check, and she lit a Chesterfield while she waited for the change.

Her world was suddenly full of Italians. Phyllis Winters and her gaudy bully of a boyfriend . . . an Italian in a wide-brimmed fedora on his way to see Phyllis's father. And one or two more in a green sedan, gloved hands on Miranda's apartment doorknob, smelling of cheap aftershave and sweat and back-alley hand jobs.

She picked up the change, leaving Jorge a good tip. And wondered again why an Italian at Gillio's gave a damn about the offing of a Japanese numbers runner.

Miranda walked out of the Moderne, waving good-bye to Marie, and reassured by her luck. Phyllis Winters was alive, at least last Tuesday.

Her wristwatch read nine-twenty. Still plenty of time to case a few nightclubs and floor shows, throw a few boxcars in the right rooms and lose gracefully, hoping to win something more important than money. But there was Betty to find, too, and that meant Chinatown, where most of the gambling was reserved for nonwhites, and the men at the tables weren't wearing tuxedos.

The Moderne made sense; Joe's place was one of the few where you could win once in a while and make it home with the money. Even if the hood of a boyfriend had blown in on a Santa Ana and the Southern Pacific, somebody local would steer him toward the Moderne. But finding where else they'd drifted would be more than one night's work—and she was dressed for the top joints, not the bottom dives.

"Sammy," Phyllis'd called him. And Vicenzo mentioned the clothes were wrong, more like Los Angeles. Miranda frowned. The only Sammy she knew of in L.A. was Sammy Martini . . . but his business was between Santa Monica and Mexico, smuggling women and drugs. Too big for a blackmail job. Too big for Phyllis Winters.

She crossed the street and walked to the corner of Powell and Sutter, dodging diners and the night shift, the streets busier than usual for a Monday. San Francisco never liked to see the end of a party.

A cable car pulled up in time for her to step on, while she threw a dime at the conductor and told him to keep the change. It lurched as it gripped the cable beneath the street, then recovered, tenaciously climbing the hill toward California. Miranda stood, holding on to the handle above her, watching the sidewalks full of restaurants and hotels and bars, full of couples and families, dockworkers and machinists, stenographers and produce men and shop-keepers. Monday night in San Francisco.

Chinatown was calling.

She began at the Twin Dragon, half-expecting to see the same fat blonde spreading out over the bar stool, and Rick with his cocky half-grin.

Waverly was empty, except for a rummy folded up between two doors, whispering to his paper bag of promises. An old Chinese woman hurried against the wind, her small feet scuffling against the alley. Discarded pop-corn gathered in the street corners, blown there with the dust and the candy wrappers and the newspapers. The wind always blew through Waverly, the refuse left behind.

Shrill laughter drifted from out of windows above her, and music played from the open doors of a few bars. Soft murmurs, staccato, sharp sounds of anger, the cooing sound of seduction and its aftermath in whatever language it was conducted.

The Chinese looked at her, looked at her again, while they blended into the night, wondering, for a moment, why a white woman in a fancy dress was walking an alley after the Rice Bowl Party.

No Madame Pengo, no little girl. Only a torn and dirty poster advertising her services, still attached to the brick edifice of the church.

No corners to catch them from the wind.

She nursed a Singapore Sling at the Twin Dragon. She knew there was a gambling room back there, and everyone was terribly polite, but she was by herself and white, and that was two strikes too many.

No one had seen Betty there, and if they had, Miranda wasn't sure they'd tell her. She was an interloper tonight. Chinatown was trying to get its heart back, after spilling it open for everyone else.

Ten-thirty. Just down the street, on Grant and Sacramento, was the Chi-nese Village, where the special drink was called the "Mandarin," and the wind didn't blow quite as hard and so the trash clinged to the bar.

A beefy truck driver from the Central Valley was taking a load off, and at first she thought he recognized Betty, but then he put his hand on her thigh and his eyes got flat and shiny. She left her egg roll unfinished and the rest of the Mandarin down his neck.

Eleven-five. She walked north on Grant, toward Washington, to the Jade

Palace, where the cool green stone and cherry-wood statues adorned the foyer and bar, and helped keep the clientele under better control. The specialty here was the "Lotus Blossom," and she hit pay dirt with the girl who served it. Betty sometimes worked the place, not often. The girl was nervous, a condition Miranda tried to help by the application of cash. It only helped a little. No, Betty hadn't been in. She thought she saw her during the Party, but there were too many people to know. She didn't know where Betty was staying or sleeping these days, whether she was alone or with someone.

Miranda drained her Blossom, leaving the tiny flower in the glass, feeling the hostile stare of the bartender, who'd kept quiet except for his eyes.

Quarter after twelve. She walked Grant for four long blocks, up the hill toward California and Old St. Mary's. The shadow of the church quieted her; the furtive steps of night workers, the invisible men and women who cleaned the restaurants and clubs, hurried by, clutching frayed brocade around their necks, their faces lined and tired, while the Bay fog, so threatening earlier, finally filled the streets, wrapping the neon chop suey signs in soiled cotton.

She passed Old St. Mary's, looking up at the clock tower, barely making out the familiar words: SON, OBSERVE THE TIME AND FLY FROM EVIL.

There were still a few couples nuzzling over drinks when she reached the Chinese Sky Room on Pine. A classier place than most, with a view of Lillie Hitchcock Coit's tribute to firemen and their apparatus.

The bartender smiled at Miranda, and she settled gratefully on a stool, the only single woman in the place, the drunks at the end of the bar too tired and too far gone to make a move. The barman with the kind eyes said he'd seen Betty, that very evening. She'd been crying, he said, that's why he remembered her. Crying and scared, tried to make a phone call, but the phone was out of order.

Miranda took out the last Chesterfield in a deck, and said: "Do you know where she went?"

He shook his head. "No. I think she turned toward Market, though. She was in a hurry."

She put some money on the counter, asked him if he's seen Phyllis. He wouldn't know, he said, he didn't work the room; it was at the other end of the building, down a flight of steep wooden stairs, in one of the Chinese basements law enforcement conveniently forgot.

He said, hope in his voice: "They're still open, Miss—if you want to try. All the games. Better than the Moderne!"

She told him not tonight.

One-forty-five. The night was colder, more empty, except for the street-lights that still glowed in the fog like their gas ancestors, the cars parked on the curb, squatting and silhouetted in the darkness. Far-off sirens pierced the wind, echoing the lonesome, mournful howl that seemed to always blow off Alcatraz.

Forbidden City was open until three. One more place to try.

She pushed her tired legs down the hill, back to Sutter, cursing her timing, her lack of a phone at the apartment. Betty liked Forbidden City, did a number for them once in a while, or filled in for one of the chorus girls.

Miranda squeezed in the double doorway, past a doorman who surrepti-tiously checked her breath and surveyed her clothes.

The floor shows were over, and a few out-of-towners, seeking the "thrill-ing Oriental experience," still clung to their tables, ready to be poured into the taxi cabs waiting outside on Sutter.

She headed for the bar, plopped inelegantly on the dark brown leather stool. The bartender hadn't seen Betty, hadn't heard of Betty. The stage man-ager was gone for the night, last show at one. Go home, lady. You can try again tomorrow.

At least she didn't have to buy a drink.

The door was heavy to push open, especially against the wind. She man-aged, the cold biting into her skin as she stood on Sutter. About three blocks to Mason. Then up the steep, steep hill to home.

She fastened the top button of the Persian lamb coat and flipped the collar up. Too tired to think, not tired enough not to worry. Maybe Betty would call her tomorrow. She'd go to her office in the morning, grab a bite on the way.

The Moderne was still open, a long black car still parked outside. Joe's room stayed available until four or five, or whenever the money ran out. Raphael had gone off shift, and a new man leaned against the door frame, bored, hoping the cold, foggy air would keep him awake.

Miranda reached the corner of Mason, staring up the angled street. Some princess she was, her and her hill of chrome and glass.

The wind was shrieking, and so were her legs. Tired, numb, her black and white dress clammy and old against her skin and her slip, she trudged toward 640 Mason Street, thinking about Betty, thinking about Phyllis, and finally thinking about Eddie Takahashi.

A squeal and roar.

She didn't remember them. But the lights blinded her, lights inhuman, cold, piercing the darkness like a knife through flesh.

She was back in Spain, and Johnny was explaining the flash before the shell hit, telling her to move if she heard a whine, move if she saw a bright light, don't be a goddamn bunny rabbit, Miranda, move your ass . . .

The force of the car flung her on the cement steps. She loved cement, loved the scrapes on her legs, the bruises on her hands and face. She embraced it, rolling her legs tight, half of her body reaching for an apartment house door, the other half compact, draped on the three steps to shelter.

The light bore down and cut across her like a razor blade, inexorable, turning off the sidewalk and heading down hill. No gun shot. The squeal screamed through the canyon.

Blind, deaf, dumb, she managed to stand, tottering on a broken high heel and an ankle that was swelling like a baseball, her lamb coat shorn of a patch of wool.

A dark green sedan.

Thirteen

She sat, or fell, back on the steps. No one opened a window; no one heard the engine, the scream of the tires. No one heard her heart beating.

Everything hurt. Her hands explored her face. It was tender on the left side, there would be a bruise. A little blood. A scrape, maybe, hope to hell no scars.

She took off her shoes, the left one, the one with the broken heel, hanging grotesquely by a strap around her swollen ankle. The right foot seemed OK, but the knee was painful. Pain was all right. It could all hurt like hell, but it still had to look good if she was going to earn a living. Living. That was the whole goddamn point.

She stood up, the silk a thin sheath between her feet and the coarse, cold sidewalk. Picked up her purse, bending over, off balance, precarious, but managing not to fall. One step. Two steps. The left foot dragged, couldn't hold her weight, not up a hill. The .22 in her purse was heavy, and inside she laughed at how useless it was. There were so many easier ways of killing somebody.

Eleven steps, twelve. Halfway there. Street still empty. Stupid, stupid Miranda. If it works once, they'll do it again. Keep doing it. Easier to change cars than a fingerprint. Next time it would be blue, or brown, or maybe black.

Eighteeen, nineteen. "Nice legs." They meant to kill her with them. Aiming for them, with all the force of a revved motor and a slope they'd love at Sun Valley. Nice fucking legs to kill you with.

Twenty-three, twenty four. Almost there.

She dragged herself up the few steps in front of the Drake Hopkins, leaned against the door. She couldn't sit again, not if she wanted to get back up. With a shaking finger, she punched the buzzer for the night doorman.

Shoes made a soft whisking sound on the carpet. Then dull thumps, as they sped up.

"Miss Corbie? My God, what happened? Are you all right?"

Leo was an old man, sixty-five and showing it. He liked the night duty because he couldn't sleep. Claimed he hadn't slept since '06. His eyes were awake now, staring at her.

"I'm OK. Need to get upstairs. Elevator work?"

"Sure, it's working. Here, let me help you—"

He put his arm behind Miranda's back and underneath her arm, helping her to stand, gently guiding her to the small, automatic elevator.

"What happened? Should I call a doctor? Or the police?"

"No." She was breathing hard. The adrenaline was catching up to her. "But you can make a call for me. Once we get upstairs."

Leo had seen too many things in sixty-five years to ask questions. He knew Miranda came home late; knew she was a private detective. And he knew to keep his mouth shut and his arm behind her back.

Leo placed her on the small stool, still in the elevator from when the building owners hired a colored man to run it. He died last year, and since they converted it to automatic, Miranda relied on the stairs.

She leaned against the wooden wall, listening to the hum of the motor, felt the cables lift them. Leo stood with his back to her, facing the door, ready to shoo away any other late-night resident of 640 Mason Street until he could deliver his charge.

A small jump before it settled. Two seconds. *Clang.*

The door hesitated, opened. Leo turned quickly to Miranda, scooping her up easily for an old man, his arm strong and secure behind her. She leaned on him, pushing herself toward the safety of her apartment.

She tried to stand up, winced and nearly buckled, but Leo caught her. He fished in his pocket for a passkey.

"At the table, please, Leo."

He turned on the light and walked her to the kitchen, gently lowering her on one of the wooden chairs. Without a word, he opened two cupboards until he found the coffee, and started filling the pot, still on the stove.

Miranda opened her purse, her fingers thick and clumsy. Her left palm was bleeding, left some blood on the cloth. She found a five, dropped it on the table.

"Thanks, Leo. I wouldn't have made it up here without you."

He flicked the burner, waited for it to catch, adjusted the flame. Then he turned, saw the money, shook his head.

"You know better than that, Miss Corbie. You sure you don't need a doctor?"

His face said she did. She must look like shit. "Maybe later. Can you phone someone for me?"

" 'Course. What's the number?"

"MArket 7237. Rick Sanders. Ask him to come as soon as he can."

"Will do, Miss Corbie. Are you sure you'll be all right? You want me to come back after I call Mr. Sanders?"

She tried to crack a smile, but it was too painful. The left side of her face felt swollen. She must have kissed the sidewalk with it. Just like Eddie.

"No thanks. Thanks for helping me. And making the coffee."

He gave her shoulder a gentle, fatherly pat and left the kitchen. She heard the door close softly behind him.

She sat for a few seconds, watching the coffee bubble to the top of the glass ball, trying to get her breathing under control.

She must've fallen asleep despite the pain and half-empty cup of coffee in front of her. She woke with a jump, hurting from the sudden movement, her hand automatically reaching for the gun on the table.

Rick was pounding on the door. "Miranda? Miranda, are you all right? Can you get to the door?"

She glanced at the clock on the kitchen wall. Ten after three. She stood up, not putting any weight on her left ankle. It looked like a ruby red grapefruit. Funny the things that go through your head in the middle of the night when someone tries to run you over.

By the time she hobbled out of the kitchen, the door was swinging open. Leo held the passkey in his hands, and Rick stood there, Rick with a blotched face, puffy eyes, and a shirt misbuttoned and hanging out of a pair of dirty trousers.

Both men stood and stared at her.

She said: "Come in and shut the door. Thanks, Leo."

Leo had at least fifty years of practice in taking a hint. Rick stepped across the threshold, hurried to Miranda. The door closed softly.

"My God, Miranda—you look like shit. I'll call a doctor—"

He had his arm around her, and she leaned against him, her body grateful to not have to carry itself. "Deadbolt and chain the door. And help me to the bed."

He made sure she could stand before leaving her, and she watched him while he manipulated the locks. Rick lived near Civic Center, by the Hotel Empire. He must've taken a taxi to make it in fifteen minutes.

He guided her through an open doorway to the small bedroom, sitting her carefully on the bed. It was stuffy, and he opened a window. The sound of foghorns drifted up from Mason Street.

"You need a doctor, goddamn it—"

"Sanders, don't fight with me. If I get a doctor, I have to explain what happened. I'll lie, he'll get suspicious—you know the routine. I don't want the cops around."

He sat beside her, gently moved a lock of hair away from her face with one finger. "You need to be cleaned up. You might even have a concussion."

She turned her head away. "I still remember my middle name."

Rick stared at her for a few seconds. "I'm going to get a cloth, some soap and warm water."

She heard him in the bathroom, gathering towels, probably looking for bandages. Probably making a mess. She wanted to yell at him, tell him she didn't need his goddamn Irish charity, tell him to get some fucking self-respect and leave her alone when she called him in the middle of the night.

She felt her cheek again. It was swollen. She wouldn't be working the clubs for a month.

Rick walked in slowly, carrying a pot of water in his hands. He managed to set it down on the rug without spilling any. Steam rose from the water, and Miranda stared at it, seeing bright lights through fog.

He knelt on the floor and wrung out the washcloth.

"Lift up your skirt, Miranda." She almost laughed. Rick was watching her. "You're still in shock, even if you don't have a concussion."

"Turn on the radio."

"What? Why do you—"

"Please, Rick, just turn on the radio."

He shrugged, hauled himself up with a groan, and twisted the knob. He waited a minute or two for the tubes to heat up, not looking back at Miranda. Static broke the silence, and he quickly adjusted the tuning until the sounds of a band broadcast drifted from the speaker, from somewhere overseas where it was already tomorrow, another day in another war.

By the time he turned toward her, she'd unsnapped her garters and taken off her silk stockings, and lifted her dress hem about four inches above her knees. The pain made her a little more awake.

Rick knelt down in front of her again. "The cloth isn't so warm anymore."

"It's still wet."

He placed a large hand around her left thigh, lifting her leg and straightening it, resting it on his right shoulder.

"Ouch! What the hell are you—"

"I'm testing your motion, trying to see if you pulled something."

"I didn't, Dr. Kildare. I'm scraped and bruised from hitting the ground hard—concrete steps."

He grunted, and applied the cloth to the side of her thigh. A bruise was starting to form. Then he rinsed the cloth again, leaving more water in it, and draped it on her knee, squeezing it so that some drips ran down the sides of her leg. He didn't look at her. She flinched from the pain.

"You've got a bad scrape and a hell of a bruise."

"Will it scar?"

"I don't think so."

He washed it three times. Miranda closed her eyes. Then he carefully moved her leg from his shoulder, supporting it with his left hand, feeling the bones of her ankle with his right.

"It's sprained."

She wanted to make a sarcastic retort, ridicule him for his ridiculous doctor act, his mother-hen attention. Instead, she just said: "Yeah."

He set her leg back down on the floor, stood up. "I'm getting more water and some iodine. I found a couple of bandages and tape in your bathroom."

She closed her eyes again. Murmured, "Thanks, Sanders."

When he came back, he put some iodine on her knee, tore off a bandage, and taped it on. The iodine stung like a bastard, and she cried out. Rick ignored her. He used the other part of the bandage and wrapped it around her ankle.

The band ran through a series of tunes from the Great War, recalled from retirement to serve again. Now the singer was emoting all over the microphone on "Hurry Home."

Miranda had forgotten about her skirt, and Rick turned toward her other leg, running his fingers along the side of it. She felt herself shiver slightly.

"What the hell are you doing, Sanders? It's my knee that's banged up." She moved to pull her skirt back down.

"You might have strained something there, too, torn a ligament. You know that, so kindly shut up." He glared at her, while he tested the extension of her leg, feeling the ankle again.

"You'll still get a couple of bruises on this leg. You can thank your calf muscles it wasn't worse."

"They saved my life."

He replaced her leg on the floor, rinsed out the cloth again, and washed her right knee. He met her eyes.

"Time for your face."

She pulled her skirt down, while from the floor he leaned in toward her, against her legs, his face close to hers.

She closed her eyes, not wanting to look into his. She felt them, though, felt them poring over her, and then the sweet relief of the warm water on her cheek, where it stung and dripped down toward her lips. She felt his finger brush the water away, and move up to feel her cheekbone.

Hurry home, hurry home. Now I know just what lonely really means . . .

Her eyelids opened, involuntarily. Rick's mouth was only a few inches away from hers. She jerked her head back from the cloth he was holding against her cheek.

"Would you shut that sentimental bullshit off, please? I can't stand these singers that warble like goddamn Jeanette MacDonald."

He turned off the radio, mid-applause. Miranda was leaning back, trying to brace herself with her arms. He sat down beside her.

"I don't think you'll have a scar on your face, but you'll be wearing a black eye for a while. Your cheek is very swollen. I'd feel better if you saw a doctor, maybe got an X-ray, but I know you won't, so you need to keep ice on it. You got any?"

"Some. Ice bag is under the bathroom sink."

She used it for hangovers. Some fucking hangover she had for a Monday night.

When Rick left, she tried to stand up. She made it on the third try.

He walked into the bedroom, carrying the ice compress and a glass of water. "What the hell are you doing?"

"I need to use the bathroom."

"Then fucking well say so, Miranda, for Chrissakes."

The lilt came back when he was angry. He set the water on her nightstand, the ice bag next to it. Then without warning, he picked her up, making sure her right side was closest to him, so she could stand the contact.

"I'm not an invalid, I can fucking walk."

"Not tonight. And shut up. If you call me in the middle of the goddamn night, then fucking listen to me."

He kicked at the bathroom door to swing it open, deposited her on the tile, closed the door again.

She looked at herself in the mirror. Started to cry, choked it back down, deep breaths. Then she peed and flushed, halfway expecting Rick to barge in as soon as he heard the noise. Every movement was agony, and it was probably four or four-thirty, and she looked like hell, like something worse than hell, and . . .

She started to cry. She leaned against the counter, the tears stinging her cheek, her left arm still dirty from the cement.

Rick tapped on the door. When there was no answer, he walked in.

Without a word, he grabbed a towel, wet it in the shower, and cleaned off her left arm. He said nothing. When he was done, he used the tail end of the wet cloth to pat around her eyes. Then he threw it on the towel rack, and picked her up again, carried her to the bedroom.

He deposited her in a chair, walked to the dresser, found a nightgown.

"Can you undress yourself?"

She nodded, feeling worse than when the car came at her. He handed her the nightgown.

"If you've got a zipper, you'd better let me do it."

He unhooked the safety at her back, unzipped the dress quickly. Then stood away, his back toward her.

She slipped out of the evening dress, lifting her legs, her swollen ankle around the bunched black and white fabric on the floor. Then she pulled off her slip, and finally unsnapped her bra. Felt the cool silk of the blue night-gown fall on skin.

"All right."

Without looking at her, Rick turned down the covers on the bed. Then helped her over to the side, lifting her legs, and tucking her in under the sheet and blankets. Finally, he pulled out a bottle of aspirin in his pocket, opened it, gave her three. And laid the ice pack on her cheek.

"You want to tell me who did this to you?"

"Italians from Gillio's—Olympic Hotel. Green sedan. They broke in this morning, left a calling card. 'Nice legs.' Tried to run me down tonight."

"Takahashi case?"

"Yeah. I'm on another—out all night looking for this girl, Phyllis Winters. Old man died at the Pickwick, stepmother thinks—knows—it's murder. Girl's been missing, she's a snowbird. Cops hushed it up at first, but now they've got an autopsy—"

"Shhh. I know about it. I'll tell you tomorrow. Today. Later. You need to sleep, Miranda. You gonna be OK?"

She let his eyes, brown and Irish, warm her for once. No defenses left. "Yeah. But—would you mind—would you mind staying here for the rest of the night?"

He shrugged, as if it were a question she asked him all the time. "Sure. May as well. You got an extra pillow for the couch?"

"Top of the closet."

He rummaged around, pulling down an old brown wool blanket and a small pillow with an embroidered pillowcase. He looked at it.

"I didn't know you embroidered."

"I don't."

He shrugged again, and tucked the pillow and blanket under his arm. Then he reached over, patting her shoulder, his lips grazing her head.

"Good night, Miranda. Try not to dream."

He clicked off the bedside lamp. She fell asleep almost immediately.

A bright yellow light and a loud thud startled her awake. Her legs were shaking, programmed to run.

Rick forgot to draw the curtains last night—this morning. She heard his voice, grumpy and thick with sleep.

"Just a minute!"

Someone was knocking on the door, urgency behind it.

Miranda flung back the covers, sharp pains in her back, neck and shoulders making her slow down. Her fingers traced the outline of her cheekbone. Swelling down a little. Thank God.

Rolling over and sitting up required strategy. She twisted herself upright like a contortionist, trying to find the least painful position. The melted ice pack still rested on her pillow, and she moved it to the nightstand, swallowed another three aspirin, and was standing by the time Rick tapped on the door.

"Miranda? You awake?"

"What's going on?"

He came in, his face bleary. "Throw on a robe. You got company."

"Who is it?"

He rubbed the stubble on his chin. "Phil."

She limped to her closet, pulled down something flannel, buttoned it in the middle, started to walk out the door.

"You'll break your goddamn ankle if you don't slow down."

Rick kept about a foot behind her. Phil was already in the foyer, hat in his hands, brown suit rumpled, smelling like stale cigarettes. Sweat dotted the deep gullies in his forehead, his gray hair damp with it.

"What the hell? Somebody do this to you, Miranda?"

His voice came out a surprised croak, his face caved in with worry and shame and what was always there when she was.

Miranda said: "I fell down some stairs in Chinatown. Rick helped me get back home."

Phil stood and sweated, the hat brim twisting around and around through his large, flat fingers, his body tense with embarrassment. His stomach, wrapped in an Arrow shirt, hung over his belt. Miranda shifted her weight, her voice more tired than angry, looking at him, trying to keep the pity out of her eyes.

"Why are you here, Phil? To tell me again to back off the Takahashi case? Or are you here to arrest me so Duggan won't?"

His coarse skin deepened to crimson. The hat kept turning. Around and around. A middle-aged man on his way to old age, still toting the desires of youth. Calling them sins just made them heavier.

"No. We can take that up another time."

Rick looked from one to the other. "I can go in the other room."

The detective blew out a long breath. "It doesn't matter. May as well come along, it'll be news soon enough." The hat brim continued to twirl, then came to an abrupt stop, and he jammed the brown fedora on his head.

"I'm sorry you're hurt, Miranda. I'm not here because of Takahashi. I got a crime scene you'll need to see, got an identification to make. We found your card. You gotta answer some questions."

"Identification—who—?"

His voice was low, and he stared at the floor. "Chinese girl. Used to work for Dianne's, goes by Betty Chow. Somebody found her in one of the empty graves in Laurel Hill. She's been strangled."

Part Three

New Year

Fourteen

The ground still stank of the dead.

Thousands of pioneers, city founders. Andrew Hallidie, the man who invented the cable car, the only mechanized transport that could tackle the hills. It allowed the rich to look down on everyone else and gave their servants transportation. Without servants, it was too difficult to tell them apart.

Brown, rich, crumbly, sandy earth. Made richer by the blue blood and red blood that poured in it; by the '49ers who never struck anything except hard rock, whose only yield was sweat and scars and forgotten memory, dreams wiped out by a dried-up creek and the hot Sonoma sun.

The wind still blew on Lone Mountain, wind from the sea to the southwest, where Sutro built his castle, his dreams embodied, and yours, too, for a dime at Playland-at-the-Beach. The dead were going, going, gone to Lawndale, as the most populous part of Colma was called, the city founded as a necropolis, a company town if there ever was one. If you worked in Colma, you worked at the company trade. If you died in Colma, they just rolled you over.

No dead allowed in San Francisco. We don't serve your kind. Have your wake, cry at the memorial service. But spend eternity to the south, even if you built the city to the north.

Cities grow, friend. The dead stay buried.

Worst of all, they don't spend money.

Fog wrapped the remaining headstones on Laurel Hill, obscuring the sun. Miranda buttoned the top of her coat, stood in between Rick and Phil, staring at the fresh-turned earth. So recently a home to someone long buried, more recently a trash pit for the cemetery workers. A grave for Betty Chow.

Cigarette wrappers and greasy paper, bits of salami still clinging to it like rotten flesh, littered the bottom and sides, churned into the soil.

Miranda stood, and looked, and smoked. Betty wasn't there anymore. Betty wasn't anywhere anymore.

Phil barked a couple of orders to the uniform cops protecting the crime scene. The photographers and lab men had left with the corpse, leaving them bored and cold and wanting off the hill, back to one of the more hospitable corners of San Francisco.

Then Phil faced Miranda, his face craggy and tired. "Couple of cemetery workers found her early this morning, 'bout five o'clock. Came out here to smoke and take a piss. The coroner's boys don't think she was killed here . . . just left as some kind of joke."

Miranda carefully put out her cigarette, half-smoked, and replaced it in the pack in her purse. Her voice was steady. "She fight back?"

The detective shrugged. "They'll check her fingernails."

A gust of wind blew a battered milk cap along the dirt path, and Miranda watched it roll until it collapsed beside a smooth, dark rock in its way.

"Hands, scarf—what?"

Again, Phil shrugged. "Report's not in yet, but not hands. No finger marks."

Rick took a step to Miranda, interrupted before she could ask another question. "What about the time of death?"

"Midnight, maybe sooner. Don't know if—well, if she was raped. Lab should be done soon, maybe by the time we're back at the Hall."

Miranda nodded, walked forward on unsteady ankles, throwing off Rick's hand at her elbow. Paper napkins from Threlkeld's Scones. Broken bottle of scotch. Lucky Strikes.

And last night, when she was searching through Chinatown, retracing Betty's footsteps, hearing her desperation, her anxiety, her fear, Betty was already dead. Tossed away. Lost candy wrappers, lost souls, all equal under the eyes of the Lord's once-sacred-now-profane garbage pit. Thank you, Jesus. A-fucking-men.

Miranda could see the small, twisted body, arms and legs cold and akimbo. The delicate cheekbones, the slim hips. The bulging, glassy eyes, where, if she was lucky, the flies hadn't gathered because they were closed, a second before oblivion. The purple tongue. The clammy blue skin. Red marks on her throat.

Death made everyone the same colors.

She spoke under her breath, words the others couldn't hear, words she didn't understand. She wouldn't recall them, couldn't recall them, but she'd spoken them before, in front of bodies of shriveled old women, their stomachs ripped open by bayonets, and men with half their faces blown away. They were always there when she needed to say them. Too many times.

Words.

Miranda turned back toward Phil and Rick, who stepped closer to her, afraid she would topple over. Not her time for the trash pit. Not just yet.

"I'll ID her at the Hall. Let's go."

Phil led the way down the hill, Rick's arm hovering behind her back. Somewhere in the fog, a seagull cried, searching for something. Miranda looked up, trying to find it, but all she could see was white.

The marble halls echoed with heavy footsteps. Cops. Prisoners. Judges, the heaviest of all, even if they weren't carrying an extra five hundred in their pockets from one of the supervisors.

Miranda said good-bye to Betty on Laurel Hill. She recognized the body on the slab, signed the form identifying it as Betty Chow, age thirty. Family unknown, profession unknown.

She sat and smoked in Phil's office, door open, the tapping of the typewriters and constant phone calls down the hall helping to drown out the voice in her head. Rick left after the identification, his face green, heading for work. Now it was question time with Phil, the man with all the answers except the obvious one.

"So you last saw her on Sunday night?"

"As I said."

"Is that when you gave her your card?"

"Yes."

"Did she try to call you?"

"Yes."

She blew smoke over her left shoulder, eyeing the clock. Nearly ten-thirty.

Phil typed more slowly than usual, reluctant to look at her. "Did you know she was a prostitute?"

Miranda shrugged, then said: "She worked for Dianne."

"Is that the only way she knew you?"

"Yes."

"Any idea why she called?"

"No."

He dragged his face up to hers, the eyes shrewd.

"Takahashi business?"

Miranda shrugged again. "I don't know. She didn't leave a message."

His fingers methodically plunked the typewriter keys. Then he swiveled the chair slightly to face her, his fingers still drumming, this time on the desk.

"There's a connection, Miranda. Don't tell me you didn't know she was working with Filipino Charlie."

"You can believe me or not believe me. But that's the first I've heard of it. Until Sunday night, I probably hadn't seen Betty for a year. I thought she was still working for Dianne. In fact, I called Dianne to find out when she quit—or if she got canned for something. Maybe you remember, Phil—Dianne's choosy."

Blood rushed to his face again. "All right, Miranda. You can go. But stick around for the inquest. And we may have more questions."

She stamped out the cigarette in his ashtray. "Report in yet?"

He stared at her for a second, then opened a manila folder on his desk. "Preliminaries came in while you were in the basement. Looks like she was strangled with a scarf of some kind. They'll check the fibers, but don't expect quick results."

Miranda stood up. "I don't expect much, Phil. Makes it easier on everybody." Her voice came out harsher than she wanted. "Was she raped?"

Phil opened it again, said slowly: "Looks like she had intercourse shortly before she was killed. Can't tell if it was consensual."

Miranda nodded, her ankle throbbing. Paused for a moment, then said: "I'm on the Winters case. Hired by Mrs. Winters. I'd like to see the report on what was found at the scene."

Phil stared up at her. "You can get that information from Inspector Gonzales."

Their eyes met, briefly, and Miranda turned to go. Phil said, "Wait a minute."

She looked back at him, surprised. His mouth was twisted in a grimace.

"And that's all, huh? Betty's dead, move on to the case that pays?" He shook his head, the sweat still beading in his hairline. "You're a cold-hearted bitch, Miranda."

She leaned forward, her hands on his desk, her voice low. "And you're a hypocritical motherfucker, Phil. Maybe that's what's wrong with you. A little too close to the apron strings, and you never got over it. Betty was a friend of mine. And you're telling me you can't tell if she was raped because she was a whore. So maybe you can tell me why the fuck I should even bother with you anymore."

His hand, the knuckles large and broken, splayed on the desk near hers, trembling. He was standing, his eyes focused on the typewriter.

"Get out of my sight. And God help you, Miranda, because I won't."

She looked at him, trying to find the man she used to know.

She said softly: "No one asked either one of you, Phil."

Miranda walked away on awkward steps, trying to protect her ankle, favoring her left leg. The detective watched her go. One too many compromises, one too many nights with the gin bottle, one too many trips to Dianne, searching for a woman with auburn hair. He stank of it.

He put both hands over his face. And crossed himself.

Gonzales was at his desk, sandwiched in a corner. It looked too small for him. The uniform she'd asked had cocked a thumb and a sneer by way of direction, and she noticed his only company was an old cop from robbery detail who was sleeping at his desk.

The scarred wooden surface was clean, immaculate. No coffee rings, no pastry crumbs. No photos of smiling wives and small children at the summer house.

He rose as soon as he saw her threading her way through the wooden gate with a limp. By the time she reached him, he'd pulled a chair from somewhere, and helped her to sit.

Miranda was still too sore to cross her legs. The concern in Gonzales's voice sounded genuine.

"What happened, Miss Corbie? Your face—"

"Won't be advertising Max Factor any time soon." She took out a cigarette, and he had the lighter, an alabaster desk model, waiting. She inhaled, thankful for the rush.

"The green sedan I told you about tried to run me down last night. I was out looking for Phyllis Winters and Betty Chow. Mrs. Winters hired me to find her daughter, that's the second case I told you about. Betty left me a message to find her, sounding distraught. Phil came this morning and told me Betty was dead. We went to Laurel Hill, I came back to ID her. He mentioned she was working for Filipino Charlie, which I didn't know. I want a full report on him, the examiner's report on Betty and Winters, and a list of what was at the scene when you found him at the Pickwick."

She took another deep drag on the cigarette, watching the end burn. Gonzales said softly: "Why are you now telling me so much, Miss Corbie? You normally like to play your cards closer."

The old cop woke up, stretched, scratched his neck, stared at Miranda, and wandered over to find coffee. She kept her voice low.

"Betty's dead. She knew something about Eddie Takahashi and it killed her. This isn't about the Rice Bowl Party or Nanking. Something else, something with money in it, something to cause a couple of Italian boys from Gillio's to scare me, and when that didn't work, to try to kill me."

She opened her purse and took out her billfold, removing the Gillio's card. Handed it to Gonzales while she shook the last cigarette out of her pack of Chesterfields. He held the lighter for her while staring at the card.

"This is what they left in your apartment?"

She nodded, searching for the series of numbers Roy had scrawled on her own business card. She found it, and handed it to Gonzales.

"That's part of the plate. Had a boy go down and get the numbers, sent him to the market to make it look natural. Somewhere along the way, one or more broke into the apartment—no noise—while I was in the shower."

Color rose in Gonzales's face. "If you had told me all this yesterday—"

Miranda stared at her fingers holding the Chesterfield. "Listen, Inspector. I'm not a child. I don't need a tail or a bodyguard, and my legal duty is to protect my clients. I'm not required to tell you anything, unless you subpoena me. But I need information, and so do you. Betty was murdered. There's a girl missing. Maybe two girls—no one seems to know where Eddie's sister is. And an informant told me yesterday that Eddie owed somebody money."

She lifted her head, and tilted it back, looking toward the window, dragging on the cigarette until the ash devoured itself and dropped to the floor.

"Filipino Charlie is involved somehow. Betty worked for him, knew something about Eddie. I want to know why Italian hit men are fucking around with dime-store Chinatown hoodlums, why they'd kill Eddie, why they'd try to kill me. Why they raped and killed Betty."

Gonzales leaned forward, his chair squeaking.

"You can't be sure the two are connected, Miss Corbie. Your friend may have been killed by a—"

"—customer. Yeah. I know the line, Gonzales. Bullshit. Betty was a professional. And she was choosy. And if she was a nice white girl from the right side of town, you wouldn't have any trouble calling a rape a rape."

He stared at the floor for a moment, then looked up. Spoke quietly. "All right. I'll look at you as a partner, if that's what you want. Unofficially, of course. Officially you are a pariah."

"Nothing new. What can you tell me?"

"About Filipino Charlie? Not much. I can do some searching and call you later. He seems to be, as you say, a minor hoodlum."

"And the Winters case?"

Gonzales scraped his chair back across the wooden floor, opening a drawer. He searched for a few seconds, while Miranda took a last drag on the cigarette, watching it burn almost to her fingers.

"I admire your ambition. For most detectives, one murder case would be quite enough."

"Not if I can prevent more. What's the toxicology report?"

He opened a gray-green folder, removed a typewritten sheet, and handed it to Miranda.

"Take a look. Winters died from an overdose of cocaine, injected intravenously into his neck. We missed the hole on the first round."

"Forcibly?"

"Not that we can tell. We think he was already intoxicated."

She nodded, looking over the rest of the papers. "So a woman could have given him the shot."

"Yes."

Miranda pointed to the paper. "This isn't very specific—keys, laundry tag, three dollars and forty-five cents, matchbooks . . . any way I can see the contents myself?"

"Certainly. I'll take you when we're finished."

"Thanks." She took out her notebook, penciled in the list of items found with Winters and a brief note on the percentage of cocaine and the state of his body when found. She handed the files back to Gonzales.

"Helen Winters made a report about Phyllis yesterday?"

He nodded. "Not my case, though. Johnson is handling it. He's been squawking about bringing in the FBI, thinks it's a kidnapping."

"Doesn't give us much time before he fucks things up. Do you have a cigarette, Gonzales? I'm all out."

He reached into his drawer, pulled out a pack of French cigarettes, gold-tipped. Miranda took one, leaning toward him while he lit it for her. Then she leaned back, her leg in pain, savoring the sweet, strong tobacco. She stared at Gonzales, and he stared back, his dark brown eyes warm and appreciative.

"Can I ask you something, Inspector?"

"Certainly, Miss Corbie."

"Where the hell do you get your money?"

He threw his head back and laughed, drawing the eyes of the old man, who'd come back from the hunt with a chipped cup of black coffee. The brown skin of his throat was smooth.

"I admire your directness. My family owns property in San Diego, where I was born, and in Mexico. I spent most of my time there as a boy, on a ranch. Cattle and real estate, Miss Corbie. They paid for me to go to Stanford, and made it easier for San Francisco to hire someone with brown skin."

The French cigarette didn't burn as fast as a Chesterfield. She gulped it, holding the smoke, before blowing it toward the window.

"Why be a cop, then? Why not go back to your property and your cows?"

His smile was easy, the wall she hit much harder. "Some other time, Miss Corbie. If you don't mind, I need to get back to work. May I escort you downstairs?"

She stood up, her ankle wobbly but holding. "Sure. How silly of me. I thought this was work."

"I didn't mean—"

"Yeah, yeah. I know."

She allowed him to take her elbow, and he gently ushered her off the floor, through the wooden gate that separated the desks, and out the door into the hallway. Neither of them spoke for a few moments while they walked to the elevator, jostled by plainclothesmen and uniforms, drunks in wrinkled suits smelling of urine, and teenagers with round, terrified eyes.

They stepped into the elevator with a couple of chatty cops and a morgue attendant. They got off on the basement, the cops following the white-suited attendant to the right, Miranda and Gonzales heading to the left.

Miranda spoke first. "Can you get me a copy of the report on Betty?"

He threw a glance at her, his fingers tightening slightly on her elbow. "I can try."

"Thanks."

They arrived at the evidence locker, a bored uniform about forty-five guarding the repository and reading a pulp magazine.

"Good morning, Peterson."

"Morning, Inspector." The uniform stared at Miranda. "You want to check something?"

"Effects of Lester Winters. Here's the case number."

Peterson looked over the paper Gonzales had brought, shoving a clip-board toward him while he read. "Sign in."

Gonzales scrawled his name, said: "Bring it over to the table, Peterson. That way you can watch me in the open."

Peterson opened his mouth to protest, and Gonzales brushed him away. "That's your job. And Miss Corbie is a civilian, a private detective. We'll wait over here."

He took her by the elbow, and directed her toward a wooden table to the left and behind Peterson's desk. Then he found a chair in the corner, sat her down. The French cigarette was done. She reluctantly dropped the butt in a rusty metal ashtray on the table.

They could hear Peterson, searching for the right box. He finally emerged, out of breath, and set it on the table.

"Here you go, Inspector. Take your time."

The gray carton was large, about two feet by three feet. Inside was a nearly empty quart of Four Roses, another empty pint of vodka.

Miranda took a handkerchief out of her jacket pocket, looked at Gonzales. "May I?"

He nodded, and she carefully lifted the bottles, searching for the price tag. "I assume these have been dusted."

"No prints."

"I didn't think so."

The name of the store had been scraped off the tag on the Four Roses, but the price was still legible: $1.75. There was no tag on the vodka.

"Winters didn't come in with the whiskey, the killers did. He wasn't a lush—the vodka, maybe, but not a quart of bourbon, even if he was expecting company. And that's last year's price on the Four Roses. Which means discount, which in this city means Martell's Cut-Rate Liquors. Three locations. The one on Powell would be closest to the Pickwick."

Gonzales raised an eyebrow. "Thank you."

Miranda said nothing, replaced the bottles carefully, and drew out a smaller gray box.

"This holds the pockets?"

"Yes."

She lifted the lid, poked a finger at the change, noticing the way the three dollars were folded, crisp and clean. She looked at Winters's wallet, noting the same care and precision in how he had his driver's license and NYK shipping identification displayed. A picture of a younger Mrs. Winters stared up at her, standing uncomfortably near a plumper Phyllis, still an awkward teenager in saddle shoes. Then she put it aside, and examined a torn cleaners' receipt.

The faded stamp read HERBERT-ROBERT CLEANERS. The address was 775 Jackson Street, in between Stockton and Grant. Chinatown. Miranda took out her notebook and a pencil, and jotted the information down while Gonzales looked on.

"We've already checked on that, Miss Corbie. It was found in his left trouser pocket. No one there knew Lester Winters or his wife, and we haven't found their mark on any of his clothes."

"Then why the hell did it wind up with him when he died?"

Gonzales shrugged. "Probably an accident. An old piece of scrap paper he picked up to write a number on, but didn't. Coincidence."

"I don't believe in coincidence."

There were three matchbooks, face down, in the bottom of the small box. Miranda picked up the first one. It was from Forbidden City. About half of the matches were used. The next one was from a club in Alameda. Nearly empty. The third booklet looked new. She turned it over.

It was from the Olympic Hotel. Where Joe Gillio owned a club.

She jotted down information about all three matchbooks, keeping her face even. Then she smiled and thanked him, sitting down again while Peterson got up from his magazine and waddled back to the storeroom with the large box. And she let Gonzales help her up, and walk her back to the elevator, up to the entrance, down the long, marble hall, and down the steps to the street.

Thick fog made the horizon line blend into the sky. A fishbowl of white. Normally fog invigorated Miranda, but now she felt trapped, standing in place. Lights in her eyes.

"So you'll work on Filipino Charlie? And see about the report on Betty?" She was shielding her eyes with her hand, fog-blind from the glare.

Gonzales nodded. "I'll do my best. And you'll let me know if you discover anything about the money Eddie owed, or information on his sister. And if you uncover any leads on the Winters case. I'll pass along any information about Phyllis to Johnson. I'll also run through those numbers on the green sedan, see what we come up with. Call your office later."

"Thanks, Inspector."

"Call me Mark."

"All right. Call me Miranda."

They were shaking hands when a rasping voice, followed by a hawking cough and a guttural spitting noise, assaulted them.

"Well, if it ain't the Mex and his girl."

Miranda turned to face him, and Duggan squinted up at her, staring.

"You finally backhand her, Gonzales? Got tired of sharing?"

Duggan was mounting the steps. Miranda clenched her fists, the pain in her ankle and legs forgotten.

"Why aren't you with the sideshow, Duggan? No more room for shrunken heads and dickless wonders?"

His heavy features compressed, jutting forward in a projection of rage. He took a step closer to Miranda, and Gonzales moved to block him him.

"We've been through this before, Gerry. Don't embarrass yourself further."

Duggan stood in front of him, half a foot shorter, stocky, thick in the middle, scars on his face, his head, and his hands. Breathing hard. Frozen.

Miranda waited and watched. He only had eyes for Gonzales. He finally looked away, hawked up a wad of yellow-gray phlegm, spitting it out so that some of it landed on Gonzales's shoe.

He took a step up and to the side, and muttered under his breath. "Watch yourself, you greasy bastard. I ain't the only one who thinks you oughta be shipped back home the hard way."

Duggan turned at the sound of the click.

"What the fuck—"

"Pick it up, you son of a bitch. Wipe up his shoes. Or so help me God, I'll blow your motherfucking head off."

She was holding the .22 against her body, aiming it at Duggan, her hands shaking. Gonzales reached over, his long fingers gently taking the gun from her.

"It's OK, Miranda."

Duggan looked from one to the other—Miranda trembling, white, Gonzales holding the gun, his hand on her arm.

He said softly: "That's one crazy fucking whore, Mex. Watch your back."

They both watched as he climbed the stairs and sauntered into the Hall of Justice.

Fifteen

M iranda stood and shook, not yet realizing her hand wasn't holding a gun. Gonzales took out his display handkerchief, wiped his shoe off, left the handkerchief behind, and took her by the arm and down the steps.

He tried to lead her to the Last Chance Saloon, the century-old watering hole for Hall of Justice habitués: cops and the accused, guards and judges, drunks who managed to stay sober long enough to walk half a block down and through the old wooden swinging doors, and found themselves back in jail by evening. Decrepit, dark with age, they squeaked and whispered about a San Francisco long gone, a gold rush Tombstone, where the only difference between the lawless and the lawful was the size of the revolver.

She shook her head, angry at him, angry at herself. It did no good to be angry at Duggan, angry at all the Duggans she'd fought over the years. Anger was their domain, their ammunition. Anger and hate.

"I'm all right. Not my usual behavior, I admit."

He still held her by the arm, looked at her with brown eyes full of worry. She avoided them, pulled away.

"I know I'm in shock. Best thing for me is a hot meal and a shot of bourbon, and some time in the office."

He handed her the .22. "If you're sure."

She appreciated the fact that he didn't second-guess her, didn't treat her like a cracked Dresden shepherdess.

He added, hesitation in his voice: "Miss Corbie—Miranda—I think you should know that Duggan had a . . . well, a heroic war record. He comes from a poor family—never had a chance at much education. He was a pretty good cop, once. He lost his brother to syphilis a few years ago, and—I—I'm not telling you this because it excuses anything—"

"Doesn't make a goddamn difference if you are. There's a lot of hurt to go around, Inspector. Try the Dust Bowl on for size. There's a hell of a lot of people with reason to be mad at the world, to give up, to give in. Most try to be more than a bully in a uniform, a home-grown fascist. Duggan doesn't. End of story."

They stared at one another for a moment, Gonzales surprised by her anger, looking sideways at her gun as if she might turn it back on him.

She said abruptly: "I'm going to eat in Chinatown and get on with my day. Thanks for working with me."

He nodded and smiled, his teeth gleaming beneath his thin mustache. "I'll call you later."

They shook hands again, this time with no interruption. Miranda turned her back and crossed the street toward Portsmouth Square, trying not to limp. Gonzales stood for a long time, smoking a gold-tipped cigarette, watching her blend into the crowds on Clay Street.

The sun was starting to crack open the fog bank over Chinatown.

Miranda sat with a plate of scrambled eggs, French toast, hash browns and sausage at the Universal Café on Washington. The late-breakfast crowd packed in around her at the counter, reaching for Tabasco sauce to enliven the eggs and sugar for the bitter coffee.

The Universal was cheap and cheery, and never closed. The kind of hospitality that was worth overcooked hash browns.

She sipped the coffee, feeling it course through her, giving her strength. No one here had looked at her swollen face twice. Another dame with a bad-tempered boyfriend or husband, drunk over the weekend, tired of hearing her complain. Will that be one lump or two?

The French toast resisted her attempt with the fork, so she brought in the knife. Reached for the syrup, and brushed the sleeve of a man in a dirty gray suit with worn shoes, who looked like he sold things no one ever needed. He didn't notice, didn't speak. Suited Miranda.

There was the French toast and the powdered sugar. The black coffee so black that cream couldn't cut the darkness. The pack of Raleighs she bought at a corner shop, to last her until she could find more Chesterfields.

Philosophy didn't matter a flying fuck to anybody. Except the walking dead, like her father, thinking life was leather-bound in a language as dead as he was. Or in a gin bottle. All kinds of philosophy there. She took a puff of the Raleigh, wrinkling her nose. Miranda had no use for philosophers. She'd never met one who could explain what she'd seen in the fields of California or the churches of Spain.

What mattered was the fact that the Winters case and the Takahashi case connected. Gonzales wouldn't believe her, wouldn't accept a matchbook as evidence of anything other than delusion. But—as she'd told him—she didn't believe in coincidence.

Italians didn't give a damn about small-time operators in Chinatown or South San Francisco. Eddie owed somebody money, and Italians tried to collect out of Miranda's legs. Cheval thought the man he took upstairs in the elevator was Italian; the woman who visited Winters was Chinese. East was east and West was west, said Rudy Kipling, and he was still right: outside of the city-sanctioned carnival called a Rice Bowl Party, they were separate worlds.

Throw in a Sicilian who squired the Winters girl around gambling joints, getting her high on coke—the same stuff that killed her father. And a card from Gillio's on her credenza and a fresh matchbook from the Olympia in a dead man's room.

Too many Italians, and too many fucking coincidences.

It meant more than one group of killers, too. The hit-runners with the sedan. The gunner who shot Eddie Takahashi. The precise plunge of the needle into Lester Winters's neck, pumping his body full of cocaine until his heart couldn't handle it. Sounded like a doctor in somebody's house, and not the Ming Chen type.

Maybe the herbalist knew something, but he was running scared and angry, trying to stalemate her . . . precisely as Gonzales suggested. The actions of a frightened bully, not a professional killer.

And there was what happened to Betty.

Miranda gulped her coffee, wishing she had some bourbon with her. She'd overreacted to Duggan. Gonzales was a cop, a rich boy from Mexico. He could handle himself. Too wealthy and isolated to understand. Making excuses.

She rubbed the Raleigh out in disgust in the ashtray. The bored man at the counter yelled something to the Chinese short-order cook in the back. The smell of burning bacon answered him. Miranda got up, careful of her legs, and headed out of Chinatown.

She took a cable car down to Powell and Market, walked down to 137 Powell and into Martell's. She found a quart of Four Roses, checked the price. Same tag, same price as the one in Lester's room.

Miranda knew better than to ask the clerk for information. A gruff, middle-aged man with a weak left eye, he yawned and waved his hands. Didn't remember anybody buying Four Roses and vodka, fancy suits walk in here all the time, it's a liquor store, lady, best prices in town, you expect me to remember who wanted a shot five days ago? You want that Old Taylor Kentucky Straight Bourbon wrapped and sent, or you gonna walk out with it? A buck ninety-five, lady, best prices in town.

She left with the Old Taylor, walked down to Market, and disappeared into the Owl for ice, an ice pack, aspirin, and two cartons of Chesterfields.

A dusty quart of Four Roses was twenty cents more than Martell's price. So they'd gone to Martell's, bought the whiskey. The vodka probably came with Winters. He and Helen were the vodka types, preferably in delicate martini glasses. Spiced with an olive, never an onion. The country-club way.

She caught one of the cars heading to the Ferry Building, saving her left leg a few blocks of pain. From the ankle up, it hurt like hell, and Miranda hated to limp.

She waved at Gladys from the elevator bank, not responding to the girl's eager look. When Miranda reached the fourth floor, squeezing out of the elevator between a portly man with a pocket watch and a woman with a baby, the noon bells of the downtown churches started to chime for lunch.

She hurried to her office, not stopping to greet the Pinkertons, hustling by the railroad offices.

Clang.

Business was slowing down, the papers said. War worries.

Clap.

Gas prices. And by the way, America, you're still in a Depression.

Bong.

It's a long climb back up the hill.

Ding.

She rested against the wall beside her door, letting the rest of the peals and claps and tolls roll over her, while the Catholics and the Protestants fought the Reformation all over again. She used the time wisely, remembering God helps her that helps herself, and took out her .22.

Just in case.

Miranda opened the door and walked in, the gun cocked in her right hand, the quart of Old Taylor awkwardly secure under her left arm, which also held her Owl bag and her purse.

The office was just as she'd left it, except for a package sitting in one of the chairs and the phone ringing. She hadn't heard it outside, thanks to the church racket, released the hammer on the .22, and limped to the desk as fast as she could.

Her hand was reaching for the receiver when it stopped ringing.

Miranda cursed, and set the gun, the whiskey, and the bag with the ice pack and partially melted ice and aspirin on her desk. She eased herself back around to the chair, sighed a little when she sat down. Put the .22 back in her handbag, unlocked her desk drawer, took out the black pistol, left the drawer open.

Stood up with difficulty, walked to the safe, and removed the newspapers from Winters's room. Walked back to the chair, picked up the package, sat down, opened the quart of bourbon, and swallowed four aspirin. Then she turned to look at the thin parcel. A note scrawled in pencil on the brown wrapping said: "This was waiting for you downstairs. Thought I'd save you a trip. Allen." There was no return address.

Miranda tore it open. A new Chief tablet. She lifted the cover, saw it was a note from Helen Winters with information, and a dark green envelope, probably with some photos.

Then she filled the ice pack up with the ice, got up again, walked to the window, opened it, and left the rest of the ice on the sill. She stood for a minute, looking out at Market Street, the ice bag cold against her face.

"So it was definitely human, and type A . . . and within the time frame, but can't tell exactly. No, I understand. Yes. Uh-huh, thanks, Edith. No, that's really helpful. What? Oh, just drop it at my apartment, will you? You're right around the corner . . . yeah, I'll be working late tonight again. Uh-huh. Yeah. Oh, I won't. Two all-day passes, Elephant Train tickets, the works. Yeah. Thanks, Edith."

Miranda dropped the receiver into the cradle, looking at the list from yesterday. So the blood was human, it was type A, and it could've been from a few days before or older. If Eddie's was also type A, just one more coincidence.

She rested the ice bag on her cheek again, setting it back on her desk and away from the list and the newspapers before she picked up the phone. She dialed the number directly, waited for the connection, the ring, and finally a response.

"Roy? Miranda Corbie. Listen, there's a woman coming over later today with a package for me. Take it upstairs, and leave it on my credenza, all right? Just make sure you lock it up again . . . uh-huh, yeah, I'm all right. No, word gets around."

She suddenly sat straight upright, leaning forward from the comfortable leather against her back.

"What? Who were they? Did they leave a name? What did they look like?"

She reached for a pencil, started scribbling below the list. "An Oriental . . . uh-huh, how was he dressed? OK. Yeah, I know. What about the—he was white? Spanish or Italian? What'd he look like, his clothes, shoes . . . yeah, Roy, but try, OK? All right. Take it easy, no one is going to be looking for you. Just tell me what you remember. Uh-huh. Good. Uh-huh. Uh-huh. Did they say they'd be back? OK. No number, no name? Uh-huh. Right."

Miranda reached for a cigarette, stretching to the right corner of her desk, cradling the phone receiver with her shoulder, which hurt like hell. "Just a second."

She set the phone down, lit the cigarette, inhaled gratefully, and picked it back up.

"OK, now listen to me. Except for the blond lady named Edith—the one with the package—don't let anyone up there, and don't take anything else to my apartment. I don't care if they say they're with the city or the City of Paris. Unless they're cops with a search warrant, you don't take anyone else up there, or deliver anything, either, and you make anyone who asks show you identification. No, you don't have to worry. You get scared, just call the cops. Yeah. No, I mean it. Yeah. Thanks . . . you've been a big help. You get anybody else asking, call me, OK? Take the package up from Edith. Yeah. All right, Roy, thanks."

Miranda inhaled the Chesterfield until she shivered, and chased the smoke with a swallow of Old Taylor. Two men were looking for her, one white, one a Chinese or Filipino from Roy's description. Couldn't be the green car boys . . . they wouldn't come out in the open.

She took another drag and swallowed one more shot of the bourbon. Laid the nine millimeter Spanish pistol on top of the desk, first double-checking the magazine to make sure it was loaded and the spring was working. Then she pulled the Kardex toward her, rifling through it until she found Bente's work number. The ice pack soothed her cheek while she waited for the ringing to stop.

"Bente? Miranda. Yeah. You got anything yet? Uh-huh. All right. Think you can by tonight? It's urgent . . . well, Betty. Betty Chow. Yeah. She was murdered. Yeah. Yeah, I know. Goddamn right, it's tied in. No, the whole fucking show. Yeah, Winters and Takahashi, the whole fucking thing. You kidding me? I was lucky to find the one I'm working with . . . no, Phil's out of the picture for good. I'm going to have to wrap it up with string and slap a bow on it. Uh-huh. Air-tight . . . yeah. Yeah, rape too, though the chicken-shit bastards won't—yeah. You too, honey. I know. Yeah, thanks, Bente. No, better make it late tonight, maybe nine or ten. Be better for you, anyway. Someplace safe . . . let's try the Moderne at nine. If I'm late, wait for me—if I can't make it, I'll phone. What? Yeah, you too."

Miranda hung up the phone, then sat back and stared at it. From her desk drawer, she took out a silver powder compact with a swan on it, opened it, and studied her face. Swelling down, bruises still visible. The phone rang, and she flung the compact back in the drawer, grabbing at the heavy receiver.

"Miranda Corb—yes, Mrs. Winters. As a matter of fact, I haven't had a chance to—What? Why? Well, technically you can, but you lose the retain—Uh-huh. Uh huh. I see. So who are they? The ones who put you up to it. Sure you do—the men threatening you to back off or else. Don't get excited . . . If you really want to find your daughter and your husband's murderer . . . Mrs. Winters? Mrs. Winters?"

She clicked the receiver a few times, waited, her toe tapping. "Operator? Yeah, the call that just came in—was it terminated on the other end? Sure, I'll wait." Miranda reached for a cigarette.

"Yeah? That's what I thought. Yeah, thanks."

She leaned back, staring at the Chief tablet still on her desk, the expression on her face making her bruises hurt. So Helen Winters changed her mind. Or had it changed for her. Miranda inhaled, absentmindedly flicked some ash on the floor. She wasn't worried about Helen. Helen could take care of herself. But somebody had found out about the hire already, somebody who didn't want Phyllis found. And without a contract, Miranda didn't have much protection.

She set the cigarette down on the Tower of the Sun ashtray, opened the Old Taylor, and waited for the shock of warmth to reach her.

Miranda shoved the pastrami sandwich aside, staring, again, at the newspapers she'd found in Winters's room. Pages of Deaths–Births–Vital Statistics. She'd been over all of them, studied the advertisements. Nothing. Then the "In and Out of This Port" column. She jotted a note about the ship movements from the Thursday paper, and found herself focusing on the *Kamakura Maru*, from the NYK line . . . Winters's company.

The report said it arrived Tuesday night, docked Wednesday, and departed Thursday. And Thursday was the day Lester was killed.

Miranda took a short inhale on the Chesterfield burning in the Tower of the Sun, then set it back down, hurriedly combing back to the small print section in Tuesday. Yes. There it was . . . TO ARRIVE. The *Kamakura Maru*, disembarked at the Ferry Building, Yokohama via Los Angeles. Large passenger carrier, 225 passengers. Docked at Pier 25.

She sat back, cigarette in her mouth, puffing furiously. Japanese ship. Eddie Takahashi dead. Winters worked for NYK, a Japanese shipping company.

She wrote "Kamakura Maru" on Winters's list, hurriedly folding the newspapers, and walked to the safe to store them, not feeling the pain in her legs. Came back to the desk, tried to take a bite of pastrami, forgetting the cigarette in her mouth, set the cigarette down again, chewed a bite of the sandwich with pickle in it, and picked up the phone, too much in a hurry to look for the number.

"Operator? I need the Takahashi residence on Wilmot Street." She pulled the Chief tablet toward her while she waited, flipping up the thin cardboard to look at Helen Winters's neat, precise penmanship. Only a few blots around the name of her lover—a lawyer with a name Miranda recognized—leaked the shrillness of the woman. Of course, Helen didn't confess . . . not in writing. She referred to him as "her adviser in this time of grief."

"What? No phone, huh? No, that's all right. Thanks."

Her wristwatch read one. She must've missed the bell.

Holding the receiver in her left hand, she searched the Kardex again with her right, almost smelling the calling card before she found it. Better call to make an appointment. Her stomach clenched as tightly as when she walked into the morgue.

She stared at the card for a few minutes, breathing hard, her tongue unconsciously running over her teeth to make sure she didn't leave any pastrami caught in between. She sat straighter, her right hand fingering the Spanish pistol next to the phone, the telephone cord pulled out to give it some slack.

She attacked the dial like a high dive into icy water, her finger plunging into the ring holes six times, the phone whining at the speed she was pushing it. She finished, hugging herself with her right arm. And waited.

The fifth ring answered.

"Dianne? Miranda Corbie. I need to see you. No. It can't wait. Betty was murdered last night. Yes. No, rape and murder. Yes. Not yet."

Miranda picked up the long, sleek black pistol, holding it in her right hand, while her voice dropped, cutting and cold.

"I wouldn't expect you to, Dianne. But you see, I'm working with the cops. So you can either see me or see them, and I think you'll prefer to see me. What? Simple. I want to know why and when Betty left. Details. Any clients to be wary of. And please don't bother to profess your ignorance of how and when and where she came across those clients and what she did with them. You're old enough to know better."

She smiled at the silence at on the other end of the phone. "Shall we say teatime? Four-thirty." Miranda leaned forward, still holding the gun. "And I don't want to see them, you understand me? Send them to another room. No, a little thing called citizen's arrest. As a matter of fact, I would, Dianne. On the contrary . . . you taught me very well. *Au revoir.*"

Miranda was still smiling, and still holding the Spanish handgun, when the door to her office swung open noiselessly.

In front of her stood a short Chinese man in his early sixties, dressed in a sharp business suit, hatless. And an Italian wearing a brown leather jacket, a fedora, and a placid expression.

There was a Smith and Wesson .38 in his left hand.

Sixteen

No one said anything. Miranda held the black pistol flat against the desk, in line with the abdomen of the older man. He wasn't smiling, but his eyes weren't the flat, animal eyes of a killer.

The Italian was a different story. He'd been trained to hold the gun and fire it, and he did it well. But that was the limit and the range of his intelligence, beyond the necessities of eating, sleeping, fornicating. He didn't have enough cunning to be or do anything else.

The older man put his hand out flat over the Italian's .38, shoving it gently downward.

"Don't need it, Bennie." His voice, as reedy as the instruments the old men played on the corner of Washington and Grant, was not unkind.

Bennie shrugged, looked at the Chinese man, looked at Miranda, then walked over and sat down in a chair, his gun on his knee. The old man, his hair short and flat with streaks of grey, said: "You mind if we sit, Miss Corbie?"

Miranda's eyes darted back to Bennie, who was staring out the window. She brought the pistol up, aimed it at the old man. "Tell him to put it away."

The older one bowed his head, quickly walked to Bennie, Miranda's pistol tracking him. He spoke clearly.

"Bennie. Put the gun in your holster, please." The Italian looked up at him as if startled from a reverie.

"Sure, Mr. Wong." He opened his jacket, already unbuttoned, and tucked the gun into a holster under his right shoulder. Looked up at his boss and whined: "Got a cigarette?"

Mr. Wong reached into his pocket, held a pack of Lucky Strikes out for Bennie.

"Only two. Tobacco isn't healthy."

Bennie shrugged, as if he'd heard it before, took two, put one in his mouth, thought for a minute on where to put the other one, finally deciding on his coat pocket, found matches in the same pocket, and lit the cigarette with a flame struck on his shoe. Then he folded his hands and looked out the window again. Mr. Wong turned to Miranda, smiled for the first time.

"You see? I am sorry about the gun. Bennie wasn't sure what we would find. I understand you had an—accident last night."

He was still standing. Miranda gestured with the pistol for him to take the other chair, and while he did, she lowered the gun to the desk, still keeping her hand on it.

She said slowly: "How exactly do you come by your information, Mr. Wong? First-hand experience?"

He shook his head. "No, Miss Corbie. I am here on an errand of my own. An errand of mercy."

Miranda felt her face muscles pull tight, her throat constrict. She tried to calm herself inside. No weakness. Weakness could kill her.

She leaned forward, eyes digging into the Chinese man's. "The kind you gave to Betty Chow?"

It was a wild swing, but she hit the Italian. His cheek twitched, his face flushed, his mouth opened. The older man sat limply, shoulders sagging. Defeat framed his features, surprising Miranda.

"It is precisely because of Betty Chow I am here, Miss Corbie. I want you to find Emily Takahashi before—before it is too late."

She stared at him. Bennie was twitchy now, agitated by the mention of Betty's name. The window no longer held interest. He finished the cigarette, dropping the butt on the floor, and lit another.

"Just who the hell are you, Mr. Wong?"

The older man looked at the gun on her desk. "I am a businessman, Miss

Corbie. Businesses, as you know, often . . . merge. Acquire others. You can incorporate, form limited partnerships. If your stock is public, you may sell investments in your business, even suffer an . . . overthrow. It is the nature of business."

Miranda reached across to the pack of Chesterfields, and removed one, keeping her hand near the pistol. She sparked the lighter with a flick of her left hand.

"You don't mind if I smoke, do you?"

The old man shook his head. "It is your office. But you should limit your smoking. It is not good for the lungs."

She inhaled deeply, then blew a stream of smoke toward Bennie, who watched, fascinated.

"I'll keep it in mind. So you want to do business. You want me to find Emi Takahashi, and you are afraid for her life. Is that the only reason you want me to find her?"

Mr. Wong raised his eyebrows. "That is the reason I want you to find her, yes. But another reason is that she owes someone money. Or, more correctly, her brother owed someone money. And they want to collect."

"What makes you think she has it?"

"The money is gone, she is gone. If—someone else—had the money, it would have been found by now."

Miranda nodded, keeping an eye on Bennie. "And you think if I don't find her first, she'll be killed. That right?"

"That is my conclusion, Miss Corbie."

"And how exactly do I know that you're not the one who wants to kill her? That you didn't just walk in here with a song and dance guaranteed to get my help, and that if I find Emily Takahashi, we won't both be murdered?"

He looked at her steadily. "That is a fair and reasoned argument. I would remind you, however, that you are the only one with a pistol showing. Perhaps it will convince you further if I tell you that Bennie and I are taking considerable risk in coming to see you at all. And not from your gun, Miss Corbie."

She took a last drag on the Chesterfield, then rubbed it viciously into the ashtray. "That's another thing. How do I know you're not using me to get rid of unwanted competition? Say two groups want this money, they're competing for it, and you want to cut the other one out. I produce Emily, produce your money, and we're both at the—mercy—of your rivals. No, Mr. Wong,

I'll need something from you, something to convince me that you're sincere. I can't risk Emily . . . or myself."

The old man leaned forward slightly. "So you have found her? You know where she is?"

Miranda kept her voice noncommittal. "Maybe. But like I said . . . first I need to understand the situation. Be convinced. For example, tell me why a Chinese 'businessman' with an Italian gun is so anxious about a Japanese girl . . . other than money."

Sweat was starting to break out on the old man's upper lip. He wiped his forehead with a yellow display handkerchief, and Miranda noticed his hands were shaking.

"Miss Corbie, I have probably told you too much already. Suffice it to say that I am not a prejudiced man. Neither is Bennie—his wife is a Filipina. Eddie Takahashi was a business associate of a . . . partner. And that must be enough for you. I've been here too long as it is."

He stood up. So did Bennie, watching him like a dog about to be taken for a walk.

"Find Emily, Miss Corbie. When you do, leave a message here." He flicked a card on her desk.

Miranda stood, too, her right hand still hovering above the black pistol.

"Who killed Betty, Mr. Wong?"

Again, Bennie's face convulsed, and Wong shook his head.

"I can say no more."

He turned to leave, snapping his fingers for Bennie to follow.

Miranda blurted, "Wait—tell me—tell me where to find Phyllis Winters. As a sign of faith. And I'll get Emily for you."

It was dangerous to mislead a dangerous man, and Miranda knew it. And it was another shot in the dark, a blind craps throw wagered on a matchbook. Wong turned back around slowly. Said, without facing him, "Bennie—go in the hallway and wait for me there."

Bennie looked from Miranda to Wong, then backed out of the room, his hand under his jacket, clutching at the gun in the holster.

Wong walked toward her, put his hands flat on her desk.

"Very well, Miss Corbie. Do not disappoint me. I do not like to be disappointed in my business associates."

She leaned forward, matching his gesture, eyes on his. "And I don't like to be used, Mr. Wong. Especially with dead friends."

They stayed in position like chess pieces, Wong searching her face. Finally, he grunted.

"Try Guerrero Street."

He turned, drawing his jacket together and buttoning it, as if he were cold, and walked out the door, letting it shut softly and automatically behind him.

Guerrero Street sang a tune, over and over again, cascading down the scale in Miranda's head. Something about Guerrero Street . . .

She gave herself a few minutes to play catch up, to realize what happened. The Chesterfield shook in her hand, and it took four strikes to light it and the Old Taylor tasted like ginger ale when it slid down her throat.

Eddie Takahashi owed money to a gangster or a syndicate of gangsters—most likely Filipino Charlie, or whoever was behind him—some of whom had—in Wong's words—moved in for an "overthrow." The same group killed Betty, maybe because they figured she knew something about the money . . . that, at least, was the implication. And somehow, Winters and his daughter were involved.

Miranda swallowed another shot, eyes falling on the card Wong had flicked on the table. It was a simple black-and-white business card: HERBERT-ROBERT CLEANERS, 775 JACKSON STREET. She sank into the chair and stared at it.

The same cleaner's receipt in Lester Winters's left trouser pocket. So much for fucking coincidence. And now it was one-thirty. Move, Miranda.

She grabbed at Helen Winters's notebook, flipped it open, hurriedly dialed a number, her foot tapping impatiently. When the butler answered, she brightened her vocal pitch, making her voice sound younger. "Good afternoon . . . may I speak to Ruth, please? Oh, just a friend of Phyllis Winters . . . yes, I'll hold."

A bored young voice sulked over the wire. "Who is it, please?"

"Ruth Landis?"

"Yes . . . who is this?" The voice held curiosity and a faint hope that something was about to dispel her ennui.

"My name is Miranda Corbie. I'm a private investigator, working for Phyllis Winters's mother."

The squeal of air breathed through teeth made Miranda hold the phone receiver away from her ear. "I know who you are! You're the lady detective that solved that baby case at the Fair last year, and your boss's murder, and—"

"Ruth, I need your help. I think Phyllis does, too. Can you meet me this afternoon?"

"Can I? You bet I will! Is Phyllis in trouble? I haven't seen her in months . . . We had a fight over Bobby Henders—"

"I'll want to hear all about it this afternoon. What you tell me is very important, Ruth, and if you have any photographs of Phyllis with friends and boyfriends, please bring them. And don't phone her mother . . . she's too upset to talk right now."

The girl giggled in delight. "Oh, sure. I'll bring photos. Where do you want to meet?"

Miranda glanced at the Chief tablet. "Let's see . . . you're at 1523 Park Street in Alameda, right?"

Awe filled Ruth's voice. "You know everything, Miss Corbie."

Miranda rolled her eyes. Getting her to talk wouldn't be a problem. "Listen, I've got an appointment downtown at four-thirty . . . how about meeting me at the Pig n' Whistle on Market and Powell, say an hour before?"

"Sure, Miss Corbie. I'll take the ferry. And thanks!"

Miranda smiled in spite of herself. "Thank you, Ruth. See you then."

The pain in her legs was gone and the ice pack forgotten on the windowsill. She stood up and opened the safe, shoving in the newspapers from the Pickwick, and crossed to the wardrobe, removing a bulky-looking coat that was lighter than it looked.

The notes on the case she locked up in her desk drawer, along with the .22. Her finger traced the length of the Spanish pistol. Then she picked it up and snapped it into the holster, and strapped the long gun under her left arm. She'd look a little stiff and unnatural on that side, but she needed the extra firepower.

At least that's what she told herself.

A gray rush of traffic fled by her on Market Street. She crossed over to Lotta's Fountain, holding her hat with one hand, pushing her legs to go faster, forgetting they'd already saved her once.

Miranda didn't own a hat with a veil. She preferred the bite of wind on her face, not hidden, not cloistered.

Hers was the generation of Gertrude Ederle, who'd swum the English Channel faster than any man. And Miranda missed those heady days, when her skirts were as short as her hair, when anything went and the world went with it, around and around and around to the sound of a jazz calliope, until it Black Bottomed-out in October '29. Then the New Morality crept in, as it always does, fingers to its lips to hush the young, herd the women back where they belonged. Skirts longer, booze banned, the Depression to end all Depressions, sequel to the War to End all Wars. The fault of women's suffrage and decadent Europe. Stay out of European Wars, the New Morality intoned. God Bless America.

Miranda leaned against the burnished gold of the fountain, comforted by its permanence, its exuberant generosity of function and form. She lit a Chesterfield, peering down Market to the Ferry Building, and spotted a Yellow Cab. She waved her gloved hand, and it responded quickly, passing a blue Pontiac sedan and a White Front street car to pull up in front of her.

The cab driver, a newsboy cap on his head and a three-day beard on his chin, looked at her quizzically, his eyes lingering on her cheek.

"Where to, lady?" His voice was softer than she expected.

"Sutter Street, between Webster and Buchanan. Matsumara Shoe Repair."

The cab driver wasn't the talkative type, and Miranda gratefully tipped him, pocketing fifty cents out of her dollar. With her face out of commission, what she had would have to last her.

The tang of eucalyptus leaves greeted her when she stepped on the curb, followed by charbroiled chicken and soy sauce. A couple of pigeons were stalking a brown and white female along the sidewalk, trying to outpuff one another for her affections. The female flew across the street to the YWCA.

Matsumara's bell tinkled at Miranda when she walked in, and the shoemaker emerged from his workroom, wearing his customary smile. It changed to surprise mixed with a little anxiety, when he noticed Miranda's face.

"Well, good afternoon, young lady! I didn't expect to see you so soon . . . your shoes won't be ready for a few more days."

She smiled, touched her cheek with her fingertips. "Just a nasty fall yesterday. I know they're not ready yet, but . . . I was hoping to talk to you, Mr. Matsumara."

He arched his eyebrows, his wide mouth turned upside down in a comical grimace. "Me? I promised you a Prince Charming, not a frog, as I remember. Why on earth do you want to talk to me?"

Miranda leaned on the counter, lowering her voice. "I'll be frank. I'm a private investigator."

"Ah." Matsumara's smile disappeared, replaced by a grave expression. He moved out from behind the counter through the little wooden gate on Miranda's right, and walked toward her, taking her by the elbow, leading her to the other end of the shop.

"Just in case my apprentice comes in through the back," he whispered. "Are you investigating the Takahashis?"

She nodded. "Eddie's murder. It's not official, you understand—I know you don't want any more trouble for your neighbor."

The little shoemaker sighed, a long, drawn-out breath. He looked older than Miranda remembered, a tired, aging man with a small business, the humor a facade and a way to fight back. He stared at the floor.

"They've already suffered more trouble than most, Miss. Maybe the truth will give them some peace. Fear is worse than anything else."

"Do you think they know where Eddie got his money?"

Matsumara shrugged. "Hiro doesn't know anything, these days. He's lost, even to himself. His wife, maybe."

Miranda reached out and put her hand on the shoemaker's arm. "Mr. Matsumara—I need to find Emily. She's in trouble with the wrong people, something about money Eddie owed someone. I think the Takahashis are hiding her."

He stared at her, his hand rubbing his chin. "I haven't seen Emily since a couple of days before Eddie was killed. And you heard what Rose—the girl who was here when you were—said. Those two are great friends—always together. Emi would find a way to talk to Rose . . . if she could."

Miranda opened her purse and found a business card, pressing it into Matsumara's hands.

"Listen—I don't have much time. There are people who want Emily found, and they may be the same people who just—who just murdered another young woman. If Rose comes in here, can you ask her to call me? Tell her what you think it's safe for her to know, enough so that she'll understand how important it is to be discreet."

He looked at her card, holding it with two hands, then met her eyes. "I'll help you, Miss Corbie, though what you think a broken-down shoemaker can do, I'm not sure."

She smiled. "You can tell me what Emily is like. The places she liked to visit, the things she liked to do. That might help."

"Rose will know more, of course . . . I'm an old man, she didn't talk to me the same way. But I know she loved fish . . . and not just to eat, you understand. They'd wander in here, picking up shoes for their mothers, dreaming of boys and houses and castles in the air. And Emi always said she wanted a place with a big garden, to grow lots of flowers, with streams and ponds for goldfish, so she could watch them swim. She was born here, of course, but I think she has a romantic notion of Old Japan in her young head . . . you know, samurai in shining armor."

His grin was a sad one. "I hope she isn't in need of one now."

Miranda squeezed his arm. "Thank you. That's a start. And Mr. Matsumara—the tailor shop next door. Is there a back entrance?"

He leaned forward, closer to her ear. "Are you planning to—what's the term—break into the joint?"

Miranda whispered back: "Yes."

He turned back toward the counter as the door bell rang, and a stout woman in blue walked in with a small boy. He waved at Miranda to follow, murmuring "Follow me," then hailed the matron with his familiar cheer, saying "Be right with you, Mrs. Ibaraki."

Miranda followed him behind the counter while he held the gate open for her. Then they both disappeared behind the curtain into the workroom, after the shoemaker gave a big smile to Mrs. Ibaraki, who was staring at them both in haughty disapproval.

He led her to the far end of the shop, where a few boxes were stored. Matsumara shoved them aside with his feet, and Miranda found herself looking at a homemade door to Takahashi Tailors.

The shoemaker whispered. "Shotsu isn't back yet, but you should hurry. I don't know what tools you use—feel free to use mine, if they help. And I don't know if it's locked on the other side. Hasn't been opened in years, so maybe we're in luck. But it will be easier than the rear entrance. If Shotsu ever comes back from lunch, I'll send him away again so you can leave through the store. Just go out my back door if I'm busy with a customer . . . it's not locked when I'm here."

Miranda turned to thank the shoemaker. "Mr. Matsumara . . . you're a sweetheart."

He blushed a brick red, looked at the wooden floor. "I'd better get back to Mrs. Ibaraki before she calls the Legion of Decency. Here's a little Japanese for you, Miss Corbie, and maybe it'll bring you luck: *nanakorobi yaoki*. It means you fall down seven times, but you pick yourself back up eight."

Miranda was already examining the lock, and taking out a small set of lock picks she carried in a cosmetic pouch. "I'll remember that."

"Oh, before I forget—most important question."

"What is it?"

"Do you still want those shoes?"

Miranda smiled, looking up from the mechanism, her face smudged with dust.

"You bet I do."

She was lucky. The keyhole was fairly large, and after a couple of tries she managed it. Now all she had to worry about was whether or not it was blocked on the other side.

Miranda positioned her right shoulder against the door, thankful the gray wool she was wearing would hide some of the dust. From the front of the store, she could hear Matsumara laughing, trying to jolly the surly Mrs. Ibaraki.

She shoved. The door moved about a foot. She cursed herself for not carrying a flashlight. She shoved again. It scraped open another foot, enough for Miranda to see there were wooden crates surrounding it, some with sewing equipment.

She shoved one more time, and the door budged about six inches. Time to step inside.

She squeezed through, stepping over one box and into another, trying to avoid any more bruises. The door was at the back of the shop, and the light from the windows in front appropriately dim, but enough for her to make out shapes until her eyes readjusted.

Miranda stepped across one more box, and looked at the door from the vantage point of a clear spot on the other side. The crates on her right, the ones she'd climbed to get through, looked old, and contained a jumble of expected shop goods: bolts of cloth, lace, remnants, sewing machine parts, buttons.

The cartons on her left, the ones she'd shoved against, were a different story.

Propped behind the older crates were large, rough wooden containers. The kind used in shipping.

Miranda hustled over to the crates, digging in her purse for a lighter. She bent down to look at the writing, stamped sloppily on the side of one furthest from her. Most of it was in Japanese. At the bottom of a string of characters were the initials, NYK.

Excited, she closed the lighter, counted the crates. About three feet by five feet, and there were four of them. She raked the lighter again, and a spot of color drew her eye.

A piece of fabric, red brocade, the kind she'd seen in Chinatown, was caught on a box corner, looking as though it had been torn. She checked the floor quickly, noting the dust on the crates was minimal, the work of weeks, not years, and that the wooden floor of the cleaners was heavily scratched where the boxes were stored.

She followed the scratch marks to the back wall of the shop, where another door—with a new lock—led to the rear entrance.

Hurriedly, she returned to the box with the fabric, gently untangling it from the corner. The edges were ripped, not cut. She tucked it into the notebook in her purse before lifting the heavy lid of the crate, holding it steady with an arm and her weight, while she flicked the lighter on again.

Nothing. Disappointed, she almost dropped the lid, barely catching it in time. Wouldn't want Mrs. Ibaraki or another of Mr. Matsumara's customers to hear a thud from the empty building next door.

She opened the other three crates. Same results. She wasn't sure what she'd been expecting.

Cursing herself again for not bringing her small flashlight, Miranda returned to the first box, and lifted and shoved the lid until she wriggled it off the box entirely, careful to lower it to the floor as noiselessly as possible, then laid it flat.

Breathing hard, and leaning into the crate as far as she could, she flicked on the lighter. A few dots of dirty white she'd missed on the first look seemed to form a line, smeared into a powder streak like flour on a pie.

Except this wasn't flour.

Miranda retrieved her purse from where she'd left it on a crate. She tore out a piece of paper from her notebook, careful not to lose the fragment of cloth. Then she folded the paper into a makeshift funnel, patiently but quickly folding and tearing until the sides were secure.

She headed back into the crate, this time stepping in it, one hand on the funnel, the other on her lighter, and carefully scooped up the small white clumps of powder. She folded the funnel as flat as possible, shaking the powder to the bottom and folding over the top. Finally, she took out her billfold, and sandwiched the makeshift envelope in between one of Mrs. Winters's twenties and a ten-dollar bill.

Her eyes hunted for white in the three other crates. Most of them had a few specks here and there, and the familiar smeared line from a sack being lifted and hauled out of the container.

Miranda checked her wristwatch. It was 2:45, almost time for her to meet Ruth Landis.

The front of the store carried more risk than the dim light of the back. She ventured closer anyway, her hands exploring the top of the counter. Probably where they checked the stuff, made sure it wasn't fake. If she'd had time, light and freedom, she'd find more powder, here in the cracks.

More cocaine.

What she found, instead, was an old Bible, tucked under the counter. Inscribed to no one, it sat there, perhaps, on the days when Mrs. Takahashi could come in and mind the tailor shop for her husband.

Miranda opened it, unsure why. Then she thought of something, remembered the little girl with the old woman's voice.

"Acts 27, 10 or 11," she'd said. Miranda flipped through quickly. St. Paul's shipwreck.

And said unto them, Sirs, I perceive that this voyage will be with hurt and much damage, not only of the lading and ship, but also of our lives.

Ships. Chinatown. Cocaine. What the hell had Madame Pengo known . . .

Miranda crept through Matsumara's door a few minutes later, trying to pull it shut behind her. It wouldn't close firmly, so she moved his boxes back in place. She could hear him in front of the shop, talking with another customer.

She found the back door, well oiled, well used, unlocked. Exited cautiously into a suddenly sunny afternoon brightening a back area of uneven open space and garbage cans that eventually led to both Webster or Buchanan on either side.

She headed toward Buchanan so she could check the lock on Takahashi

Tailors. The back door sported a new padlock, as well as a new door lock. No more than a year old, more likely a few months.

The smell of tempura was drifting toward her from the Ginza Café. Miranda walked through their narrow alley, skirting more garbage pans, and interrupting more pigeons hungrily pecking some discarded rice. From the top of a roof nearby, a raven croaked his annoyance.

She looked up at it, shielding her eyes from the glare of the sun.

Maybe she'd found some truth at that.

Lester Winters was killed with cocaine. His daughter was addicted to it. Eddie Takahashi's empty storefront had stored it, in bags inside crates—containers from Lester Winters's shipping company.

Cocaine. The happy, helpful drug that gave you energy, making your eyes bright with excitement, your luck unstoppable, your sex appeal unmistakable. Until you looked in the mirror the next morning, or at whom you'd fucked the night before.

Nothing another line wouldn't solve. Everything looks better through a haze of white powder. *I get no kick from cocaine,* the song ran. Brother, you might not, but plenty of people with plenty of money did.

The raven cawed again, and Miranda hurried to catch the White Front, heading back downtown on Sutter.

Seventeen

The Pig n' Whistle was packed with shoppers and teenagers. Miranda checked her watch for the fifth time. 3:22.

She scanned the tables, her eyes lingering on well-dressed girls of the right age. None showed any interest in her, and none were there by themselves. The Pig was a place for boisterous groups of high school kids and matrons with tired feet, who could just manage the walk down from the shopping district at Magnin's or The White House or City of Paris to refuel on Black Forest Cake, blueberry pie, or an ice cream sundae.

Afterward, buoyed with cream and sugar, they'd stop across the street at the Emporium, before heading back home to the Peninsula or across the Bay or to Forest Hill, where they'd climb the steps and walk through a wide, imposing door, throwing the packages at their maid before settling down on a settee with a Manhattan. Martinis were so terribly '39.

A harried waiter hurried up to find what she wanted. Did Madame prefer a table, a booth, a counter seat and soda at the fountain? Apple pie à la mode, strawberry shortcake, hot fudge sundae, a sugar doughnut?

She winced at "Madame." Hurt worse than the swollen cheek. Mademoiselle would like a goddamn table, please, in a dark corner facing the door, and a piece of Boston cream pie with black coffee. And never mind the fucking bruises, buddy, just shut up and serve. She slipped him a dollar, which accelerated the appearance of a table against the back wall, facing the door, not dark enough, but what the hell. It was a bakery, not a bar, and bakeries weren't built for hiding the bruised faces of women.

Miranda hoped Ruth Landis wasn't the late type. She had too much to do, too much to think about, too much to figure out, and too much to plan. Laughing girls only reminded her of the two she needed to find. And somehow, she didn't think either one was laughing.

The coffee arrived quickly, sloppily poured by a waitress with one eye on the clock and the other on the beat cop at the soda fountain. Miranda wiped up the spilled brown liquid with a napkin. The cop wasn't one she knew or recognized, and as soon as he picked up his cinnamon roll, he waved good-bye at the waitress over the tumult, who nervously cleaned her hands on her apron, running them down her stomach under her breasts, unconscious of her own desperation.

Hell, aren't we all? Miranda thought. The pie arrived. 3:30 on the mark.

She started to eat.

She was on her third cup of coffee fifteen minutes later when a plump brunette in glasses walked in, holding a City of Paris shopping bag and trying to look mysterious.

Miranda lifted her hand up to catch the girl's attention. Ruth blushed, looked around, and scurried toward the table.

Her voice was breathless. "I'm so sorry, Miss Corbie, I had to tell my mother that I was taking the ferry over to San Francisco because of a new hat." She started to take the hat box out of the bag. "It's really a dream—"

"I'm sure it is, Ruth, but we don't have much time. You want a soda or something?"

Ruth wasn't accustomed to women who didn't dither, but she was a quick study and closed her mouth. "Root beer float. I brought some pictures."

Miranda smiled for the first time. "Good girl."

The first waitress was on break, so she flagged down another one, a skinny woman in her forties, with yellowed skin and large pores. "Root beer float, please, and I'd appreciate it if you could get it here quickly."

The waitress looked her over, lingering on the bruises. "Sure thing, ma'am. Hurry is our middle name." Her walk back to the soda jerk was anything but.

Miranda remembered not to swear in front of a teenager.

"Mind if I smoke?"

"Oh, not at all, Miss Corbie. I like to smoke, too . . . when my father's not around. He's a doctor, and he's against everything fun and modern and—"

"Most parents are. But he's right about smoking. Don't start, because once you do, it owns you." Miranda lit a Chesterfield with the matchbook on the table, leaned back, keeping her voice low.

"I've got to leave in less than thirty minutes—"

"I'm so sorry, Miss Corb—"

"Don't worry about it, Ruth, I appreciate you meeting me and you were inventive about getting down here. You're a smart young lady."

Ruth blushed again. "I—I recognized you from the papers."

"That's good. With this cheek, I wasn't sure if you'd be able to."

The girl stared at her, awe-struck. "Was it chin music, Miss Corbie? Did a bad hombre try to bump you off?"

Miranda sipped her coffee. "You've been reading too many magazines. Let's talk about Phyllis. You're a couple of years younger than she, right?"

"I'll be seventeen in May." The tone was defensive. Miranda ignored it.

"And you've known each other for how long?"

"Oh, gee—I'd say—I'd say almost ten years. Since second grade. We were at Sacred Heart together, too—I still am, anyway."

Miranda leaned forward. "Ruth—I need you to be as frank as possible. What you tell me is very, very important—possibly for your friend's safety."

The girl reached up to touch her hat, as if for reassurance. "Oh, no, Miss Corbie—is Phyllis—is Phyllis—?"

Miranda said smoothly: "I can't go over the details with you—by law. But it's very serious, and we need your help."

Ruth thought for a moment, as if considering something. Then she looked up at Miranda, and said simply and directly: "Ask me anything."

Miranda was relieved. Adolescents were such a strange mixture of child and adult, and right now she needed the latter.

"Did Phyllis get along well with her father and stepmother?"

The girl thought about it for a moment, while fidgeting with her fork. "She loved her dad. I can't believe Mr. Winters is dead—doesn't seem real somehow. I figured we'd make up, you know, after fighting about Bobby Henderson, as soon as I found out about him dying and all. But Phyllis never called."

"What about Mrs. Winters?"

Ruth frowned. "Off and on. Sometimes Phyllis acted like they were really chummy, going shopping together. But most of the time she . . . well, she hated her, Miss Corbie. Said she'd trapped her father, and never cared for him or Phyllis, and—and a lot of hurtful things."

Ruth leaned forward and whispered, shielding her mouth with her hand. "She even said Mrs. Winters had a boyfriend." Then she shook her head and snorted at the disclosure. "At her age!"

Miranda made a couple of notes in her notebook, taking a last inhale on the Chesterfield before rubbing it out in the ashtray.

"You say you fought over Bobby Henderson. Tell me what happened—and when."

Ruth giggled, then remembered herself, trying hard not to look like a virgin. "Bobby graduated last June, from S.I.—St. Ignatius. Phyllis was supposed to graduate then, too, but had to stay an extra half-year because of grades. He was in the rowing club, got a letter for it."

"Were they boyfriend and girlfriend?"

She hesitated. "Well—kind of. They went out for sodas and stuff, and we always thought they were sweet on each other—at least Bobby was. But then when Phyllis came back from summer vacation to finish, she sort of—changed a little. She said she wasn't sure what she was going to do after graduation, didn't want to stay home and be near her stepmother. She was skipping a lot of class, and didn't want to, you know, have sodas or go dancing with us, and we figured maybe it was another boyfriend, someone older. This was, oh, a couple of months before she was supposed to graduate—for good this time, in December. Phyllis turned eighteen in October, and we thought maybe she was just, you know, exercising her independence."

Ruth leaned forward again, speaking in a stage whisper. "But she wasn't, Miss Corbie. She was meeting someone. She'd been going with Bobby, and he found out, and they had an awful row. And all of us like Bobby, and I flat-out told Phyllis that if she didn't treat that boy right and hang on to him I'd take him away from her. And that's why we fought, because she laughed at me, and said some awfully mean things about him, called him a little boy, and told me I was too fat to get him and called me a four-eyes."

The girl's eyes sparkled with rage and pain. The paper napkin she'd been holding lay twisted on the tabletop.

Miranda's voice was gentle. "I'm sorry, Ruth. Try very hard not to be angry at Phyllis. I'm sure she didn't mean it."

"Then she shouldn't have said it!" The voice came out sharp and loud, and a mother and ten-year-old daughter at the table behind them turned to stare. Ruth covered her mouth. "I—I'm sorry, Miss Corbie."

The waitress crawled from the soda fountain, which apparently had nothing better to do than to produce the long-delayed root beer float. The interruption gave Ruth a chance to calm down and focus on something other than her outrage.

Miranda waited for the girl to take a few sips and said: "Did anyone ever see her with another boy—a man?"

Ruth lifted her head from the tall glass, looking at the ceiling and thinking hard. "You know—Bobby might have seen them together. You might ask him. Here's his picture, and a few of Phyllis."

She removed an envelope from her bag, and slid it across the table to Miranda, then applied herself to the root beer. Miranda studied the pictures of a smiling Phyllis next to a few other girls, and a tall, athletic boy with brown hair, wearing a letter jacket and a confident, if stupid, look on his face.

"Where is Bobby, if I want to speak to him?"

"Oh, he works in his father's hardware store, in Alameda. Henderson Hardware." The girl was blushing furiously, not looking up from her drink.

"Do you see him regularly?"

Ruth was trying to be nonchalant. "His store is close to where I live . . . I see him sometimes. But I'm dating George Adams now."

Miranda smiled at the bravado. "Will you give him a message, ask him to call me? Here's my card—one for you, one for Bobby. OK?"

The girl took them eagerly. "Sure thing, Miss Corbie. Do the pictures help?"

"Very much. Mind if I keep them awhile?"

"Oh, no. Please do. Did you need to know anything else?"

Miranda checked the time. 4:17. And she needed to make a call before walking in on Dianne.

"Yes . . . did Phyllis like to gamble, do you know? And other than Bobby, what kind of boys—men—did she like . . . her favorite Hollywood stars?"

A slurping sound from the straw signaled the end of the root beer float. Ruth wiped her face with another napkin, frowning.

"I don't remember Phyllis talking about it much, except in pictures. Sometimes we'd talk about what kind of gambling we'd do, if we were rich and walked into one of those terribly chic clubs where they play cards and roulette in the back. She liked the idea of roulette, I remember . . . but that was a long time ago, last year sometime. I think we were watching *King of the Underworld*. She thought Humphrey Bogart was dreamy."

Ruth wore a disgusted look on her face. "I think he's ugly. Now, Clark Gable is what I call a real he-man. I just loved him in *Gone With the Wind*! I've seen it five times already . . . I wish I looked like Vivien Leigh!" A deep sigh of realization that she would never look like Vivien Leigh rose from her chest.

Miranda asked: "What about radio? What did she like?"

"Lots. *Gangbusters. Myrt and Marge*, though sometimes that was boring. *Hollywood Hotel*, while that was on, and oh, *Lux Radio Theater*. And that Orson Welles and the *Mercury* or *Campbell's Playhouse*, whatever it is—the one who scared us all about Mars—she likes him a lot."

Miranda made a few more notes. "Thanks, Ruth. One more question. Did Phyllis know anyone on Guerrero Street, or ever go there?

Ruth's glasses fell sidewise a little, when she wrinkled her brow. She pushed them back into place and said: "If she did, she never told me."

Miranda stood up, took out fifty cents, left it on the table, and scooted her chair back in, while Ruth stared at her, wide-eyed.

"Be careful, Miss Corbie. Do you—do you have a gun?"

Miranda smiled down at the girl. "Don't worry about me, Ruth. Just be careful going home. Don't talk to any strangers—especially men. OK? Promise me, now."

The young girl looked solemn. "I promise, Miss Corbie. Thanks for the soda. Shall I tell Bobby to telephone you?"

"Yes—thank you, Ruth. You've been a big help."

The girl's eyes were anxious, and her face suddenly looked older. "If a gink tries to put the screws to you, give 'em the gate, OK, Miss Corbie?"

Miranda laughed, and said: "You bet I will."

She pushed through the crowds on Powell, past the Owl, the Clinton Cafeteria, and turned right on Ellis, heading for John's Grill. Her stomach growled when the aroma of charred steak drifted past her, and she shut the door of the small phone booth, her shoes pressed firmly against the wood of the door to hold it closed.

Miranda opened a pocket change purse, extracted a nickel. She perched on the narrow oak ledge in the corner, staring for a moment through the scratched and dirty glass at John's afternoon crowd, envying them their steaks, their drinks, their leisure.

She shook herself. Dianne was ahead. She wanted her stomach empty, her thoughts as clear as ice.

The nickel dropped, and an operator fresh from a break answered in a chatty voice.

"Number, please?"

"Sutter 9764."

"Hold one moment."

Static ran through the cord and into Miranda's ear, and she held the phone away from her until she could hear a tired male voice making a half-hearted attempt to communicate.

"Oceanic Hotel. Hello? This is the Oceanic Hote—"

"I need to leave a message for room 256. Can you take it?"

A pause filled the low static hum between them. "Yeah, lady, I can take it. What you got in mind?"

The Oceanic was one of the hotels the city tried to scratch over. The only thing shiplike about it was the size of the rooms, as big as a cot and a sink and usually rented by the hour, or even every twenty minutes. But Bente insisted on living there, so she could be near the waterfront . . . and near the men the waterfront had killed but didn't know it yet.

"What I have in mind, buddy, is that you take the pencil out of your ass and write me a message to room 256. Think you can handle that?"

The voice, as gravelly as week old coffee, harrumphed in fictional offense. "Go ahead, lady, I ain't got all day."

"Nine P.M. Moderne. Still on."

"Nine . . . OK. How the hell you spell the other thing?"

"Modern with an *e*. M-o-d-e-r-n-e. Club Moderne."

He snorted. "You lucky I ain't chargin' by the word like Western Union. So you're a Frenchie, eh? Won't be long now 'til you're all speakin' German. Bunch of queens, those French. Serves the bastards right—"

The phone made a satisfyingly loud clang when she slammed it on the receiver. And wondered, again, why the hell Bente lived at the Oceanic Hotel.

She turned left at Stockton, a right on O'Farrell, the precision of her steps and the directions driving her forward, easing the knot in her stomach.

Betty was dead. Three words, around and around and around.

Some horns blared, and a jukebox from a corner bar was crooning an old Ruth Etting tune, while she stepped over spit and Baby Ruth wrappers and crumpled race pages.

My heart is sad and lonely . . .

Betty was dead.

Raped.

Strangled.

Gone.

Like Eddie.

Like Johnny.

Body and soul.

She leaned over, her back against a bank across the street from 41 Grant Avenue, clutching her stomach, staring at her shoes to keep it down. Bile bit the back of her throat, and she looked at the creased leather, and thought of Matsumara, thought of Bente, thought of Rick, willing herself not to vomit.

A man in a well-cut business suit touched her elbow.

"Miss? You need some help?"

She pulled herself up, met his eyes, kind, concerned. Fatherly eyes.

The kind she never knew.

"Yes—thank you. Just a bad lunch. I'm—OK."

He brushed her elbow again, said: "Are you sure? I can call you a taxi, or—"

"No. Really, I'm all right. Thank you for checking."

He smiled at her, touched his brim, and for a second she could see herself in a checkered-print housedress, young and naive, fixing his pipe and telling him about the glee club, while a vaguely kind woman lingered in the background, making apple pies.

Miranda stared after him, wondered what he thought of the bruise on her cheek. Took out a cigarette, lit it with shaking hands on the fourth try.

The nicotine calmed her, gave her focus.

Dianne was waiting inside the ornate building in front of her, a gray-stone 1912 that looked like another bank. A temple to money.

In a sense it was.

She'd find her there, draped artistically over a chaise lounge, recalling the good ol' days of the Barbary Coast and the high-priced whores that controlled the men that controlled the city.

She'd be drinking tea, her finger daintily crooked, her fat face smooth from care or concern, a thick illusion of youth covering it and shielding it from time.

Dianne's finishing school and escort service.

Time to talk.

Eighteen

The air was heavy and cool inside, perfumed like a Southern mansion. Miranda half-shuddered, anticipating the macabre brush of Spanish moss against her cheek.

The butler greeted her, recognition warming his eyes for a moment. Then they fell back to the floor, where Dianne liked to keep them.

"She expecting you, Miss Corbie?"

Miranda nodded, looked around the foyer. Not much had changed. Still the hunting scenes on the wall, Merrie Olde England as transferred through the Confederacy. The red velvet seemed plusher, the carpet thicker. A faint odor of expensive Cuban tobacco mixed with magnolias and good English tea. And the acrid smell of crisply folded greenbacks.

"Yeah. How've you been, Franklin?"

The black man shrugged imperceptibly against the tight white cloth of the uniform. "I can't complain, Miss Corbie."

Miranda stared at him for a minute, wondering if he ever wondered what the hell a Howard University summa cum laude was doing in 41 Grant Ave. Her fingers drifted toward the cigarettes in her purse, until she remembered Dianne's "only for the gentlemen" rule. She clenched them together, kept them at her side.

"Show me in, please."

He nodded, leading her down a long corridor with old paintings in tarnished frames, the women in them seemingly unaware of their plunging décolletage, the men holding riding whips, modeling tight trousers and loose cravats.

The hush of a library filled the house along with the scent of decay. Aristocracy died slowly, lingering in the enjoyment of the expiration.

Franklin opened the door to the sitting room.

Wine-colored draperies matched the chaise and the Victorian furniture and the glass in Dianne's hand. Miranda squinted a little, adjusting her eyes to the color-tinted shadows her hostess lived in.

Franklin looked from one woman to the other, bowed, and retreated backward to another room of the house.

She appeared no older than Miranda remembered, her face as smooth as the past she'd wiped clean. Dark hair curly, soft, framing the large eyes and the small mouth, the features that of the pretty girl of yesterday, when women buttoned their shoes and wore hour-glass corsets their lovers loved to unlace, when they spoke in soft tones, and wore their hair upswept, daintily seated on nothing faster than a bicycle.

One hand was holding a half-empty wineglass. Her other, adorned with large rings and dark stones, waved vaguely in the direction of a horsehair chair near the chaise. A bone china teacup with a chinoiserie pattern rested on the tea service tray in front of her.

"Please, Miranda . . . sit down."

"I'll stand."

The words came out more harshly than she intended, and Dianne opened her eyes very wide, until Miranda felt that she might fall into them.

"Why on earth do you want to make yourself uncomfortable? And I'm sorry to hear, my dear, that you've been smoking again. A pity. You have such a lovely voice."

Miranda swallowed with difficulty, shifted her weight. "This is business, Dianne, or I wouldn't be here."

The older woman brought the glass to her lips and sipped, the dark purple of the wine bloodying her small white teeth. Soft Southern cadences dripped from her mouth like acid from a glass pipe.

"Oh, yes, forgive me. I'd almost forgotten how we parted. And still, Franklin made us tea."

She set the wine down and leaned toward the low table in front of her, pouring from the matching china pot. Miranda smelled the familiar bitter tang, watched the steam from the dark brown liquid rise and envelop her hostess.

"As I said, a pity. You had such promise. If only you'd learned to be a lady . . . and a real woman. But that, I'm afraid, is beyond you, my dear. You'll never let anyone in, will you?"

Miranda felt herself, like always, diminish in front of Dianne. Her eyes lost themselves in the Oriental carpet. From outside, the shriek of a car horn penetrated the wall. For a moment she could smell the sea, hear the barkers on Treasure Island. And remember the license in her wallet.

She raised her face to Dianne, and said: "Who I am and what I do and what I become ceased to be your business a long time ago. I didn't expect to see you again. I'm here because of Betty. And I suggest you ditch the Scarlett O'Hara act and tell me what you know about it."

Miranda walked to the chair and sat, crossing her legs while watching the other woman unsuccessfully hide her anger. From this distance, the tiny wrinkles glistened with oil in the crevasses, and the hair dye was starting to fade to white along the scalp.

Dianne picked the china cup up carefully. "You were always an ungrateful little bitch. I took you in when you had nothing, were nothing, a sobbing little girl of thirty-one crying over her poor, departed John—"

"Should I knock on door 103, Dianne, and make a citizen's arrest? No mirrors in jail cells. And they'll look up your birthday. The real one."

The older woman quieted, swallowing the rest, the dark eyes sad and reproachful now. "You would, wouldn't you? After everything. You've become hard, Miranda, hardened and cruel. No wonder you walk in here sporting a bruise . . . and act as though it were a mink stole from Magnin's."

Miranda smiled for the first time. "Back to the Brave Little Woman, now, are we? As entertaining as your role changes are, I want information, and the sooner you give it to me, the sooner I leave. Why did Betty go? Besides the obvious."

Dianne leaned forward, the feathers on her robe lapels waving daintily with the motion, and poured from a small decanter into the teacup. She always needed something to take the tang out.

"That was several months ago. How do you expect me to remem—"

"Six months ago, you said. And you remember every cent ever brought into this house, and I'm sure Betty delivered her share. Why did she quit?"

Dianne stared at the warm brown liquid critically, then drank. She didn't bother to sip this time.

"She came to me—a Chinese—no parent, no relatives—"

"I've heard the philanthropy angle. What did she say?"

"Something about new work. I thought she meant singing, chorus line—something like that. That was my impression, at least. She said she didn't need to be an escort any longer. That was all."

"Was she happy about it, excited?"

The decanter was pouring faster, out of the bottle and into the teacup, and down Dianne's throat. "How the hell should I know? Too much competition these days, especially with the Orientals. New ones in town. Thought maybe she wanted to work for one of her own . . . not that they'd be as good to her as I was. Ungrateful little bitches. All of you"—she waved her right hand around the room as if pointing out a crowd—"ungrateful little bitches."

The gentle Southern accent was slipping away. Dianne used to hold her liquor better.

"What about customers? Anyone rough on Betty?"

She shook her head, the jet black ringlets bouncing. "Mostly other Orientals, some white men on the sly. She never complained. Unlike you, she was a professional. Made the customers happy."

Which meant she made the customers. Dianne gave you the illusion of choice, but her insinuations of what she expected from you—and what, she hoped, her clients could expect from you—were very clear.

Miranda thought a minute, asked: "Was she male only?"

Escorts were provided for both genders, and sometimes the same gender . . . if the party was in Pacific Heights or Nob Hill, and the price was high enough.

"Hell, yes. I don't have any Orientals who'll do drag."

"All right. She leave a forwarding address, tell you where she was staying?"

The smell of apricot brandy was overwhelming the tea leaves. The older woman's face was starting to cave in like an overripe piece of fruit. Miranda wanted to leave before the worms crawled out of it.

"Chinatown, I should imagine. Same place I picked her up, last row in a chorus line, scared little thing. But pretty. I invested some time and money into that one."

Miranda stood, her leg shaking with a pain spasm. It helped clear the miasma that always cloaked and protected Dianne. Red-lit, sweetly scented, it swirled like summer fog, pinwheeling through dreams and fancies and fantasies, crashing back to Earth in an alcoholic haze and bruises on a teenager's breasts.

Miranda drew a breath, and said: "I hope I never have to see you again."

Dianne was pouring more brandy, and set the decanter down slowly, leaning back, her eyes narrowed and trained on Miranda's face.

"You were my biggest loss. Beauty, hell yes, but you're an empty woman. No fire. Maybe at one time, but not anymore. And one day, honey, you'll wake up to a cold bed and a hell of a lot of wrinkles, with no money and no one to keep you warm at night. And you'll wonder where the hell it all went."

She shook her head, while the ringlets danced.

"It's gone before you know it. So what's wrong with making a little money with it? What's wrong with putting aside a nest egg for the day no one will look at you twice? But you never understood. Because you're there already. Dead. You're deader than Betty. Who killed you, Miranda? Who the hell killed you?"

Miranda felt the blood rush to her face. Dianne had already dismissed her, was looking at the decanter again. She turned on her heel, walked through the door, back to the foyer, and into the waiting arms of Duggan.

The handcuffs hurt like hell.

Miranda's hands were large, and so were her wrists, and Duggan relished fitting them on her, his eyes bright with barely suppressed excitement.

"Think you're so high and mighty, you and the Mex. Can't parade around my town, not a fucking chance. You're getting arrested for solicitation, lady, and you'll lose your license. Ever hear of the moral turpitude clause?"

He was by himself. No partner. Franklin hovered at a distance, his hands clenched together, unsure what to do. Miranda looked him in the eyes steadily, not giving Duggan the satisfaction of a flinch or a response.

He grabbed the chain in the middle of the cuffs, yanking her viciously toward the door. "C'mon."

She stumbled, her leg still in pain from earlier, but managed not to fall down. "You're arresting me for what?"

"You heard me. Pandering. Solicitation. As in prostitute. As in whore."

Miranda turned back to Dianne's butler, searching his eyes, hoping he'd remember. "Franklin—please call Rick."

Duggan snapped her backward with the handcuffs again, making her stumble toward him. "You got nothing to say to the nigger, lady. He your pimp or something? Niggers and whores, always together."

He slammed his boot down on the floor toward Franklin. "Get your ass back to the kitchen, shine, before I give you some blue to go with the black."

Franklin left his eyes on the floor, took half a step backward. Duggan yanked on the handcuffs again, and this time Miranda lost her balance. He laughed, holding her body up by the wrists while she dangled, scrambling to get her feet back under her. Her wrists felt sprained, but she didn't cry out, and righted herself after a few seconds.

Duggan pulled again, not quite as hard. She followed him into the street, her eyes blinking in the sudden shift from dark to light, and to a police car, parked about five hundred feet down the block.

He unlocked the door with one hand, shoved her into the back. She hit the other side of the door with her shoulder, but was able to avoid her cheek. Then he climbed into the driver's seat, checking her in the rearview mirror.

"What's wrong, lady? Cat got your tongue? Or don't you use it unless you get paid?"

Miranda leaned back against the seat and closed her eyes, trying to fight the pain all over her body, the sickening feeling in her stomach.

Maybe Duggan was shadowing her, maybe she was too tired and too beat up to have noticed. But if Franklin phoned Rick—and he remembered which Rick—maybe she could get to her lawyer before Duggan got her alone in an examination room. A whole hell of a lot of ifs. Franklin would have to tell Dianne. She'd help, because it meant her business. And she'd made plenty of payments to the Policemen's Fund over the years.

The car stopped suddenly, and Miranda lurched forward, hanging on to the handle on the car side.

Duggan turned to look back at her, savoring it. "Time to get out, sweet cakes. You ain't gonna get no sympathy here."

She braced herself, while he came around to her side, opened the door, grabbed the chain again, and almost yanked her off her feet. They drew a few looks, but the heads turned quickly away. Just another cop and a whore.

She half-stumbled and half-ran up the stairs to keep pace with him. He led her past the elevator and down the hallway toward the booking area and offices, head high like a triumphant general or a hunter with a dead animal. No sign of Phil. No sign of Gonzales. Collins, the cop who'd questioned her after Eddie Takahashi, walked by and looked her up and down. Then in a low voice to Duggan, said: "About goddamn time."

No friends at the force.

He kept her in isolation. No food, no water. Came in about every twenty minutes just to stare at her. He slapped her cheek once, the one already bruised, but watching it swell up again must have made him uneasy. So he backed off, put the bright lights on, and made sure there was as little air in the room as possible.

She tried to concentrate on figuring out what time it was. Say 5:15 at the most when Duggan arrested her. She'd been here for probably two hours.

One Mississippi.

Two Mississippi.

No clocks in interrogation rooms, nothing to mark the time except for your pain.

If only Franklin called Rick. And remembered the Rick to call. And Rick called Meyer. Duggan wouldn't let her call anybody.

He'd try to nail her on the moral turpitude clause in the law regulating investigators, even if he couldn't get the pandering charge to stick. She couldn't afford to say anything. He'd twist her words like he'd twisted her wrists.

She could see him outside, pacing, peering through the frosted glass, waiting for her to crack before he brought her before a judge.

One Mississippi.

Two Mississippi.

She sat up straighter. Fuck the pain. Fuck Duggan. Fuck all the bastards.

Miranda put her hands on the table out flat and heard herself laugh. She'd met Franklin when she started at Dianne's. He'd improved her table manners, taught her how to mix a julep according to Dianne's recipe, and once, after a long night and a messy party, sang her an Ethel Waters song . . .

She laughed again, and Duggan came in, piggish eyes narrowed and suspicious.

"You think this is funny, bitch? Is that it? You ain't got nobody—hear?"

Miranda stared up at him. Her voice came out soft.

"'s wrong, Duggan? Don't like my face?"

He crossed over, grabbed her hair close to the scalp and pulled, put his mouth to her ear until she could feel his breath burn her skin like steam from a sewer grate.

"Your face ain't gonna be the same, lady. Not when I get through with you."

He flung her back toward the table, but she caught her head on her forearms. Let it rest there. Duggan stood over her, breathing hard, drawing out the little air left in the room. Then she heard him leave, banging the door behind him.

Miranda sat back up. She laughed again. Couldn't stop laughing.

What did I do . . . to be so black and blue . . .

She didn't see him again. Eventually dozed in the chair, propped upright. Opened her eyes when she felt a touch on her shoulder, and saw her attorney, standing in front of her. With Rick and Gonzales.

Franklin.

Rick was holding a glass of water to her lips. "Drink this, Miranda."

Her lips were dry and cracked. She sipped the water, felt them burn. Drank the glass slowly, savoring it like scotch.

Her voice came out a croak. "What time is it?"

Meyer looked at his pocket watch. "Eight o'clock, sweetheart. I'm sorry I couldn't get here sooner."

She looked up at Rick. "I've got to meet Bente . . ."

"You need to get home, Miranda, or you'll wind up in a hospital."

"St. James Infirmary."

"What?" They looked puzzled. Gonzales looked away.

"Nothing. Just give me a shot of something. I'll be OK."

"But your cheek—"

"Never mind my cheek. I've got to get to my office, then to the Moderne."

The men looked at each other. Rick pulled out a flask from his inside jacket pocket, handed it to Miranda. She drank it down, felt the liquid loosen her aching muscles, numbing the pain.

"Cigarette?"

This time it was Gonzales, offering her one of his French gold-tips. He lit it for her, his eyes angry and upset. Rick didn't look happy, either, especially when looking at Gonzales.

Meyer rested his plump hand lightly on her shoulder. "The charge has been thrown out, my dear. No habeas corpus necessary . . . Duggan violated section 849 by not taking you before a judge—and there was one available, I checked. He also violated section 149 of the penal code with an assault on you, as reported by Mr. Franklin Hayes, who contacted Mr. Sanders about two hours ago. One call, and an explanation of your case, as provided by Mr. Sanders, and the new chief agreed that we'd just pretend it didn't happen. The best outcome, I think."

"He has been temporarily relieved from duty, Miss Corbie." Gonzales's soft accent felt like a caress after Duggan's rasp. "He'd staked out Miss Laroche's residence on his own initiative, anticipating your visit. Miss Laroche has agreed not to pursue any claim against him, as the matter is being dropped."

Dianne and her reputation. Escort services advertised, she used to say; whores did not. Miranda inhaled Gonzales's cigarette, the stronger tobacco helping to revive her. At least she wasn't so incompetent that she'd failed to see a tail.

Her attorney cleared his throat and said: "The new police chief was also very unhappy to receive a call from Leland Cutler."

"You phoned Cutler?"

Bialik shrugged, his paisley vest expanding with the gesture. "He owes you, Miranda. Given this Duggan's propensity for theatrics, I thought it would make you reasonably secure for the future."

She took another swig of Rick's whiskey, dropped the cigarette in the ashtray, and put her hands in front of her on the table, pushing herself up and trying to stand. Gonzales moved to help her, but Rick was closer and lifted her by the elbow.

She stood, looked at Meyer Bialik and his formal suit, his eyes and smile benevolent. The other side of her face was too swollen to see properly.

"No worry on the moral turpitude clause?"

He shook his head.

She turned to Gonzales. Lowered her voice. "Did Phil know about this?"

"Phil is on a leave of absence, Miss Corbie. Since this morning."

Fuck. Probably drinking again.

"I've gotta get to Bente and the Moderne. Can someone take me to the office in a hurry?"

Gonzales said: "I will drive you in a police car, Miss Corbie. It is the least we can do."

Rick said quickly: "I'll go with you, Miranda."

Bialik looked at the two men, amusement playing across his good-humored face.

"I shall dine in Chinatown tonight, gentlemen, so don't bother yourselves with me." He bent over, took Miranda's hand, and kissed it. "I'll send you the bill, but it won't be much."

"Thanks, Meyer. With this face, I'll need to keep it in the bank."

"*Jamais*, my dear, *jamais*. *Adieu*, gentlemen." He waddled out of the room, his cane tapping on the floor in a jaunty rhythm.

"Can I collect my things?"

"They're here, Miss Corbie." Gonzales gestured to a box in the chair opposite from where she'd sat, and lifted it on the table. "I had them brought to you."

She looked at him. "Thank you, Inspector."

Rick said, a bite in his voice: "Can we get on the way, if you're going to insist on not seeing a doctor?"

Gonzales held the door open for them both, while Rick's hand hovered protectively near her waist. She glanced back at the small, airless room.

"Thanks, Franklin," she whispered to herself.

Nineteen

Miranda tried to shove the tiredness out of her body and concentrated on the pain. The side of her face felt like a lead balloon. Too heavy to smile. Not that she had much to smile about.

Rick sat on her right, looking at her every few seconds when he wasn't watching Gonzales's eyes in the rearview mirror.

The detective maneuvered the large black Ford out of the Hall of Justice parking lot, and turned left on Jackson. He was taking the long way, and Miranda figured he had something to say.

"I have some information for you, but I'm not sure that Mr. Sanders—"

"—Mr. Sanders knows when to keep his mouth shut and his pencil in his pocket, Gonzales. Tell Miranda what she needs to know, and all of it is off the record." No Irish lilt in the voice today.

Gonzales flashed a glance at Rick, came back to Miranda, and passed a man on a bag-laden bicycle rolling down Grant Avenue.

"We ran down the numbers you gave us this morning, Miss Corbie, cross-referenced them with late-model sedans. We have not located the car, but we think we found a match to one registered in Los Angeles and reported stolen. So it seems your visitors may not be local."

"Any reports on the grapevine about L.A. muscle moving north? Italians, maybe even Sammy Martini?"

Gonzales shook his head, stifled a mild expletive when two teenagers jumped in front of the car and jaywalked across Stockton. Caution made his voice rougher: "We've heard something about Los Angeles. Something to do with drugs, nothing to do with killers. And nothing to do with Martini."

Miranda glanced at Rick, who was staring at her. Came back to Gonzales's eyes in the mirror. "They're connected. L.A., Filipino Charlie, and Gillio's boys."

They were moving through the Stockton Tunnel, and Gonzales shook his head. "I can't hear you properly. Just a moment."

He pulled over to a parking space a block and a half later, in front of one of the ubiquitous cheap hotels that lined the area up the hill from Union Square. The space was big enough not to parallel park, and once the large car was secure, he turned around in the seat to look at Miranda.

"I thought I heard you say something about Filipino Charlie and Gillio's . . ."

"You did. And Los Angeles. It's all tied in, the Winters case, Eddie Takahashi . . . and probably Betty. Don't ask me how, I don't know the specifics yet. But Winters was carrying a matchbook from the Olympic Hotel in his pocket when he was killed. These boys from L.A. left me a calling card from Gillio's at the Olympic Hotel. And Helen Winters called to tell me to drop the case . . . Why? Maybe she got a calling card, too."

Rick pushed his hat up from his forehead and gave a low whistle. "That's a big leap, Miranda."

Gonzales nodded. "One matchbook, three murders? Slim evidence, Miss Corbie."

She looked from one man to the other, impatiently. "Look . . . I don't like coincidences. Men in a green car followed me after Eddie was killed. Then they tried to kill me. A Chinese business associate—what business, I don't know—of someone connected, probably Filipino Charlie—walked into my office with an Italian gunman today, and asked me to find Eddie's sister . . . because Eddie owed them money. And the man knew something about Betty's death and Phyllis Winters's disappearance."

"Could be word on the street. Doesn't necessarily mean they were involved."

She shook her head stubbornly. "No. You're wrong. And if you don't believe me, go down to Japantown. Visit the empty storefront belonging to Eddie's family. Except it's not quite empty. Because inside you'll find cargo boxes from Lester Winters' shipping line that used to hold bags of cocaine."

Gonzales made a sudden move, as if he might sprint out of the car. "Are you sure it was cocaine?"

Miranda opened her purse, carefully removing the envelope with the white powder. "Test it and see."

Gonzales took it from her gingerly, while Rick leaned forward to look. Gonzales placed it next to him on the car seat, then looked up at her, his face holding admiration.

"Thank you, Miss Corbie. Miranda. That dovetails with what we heard about the Los Angeles connection. Cocaine and heroin, moving north in large quantities. Perhaps—perhaps that matchbook means more than I thought."

Rick looked dubious. "I've never heard of Italians mixing with Oriental gangs, Miranda."

"Nor have I. But the man that paid me a visit mentioned something about unwanted business associates moving in on them. I don't know whether that's the Italians, or the Los Angeles boys. Or both. We don't know why Winters was killed, even if we can guess how he fits in. And we don't know where his daughter is, or Eddie's sister. But this Mr. Wong, as he called himself, said that if we didn't find Emily Takahashi, she'd wind up like Betty. That's enough fucking coincidence for me."

Gonzales let out the clutch, and moved the car back into traffic. "Winters looks like a very professional job. Similar to a killing in Seattle last year. A man known as Needles, former nurse at a hospital in St. Louis. He was supposed to be hiding out in Portland."

Rick asked: "Think he traveled south?"

"Possibly. Yet Takahashi was shot and Betty Chow was strangled."

"And raped."

Miranda stared out the window at the shoppers on Market, while Gonzales pulled into another spot about a block away from the Monadnock.

He flicked a glance at her, while Rick looked down at the car floor.

"And raped. And the men in the car—if they are the same as those we have been looking for earlier—"

"You mean the hit-runners that killed the old man last week?" Rick leaned forward. "We've been trying to get more information out of you guys ever since."

Gonzales shut the engine off, turned around to face them again. A street-car rumbled by, and he waited until it passed before responding.

"We have little to go on, Mr. Sanders. Other than the victim, an old man, retired from the gas company. From a fender at the scene, we believe it was a '39 Dodge coupe, not an Oldsmobile sedan. The car that tried to run you down was an Oldsmobile, Miss Corbie. Large four-door model. Belonged to a real estate agent in Santa Monica. The earlier hit-and-run seems like a genuine— and unfortunate—coincidence."

Rick grunted. "Maybe. But Clarion Alley isn't known for its traffic problems."

Miranda turned toward him. "I thought it was Seventeenth Street."

"Clarion. Off of Seventeenth."

Gonzales said: "I'll follow up on the cocaine immediately. Regan in Narcotics will appreciate the lead."

"See if he can find us one between Lester Winters, Filipino Charlie, and Joe Gillio." Miranda gathered her purse and the Spanish gun, still in the holster, and started to open the door. "Thank you, Inspector."

He jumped out, opened it for her before Rick was around the other side of the car. Took her hand, and she could feel the warmth in it.

"I'm sorry, Miranda. Duggan . . . what he did to you . . . I'm sorry. He'll probably be suspended because of this—deservedly so. But I ask you—please don't judge him too harshly. He used to be a good cop."

"And now he's a son of a bitch who's goddamn lucky she's not charging him with assault and battery. C'mon, Miranda." Rick was standing impatiently at her side, Irish pugnacity aimed full force at Gonzales.

The inspector bowed his head, hair perfectly in place, smelling of French tobacco and aftershave. "You're right, of course. Please be careful, and stay in touch. Call me directly with any information, or if you need . . . any help."

Miranda shook his hand quickly. Rick stuck his own hand out immediately, gave him one quick jerk, and took Miranda by the elbow, around the police car, and on the sidewalk.

Gonzales stood next to his open door, watching them, and lit a French cigarette.

They didn't say anything on the way to the Monadnock. Miranda could feel Rick's irritation and impatience, and was grateful that he kept quiet.

The lobby was busy for past eight o'clock on a Tuesday. Gladys wasn't working the magazine stand. Miranda was grateful; the fewer people who saw her face, the better.

She caught a few sideways glances, as people in the elevator tried not to stare, tried not to speculate on the woman with the dark bruises and circles under her eyes. None of their business if her husband gave her a slap now and again.

Not much noise on the fourth floor. You'd never know if the Pinkertons were busy, anyway. She and Rick walked by, catching a whiff of expense account on the way to her office.

She unlocked the door, while Rick waited, muscles tensed, anticipating someone to fight other than himself.

Miranda walked in, threw her purse on the desk, and finally collapsed in her chair, the leather caressing her, supporting her. She set the holster in front of her, and removed the black pistol, examining it for any damage.

Rick took off his hat, sat across from her, lit a cigarette. And asked: "Why the hell are you here, Miranda? You're hurt. You've been through hell. I could blast Duggan and those bastards through the roof—get an investigation, get the boss involved. We've been looking for a cause for two months."

She carefully replaced the gun in the holster. Unlocked the drawer with the Old Taylor, and pulled out the bottle and uncorked it. Wiped the top with her sleeve and took a long drink. Wiped it again, and offered it to Rick.

"I'm not it, Sanders. As despicable as Duggan is—and nobody wants the son of a bitch to suffer as much as I do, right now—I don't want to make waves with the cops. Makes it hard with the prison board when I renew my license. And Dullea's new in the job. Let's see how he handles things."

Rick took a pull on the bottle, put it back on the desk. "Bastard should lose his job."

"Yeah. He should. And short men with small mustaches shouldn't invade countries, either. Let's concentrate on what we can actually do, OK? You want to go to the Moderne with me, see Bente?"

His face twisted in a comical grimace. "Sure, Miranda. May as well. Beats getting a call from you at any hour of the goddamn night, and I may even find something to write about and keep myself from getting fired."

She pulled the purse toward her, took out a Chesterfield. Said, without looking at Rick: "Thanks, Sanders. For last night and tonight."

He leaned forward in the chair, then awkwardly picked up the bottle of bourbon.

"Don't mention it."

Miranda felt her face melt a little, fleetingly soft, like a cloud across the moon. Then she lit the cigarette with the Sally Rand lighter on the desk.

And said: "I won't."

Marie was working coat check at the Moderne again, said she'd deliver the message to Bente personally. They shouldn't be too late. It would depend on what Bobby Henderson had to say, and what messages were waiting.

Rick leaned on the windowsill, looking out into the San Francisco night. A light drizzle was falling on Market Street, the neon of the nearby bars and restaurants cracking and popping as the electricity surged through the overhead wires into the rooftop signs and blinking pink and yellow advertisements. A streetcar passed, and Lotta's Fountain flashed like a fan dancer, its burnished gold refracted by the droplets and the White Front's bright yellow light.

Rick stood, and smoked, and tried not to think about Miranda.

She was on the phone with the answering service, the ice pack on her cheek, filled with cubes from the Sweet Spot Tavern, around the corner toward Mission.

"So that was the only message? From Rose Shiara. No, that's fine, thanks." She hung the phone up slowly.

Rick turned toward her. "Who's Rose Shiara?"

"Emi Takahashi's best friend."

"You gonna call her?"

Miranda tried to shake her head, then said, "No. I'll phone her tomorrow." She was searching her notebook, the one she carried in her purse.

"When are we leaving for the Moderne?"

"In just a minute. I need to try to reach Bobby Henderson."

She was starting to slip. To fall. The well was deep, and no light reached the bottom. The girls were probably dead already, as dead as she felt. As dead as Dianne said she was.

Her fingers dialed the operator by rote, by habit, no faith implied.

"Alameda, please. I'm trying to reach a Mr. Henderson, of Henderson's Hardware. No, not the store. His home. Yes, I thought there might be . . . but I thought perhaps you'd know which one he was . . . uh-huh. Oh, I know, all those names, every day! I don't know how you girls manage so well . . . do they give you memory tests, or something? I ask because a cousin of mine wants to move to the city and has always wanted to be an operator . . . uh-huh. Topeka. Well, not as big as San Francisco. Oh, sure, I don't mind waiting."

She looked up from the phone, gave Rick a lopsided grin. "I'm sorry, what was that? She did? Oh, thank you ever so much! No, a plumbing problem. Uh-huh. Oh yes . . . it's terrible when that happens. Well, have a good evening—and thank Alice ever so, would you? Yes . . . you, too. 'Bye, now."

Miranda leaned back in the chair, one hand covering the mouthpiece, while she picked up her cigarette and puffed furiously before setting it down again.

"Mr. Henderson? How do you do. My name is Norma MacIntosh. I'm an admissions officer for Stanford University, and I'd like to speak to your son Bobby. Yes . . . yes, we have. That's why I'm calling. Well, we call after the dinner hour to make sure we can reach our prospective students . . . you know how busy young people can be, and I understand Bobby works in your store . . . yes . . . athletic scholarship. Certainly. I'd like to speak to you and your wife later, but I really must speak with him first . . . yes . . . thank you for understanding."

Rick crossed from the window, and sat in the chair opposite from Miranda and watched her. She kept her eyes on the bottle of Old Taylor.

"Bobby? Listen, please don't let on, but this is Miranda Corbie, the private detective. Yes . . . did Ruth contact you? No, she wasn't pulling your leg. And please—I had to tell a little white lie to your parents, so keep pretending I'm from Stanford. Yes . . . that's it. Can you get to a private phone? You have another extension? Oh, she does . . . How about a pay phone nearby? All right. Then I'll just ask you a couple of questions about Phyllis, and maybe we can talk tomorrow. Is that OK? Good. Hang on for a moment."

Miranda picked up the cigarette and inhaled until the red end met her fingers, and she dropped it in the ashtray, returning to the phone.

"All right, Bobby. Just answer as best you can, and try to make up something clever about Stanford and their crazy admissions policies, OK? Great . . . and thanks. What was Phyllis's favorite movie magazine? Uh-huh, good. Favorite radio shows? *Gangbusters*, uh-huh . . . *I Love a Mystery* . . . OK. Did you ever see the man she was with? Just say yes or no. All right. Was he a lot older? Uh-huh. Fancy dresser? No, don't say too much, I'll guess. Gangster type, right? Maybe looked Italian? OK . . . no, that's good. Keep it easy, I'm sure your parents are listening. And this was when? Uh-huh . . . that's perfect. Just a few more questions. Ever see his car? Sedan, huh? Dark color? No . . . a Dodge coupe, you say? Very good, Bobby, that's a big help . . . yeah. What kind of food did she like best, sandwich, that kind of thing . . . uh-huh. Right. OK, last one: Did she ever mention Guerrero Street? . . . No, that's OK. It was a long shot. You've been a big help. No, phone me tomorrow . . . yes. And listen, thank you! And I hope you do get into Stanford . . . all right. 'Bye."

She settled the phone into the cradle, and met Rick's eyes.

"Let's go see Bente."

Marie only flinched a little when she saw Miranda's face, and was too well bred to mention it. "I gave her the message, sugar—she's only been here for about half an hour."

A high-pitched buzz of excitement told them how busy the main floor was before they walked in. With a shock, Miranda realized it was the night before Valentine's Day.

Foil and papier-mâché hearts hung from the ceiling, while the women draped their cleavage in red velvet, powdered and sparkling with diamonds or rhinestones, depending on how far away they sat from the orchestra. Men in double-breasted dinner jackets with crisp white display handkerchiefs leaned forward, eyes glistening, lighter flames lit.

Valentine's Day held promises kept in small hotel rooms or posh penthouses, beach chalets and riverfront cottages . . . or the new luxury Pontiac, latest model, wide-open rumble seat.

Promises broken the next morning . . . when the glass slipper slipped and splintered on the floor.

The orchestra was playing everything from "I Love You Truly" to "Moonlight Serenade," all at the same time. Nobody gave a damn. I only have eyes for you, dear. You and what's between your legs.

Bente was tucked in a corner far away from the would-be Romeos, hiding behind a plant. Miranda saw Jorge in the distance, caught his raised eyebrow and the look he gave to Rick. Poor bastard. As if she hadn't put him through enough already.

Miranda slid into the seat next to Bente, who stared at her.

"What the hell happened to you?"

"Car tried to run me over, and a cop slapped me."

"You look like shit."

"I know."

"Go to the doctor?"

Rick interrupted. "She refused."

Bente turned her large brown eyes on him. "Oh—hello, Sanders. How you doing?"

He shrugged, and Bente came back to Miranda with the relentlessness of a pit bull.

"You better go to the doctor."

"Quit grandmothering me and talk."

Bente frowned, hitched her evening-gown strap a little higher. The blue shimmer was tight against her large breasts, and looked like it might fall down at any moment.

"I got your message at the Oceanic."

"That's a fucking miracle."

Bente pointed a finger at her. "Listen—I won't bitch to you, you don't bitch to me. Got it?"

Miranda lit a cigarette, waved her hand, grinned with one side of her face. "Yeah, yeah. So what's the score?"

Her friend leaned in over the table, her breasts resting on the top. Miranda noticed Rick trying not to stare. "That Parker you mentioned. The waterfront cop . . ."

"Yeah?"

"He's OK. And out here to investigate Winters, except Winters turned up dead."

Miranda inhaled, reached over to take a drink of Bente's sloe gin fizz. "So Parker's on the up-and-up?"

"From what I could tell. I mean, he's not a party member . . . but then, neither are you."

"You know what I believe in, Bente."

She snorted, her décolletage quivering. "Not much. But you're an old pal from Spain, Randy. And your heart's in the right place."

Miranda flinched at the nickname, turned her head quickly to signal a waiter. It was Jorge. He danced to the table, sinuous and lithe, hips loose, trousers tight.

"Miss Corbie?"

"Your best bourbon, Jorge. Neat."

He nodded, turned toward Bente. "Another cocktail, Miss?"

"Make it a double martini. I'm tired of fizzes."

"And the gentleman?"

A sneer lay behind the polite veneer, as Jorge took in Rick's rumpled suit. Rick stared at him, hard-eyed. "Scotch on the rocks."

The waiter nodded, turned back, warmth in his voice and face. "Anything else, Miss Corbie? Dinner, perhaps?"

Miranda recognized the hollow feeling in her stomach as hunger. She shook her head. "No, thanks."

He smiled, nodded, glanced at Bente's chest and then at Bente's eyes, smiled again, more slowly, and walked off, bouncing on the balls of his feet. Bente's eyes followed him.

"He's available. Almost always."

Her friend raised her eyebrows. "Is he worth it?"

Miranda shook her head. "I wouldn't know."

Rick had turned a shade of deep crimson, and cleared his throat. Both women looked up at him.

Bente said: "What's wrong with you, Sanders? Want some fizz?"

He lit a cigarette, said: "I'm just wondering what the hell I'm doing here."

She grinned at him affectionately. "Helping to take care of Randy. Same as always."

Another waiter appeared with drinks before the silence became too awkward. Miranda held the bourbon in her mouth, savoring the feel and memory of it. Rick gulped his scotch.

Bente stroked the side of her glass, making a pattern in the moisture. Without looking up, she said: "Who killed Betty?"

"I don't know. But I will. Any idea what Parker was investigating?"

"Far as I know, he still is. Smuggling, of some sort. Always the problem with shipping lines. Could be legal stuff nobody wants to pay taxes on, could be looted art, could be drugs. With the war, things are worse . . . more goods to be looted, more smuggling. Looks like Winters was playing that game, and Parker was onto him."

"Maybe that's why he was killed—he wanted out. Maybe he was even blackmailed into it somehow, or got in too deep. And maybe his daughter was used against him."

"What about his old lady?"

"Helen Winters? She called me today, told me to keep the money, quit the case."

"You think she knows something?"

Miranda swallowed another mouthful of whiskey. "I think she was warned off. And she might guess something. She's having an affair, didn't get along with her stepdaughter . . . has her own reasons to stay quiet."

"Yeah . . . six and a half inches of reason."

Rick choked on his drink.

Bente eyed him quizzically. "What's wrong, Sanders? Can't hold your liquor?"

Miranda said, "Can you keep digging on Winters, Bente? See what you find out on the smuggling angle, or any reports on the missing girls?"

"Sure thing, Miranda. Been hearing about something foul on the waterfront . . . nobody'll talk, though. So it's big."

"Be careful, for God's sake."

"Tell it to the Marines. I'm not the one who looks like Schmeling after the Louis fight."

"Might be able to use you on a job soon."

"First get your face fixed. But when you need my tits, just let me know."

Rick swallowed the rest of his scotch. Miranda stood up, said: "My tab tonight. Call me, leave a message with the service."

"Right-oh."

She looked at Rick. "You ready?"

"Where are we going?"

"To find Phyllis Winters."

Twenty

Sometimes she followed her instincts, winding past the small tables and the stares of men, their fingers tracing the line of her hips through a tight pale yellow gown, moving in time to the music, the rhythm, following the scent, that feral smell of desire, of sweat on skin.

Sometimes the journey was longer . . . through smoke-filled jazz clubs on the east end of Fillmore, or Irish bars with long, low wooden counters, scarred with the sobs of tearful wives and calloused hands, spit hawked and left on the sidewalk outside the door mutely venomous. "Catholic bastards," it said.

Sometimes it was over quickly, a sidewalk job, a back-alley quickie, the hand on the thigh, groping upward, blind and seeking comfort, a warm place to hide, a nipple to suck.

Sometimes she felt sorry for them.

And then she'd remember their wives, the tired age lines, the sagging stomachs from too many children, the thick waist and bent posture from making do when making do was necessary, hiding underneath a coiffure by Marcel, or a City of Paris dress. And the hands and the mouth never reached their destinations, what passed for manhood a pathetic, shriveled organ, plumped by illusion, fed by fantasy, returned to its natural state . . . shrunken, old, decayed.

She usually worked the rooms on Valentine's Day. Worked the clubs and the dance halls, called in by the women that were tired of waiting, tired of the cold, tired of being tired.

Tonight she was seeking something else, her face swollen and misshapen, her suit rumpled, her body dull. The holster under her left arm weighed too much, but the weight propped her up, kept her going.

And she wasn't alone.

They made the rounds. Bal Tabarin, Golconda, even La Fiesta, where Don Aldino and His Gauchos offered a tango about as sensuous as an assembly line.

A flash of the picture, a quick stare at Miranda, averted eyes, blank, bland, empty.

No girl, no dice.

She swallowed the repertoire of Goodman and Miller and Dorsey along with watered-down booze and curious, eager looks from men who were excited by the bruises on her face.

No, ain't seen your friend, girlie, but I'll be your friend if you want me to. I go for a fighter. And I won't treat you so bad like your old man, neither . . . I like your face. Like the whole package. How 'bout letting me unwrap it some?

Rick handed out half dollars and dollar bills, his hat pushed back on his head, sweat on his brow, not used to the heat, the friction. One of Helen Winters's twenties gone, evaporated like the ice cubes in a highball glass. Look for Phyllis Winters, ask about Phyllis Winters. Can't ask about Emily, not at the same clubs.

White and yellow don't mix, unless it's in a cocktail or a Rice Bowl Party, Mister, you won't find Orientals here, taste runs in that direction, try Chinatown. Get yourself a real China doll, Mister, ain't I funny? Should be on the radio . . .

No girl, buddy. No, I'd recognize her . . . I go for blondes. You try Chez Paris? What about Vanessi's?

And then it was midnight, and the bells chimed out from every chromium door in the city, twined with the reproach of stone church towers and the workaday clangs of cable cars, still running into the night.

The city sparkled, her neon winking, shining like a bride on her wedding day. It was night, and the double-lit street lamps danced a fox trot in the fog, and south of Market the overnight to L.A. pulled from the station, rumbling through the rich and fertile land just south of San Francisco, orchards stretched and sleeping, the only light the lantern of a farmer, worried about his crop.

Whistles blew, and longshoremen strode across the piers, unloading cargo from a ship pulled in, crew tired, while the smoke poured from the factories on the shore, paper and glass and steel and aluminum, machine parts made by men bent in a perennial hunch, working through the night, coffee and a cigarette their only companions.

Horns on Nob Hill blared while chauffeurs maneuvered long sleek autos from the Top of the Mark, the new spot for socialites to view the city, their city, the lights and the noise and the hum and the life of it all beautiful, throbbing, more sensual than the perfunctory grope of a banker's son, drunk on gin, eyes on the waiter, hands on his date.

On the way to the apartment, a kiss, a strip, a shove and a grunt, hands soft, nails white, it'll all be over with in a minute, honey, you don't know what you do to me.

It's what you don't do to me that's the problem.

Middle-aged housewives in print nightgowns, wool covers pulled over pendulous breasts, stir in their sleep, nudging their husbands, scooting beneath them on mended flannel sheets, hoping the kids aren't reading a comic book under the covers, listening through the thin walls.

The ferries lay docked on the water, harbor lights left over from Christmas, while young Italian fishermen hold hands with the girl from down the block, eyes shining as dark as her hair.

And still the city shimmered . . . Treasure Island unlit, a promise in the night, a black pearl next to a pirate's chest of yellow, pink and green. Out on the Bay, a foghorn moans in ecstasy, the sound floating upward, blending with the sighs from open bedroom windows.

Midnight, Valentine's Day, 1940.

Rain was hitting the windows in sheets, while Miranda poked at the hamburger steak and baked potato in front of her. The Nite Hawk was out of the way of everything, tucked on a corner of Market and Sixteenth streets, where holidays didn't matter and neither did your clothes.

A drunk sat in the corner, staring out the window, cradling the sugar shaker in his hands like a baby.

Rick said: "I'm getting sick and goddamn tired of telling you to eat. You need energy. Why the hell you thought you'd find it here, I don't know."

His nose was red with irritation and effort and exhaustion, and he reached into his overcoat pocket for his flask and handed it to her.

"Here. Have a drink."

She couldn't explain; he would dismiss the instinct that drove her forward. So she chewed the tough meat, and ate one of the pickles, and thought about Phyllis Winters and a green sedan.

"Rick, where did you say that hit-and-run was? An alley, wasn't it?"

He leaned back, exhaling smoke into the air. "Clarion Alley. Not too far from here, as a matter of fact. Why, Miranda? You heard what Gonzales said. Two different cars."

She leaned forward. "Yeah . . . but you didn't hear what Bobby Henderson said. He thought Phyllis' boyfriend has a Dodge. What if it's the same one?"

He shook his head, defeated and tired. "Then where the hell does the sedan come in, Miranda? Remember—the one that tried to run you over? If you need a reminder, take a look in the goddamn mirror."

She was already pulling out the *Chadwicks* street map, her finger tracing an intersection. "We didn't turn up any more leads on Phyllis downtown. And the only one we've got is Guerrero Street. And Guerrero Street intersects Seventeenth here—just a block from Clarion Alley."

He yawned, his arm rising to cover his mouth, but too slow, too exhausted. "It's after midnight, for Chrissakes. I've gotta work tomorrow morning. Let's go back home. And you need a doctor. You promised—"

"I promised I'd find Phyllis Winters and Emily Takahashi. And I don't have much time. Emily is safe for the time being, I think . . . but Phyllis is expendable. Her father's dead. She's young, addicted to coke and high times. I can't afford to sleep."

He yawned again, this time managing to cover himself, his mouth hanging frozen for a moment in an open rictus.

Miranda said: "Go home. Really, Rick. You've saved me enough for twenty-four hours. You've met your knight-in-shining-armor quota."

He knew she was telling him what he wanted to hear, caught at the gentle sarcasm in her voice, but also heard the gratitude. Warm, affectionate even. He stared at her, at the red-brown hair falling to her shoulders, the long neck and curve of her jawline. The eyes, frank, deep brown, always in check, always in hiding.

He wanted to ask her when she would ever be herself again, ever let herself be close to someone. To a man. To him.

He took another shot of rye instead, stood up from the Formica table, and shoved the chair in. The short-order cook scratched his beard from the kitchen, watching, and poured more pancake batter on the grill.

"Goddamn right, I have. Go to the doctor, Miranda. I can't be your fucking nursemaid—"

"—no one asked you to, Sanders—"

"—and if you won't take care of yourself, how the hell do you expect anyone else to?"

"I don't."

They stared at each other, the cigarette smoke forming a halo of gray around Miranda. Rick pushed his fedora back again, and said, more softly: "This is where we always leave it."

She said: "Go home. Get some rest. I'll call you tomorrow."

He shook his head, the corners of his mouth pulled down. Said, blurting it out: "That pistol of John's still work?"

She looked at him steadily out of the one good eye. "Yes."

He nodded, took off his hat, held it in his hand, hesitated awkwardly, then came back around to her chair, where she still sat. Bent down to her good side, gave her a peck on the cheek.

"Good night, Miranda. Happy Valentine's Day."

The cigarette smoke from the Chesterfield swirled around him, and she watched as he walked out the door into the rainy night, the screen door slamming shut behind him.

Where they always left it.

On the floor, in the air between them. Friends and not friends. Lovers and not lovers.

She stabbed the meat with her fork, breaking it into small chunks, watching it crumble. In the corner, the drunk rocked his sugar shaker, watching the window, the lights of the Market Street railway cars raking past the Nite Hawk.

The cook was standing at his back door, staring out into the night. The haze from his cigarette blended with the smoke from the grill.

She wouldn't see Rick for a while, he wouldn't call, wouldn't return her messages. Then one day, he'd phone, how's everything, Miranda, you got a story? I heard you're in it again.

And they'd dance, and they'd dance, and they'd dance.

Rick Sanders and his motherfucking Irish lilt. Sounded nothing like Johnny, looked nothing like Johnny, but was part of Johnny's world, part of her world, remembered her perfume in New York, and helped her when she needed help, all the time wanting more, wanting what she couldn't give.

It hurt her, twisted her guts, made her ache inside.

Close and not close enough. Friends and not friends. Lovers and not lovers.

She rubbed the cigarette out in the tin ashtray, threw a quarter on the table.

And Miranda walked out into the black, her coat wrapped to keep out the rain drops, pistol heavy in the holster.

She walked down Noe a block to Seventeenth Street. Past rows of Victorian houses and rooming houses, their wooden frames staring with disapproval at the woman walking, her heels click-clacking in the darkness.

Like their queen, they were not amused.

The neighborhood survived the Quake and Fire, and so it judged the new world harshly, watching it deteriorate, as the rooms got cheaper and the company less elegant. Immigrants, San Francisco's unwanted, mostly, who couldn't afford anything else, and needed something close to the railways, close to Bethlehem Steel and Hunter's Point.

Corner markets, a few pharmacies scattered the darkness of Seventeenth Street, as Miranda walked the five and a half blocks to Valencia and Clarion Alley. A Polish church here, a German church there. A Jewish kosher market. Catholics and Jews, shunted from the restricted sections, right skin, wrong religion.

It was an uneasy relationship, suspicion running on both sides, little unity in sharing a target on your back. And saintly Father Coughlin let the radio world know how much Catholics owed Hitler, in helping exterminate the Communist/Jewish/Nonwhite/Liberal/Franklin Roosevelt New Dealers of the World.

There were some younger rabbis who had championed the '34 strike. Friends of Bente, who didn't turn a deaf ear and a blind eye to the Old Country, fast becoming the New Country, one nation, indivisible, with a concentration camp for all.

Miranda admired them, worked with the Abraham Lincoln Brigade in New York, when wealthy Jews were among the few people who tried to save the Spanish Catholics from fascism. Giving aid and succor to people who might—and probably did—hate them. Still didn't make them "Christian" enough.

The cigarette nearly burned her fingers, and Miranda dropped it, cursing. So much for God.

She looked up and down the street, the rain turning to drizzle, street lamps mirrored in the asphalt. She scanned for cars or footsteps or men. And kept walking.

Clarion Alley was a dark, dingy little byway, barely big enough for a car. A couple of trash cans lined the side, leaning drunkenly against a brick building, their mouths caved in like toothless old men.

A man whose name she couldn't remember had been killed here. A gust of wind blew from the south, lifting a torn piece of newspaper from something rotten and vegetal by the trash can. He'd been a gas company worker. That much she could recall.

Wong said Guerrero Street. Clarion Alley was tucked behind Seventeenth, between Mission and Valencia. Guerrero was a little over a block away, and it was the middle of the night, a Tuesday, early morning Valentine's Day in San Francisco, so to Miranda it made sense that she should focus on Guerrero between Seventeenth and Eighteenth. If anything made sense at all.

Either the hit-runs were connected, or they weren't.

If they were, the old man was killed because he discovered something.

Maybe something to do with gas service.

She frowned, digging out another cigarette, and loosened the gun in the holster under her arm.

She could wait until morning, call up the gas company. Get his name from the paper.

But she was here. No time like the present, even when the present was one o'clock in the morning, and the streets were as wet as a stepdaughter's tears.

Miranda headed back toward Guerrero Street, looking for rooming houses or empty, sad flats. Temporary storage was always the name of the game . . .

move around, don't let the cops get too close, not unless you're a well-heeled accountant to the criminal stars, or a lady with a long-running escort service.

Yellow light from a twenty-four-hour market carved a pie slice out of the black sidewalk on Guerrero and Dorland Street. Miranda headed in that direction, backing against the stairway of a tired-looking Queen Anne when she heard the whine of a car engine behind her.

It passed by in a hurry. She didn't see any faces turned toward her. No glint of gun metal, sparkling like ice.

She still hurried to the store.

An old man in a faded suit dozed on a stool, listening to the sounds of a faraway orchestra. Magazines lay strewn on the counter, left there when he'd grown tired of reading them. A hand-lettered sign read KOSHER MEATS AND CHEESES—HOMEMADE SANDWICHES—CAKES.

He hadn't opened his eyes when the door bell jingled, so Miranda cleared her throat.

He didn't fall off the stool, but looked at her, still half-asleep, puzzled.

"You want some aspirin, lady? Somebody hit you? Got a pay phone in the corner . . ."

"I'm OK. Car accident this morning. Listen, I'm sorry to bother you, but I'm looking for someone. She might be in trouble."

That made him hop off the stool for a closer look. He put his hands on the counter, stared at her.

"Lady, you look like you've seen enough for two. Why you chasing more?"

Miranda fished the photo of Phyllis out of her wallet. "This girl. She's in danger."

He scrunched up one side of his face quizzically.

"You a cop?"

"Private detective."

"Not what I want my daughter to do, you understand me. Too dangerous. Look at that face . . . Here, let me get you some ice."

Miranda leaned against the counter, looking around the tiny, cluttered market, took out a cigarette. This was going to be a while.

After a few minutes, he came back with a stained ice bag filled with cubes. "Here . . . put this on your cheek and it won't hurt me so much to see it."

"Thanks." She held it to her face. "Have you seen that girl?"

The old man stuck a finger in his ear, turned it around twice, frowned, and shook his head slowly.

"No. I don't think so. What kind of trouble?"

"Men trouble. Bad kind. She's with a flashy-looking Italian."

He thought it over. "Italian stopped by last night. Not flashy, like yours. Bought three or four sandwiches and some magazines."

"Do you remember what he bought exactly?"

The shopkeeper sighed, leaned on the counter. "My days and nights get all mixed up. I think it was . . . maybe nine, ten o'clock. Not like this, you understand. I remember because I never seen him before."

"You remember the magazines?"

He shambled out from behind the counter, and walked toward the magazine rack, thumbing through *Life, Time, Good Housekeeping, Family Circle, Saturday Evening Post,* and then a small section of movie fan magazines.

"I think it was some of these. Radio and TV stars. He don't seem like the type, you know what I mean? Not the type to read anything more than the paper, and maybe a racing form. Yeah . . . I remember Shirley Temple on the cover of one."

"What about the sandwiches?"

"I don't remember, lady. Nothing stands out. Pastrami on rye, headcheese, ham and Swiss . . ."

"One was a ham and Swiss? You're sure?" Phyllis's favorite sandwich, according to Bobby.

He shrugged. "Seems right, but it's getting on two o'clock in the morning. How's the cheek?"

She took off the bag, felt her face. "Much better—thank you. All right . . . this Italian. Did he say anything about where he was, where he was staying?"

"Guerrero, I think he said. Talkative, he was. Said he just moved in, house was empty for a while."

Miranda tried to keep her voice calm, nonchalant.

"Any idea where a house like that might be?"

"Couple of places. One up the street by Seventeenth, one down by Eighteenth. Don't know if somebody moved in, but they've been empty."

"Color to the house?"

He shrugged. "Everything is gray in San Francisco after one o'clock in the morning. One has a boarded-up window at the bottom, if that helps."

"Is that the one by Seventeenth?"

"Yeah. You sure you don't want any aspirin?"

She bought a small bottle. Tried to give him a dollar, but he wouldn't take it.

"You come back when you're hungry, try a sandwich. When you can chew good with that cheek."

Miranda thanked him and headed back into the darkness of Guerrero Street.

The house was still.

Green-gray, it clung to the lot with desperation, neglect seeping through it from all sides. A gap in roof tiles on the cylindrical turret, the boarded-up window, the stairs covered in mildew. A drip from the broken gutter hit the ground, thudding like distant gunfire.

The house waited, silently, dreaming of better days.

Miranda blended into the shadows by the boarded window, away from the sputtering street lamp a house down, away from the occasional car light that meandered down Guerrero. She unbuttoned her coat, reached in, took the pistol from the shoulder holster, her left breast and shoulder sighing with relief.

This was trespassing. On a case she'd been fired from. She could lose her license.

But only if someone found out who wanted her to.

And maybe Duggan had done her a favor. Maybe they'd let her alone for a while.

She walked around the house to the rear fence. It was mostly intact, except for a rotten board. It would be tight. Try the other side.

A car drove by, the sound of shrieks and laughter incongruous in the somber neighborhood. She froze against the fence, the gun at her side, and then cautiously walked under the tree near the window, around the front steps, toward the other side.

She peered inside the window, wiping it first, fingers smudged with wet dirt and coal dust.

A very faint light seemed to trickle down a main stair. Nothing she could see definitively from below.

Miranda walked to the back, where the house was closer to its neighbor. A small gate opened into the rear yard.

She leaned against the wood, listening for the heavy breathing of a sleeping dog or the rattle of a chain.

Nothing.

She propped her handbag against the corner of the house, on the damp ground out of the light. Then, gun in hand, she slowly opened the latch of the gate. It was rusty and it squeaked, but it swung open, protesting, and she was in.

Overgrown weeds. Yellow mustard, a few California poppies. The smell was sweet—eucalyptus and elm, borne on the post-rain breeze from the Western Addition.

The back of the house offered two more windows and a door.

The window wouldn't do much good. It would face the rear of the stairs, and she thought the light was on the first floor.

Taking breaths to calm herself, make herself alert and ready, Miranda moved toward the door.

Old paint flaking off, leaving an exposed gray, the doorknob tarnished.

She tried to turn it, and it responded, squeaking again, but offering no lock, no resistance.

She cocked the Spanish pistol, moving the safety into position. The noise sounded deafening, and she stood still, waiting. Counted a minute.

No noise. No steps. No light.

Miranda slid inside the house, waiting by the door for her eyes to adjust to the darker interior. Enough light was coming from the windows to let her see there wasn't much furniture; even the kitchen looked barren. No carpets.

She stepped heel to toe on the wooden floorboards, as noiselessly as she could. Made her way to the back of the stairway and around the front, an old, ornate balustrade missing some rails.

A faint, very dim light landed at her feet.

She breathed again. And started walking up the stairs.

The fifth one creaked, and she stopped. Belch of a foghorn made her bring the gun up. She lowered it slowly.

Too shaky, Miranda. Steady. Shaky can kill you.

Top of the landing. Light was brighter, sliding underneath a crack in a door. Cigarette smoke and liquor made a dense cloud of scent, like a cheap bar on the wharf.

She sighed, thought about it, thought about the hat she wanted at City of Paris. Thought about Paris. And New York, and Johnny. And Betty.

She bent down to the keyhole. She couldn't see much. Maybe a bed.

Miranda held the pistol ready in her right hand, tried to open it, slowly, carefully, with her left.

It was locked, and the clicking noise made her hold her breath, waiting for a sound or a bullet from the other side.

Nothing.

She pulled a hairpin from her hat. No pliers, but maybe she wouldn't need them. She worked the pin around the keyhole for about five minutes until she could hear a couple of clicks in the silence.

Deep breath again.

Tried the doorknob.

This time it responded. She opened it, keeping her hand on the knob and turning it back around manually so that it wouldn't recoil and click again.

Waited, breathing hard.

Let her eyes adjust.

Nothing.

She shoved it open, just enough.

A light with no shade was on the floor next to a bed with no headboard or frame. Sandwich wrappings, coffee cups, and movie and radio magazines lay scattered, along with a few clothes. An old radio lay on the other side of the bed, static droning from the torn speakers.

A blond woman was strewn across the mattress. Bruised, naked.

Phyllis Winters.

Part Four

Valentine's Day

Twenty-one

Somehow she woke the girl, kept her from screaming, ignored the tears and lethargy of the drugs, and coaxed and bullied her into getting up and moving. Wrapped her in a man's jacket hanging over a closet door-knob, hustled her down the stairs, still ignoring the sobs and shrill objections, the demands for food and "Where's Sammy?" over and over and over again.

Didn't take the time to count the bruises on her legs and breasts and inner thighs, or think about the terror that shook her too-thin body when she froze outside, paralyzed, and tried to run.

The wind was cold, and the fog wrapped and enveloped them, and Miranda hoped it would make them invisible to the occasional car on Guerrero Street, or to the men who had used the house, used the girl's body, and could return at any time.

She pulled her, pushed her, until they reached a streetlight by the old man's market.

Phyllis was quiet, now, docile and compliant, her eyes half closed, her naked legs broken out with goose bumps that looked like a child's chicken pox.

Miranda held her upper arm tight, but the girl wasn't complaining anymore. She let go for a moment, hoping she wouldn't have to chase, not tonight, not with her leg. Put the pistol back in her holster, never taking her eyes from Phyllis.

What was left of her.

The old man was dozing on the stool again when Miranda pushed the girl through the door. He woke up suddenly, his forehead wrinkling, and held a hand to his mouth.

"My God! What—who—?"

"You got a blanket? She doesn't have any clothes."

He looked again, his eyes squinting as if he were blinded by light. Then he shook his head, and moved.

"Right away, I get you something."

While he rummaged in the back, Miranda held the girl up. She was staring at the movie magazines, her jaw slack, her blue eyes unblinking. The old man came out with a thin wool blanket, patched here and there with discolored fabric, and handed it to Miranda, not looking.

"You need the police, maybe?"

"Yeah. Tell them Miranda Corbie found the Winters girl. You got some coffee somewhere?"

He grunted. "I get you coffee. Maybe put something in it, yes?"

"Not too much. Can we stay in the back while we wait? I don't want anyone to see her."

"This way."

He led them through a gate to the register area, and from there past a faded black curtain, the fabric stiff. Crates and boxes filled the small room. A couple of moths fluttered around a single yellow lightbulb, banging themselves against the glass. She steered Phyllis to the saggy cot with a rumpled sheet, holding up the rear wall. The door on the right led to the toilet, orange rust stains along the edges of the upraised seat.

Miranda put gentle pressure on her shoulder until the girl sat down, her body responding automatically.

The old man nodded, back turned, while Miranda wrapped the blanket around the girl. Then he pushed his way through the curtain. Miranda could hear him by the food area, pouring something into a cup. Phyllis's eyes were closed again, her mouth still slightly open.

He returned, out of breath.

"Coffee. Strong and old. I added something to it, not much. I go to call the police now."

Miranda took the coffee from his shaking hands.

"Thank you. I'm sorry to troub—"

"Hush, young lady. I go to call."

She listened for the reedy tones of the old man's voice, his accent stronger than earlier tonight. Phyllis's head was drooping, slack. Miranda stood up, and tried to push her back, to make her recline.

She was surprised when the girl grabbed her arms, fought her. An almost-awareness wrenched her face. Panic and fear. The odor of urine rose from the cot.

"No . . . no more."

The girl clung to her, as limp as a rag doll, the white skin on her thin arms translucent between the bruises.

Miranda held her, stroked her hair, dry and brittle. Held her, and murmured words that meant nothing, words she had said before to other women, women who lived in small Spanish villages, who had been left behind, who had no one to hold them, no one to help them.

Women who fought their own wars.

With pitchforks and kitchen knives. Jagged bottles and empty fists.

Until they lost or died, the bottle dropping from fingers pried open, the knife falling, falling, falling, their mouths open and shrieking a name.

Spoils.

Conquered.

Broken.

Like their little houses. The roofs torn, the doors broken down.

Like the house on Guerrero Street.

The Hall was warm, quiet, subdued.

The matron pried Phyllis from Miranda. A squat woman with eyes that weren't unkind, but had seen too much to be generous. The girl wouldn't let go at first, shaking, then shrunk into herself, refusing to speak. She'd said nothing to Miranda since the store, had gone quietly into the police car, the shock protecting her from self-consciousness.

Then Helen Winters hurried in, breathless, her veil askew, her nails chipped, heels tap-tap-tapping on the marble floors. The girl looked back at Miranda before she retreated, before she shut down everything that happened to her and everything that would happen to her.

Head slack, eyes blank, she turned and walked in infant steps to her stepmother.

The attorney with Helen glanced at Miranda, and glanced again, whispering something to his mistress while she threw her arms open, ever the sacrificing mother, ever forgiving. She'd seen *Stella Dallas* at least five times.

Miranda recognized him from his run for a board of supervisor's seat. Phyllis held herself like a bird with two broken wings. She wasn't recognizing anyone.

Mr. Would-be Supervisor discussed business with the cops; Johnson wasn't in yet. He'd be disappointed at not getting to call in the FBI.

Miranda leaned against a wall, a Chesterfield between her fingers, watching the scenes unfold. Attorney, mistress, stepdaughter. Dead father. Dead husband. Cops caught by surprise. The girl would need time, and care, and patience. She'd get the time, once Helen stuck her in a mental home. The other two would depend on where they put her.

The attorney would keep most of it out of the papers. And he'd keep Helen Winters out of jail, for anything she knew or didn't know about her husband and the drugs and the Italian named Sammy. And soon Miranda would get a check in the mail, made out for the full amount of her fee and a little more, while everybody pretended that Helen had never called to cancel the contract. Step right up, lady, we can erase your memory with money. Only five hundred dollars for a new history, a bargain at any price. Don't bother to not cash it, girlie, you won't be able to testify anyway.

Nothing to testify about.

There was still the little matter of who killed Lester, but Mr. Would-be Supervisor would make sure the press got the right script about the forgiving little woman with the wayward daughter and blackmailed husband. He'd been caught in a trap, murdered by smugglers and thieves. No one would find out if Lester was guilty or not.

He was dead, after all. Yesterday's news. And nobody much gave a shit who killed him.

Just like Eddie Takahashi.

Miranda dropped the cigarette and rubbed it out into a gray streak in the marble. The attorney finished his conversation with one of the cops, and hurried after Helen and Phyllis, closing ranks on the girl, surrounding her, already telling her what happened until her reality would be swallowed up by theirs, wholly owned, never regained.

Miranda watched the family reunion and hasty departure until the echo of Helen's heels bounced against the walls and drifted on, blending into the low hum of nightly business at the Hall of Justice.

Click-clack. Click-clack.

So many nails in a coffin.

Phyllis had tried to escape once. Too young to wait for adulthood, too young to be patient. And now she'd live a half life, of doubts and self-loathing, pretending and hiding. Drowning them out, perhaps, in secret bottles. The marble hall lit with gold would always seem dark to her. So would the dances and the bands, the clubs and the clinking glasses, and the touch of the man, the safe man, the older man she'd be told to love and dutifully spread her legs for, all thought, all feeling, all pleasure locked up with the pain.

Miranda leaned against the cold stone, her eyes closed. Then she shook herself and lit another cigarette.

And phoned Rick.

Cops slouched through offices and dully lit corridors, waiting to process the knife fights and split lips of a lovers' evening, spell broken with dawn. Tonight and tomorrow night. Bubbles bursting along with zippers and fasteners, remorse and tears running like the rain.

Jokes about another St. Valentine's Day massacre. Then the arrival of the boyfriend or husband, hat in hand or spitting angry. And the girl with the black eye would shuffle out with him, sorry for making a fuss.

Lesson over.

Just another lovers' spat.

Miranda sat at the desk and smoked, watching the cops drift by along with the nicotine. Johnson had come in for his stake, marked his territory, barking orders at no one in particular, and then turned on the siren on his way down to Guerrero Street. Noise always made the Johnsons of the world feel better.

Rick was down there already, waiting for him. He'd come awake at the information, rapped out a "Got it" to Miranda over the phone. She didn't expect to hear from him. She'd just read the papers the next day. Today. This afternoon.

She wasn't sure why she was waiting. Someone to talk it through with, someone to throw around ideas. Someone to fill an empty space. Gonzales drove straight to the house on Guerrero when they called. From a warm bed. Or wherever he was when they phoned him.

Miranda took a deep inhale of the Chesterfield, feeling the soothing bite of the smoke hit her lungs. The night shift was always understaffed, half on the take and the other half asleep. At least Grogan was one of the sleepy ones.

"So you think we're talking Sammy Martini here?"

He held a fist up to his mouth and yawned. "You heard Johnson. Girl hasn't identified anybody, and all we got is your description from hearsay and you sayin' she said 'Sammy.'"

"Don't you know anything, Grogan?"

"Yeah. I know I wanta go home. So quit asking me questions."

She leaned forward, pointing the cigarette at him.

"Listen to me, goddamn it. The girl was passed around when he got tired of her. On her way to getting dumped, or sold, or traded. Or murdered. They stashed her at that house, ran over the old man when he found out what they were doing there. That sounds like Sammy Martini to me."

"He's L.A.'s problem, Miranda, why the hell would he move up here?"

She looked for an ashtray, couldn't find any, and bent over the desk close to Grogan, stamping the cigarette out in a hole near the typewriter.

"Because he is L.A.'s problem. Because things got too hot, and he found fresher water in the Bay and fresher meat in San Francisco. Because he's got a partner or more than one working out of the Olympic Hotel or Chinatown."

"Chinatown?" Grogan shook his head, swallowed some cold coffee out of a jade-colored mug. "Now I know you're nutty. You won't find Aye-ties workin' with Chinks."

Miranda sat back, studying him. "Spoken like a typical cop."

He waved his hand at her. "Why don't you go home and get some sleep, for God's sake? You seen Johnson already. Gonzales'll be the one to tie this in with the murder and the drugs. You can talk to him later, he'll be at the house for a while. Along with your other boyfriend, the reporter—how many you stringin' these days, Miranda?"

"Go to hell, Grogan." She stood up, with difficulty. "Rick's the best goddamn reporter in the city."

"And you're pissed off at not going along."

"It's my fucking case."

"And the city's, sweetheart. Don't forget it."

Her mouth twisted up on the side that wasn't swollen. "How could I forget? So nice of you boys to let me share."

Grogan grinned. "Don't mention it. But go home. You look like shit."

She put both hands on the desk, leaning over to face him. "Tell me one thing. Has anybody seen Phil?"

His face got noncommittal, cautious. "He's around. That's all you need to know, Miranda. Go home." Grogan opened a drawer, busied himself with feeding fresh paper to the typewriter.

Her hands curled up into fists, resting on the desk. She rapped the scarred wood with the knuckles of her right hand.

"Yeah. You're right. That's all I need to know. Along with when Duggan gets out of the psychiatric ward and decides to come after me again."

Grogan looked up from the typewriter. "Go home, Miranda. The Fair'll be open soon."

They stared at one another. Grogan dropped his eyes first, started to type. She watched him for a few seconds, then said softly: "Back to the Fair and the Gayway, the pickpockets and the pimps. Where I belong. Not exactly the kitchen, but not the boys' club, either. Thanks, Grogan. And fuck you, too."

She turned and walked away. The clack of Grogan's typewriter never missed a beat.

5:30 A.M. by the clock on Old St. Mary's. Chinatown, already long awake in the gray-black dusk that passed for dawn.

Miranda decided to walk home, taking the same route of four days before. No drunken sailors, no brass band.

No Rice Bowl Party.

No Eddie Takahashi lying dead on Sacramento Street.

Pallid red light from Buddhist altars spilled over the black tar, a Chinatown dawn two hours early. Her footsteps drowned in car honks and wooden shutters opening, an occasional pigeon still cooing from last night. Before her, San Francisco lay there and winked, redolent and glistening with sin and lamplight, forever a girl you didn't take home to Mother.

Men in work uniforms leaving for the factories on the east side of town, men with heads bent, arms and minds tired from repetition on the assembly lines, straggling in after the night shift and a beer at Tomasso's.

The White Fronts and the municipal buses and trains rumbled by, the concert accompanied by an occasional clang from a cable car. Miranda walked steadily on sore legs, waved to No-Legs Norris on Grant and Bush, who shook his head in response to her questioning hand. He'd hear about Phyllis Winters soon, if he already didn't know more than she did.

She thought about the cops. Gonzales, Duggan. Johnson and Grogan. Phil.

The boys' club. They loved her and hated her, used her and ignored her, tried to forget she existed, tried to keep her where they thought she belonged. One or two hoping he'd be the one.

Maybe some day she'd meet a cop she wouldn't have to say "fuck you" to. But she didn't think so.

She crawled upstairs, the elevator out. Roy was the doorman this morning, old Leo sleeping one off in his own small apartment bed.

No one, Miss Corbie. Yes, he was sure. No one tried to come upstairs or deliver a package, no one asked for her at all.

Her feet trudged the four flights up. Skidding, heavy, sore. A man ran down beside her in a hurry, business suit rumpled, late for trading on the stock exchange. Wheat or oil? Just call Marvin.

He tipped his hat, left it perched sideways. She couldn't remember if hers was still on her head; stopped, felt, found it.

The door opened, and the smell of warm wood floor and shut-in apartment air rushed to meet her. A package lay on the credenza. She turned it over, making sure it was from Edith.

Eddie's bloody bandages, safely wrapped. She walked to the window, shedding her coat and bag as she went.

She pushed up the sill, the noise rising, filling the apartment. Whistles and clangs. Car horns in basso profundo and tenor. And the sound of voices, everyday people, asking directions, reading the headlines out loud, ordering coffee and doughnuts, how about the horses, buddy, muddy track and all, you got a tip for Tanforan today?

Miranda drank it in, closing her eyes, the Spanish pistol still in the holster, tight against her left side. She smelled the air, newly cleaned city of sailors and seagulls, full of possibilities and the promise of the morning.

And thought of the promise she'd made to Wong.

Emily Takashashi was out there, somewhere. Maybe underground or in a tunnel, left in a copse of Golden Gate Park or on a beach in Pacifica. But not according to the air, the thin warmth on her battered cheek. There was still a chance.

Not much of one for Phyllis. Alive and dead at the same time. Still, she was young. Never young enough to forget. But maybe old enough to make a life.

At least it was pretty to think so.

Miranda reached around to her left, and pulled out the pistol, holding the heft of it in her hands. She remembered the last time she'd killed a man with it.

She still wasn't sorry.

She left the window open behind her, opened the bedroom door, and opened that window, too. The gauze curtain billowed with the up draft and the energy of the voices below.

She unbuckled the holster, carefully setting the gun down on her nightstand, the symbol of the International Brigades carved into the leather, the rivulets smooth with time and her fingertips.

Miranda let them run over the crevices again, tracing the outline.

She stripped off the rest of her clothes, and climbed into bed, facing the pistol and the open window.

Her eyes closed, and she slept for three hours.

Twenty-two

By the time she got back to the Hall of Justice, cheek still swollen, dressed carefully in a dark blue two-piece suit, with a wool coat in case of more rain, and a stomach full of jelly doughnut and bitter coffee—they'd decided how to handle her.

Johnson was nowhere to be seen, but Gonzales met her in the hallway, greeted her warmly. The suit was crisp, the hat clean, and he smelled like expensive tobacco and well-worn leather. He didn't look as if he'd spent the night on Guerrero Street.

"Miss Corbie—we have some news for you."

Miranda reached for the cigarette case in her coat pocket. He held the lighter out before it was in her hand.

"I would offer you one of mine, but I think you prefer Chesterfield, do you not?" His voice held a certain admiration. She leaned over the flame, briefly looking up into his eyes.

"I like the simple things, Inspector."

They stood together, awkward, while he opened his mouth as if he wanted to say something. He checked his watch instead, took her elbow.

"May I?" he asked softy.

Miranda shrugged. He steered her into an empty interrogation room.

She walked in, looked around, and recognized the table. Same scratches, same stains. No Duggan.

This time four chairs huddled around it, one filled by Regan, the narcotics detective, and Parker, the waterfront dick. Both of them stood when she entered, Parker unfolding himself from the chair, all legs and knees and plaid flannel shirt.

Miranda stared at him and said: "I hear you're investigating Winters. Would've been nice to know that a couple of days ago."

The barely perceptible squint reminded Miranda of William S. Hart or Tom Mix. "Old West" draped off Parker's lanky brown shoulders like dust on the wooden sidewalks of Deadwood. She expected to hear the squeak of leather and the clatter of rusty spurs.

He turned toward a bucket someone had dug up from somewhere, possibly the morgue, and spat out a wad of tobacco. The white enamel side rang with the force of the ejaculation.

"I *was* investigating Winters, Miss Corbie. Case will be closed, now, thanks to you."

If he'd been wearing a Stetson, he would've tipped it. But the look on his face wasn't exactly ice-cream social.

Regan leaned forward, hands on the table, twitchy. Acted like he snorted the stuff, but clean, as far as Miranda knew.

"That was some find. The Takahashi place. It was coke, all right—and traces of opium and heroin, too. It all adds up."

Miranda sat down across from him, crossed her legs. Coffee cups in various states of cleanliness sat in front of each of the men. Parker and Regan took chairs, Parker's knees jutting up like spikes.

Gonzales asked: "Can I get you some coffee, Miss Corbie?"

She shook her head, and he pulled out the chair next to her, carefully laying his fedora on the table.

"Adds up to what? And why is the case closed? Winters was murdered. Seems like you'd want to—"

Gonzales interrupted, his voice smooth and even. "We're here to bring you up to speed, Miss Corbie. The San Francisco Police Department is much indebted to you. By the way"—he turned to Miranda, and removed the gold cigarette case from inside his suit jacket—"you were in the morning edition. Officially, you called in a tip that we investigated."

She blew a stream of smoke toward the ceiling, and looked up at it, her wide-brim hat hiding her eyes.

"I know how it's played, Gonzales. I just want information. You can take the collar. Ink doesn't much matter in my business."

Another wad of tobacco rang against the pot. "And exactly what business is that, Miss Corbie? I heard you handled divorce cases." Parker's eyes crinkled like he was staring at the prairie sun.

"I handle cases, Parker. All kinds of them. What's your role? Shouldn't you be on a ship?"

Gonzales interrupted again. One of his French cigarettes dangled between his fingers, still unlit. "I asked Inspector Parker to join us earlier. He's remained out of courtesy to you, Miss Corbie."

Miranda stared at Parker's short brown hair, wetted down on a bony skull with something that looked like bear grease. Maybe he was planning to run for office. Cowboy acts always got a lot of votes.

"Thanks. So what the hell is going on? I get down here and Gonzales tells me there's news. What about Phyllis Winters? She ID Sammy Martini?"

The detective shook his head. "Phyllis Winters so far will not identify anyone. She also refuses to explain who Sammy is. Her stepmother has admitted her to a sanitarium in Marin, and our hands are tied at the moment. But you'll be interested to know that the Guerrero Street garage contained a green Dodge coupe . . . the same one used in the hit-and-run killing of Leroy Jones, in Clarion Alley. And it was registered out of San Bernadino to a known associate of Sammy Martini's, a Giuseppe Coppa. The house was rented in his name as well."

"That's it, then—you put out a dragnet for Coppa and Martini?"

Gonzales inhaled his brown cigarette, and shook his head again. "We're taking care of it. We've notified Los Angeles, and Parker here is working with the FBI on the drug smuggling. We want Martini for questioning, certainly. The evidence isn't conclusive. All we have is the Coppa link and your testimony that the girl was asking for a 'Sammy.'"

"And the description. And the drugs. And the fact that Phyllis Winters was fed coke and fucked until he got tired of her. At which point he whored her out to whoever knocked on the door."

Gonzales studied the floor. Parker's thin lips pulled tighter, and Regan drummed his fingers. Miranda rubbed her cigarette viciously into the table, and then flicked it into Parker's slop bucket.

"I knew as soon as she said 'Sammy.' It's his M.O. Drugs and whores, whores and drugs. The Mann Act, gentlemen. What *Spicy Detective Weekly* calls "white slavery." So don't tell me you're taking care of it when you don't have a dragnet out for fucking Sammy Martini."

Gonzales still said nothing, his face red. Regan leaned back, spoke conversationally.

"You know how these wops operate. Everything's in the family. We're getting the goods on the small fry, moving our way up. For fuck's sake, these are businessmen we're dealing with. Everything you've heard about Sammy Martini is rumor . . . legally speaking. He owns clubs in Santa Monica, two in San Diego. You can't walk into Bank of America and demand to see A. P. fucking Giannini, you know?"

Parker's drawl drifted across the table, a knife-edge to it. "We ain't convinced, Miss Corbie. This smuggling gang is big—we're talking crews overseas, crews in Los Angeles, crews in San Francisco. Chinese tong at the head of it—usually is out here. Martini's men tried to muscle in on new territory, stole Winters's daughter to bargain with. But I do know one thing—I ain't never seen a Chinese gang working with one of them Aye-talians. And we got Chinese involved here."

Miranda opened her cigarette case. She was down to two. Gonzales clicked his lighter for her, but she ignored him, took out a book of matches from the Club Moderne, and struck one on the table. She leaned back and looked at the ceiling again, inhaling until the end of the stick glowed red.

"The NYK was a Japanese line, last I checked. And Takahashi is a Japanese name. To be perfectly clear, Parker, we've got Japanese, Chinese, and Italians involved."

The smoke was drifting toward the door, curling into vague shapes before losing focus. Miranda watched it for a few minutes. No one said anything.

Then she lowered her head and faced them again. "Welcome to the melting pot. Though I guess you figure the Chinese don't melt."

A rap on the door broke the tension until Phil walked in behind it. He froze when he saw Miranda. Passed a hand across his forehead, stood against the wall behind Miranda and Gonzales.

His voice was hoarse. "You having a conference?"

The detective uncrossed his legs. "No, sir. Just updating Miss Corbie on the case."

Phil grunted, studied his fingernails. "Go ahead."

Parker spit again. Regan cleared his throat. "Thing is, we don't know if Phyllis Winters will press charges. In fact, with Sutherland as her attorney, we figure she won't—they don't want the girl in the papers, and I can't say as I blame 'em. And without her testimony, we ain't got much of a case against Coppa or Martini, if it even goes that far. They can claim the car was stolen out of the garage—hire a good lawyer—pay off the jury—and we're back to square one."

The tall brown man took out a can of tobacco from his leather jacket, pinched off a wad with two long, bony fingers, and stuck it in his cheek. His voice was slow and deliberate.

"Got a good case on Winters working with this Jap boy, though. The Bureau will keep on it, they're down at the pier with Johnson, lining up crew. NYK will cooperate, of course. And it's a matter for the consulates, too, Miss Corbie. Japan don't want no more stink with the U.S., especially after the *Panay*, and they'll help us nail the smugglers on their end."

Gonzales added: "We believe Martini is back in L.A. now. And we are also searching for the two men in the green Oldsmobile—the ones that tried to hit you. We think whoever killed Jones hid the car, and tried to confuse the trail by ordering up another green car—and using it."

Miranda was staring at her cigarette critically. "And who might the two men be?"

The detective hesitated, his normal smoothness a little unsure. "Possibly Noldano and Capella, two men linked to Martini. Both wanted on hit-and-run charges in Santa Monica. We think they stole the Oldsmobile and drove it up here at Martini's request. They are also tied to drug interests in the south, mostly marijuana from Mexico. And prostitution rings."

Regan grinned at her, his eyebrow twitching. "They threw some big boys at you, Miranda."

"At least a big car. What about Winters?"

Parker shrugged. "My business is the smuggling. Figure Winters was in it up to his eyeballs. Maybe he didn't like workin' with the Chinese, brought the Aye-talians in, and it backfired on him." A wad of chewed tobacco hit the side of the white can, leaving a dark yellow streak as it slid to the bottom.

Gonzales said: "'Needles' Trakey is out and known to be operating north of Monterey. He's freelance, and the hit on Winters looks like his work. We're hoping to pick him up."

He gave Miranda a small smile. "At least Winters's daughter is safe. Thanks to you."

From behind him, Phil grunted. Regan jumped; they'd forgotten about him. He was still slouched against the wall, still wearing his hat.

"Don't overdo it, Gonzales. You don't want Miss Corbie walking down to her pet newspaper and demanding a retraction."

Miranda let go of the cigarette end and watched it fall to the floor. She rubbed it with the toe of her shoe.

Her voice was even. "You know me better than that, Phil."

Gonzales looked at Parker. "Why don't you lay the rest out?"

Parker repositioned the tobacco in his cheek. "I been investigating Winters for a while. Crew on different NYK ships he was responsible for got suspicious. Missing paperwork, Winters acting funny, showin' up at night. There's been a lot of junk comin' into L.A. from foreign countries—their war been makin' it easier to get it out."

Regan interrupted. "The tailor shop proved he was working with Eddie Takahashi. Makes sense, 'cause Takahashi was a Jap and NYK's a Jap shipping line. He could speak the language. And we figure whatever gang Takahashi ran with—maybe Filipino Charlie—was behind the operation up here. I mean, the kid was young, too young to be too important, know what I mean?"

Miranda studied her fingernails. "Yeah. I know what you mean. So did you pick up Charlie?"

"Yeah. Late yesterday. But we had to let him go. He's never been involved in anything real serious. And he's got alibis for everything. You know how it goes."

She nodded, still looking at her hands. "What about Wong?"

Regan shrugged. "Gonzales gave us the information, but we ain't found him yet. You know how many goddamn Wongs there are in San Francisco? Fucking bastards breed like flies. He's a lot more likely than the wop, I'll say that—slant-eyes stick together—right, Parker?"

Parker leaned back, laced his hands behind his neck, what passed for a grim smile on his face.

"That's the way we figure it. Y'see, Winters wanted more money. He tries to deal with the Aye-ties, and they up and kidnap his daughter almost four weeks ago, only she don't know it's kidnapping. Willing, you might say."

Miranda took out her last cigarette. Gonzales held out the lighter, his eyes on hers. This time she used it. She sat back up, took a long drag. Looked over at the cowboy.

"You might say that. But I guess wherever you're from they marry 'em off when they're ten."

The thin, stoic line of Parker's mouth grew wide with indignity. "Now, see here, lady—"

Phil interrupted him. "You're wrong already, Parker."

Silence slammed into the room. Regan cleared his throat again. "Goddamn airless closet gets to me. Can we finish this up?"

Gonzales's face was red. "Parker and Regan believe Winters was shopping his services to another combination. Martini, it seems. The gang he worked with up here was Oriental. We're watching Ming Chen, by the way—we think he may be an outlet for Chinatown drug traffic."

Miranda nodded her head and took a deep drag on her Chesterfield. "So you think Filipino Charlie or Wong or a mysterious Oriental Chinatown tong murdered Winters because he was bringing in an Italian takeover for more drug-smuggling money. Is that it?"

Regan was the only one to respond, and he looked delighted. "That's it exactly."

Parker rang his bell again, squinting his eyes at her. "You see something wrong with that, Miss Corbie?"

Miranda shrugged. "Not if you like reading *Dime Detective*. I'd like to know why you think a Chinese gang murdered Winters when an Italian visited him that night."

Gonzales leaned forward. "An Italian? How did you—"

"Elevator man told me."

Regan was draining his cold coffee, and nearly spit it out. "A dinge? You're takin' the word of a—"

Phil said: "Never mind, Regan. I'll tell Miss Corbie."

Regan wiped his mouth. Gonzales took out another cigarette. Miranda noticed his hand trembling. She watched Phil make his way around to the other side of the small table. Facing her.

She turned toward Gonzales. "Did you get anything on Joe Gillio?"

His mouth was open to respond, when Phil laughed harshly. "What sort of fantasy is this? Joe Gillio is a respected businessman, Corbie. You oughta know better than that."

She was still looking at Gonzales. "Joe Gillio was a bootlegger, Phil. You're the one who ought to know better."

Regan stared up at Phil, puzzlement on his broad face. "What's this about Gillio?"

Miranda flung around in her chair toward the narcotics man. "He's an Italian, Regan. You know, they like it all in the family. Just like the Irish."

Regan's mouth opened and shut like a fish.

Phil stood with his hands balled into fists, and stuck them into his pockets. "So here's who murdered Winters, Miranda—"

"—Needles, you just said so."

"Not by himself." Phil leaned forward, his eyes too shiny. "He had help. Your old friend. Betty Chow."

Miranda lost her breath. "What? What the hell are you—"

Gonzales's voice was low. "The maid at the Pickwick identified her picture as the Chinese woman who saw Winters that night. We believe she was working with whatever Oriental gang Takahashi was moving in."

Phil was breathless, excited by his triumph. He took his hands out of his pockets, started to walk around the table. "She was part of them, Miranda. She helped kill Winters. And then they killed her. The end, as they say in the movies."

He circled back until he stood in front of her again, his legs apart, his gray hair curly and slick with sweat. Miranda finally looked up at him, kept looking until he passed a shaking hand over his face and turned away to light a cigarette.

She ignored Parker and Regan, and stared at Gonzales.

"And Eddie Takahashi?"

Gonzales focused on his cigarette. "Same thing, Miss Corbie. Part of the gang, the gang killed him. You say he owed someone money. He didn't pay."

Miranda looked around the table. Gonzales wouldn't meet her eyes. Regan nodded his head energetically. Phil was facing the wall, his cigarette forgotten between his fingers. Parker hawked up a large wad of phlegm and spit it in the bucket.

It was still ringing when she scraped her chair back and stood up.

"Oh, Eddie paid. And so will his sister. She's been missing since he was murdered. But she doesn't fit your neat little summary too well, does she?"

Phil coughed, and waved a hand dismissively without looking at her. "She got the money and she ran away with it. You'll probably find her in a whore-house in Japantown. Your job, not ours."

The other cops looked at him, and looked away again quickly. She pulled her gloves on tighter, paused, and turned to Parker.

"You could use a bigger slop bucket. Try about six feet deep."

The door banged behind her.

Twenty-three

The air was fresh and clean, with the kind of false heartiness that surrounds college football games. Flower hawkers in Portsmouth Square next to the bail bonds office. Violins shrilling from jukeboxes and gramophones, while tenors and sopranos whined about Soft Lights and Sweet Music because It's a Big Wide Wonderful World and Love is Just Around the Corner.

Miranda got out the cigarette case and leaned against Lotta's Fountain. "My Baby Just Cares for Me" tinkled from a piano and a gin-scratched voice somewhere up Kearny. Get drunk enough and you'll believe it, lady.

Solace was empty. No more sticks. Maybe Gladys stashed a few packs of Chesterfields for her. She watched the traffic go by, men nervously eying the flower stands. Roses and candy time, gents. Buy her a heart-shaped box and show her how much you care. Women don't ask for much.

Piano keys crashed, and someone put on a scratchy record of Ruth Etting, singing about tenderness and heroes.

Some hero. Etting was just another show business broad who married a gangster. Miranda hurried across Market Street, dodging a yellow cab in the middle of the crosswalk. Back to the office. Another cigarette, a shot of Old Taylor. It was Valentine's Day, after all.

A box of these chocolates will make her forget that shabby dress, gents, right this way, buy the little lady something you can afford—she'll never know the difference.

Miranda walked into the Monadnock lobby, trying to shut out the voices and music in her head. Coffee and bourbon and a smoke. That's what she needed. Fuck the chocolate.

The song followed her, relentless, mournful, teary. Women crying over what they don't have, never will have. Her own needs were simple. She wanted the truth.

Not the fucking fantasy the fucking cops dreamed up. Don't rock the fucking boat, lady, get out of it—women and children first. We've got businessmen to protect. Gotta protect 'em from whores, lady. Whores like Betty Chow.

Whores weren't supposed to like it soft and gentle, tinkling piano and sad refrain.

Soft and gentle. Soft-and-fucking-gentle, eighteen years old, gang-raped and left to die a couple of years later, anonymous whore in an anonymous bed, drugs or beaten up. Soft and gentle Sammy Martini, who ran the biggest prostitution ring in L.A., importing twelve-year-olds from Mexico. He liked to handpick the girls. If Sammy fucked them, they brought more on the open market. Good Housekeeping Seal of Approval.

But hell, Phyllis thought she was in love, and that's all we want, isn't it, love on Valentine's Day or any other day. Our only happiness. That's what the songs tell us.

Miranda rubbed her temples, tune louder, words more insistent. Our whole big, wonderful world of happiness. Phyllis and Betty and Miranda, oh my. Throw in Dianne, too, maybe she loved someone once before she had the tumor removed. And beware, my lord, not of jealousy, but of the green-eyed monster called Love, the one that all the singers sing about, the reason for holidays and sunshine and dancing, the red of the roses and the blood on the sheets and all the nice green money it makes us, because if you ain't got it, sister, you're too old or too fat or you use the wrong deodorant, and you'd better change your ways, because there's more of you than us, and you'll want to have babies and a family, that's what you're made for, you're love, love, love, love, love, The Glory of Love, Easy to Love, There is No Greater Love, and if your love isn't here to stay, then sister . . .

. . . *it's all so easy, try a little tenderness*

You may as well dance with the maggots.

"Miranda? Miss Corbie?"

It took her a second to realize someone was talking to her. Another to realize that it was Gonzales. She looked over at the lobby stand. Gladys was staring at her, worry on her face, handing change to a lady in a turban. Miranda started walking toward her, Gonzales following.

"Miss Corbie, I am very sorry—"

"You say that a lot, Gonzales. First with Duggan, and now with what? Business as usual?"

"It is not business as usual. Lieutenant Holden was out of line."

She studied him for a moment. "You agreed with the theory. How Phil delivered it shouldn't make that much goddamn difference."

Gladys was craning her ear toward them while pretending to powder her nose, and studiously ignoring the old man in the dirty suit who was pawing through various photo magazines. Gonzales plucked at Miranda's jacket sleeve, but she flung up her arm and leaned against the counter.

"Gladdy—you got any Chesterfields?"

Gladys flipped a blond curl off her cheek, and looked back and forth between Miranda and Gonzales, throwing out a smile with a lot of teeth.

"Sure, honey, let me look, hang on a second."

She turned to open a storage cabinet, and Miranda felt Gonzales next to her.

"Please . . . if you'll hear me out—"

"How the hell did you get here so quickly? Drive?"

He nodded.

Gladys faced them, empty-handed, a little red in front of Cesar Romero.

"Honey, I'm sorry. We're expecting another shipment this afternoon . . . I thought I put some away for you, but Sophie musta sold 'em."

Miranda sighed. "I'll check back later. Just give me some Raleighs. Thanks, Gladdy."

"Don't mention it, sugar."

The blonde drank in Gonzales, then crooked a finger for Miranda to come closer. She said in a low voice: "You sure you're OK? That cheek looks bad, and so did the look on your face a minute ago. You want me to call somebody?"

Miranda opened the pack of cigarettes and noticed her hands shaking. "I'm all right, Gladdy. Thanks for asking."

Gonzales performed his lighter trick, had it lit and ready by the time the stick was in her mouth. She pointedly turned back to Gladys and slapped a dollar on the counter. "A decent lighter, please, Gladdy. Mine are always blowing out."

The counter girl's eyes grew bigger, darting back and forth between them like a tennis match. Then she pulled a thin chromium and black enamel lighter off a display card, and handed it to Miranda.

"Here's a Ronson Majorette. Can't go wrong with this. And it so happens we've got it on sale for one dollar even. Comes full." She winked at Miranda, snuck a glance at Gonzales. He was still staring at Miranda, his face drawn.

"Thanks, Gladdy. I'll see you later about the Chesterfields."

Gladys nodded, while a bald man in a gaudy suit cleared his throat impatiently, waiting to buy a pack of Chiclets. Miranda picked up the lighter, and lit the Raleigh on the way to the elevator. Gonzales followed behind her.

She pushed four. The Monadnock's newly automated elevators were full of holiday travelers, desperate to reunite for Valentine's Day. Overnight train to L.A. or Coos Bay, a quick hop to Santa Rosa, or Cloverdale, or Sacramento, or Stockton. Chocolate hearts in hand, beating to the tune of "Moonglow." Isn't it romantic?

Gonzales squeezed in next to her. He was persistent, she'd give him that. They rode up in silence, while the women chatted about plans and the men worried about time. "Gotta Get A'goin' to the Golden Gate, to My Fair One at the Fair," ran the cheesy song. Oh, wait—that was last year. No Fair ones this February, no fucking fair, in fact. Say it five times fast enough, lady, and you win a ticket to Midget Village.

Miranda took a drag on the Raleigh, and the elevator doors opened as if they meant it. About five people stepped out, and she followed, threading through them when they bunched in the hallway, trying to decide which way to walk. She could hear Gonzales's footsteps behind her.

Allen's door was open, and he looked up at her when she walked by, looked up again at Gonzales, leaned back in his chair and grinned. Miranda ignored him. When she stopped to get her keys, Gonzales moved beside her, still silent. She shoved open the door, glad to see her chair, unlocked the desk drawer, took out the bottle of Old Taylor, and sank into the leather. Dropped the smoked cigarette butt into the Tower of the Sun ashtray, left it smoldering.

Miranda unscrewed the bottle, took a long drink. Wiped it with her hand, screwed it back on, and shoved the bottle forward on the desk.

"Don't stand on ceremony, Inspector. Take a drink, if you want one. You could use some bourbon."

He looked at her, a little sad, a little embarrassed. Shook his head. "No, thank you, Miss Corbie."

She shrugged, reached out to pick up the bottle, repeated the ritual. Then she shut the Old Taylor in her desk drawer, leaned back in the chair, and looked at him.

"Battlefield courage. I imagine you don't know many women who take it that way."

"Are you fighting a war, Miss Corbie? Is that what you think?"

She lit another Raleigh with the new lighter. "It's not what I think. It's what is, as the philosophers say."

He shook his head, leaned forward with his hat on his knees. "I'm sorry. Holden was out of line, as I said. I did not intend for you to be subjected to that."

She blew a smoke ring toward the window, frowning at the thin line of gray. "Phil's the least of my worries. Frankly, I'm more disappointed in you."

"Me?" The shock made him rise from his seat, and his fedora fell to the floor. He picked it up, threw it in the chair, and walked to the window, then paced back to the front of Miranda's desk.

Gonzales drew a hand across his forehead. She could see sweat glistening on it. "How have I disappointed you? I've risked much, working with you, sharing information, trying to protect—"

"—and that's the fucking problem, Gonzales. Protect. You, Phil, every fucking man I meet tries to protect me. From what? My job? My life? Because it is my life, goddamn it, I've fought for it and earned the right to call it my own. *My* life. Not yours. Not my father's. Not Phil's. And I'm damn good at what I do, too damn good to see what I saw this morning."

She was standing, now, her face white. Fists clenched, cigarette forgotten.

"You think Parker doesn't want to hush this up? He was investigating Winters, and the man turns up murdered. That doesn't look so good on his record. So easy answers, Gonzales, easy targets. The usual list of public enemies. Don't look farther than Chinatown, we've got Chinese involved. Or is it Japanese? God knows, none of you motherfuckers bother to recognize the difference."

She sank back into her chair, not looking at him. Pried the Raleigh out from between her fingers, took a long drag. Gonzales stared at her.

"I do know the difference, Miss Corbie. I didn't report your Gillio theory because I don't think it would have been accepted. Not because I didn't accept it. I'd like to find a connection between Martini and Gillio and Filipino Charlie and your Mr. Wong."

Miranda didn't bother to face him this time. Her voice was weary. "Then why didn't you say something, Gonzales? Why toe the party line this morning? I expected . . . I expected more from you."

He reddened, didn't speak for a minute. Headed back to the window, opened the ledge. Miranda smoked in silence, staring at the opposite wall.

Gonzales hesitantly moved to the side of her desk. "Perhaps I could use some of that bottled courage. Do you mind?"

She pivoted the chair, opened the drawer without looking at him, handed him the bottle, her fingers brushing his.

Gonzales took it from her, unscrewed the top, and drank for a few seconds. He replaced it, handed the bottle to her. Miranda locked it back in the drawer. He resumed his seat.

He studied his fedora for a minute. Miranda blew another smoke ring.

"Your friend—Betty—"

"—was not a killer. Maybe she was there that night—the thought had occurred to me—but it wasn't to help kill Winters. Betty was . . . a good girl, Gonzales. Maybe that's hard for you to understand."

He shook his head. "It is not."

She looked at the half-smoked cigarette between her fingers. "Then you're in the minority. They're railroading her. Because she's Chinese, and not from one of the ruling families. No family to speak of, actually. She's a dead escort, which in their eyes makes her a dead whore. So she may as well be a dead accomplice to murder."

Miranda rubbed her eyes with her thumb, and turned to him, speaking softly. "I'm going to clear her name."

Gonzales hesitated, dusting imaginary specks off his fedora. His voice was heavy.

"That will be difficult. There is word from the top, Miss Corbie. The new chief does not want the department to . . . to spend too much of its resources on the Winters affair. He wants an answer quickly."

"And he doesn't give a fuck whether it's the right answer. So you and Phil wrapped one up in a bow, and handed it to him. Strictly Chinese affair. Let the Orientals kill themselves, and serves Winters right and all that."

"The maid testified—"

Miranda jumped up from the chair, strode toward the safe. "Fuck the maid! She testified that she saw a Chinese woman in the same dress as the picture you showed her. And maybe it was Betty—but that doesn't prove a fucking thing, Gonzales, and you know it!"

She unlocked the safe door, took out the list she'd written and the newspapers from the Pickwick. Crossed the room, and threw them on the desk, scattering the sheets of newsprint.

"I've heard the tune. It plays whenever the wrong class of people get murdered. And the cops only listen to the wrong class when they incriminate one of their own."

He stood up, his voice rising. "I interviewed her myself, Miss Corb—"

"So what? Did you talk to the elevator operator? Cheval, who saw a flashily dressed Italian go up and not come down? Or don't you talk to Negroes?"

"I speak to whomever—"

"Did you pin the maid down on her times? On whether she'd cleaned the room? I found these newspaper sections in the trash can, and they had one thing in common—ship arrivals. And you probably didn't bother to ask Estelle about the stationery, either."

"What about the stationery?"

Miranda gave him a withering look. "He used it, Gonzales. Winters wrote someone that night. But I forget, you're the delivery boy for neat and tidy packages."

He was staring at the floor. "That's not fair. Obviously, I wouldn't have come here, leaving behind my work, the men laughing at me, chasing you to tell you—"

Miranda twisted her cigarette in the ashtray, walked up to him, looking him square in the face.

"Just why the hell did you come here, Inspector?"

For a moment, their eyes locked, hers uncompromising, direct and honest. Before Miranda could react, he grabbed her shoulders with both hands, pulled her to his chest and had his mouth on hers, hot and angry, trying to open her mouth with his.

She parted her lips without thought, responding to the warmth and pressure of his body. Responding to something inside of herself. For a moment, she enjoyed the scent of expensive European tobacco and sweat, his tongue devouring hers. Not knowing where she was. When she was. Who she was.

A church bell south of Market rang the half-hour. Miranda wrenched herself away from him, breathing hard. And threw everything she had into a right cross to his nose. Gonzales staggered backward, starting to bleed.

She was shaking. Walked to the desk drawer, pulled out the .22.

"You miserable bastard. I liked you, Gonzales. But that wasn't enough, was it?"

He was covering his nose with both hands and his display handkerchief. The eyes that met hers no longer angry. Full of pain. Embarrassment. And something more underneath. As always.

She cocked the .22. And pointed it at him.

"Get the fuck out of my office. And out of my sight."

He groped at the chair, picking up his hat with one hand. Red was seeping through the handkerchief.

"There's a lavatory on the first floor. I hope I broke your fucking nose."

He looked up at her, shook his head slightly. "It's not broken."

She sat in her chair, still holding the gun. He was standing before her, searching her face.

"Too bad." She said it lightly. Then she waved the gun a little. "I meant what I said. Get out of my office. You're useless to me."

The words seemed to hit Gonzales harder than her fist. She watched him curl. Kept her face away from his eyes. Put the gun on the desk. And lit another cigarette.

"I thought—I thought—"

"You thought wrong. About a lot of things, obviously."

He stood, smaller than a few minutes before, unsure. She saw him hesitate, saw him gather the tattered remnants of his ego around him like his camel-hair coat. Handkerchief still to his nose, he made a little bow.

"If events should prove otherwise—if you need help—"

"I'll call for Superman."

This time he nodded, turned to go. Stopped halfway to the door. Didn't look at her.

"I'm . . . sorry, Miranda."

She blew a smoke ring to the corner. "You say that an awful lot, Gonzales."

The door closed slowly, automatically, while she heard his footsteps retreating down the hall.

She sat in the chair, stared at the wall.

Happy Valentine's Day.

She didn't hear Allen tap on the doorway, and only looked up from the list on the desk when she caught his "You in, sweetheart?"

The Pinkerton man was holding mail; he grinned at Miranda and said: "Thought I'd deliver you your Valentines."

Miranda stretched and yawned, mumbled "Thanks."

Allen set the thin stack of bills and miscellaneous flyers on the desk, and stood over her, looking down.

"What happened to your face, kid? That's your meal ticket."

She touched her cheek without thinking about it. "It was worse yesterday."

"Somebody swat you? John you're chasing?"

She shook her head. "Bastards tried to run over me. And a cop took a cheap hit. This is a big one, Allen. New chief wants it shut down."

The detective took Gonzales's former chair, crossed his legs, and lit up a Camel with a match struck on his thumb. He looked at Miranda, added: "Trick they teach you when you get to be a Pinkerton."

"They teach you to talk like Cagney?"

Allen threw back his head, laughed until his belly quaked. "You're a funny girl, Miri. And a good kid. And not a bad shamus in your own right. You in over your head?"

"I've got to find a missing Japanese girl. Find out who killed her brother and why. And clear the name of a friend who was murdered." Her eyes were steady on Allen. "She was an escort."

He whistled. "Oh, is that all?" Took another drag on the Camel, and stood up, stretching. "I've been worried about you. Don't like to see you get hurt."

She shrugged. "Part of the business. That bald head of yours has taken a few blackjack imprints in its time."

"Yeah, sweetheart, but it was never very pretty to start with. Me, I got a long life in the business no matter how ugly I get, you know what I mean?"

Miranda sighed. "Yeah. I know what you mean."

"You need any help—off the record? We're not real busy just now. Everybody's out spoonin'."

She grinned at him. "Why aren't you? Wife mad at you?"

He shrugged. "Her old lady's stayin' with us. You know how it is."

"I can imagine."

Miranda dug in her purse for another Raleigh, looked at it with distaste, and lit it with the new Ronson. She said slowly: "I could use some information."

He gave his cigarette a deep inhale, then rubbed it out in the Tower of the Sun ashtray. "What have you got in mind?"

"Any connections between a numbers racket gangster named Filipino Charlie, Joe Gillio, ex-bootlegger, and Sammy Martini."

Allen's eyes widened. "Sammy Martini is big. He involved in all this?" He gestured to her face with the hand holding the cigarette.

"I think he's behind most of it. Also, a Chinese hood named Wong. On the genteel side. Runs with an Italian gun named Bennie."

The Pinkerton op scratched his eyebrow. "Either you're nutty or something is going down in San Francisco." He thought for a minute, then nodded. "You've got me for half a day, Miranda." He checked his wristwatch. "It's a little after twelve. I'll see what I can get you from our vast Pinkerton resources before five."

She looked up at him gratefully. "Thanks. I appreciate it."

The detective was already on his way out the door. "Don't mention it, kid. And really—don't mention it. They get hot and sweaty about this stuff. But hey—it's Valentine's Day." He grinned at her before vanishing behind the glass.

She smiled after him. Took a deep drag on the Raleigh, which satisfied much less than the Chesterfields. Reached out to pick up the stack of mail.

On the top was an envelope from Rick. She picked up the Treasure Island letter opener, slit it open. Inside was a Valentine's Day card.

It was one of those stupid cards with birds and roses and cupids, simpering and sighing, big-eyed and coy. The printing read BE MINE and it was signed, "Rick—Your Funny Valentine."

Just the kind of card she hated. Why she hated Valentine's Day. Why, at this moment, she hated Rick.

She pushed it aside to look at the other mail. An ad for a print shop, business cards on sale. Flyer for a bakery down the street. And another envelope, a little dirty, with handwriting she didn't recognize. It felt empty.

She slit it open carefully. Turned the envelope upside down and shook it. Out fell a crumpled receipt of some kind.

She spread it open.

It was a receipt for a dress to be picked up from Herbert-Robert Cleaners. Miranda was long overdue for a visit to 775 Jackson Street.

Twenty-four

She caught the Powell Street Cable Car in front of the turnaround at the Owl. Her stomach lurched when they climbed past Union Square, and she remembered how hungry she was.

The irresistible smell of sourdough pancakes and sausage drifted from Sears Pancake House and across the street to the swanky, shiny Sir Francis Drake, home away from home for those who liked ice water out of a faucet and the fresh, clean smell of an indoor golf course. Miranda's stomach growled, and led her through the double doors of Sears.

The counter was nearly full, but she found a stool at the end of the curve. A thin young man with acne and a too-big apron poured coffee for her. She stared in the cup, swished it around, watching it lap the sides like an oil spill. Two eggs, two sausage, two hotcakes, sunny-side up. Keep your sunny side up, young lady, this is the sunny side of the street.

She reached for the discarded *Los Angeles Times* someone had left behind, hoping the coffee would make her sharper, more focused. Sharp enough to find out where the receipt came from. Winters was dead, but thought enough of the place to carry around a card in his pocket. And Wong had flipped a card on her desk as either a promise or a threat—maybe both.

She sipped the coffee, watching the short-order cooks, and lit a cigarette, still chewing down the pack of Raleighs. The L.A. paper didn't offer much.

Phony War still phony to everyone except the fleets getting sunk by U-boats. And the Finns, of course, gasping on their skis, holding the Mannerheim Line against the Russians. They were almost done, almost finished. The headline bleated FINNS HOLD RUSSIANS BUT BEG WORLD AID.

The world wasn't listening. Not much. It was more concerned with Artie Shaw marrying nineteen-year-old Lana Turner a couple of days ago. However would Betty Grable take it? Answer on column four.

She flipped the paper to the top, caught an article about two Maryland women who were dragged from jail and almost lynched. They were Negroes, and wanted for questioning, and that's all it took to be guilty of murder in Snow Hill, Maryland. They liked their snow pure white in Snow Hill.

The plate arrived, and Miranda set it on top the newspaper. Poured maple syrup over the sausage and pancakes until they were swimming in it. Tabasco sauce on the eggs, along with salt and pepper. The kid refilled her coffee.

No one bothered her, no one talked to her. She was alone, in her sea of syrup and sea of people, the lunchtime conversations loud and hushed, while she drowned, surrounded, alone in the sensual joy of eating pancakes the way she liked them, drinking coffee so bitter it couldn't cry any more.

She looked down at the headline, chewed a piece of sausage. Asked for another cup.

The Herbert-Robert Cleaners was only big enough for one name. Miranda looked around the dimly lit shop, hearing the whirr of machinery in the back, watching the woman with the straggly gray hair rifle through the hanging clothes on long racks, searching for a fat lady's evening gown. She finally found it. The fat lady found fifty-nine cents, paid, and left. The gray-haired woman moved her bored eyes to Miranda.

"I need to pick up this dress."

The woman squinted at the receipt. "Be right back."

The shelves at the front were lined with clothes bundled in paper and string, stacked and waiting. At the rear, Miranda caught a glimpse of a Chinese woman pushing a large cart toward one of the machines. The woman leaned against the cart for a moment, wiping her face with her sleeve.

The counter woman appeared from behind a rack of dresses, holding a red brocade number with a small matching jacket. The bodice was low-cut, an evening gown of the type that was common in Chinatown, an imitation of an expensive design at Magnin's or City of Paris, remade with more traditional Chinese fabric.

Miranda held her hand over the dollar on the counter. Not too much. The woman looked down at the money, and up again at Miranda, her face not bored anymore.

"I'm picking this up for a friend of mine, and I need to know where she wants me to take it. Can you look it up for me?" Her voice was slow, careful.

The woman leaned against the counter and looked at her thoughtfully, tucking her hair back into the knot before more escaped.

"If you're her friend, you'd know where to take it, I expect. Maybe I shouldn't let you have it."

Her eyes were drawn back down to the dollar. Miranda moved her palm aside to reveal another dollar bill below the first one.

"I'm a friend. She works during the week, so I need to know where she wants it. Did she drop it by herself or have it picked up?"

The woman tore her eyes away from the money, and moved toward a large metal file box next to the cash register, throwing the dress on the counter.

She mumbled: "Don't suppose it'll do any harm. Can't be too careful in Chinatown, lady."

The calluses on her thick fingers caught at the various receipt books, until she found one close to the top.

"Says here it was picked up on Monday afternoon. House at 110 Cordelia Street."

Miranda shoved the money a little closer. "Say anything else?"

The woman's eyes narrowed, but she looked down at the counter and licked her lips.

"Nothin'. Clara picked it up."

"Clara's Chinese?"

The woman put her head to the side, asked suspiciously: "How'd you know that?"

Miranda gave the money one more shove, then released it. "Because Mr. Wong sent me here."

The woman slapped her hand on the two bills and slid them off the other side of the counter, pocketing them in one of the folds of the dingy yellow uniform she wore. Not much of an advertisement for Herbert or Robert.

"Don't know a Mr. Wong, lady, but that's all right. I don't work the weekends or the night shift."

"You think Clara might know him?"

She shrugged, her interest lost. "You can ask her. Clara! This lady's got a question."

The gray-haired woman left with noise and without undue haste, letting Miranda know that she knew she wasn't needed anymore. She shoved a tuxedo shirt aside and vanished into the back, no doubt dreaming of a new apron and a bottle of peroxide. Miranda lit a cigarette and waited.

A small woman about forty emerged, her face damp with sweat. The same one Miranda had noticed earlier. The doorbell chimed, and the gray-haired counter worker came out to the front of the shop, chatting with the customer, a harassed-looking mother picking up four bundles of play clothes.

Miranda motioned down to the opposite end of the counter, and Clara followed her, face expressionless, body stiff with anticipation.

Miranda gestured to the dress, which still lay where the other woman had thrown it.

"You picked that up at 110 Cordelia."

Clara nodded, waiting.

Miranda took a drag on her cigarette, looked over Clara's head into the back, and said casually: "You pick it up from Mr. Wong?"

The woman froze, her eyes darting for a way out. The other woman's attention was still focused on the customer.

"Look—I'm working with Wong. He knows me. I'm trying to find someone for him."

Clara's chest moved up and down in excited breathing, her hands shaking even while holding on to the counter. Then she shook her head.

"Can't help, Miss. Can't help. You go now. You go!"

Her voice was rising, and it was only a matter of seconds before the other woman would hear. Miranda pushed a dollar into her hand, adding in a low voice, "Betty Chow was a friend of mine."

The woman held a trembling hand to her mouth and pressed it tight like a gag. When she finally dropped it, there was an imprint across her lower cheeks. The dollar tumbled out of her palm, ignored. She looked at Miranda, terror pouring out of her eyes with the tears.

Then she turned and ran back inside the cave of Herbert-Robert Cleaners.

———

Cordelia was one of the small, forgotten byways of San Francisco, probably an alley for bilge water and quick assignations with sailors long before '06. It tunneled between Broadway and Pacific, running parallel to Stockton, and contained mostly garbage cans, alley cats, rats, and pigeons.

Neighborhoods in San Francisco varied on a block-to-block basis, the smallness of the city masking fissures that cracked open and ran deeper than the fault line. Chinatown was circumscribed, cut off, a matter of legal record. Here, you could live; here you couldn't.

Everywhere else was open to debate, tradition, and wallet books. Italians, Spanish, Chileans, Mexicans, and Peruvians clustered along the Bay front and Telegraph Hill and North Beach, which the Chamber of Commerce had tried to rename as the Latin Quarter. Time to capitalize on all that hot Latin blood for the million and a half visitors to the Pageant of the Pacific, the World's Fair to end all World's Fairs, by the city that knew how to put one on and put one over.

Cordelia Street was close enough to Chinatown to spit, if the wind was with you. And smack-dab by North Beach, with Italian restaurants and clubs and gambling joints. And only two blocks from the International Settlement, the new ode to the Barbary Coast for the new twentieth-century hell-raiser.

Whatever you wanted you'd find at the International Settlement. Made to order. Pleasure or pain, take your pick, you can have both, if that's the way you like it.

Fancy nudie joints like the House of Pisco made Sally Rand look like St. Theresa. You could order up women like a T-bone steak, lean or juicy, tartare or well-done. Everything from tough and stringy to milk-fed veal, all available, all open, all the time.

Give the gentleman what he wants and keep the sin confined to a two-block stretch of Pacific Avenue, so those million and a half visitors will know where to go when they get sick of The Gayway and Midget Village and the Tower of the Sun and the pale-faced madonnas with the glued-together thighs hanging in the Treasure Island Art Collection. *Pacifica* was a nice sculpture, but her nipples were too small. Best try Pickles O'Dell, fourth bar from the left.

Some respectable joints like the Monaco operated at the Settlement, too, a hall of mirrors reflection of the Naughty Nineties. Their brand of sin was inspired by Metro-Goldwyn-Mayer, the film company that held God's ear. According to Louis B. Mayer, second only to Moses and possibly Jesus as a prophet, the Earthquake was a punishment for our wicked ways. So Clark Gable reformed, and Jeanette MacDonald lived to sing "San Francisco" again, and Spencer Tracy tugged at the collar around his neck and blessed them both. And went back to the bottle under his cot.

Hollywood liked to celebrate anniversaries, and hell, an earthquake and fire were still big news thirty years later, but no sense in scaring off tourists. That good ol', bad ol' broad the natives never called Frisco was a sober, God-fearing city now, as scrubbed and clean as Shirley Temple's puberty. So the Monacos and Diamond Horseshoes batted their eyes and flirted, fronting for the real International Settlement that lurked behind the chromium and glass.

And the tune went out from the land. And the tune was good, and milk and honey came to the land. And the tune was "Sing, you Sinners."

Miranda stood at the edge of Broadway, looking down Cordelia Street. A couple of houses still squatted in the alley like an old woman taking a pee. They lingered, cheek by jowl to hash houses and bars named after Mike or Sam, mostly with the neon burned out, mostly with liquor spiced up from old bootlegging supplies and rubbing alcohol.

110 Cordelia was the better off of the two, at the more respectable end of the street near Miranda, away from Pacific Avenue and the run-off from the International Settlement. Pierino Gavallo's little foray into rebuilding the Barbary Coast into fun town, sin town, buy-what-you-like town came with a set of streamlined blueprints and arches at each end of Pacific Avenue, the old Terrific Avenue of the ghosts who roamed the gold-dust-sprinkled slats at Tar's, the one lone bar still shipwrecked from the Old Coast. It lingered there, looking inward, next to chrome and steel, curves and lines and violet-colored lights, wrapped in its memories of the old days. People came in for a drink to say they'd seen it, then left for more excitement down the street at the Conga Club, where the dance wasn't the only thing to get in line for.

The International Settlement. Gavallo had a few partners in his venture. Joe Gillio was one of them.

Miranda inhaled, trying to find some taste in the Raleigh. She could stake out the house if she could enlist the tavern across the street from it, hire out a back room, and keep watch. But talking her way into it would take time, and time is what she didn't have.

She leaned against the brick wall of a barbershop kitty-corner from

Cordelia. It was close to two o'clock, and she couldn't stay much longer—she'd already drawn unwanted attention from two sailors and a drunk. Make that three drunks.

The house was a wood-frame cottage that probably looked like a shanty when it was new. The years hadn't been kind, but it nodded to livability. Someone had even dabbed some brown paint by the front windows.

She figured she was supposed to be here. She was looking for Wong.

What she saw was a hawk-nosed man in a fancy green suit and a broad-rimmed fedora.

Miranda disappeared into the barbershop, keeping her eyes on the Italian. The customer in the chair opened his eyes in surprise, and the barber paused, razor in mid shave, staring at her.

"You lookin' for somebody, lady?"

"Yes. I mean, no, sorry."

She walked out, turned left toward Market. He was walking down Broadway, and she was now behind him.

She recognized the face. It was Sammy Martini.

The red brocade dress was small and light in the paper bag. A woman out for a stroll down to the shops. Only a few people looked at her twice. She tilted her hat, making her cheek look less swollen. The makeup hid the blue-and-green bruises.

Martini didn't turn around, walked with a light step, his hat worn low, his hands in his pockets. Sure of himself. At ease. And he didn't walk far.

Once across Stockton and halfway to Grant, a dark sedan pulled up next to him. It double-parked, but the taxi driver behind it quit honking when the guns in the back climbed out.

They both flanked Martini like Great Danes around a terrier. Miranda watched from the front window of a small bookshop as he nodded, grinning at the men, and gestured for them to go back into the car. They obeyed and drove off, making an immediate right on Columbus.

The bookstore clerk was walking over, smiling, helpfulness incarnate. Not a neighborhood for readers, unless they were selling pornography. Valentine's Day Special. Miranda stepped outside quickly, keeping Martini in her sights.

The traffic was getting thicker, and she almost lost him, thinking he'd hopped a streetcar. She maintained half a block distance; he stopped once, turned around, shading his eyes. Then lit a cigarette. She kept walking, looking in the occasional store windows, fussing with her bag when she walked in front of a bar. The streets were getting a bit rougher, despite the new lift to the baggy eyes of the Coast. Martini turned on Columbus, probably headed the same place as the six-foot bodyguards he carried around as lucky rabbit's feet.

He disappeared into the crowds under the arch, tourists getting their pictures taken with the Brownie, someone yelling to make sure the words "International Settlement" got in the photo. Miranda thought she saw him saunter into one of the clubs.

Looked like the Covered Wagon, a shady little cocktail lounge. Where the West was still wild, and wagons were the only things that stayed covered.

She turned right on Kearny and caught a yellow cab.

The driver spit out the window, and sped past the crab shacks of Fisherman's Wharf and Fisherman's Grotto Number Nine and DiMaggio's Restaurant, headed toward the Aquatic Park Casino. Passed the giant PG&E petroleum reserves by the waterfront. Miranda craned her neck, staring up at the huge tank, replaying memories of her old boss, bastard that he was, and the even worse bastards that killed him.

She told the cabbie to take a trip back over Nob Hill, down past Mason, and over to Market, a roundabout way to get to her office, which would let her know if she had a shadow.

He was a taciturn man with a three-day-old beard, eyes indifferent to passengers, not indifferent to extra money. Slammed on his brakes when a truck loaded with herring slowly pulled out of one of the fisheries.

Miranda held a mirror up to check the cars behind them. No one had stayed with them more than a block.

They careened past the glittering, boatlike casino, opened last year or the year before to high hopes and little money. No one gambled in the Depression. The stakes were too high, and the odds too low.

The upper crust considered Aquatic Park not upper or crusty enough to earn their green backs. They played in well-heeled dives that looked like the Warner Brothers's idea of a gambling den, places like the Moderne, with the patina of bootleggers still shiny at the edges.

He hung a left on Van Ness, got caught in traffic, passed a couple of other taxis, people visiting the car dealers, ogling the new models, college kids seeing how many could squeeze in the new rumble seats.

Still no car behind them.

A glass truck tried to change lanes and trapped them, so he switched on the radio and a few seconds later the sonorous tones of H. V. Kaltenborn discussing the world filled the car. The driver made a noise of disgust and turned the dial until he found someone singing opera, then laid on his horn, finally working his way around the glass truck.

He swung around until he could head north on California, crawling up the hills toward the mansions, Grace Cathedral, the Fairmont, and the Top of the Mark, Old San Francisco, Railroad San Francisco. The smell of gold still perfumed the atmosphere of Nob Hill, not quite a hundred years later.

He hung a right at Jones, then a left at Sutter, and a left again at Bush, again stalling behind a streetcar, his fingers tapping his steering wheel as if he had somewhere to go.

Miranda watched him, smoking her Raleigh in silence, and every few seconds, checked the pocket mirror.

He finally headed down Mason, past the apartment, and at her bidding slowed down to a trot. She leaned back against the seat, her hat pulled low over her eyes, looking for parked cars or dark windows, or men who looked like they had too little to do, their eyes sharp, their fingers twitching on imaginary triggers.

Still nothing.

She shrugged, told him to get her to the Monadnock. He stepped on the gas.

The phone started ringing when the key was in the lock. She cursed, dropping the dress, shoved the door open, picked up the bag and ran.

She lifted the receiver, shoved the bag under the desk, and faced toward the still open door.

"Miranda Corbie, Investigations."

The voice at the other end was young and hesitant.

"Miss Corbie?"

An image of a girl, immaculately dressed, bringing in her mother's shoes.

"Is this Rose? Rose Shiara?"

Miranda sat in the leather chair, opening her purse and taking out the .22.

"Of course I remember you. And thank you for calling. Did Mr. Matsumara explain that I'm trying to help Emily?"

Miranda pulled out Helen Winters's Chief tablet from the desk drawer, and dipped the fountain pen in the well, poising it above the paper.

"Uh-huh. Yes, that's right. It's very important, Rose. So if you know anything—"

Disappointment shadowed Miranda's face, and she set the pen down. "Yes. I see. I was hoping she'd told you. No, no, it's not your fault. Uh-huh. Uh-huh. Okay."

Deep sigh. She picked up the pen again.

"All right. Anything at all, any personal fact you can tell me? Uh-huh . . . tea ceremony. Yes, Mrs. Takahashi mentioned that to me. Okay. Relatives in Burlingame . . . uh-huh . . . own a grocery market? Importers? Were they close? All right. No, that could be important. Any more personal things, favorite movie star, that kind of—oh, she did? Gardening, huh? And fish. No, that's interesting. You never know what can help, honestly. You've been wonderful. If you hear anything at all . . . Yes, please do. And Mr. Matsumara probably told you that you can't let—yes. Well, it could be dangerous. So please, Rose—be careful. If you see anything odd, someone tries to follow you, you'll call—yes. Call the police. Then call me. Okay. Thank you again. I'll let you know. 'Bye."

Miranda sat and frowned at the notebook, at the words "garden" and "fish" and "tea," while holding the .22 in her hand, the door still open. She sighed, stood up, and stretched, and walked from behind the desk toward the door to close it.

Footsteps tapped and skidded, uneven and off-balance, close by her office. Before she could look out into the hallway, a gray-haired man in a wool jacket, covered in pipe ash and the stench of a three-day-old bender, wavered into her office, hitting and banging the door against the wall stopper.

Her father.

Twenty-five

S ome of the red lines tattooing his nose and cheeks were new. She was surprised at how old he looked. How long—a year ago?

His hair was still parted on the extreme left, carefully combed, oiled and full of bits of dry, flaky scalp he didn't see when he looked in the mirror. She wondered for a moment what he did see.

He weaved toward the desk chair, bowing to her, and nearly toppling over, collapsing in the seat until he could assume a more professorial posture.

Miranda stared at him from the door, then slowly closed it and walked back to her desk. She was still holding the pistol.

"What the hell do you want?"

He gazed at her mournfully, shaking his head with disapproval. "Ah, Miranda. Your father comes down from th' hill to see you, to make sure y'r all right, and you disappoint him. Not the first time. I taught you better than that."

She sank heavily in the leather seat. "You didn't teach me a goddamn thing. What do you want?"

The head-shaking intensified until he was close to falling over. Then he drew himself up like a Roman senator about to make a speech.

"I taught you English, young lady, the King's tongue, and the language of

Shakespeare. Made sure"—he waggled his finger—"made sure you had 'n education. An' you choose to be vulgar, like those people you work for."

His voice took on an exaggerated pitch, while he thrust his hand out and gestured at her. *"How sharper than a serpent's tooth—"*

"For fuck's sake, drop the John Barrymore act. You only remember me when you're drunk and desperate and want money. Is that what you're here for?"

He dropped his hand slowly into his lap. She noticed his pants were dirty, and covered with ash and chalk dust. His eyes were large and brown. Her eyes.

"You will kindly r'frain from using the language of those whom I would call *hoi polloi*, if the very usage of Greek did not ennoble them far more than they deserve. Can I not see my own daughter—whom I named after that glorious, bright creat're in *The Tempest*, and who has become my own Regan— can I not see her without stepping in her wasted life, her verbal trash?"

He was starting to work himself up, saw the look on Miranda's face, noticed the gun in her hand, and burbled back down into less angry dramatics. He brushed off his suit, smoothed his hair.

She said, wearily: "You need money. I suppose you saw me in the paper."

He made an effort to sober up. "I was reading my Hopkins, preparing for a class. I noted that you were involved with finding a missing girl. I was worried."

Miranda leaned back in the chair. The laugh hurt her lungs.

"Worried? Who the fuck—excuse me, Cotton Mather, who are you trying to put one over? This is me you're talking to. Your so-called child you haven't seen or contacted since the Fair opened last year. And precious few times before that. The daughter you never wanted, a sensation you made perfectly clear to me, over and over again, in dactylic hexameter or fourteen-line sonnets, whenever you bothered to climb down from the Ivory Tower."

She lowered the gun but didn't let it go, pulling a cigarette out of her purse and lighting it one-handed with the Ronson lighter. Inhaled until the pain went away.

"You never wanted me. You didn't like me as a child, and don't like me now, except in some sort of Grand Guignol fashion where you can martyr yourself to your art and your writing and your teaching, and pretend to be King Lear. Oh, and there's the money. That's a new twist, I suppose, since my notoriety has caused you both discomfort from the fossilized old bastards at

Berkeley . . . and comfort in the form of, shall we say, liquid assets? So let's get down to business, Pops. How much do you want to go away?"

His face was blue with shock and repressed anger. Not drunk enough to hear the truth. Not yet.

"How . . . dare you. You at least have an eloquence you owe me. You could've gone to Berkeley or Stanford, married, and been a decent woman. You—and you alone—have chosen to live like this, wasting whatever gifts God gave you, unfit for decent company. Is it any wonder I don't see you? Tenure doesn't protect a man forever, not if his daughter's no better than a who—"

"Watch your mouth, old man. You managed to kill off my mother. I've often wondered if I should return the favor for her."

Miranda was halfway out of her chair, breathing hard, her eyes swimming. Very carefully, she laid down the .22 still in her hand. Calmed herself, checked her breathing. She opened the desk drawer, took out the half-empty bottle of Old Taylor, and handed it to him contemptuously.

"Here's your mother's milk, Pops. Suck down some of this, and I'll get you what you came for."

His hand shook when he reached for it, his eyes full of loathing and greed. He'd be on the stuff for a week, until he got sick. One of these days he'd die of it.

Miranda walked to the safe, while he quickly unstoppered the bottle and swallowed about four gulps of the bourbon. She fished out a hundred-dollar bill. The annual tax.

She thrust it at him and removed the bottle from his other hand, where it hung limply, his head drooping, his shoulders slouched. She put it back on the desk.

"I thought perhaps—perhaps there had been a reward . . . My salary has—"

"No explanations necessary, Pops. Go buy your brandy, read your Shakespeare. It's my filial duty to make sure you're in the clover. As you've explained before. Maybe it'll help you shuffle off your mortal coil."

He looked up at her, the eyes brown and large. "Miranda. A good Latin name."

"So you've told me."

He stood up, unsteady, grasped her arm. She flinched, then relaxed. Walked him to the door.

He stooped, the haze of the bourbon settling on him for a while, his face placid and dreaming.

"I'm teaching modern poetry. Hopkins reminded me of you."

They were at the doorway. Miranda cocked an eyebrow. "In what way? He's not vulgar."

He braced himself on the door frame, and for a moment, his voice was that of the teacher, sonorous, charismatic, Henry Irving in front of the chalkboard, reciting verse like he lived it.

"The poem you liked a long time ago. Remember?"

She shook her head.

"We substituted your name. One Christmas, perhaps the only Christmas . . . '*Miranda,* are you grieving/Over Goldengroves unleaving?/Leaves, like the things of man, you/With your fresh thoughts care for, can you?/Ah! as the heart grows older/It will come to such sights colder/By and by, nor spare a sigh/Though worlds of wanwood leafmeal lie . . .'"

Her hand dropped from his arm. He turned to face her, eyes shining.

"*It is the blight man was born for. It is Miranda you mourn for.*"

He bowed, kissed her hand, and wavered back into the hallway, the hundred dollars in his pocket. Miranda watched him go, the cigarette burning its way toward her fingers, not feeling the tears on her cheeks.

.

The Old Taylor bottle stood empty and the Raleigh packs lay crumpled on the desk. Miranda smoked the last stick, letting it linger, finally stamping it out in the ashtray, rubbing the burned gray dust around and around the circular indentation.

No Memory Box, no sirree, don't need one when you've got a bottle of bourbon and your old man stops in to grift a hundred bucks.

Christmas, 1918. Only Christmas she remembered with him. Snow in New York, the flurries swirling through the honking traffic and the rumbling trains, Miranda's eyes big and wondering, staring at the men in the funny pants, the men missing a leg or an arm, back from the Great War, the War to End All Wars.

Marching. Yelling. People always yelling, fighting, never smiling, wrapped against the cold but breathing it out, never warm, never inviting. Old Mrs. Hatchett. Miranda thought the sour old woman would cut her head off if she disobeyed.

Pinafore dirty, shoes scuffed. Poor relation, they whispered, and she didn't know what it meant, but she knew she didn't want it to mean her.

His hair shining, voice mellifluous, preparing for the speech on Hopkins, Gerard Manley. He was always correcting Miranda, that peevish tone, that turned-down grimace, when she carefully said "Gerald" instead of Gerard.

Christmas Eve. Rum punch, and he didn't correct her anymore. No tree to speak of, something small and wretched and more brown than green, something found by Hatchett and brought in with triumph, an ode to parsimony and a testament to thrift.

Miranda loved it anyway. Traced the dried and crackled branches with her fingertip, felt the life still in it. She sat by it on Christmas Eve, the only company in the house she liked, other than the cats in the alley behind the boardinghouse, and those she couldn't smuggle in.

She saved them bones from the chicken leg for Christmas Day, ate her baked potato sitting under the tree. Her father didn't notice. Speech over, time to celebrate. Another rum punch or hot toddy. Hatchett dipping into sherry, dropping a curtsy, nodding to sleep.

Under the tree was her space. She fell asleep, not dreaming of sugarplums, not dreaming at all.

She woke up on the floor, not in the attic room they usually confined her to. Opened her eyes to Christmas morning. Ten years had taught her not to hope too much.

There was a torn box, hastily wrapped with brown cardboard peeking through. She recognized it as a pair of used ice skates she'd seen in a pawnshop window, and for a moment her heart was full, under the bent and brittle tree, as she carefully opened the box while her father lay stretched on the chaise lounge, snoring, a bottle near his hand.

Mrs. Hatchett from the kitchen, sherry still on her breath, making the disapproving noises she always made. No, you can't go out. No, you can't skate until your father wakes up. If you're not quiet . . .

The threat stilled her, and she waited under the tree, staring at her father, willing him to wake up. Breakfast was cold toast and sausage, and lunch was tepid tomato soup and crackers. Still he slept, and the light was fading, and when they took the train back to San Francisco there wouldn't be any snow to skate in.

The sighs and plaintive longing bothered Hatchett. Miranda sat and traced the scars on the bark, over and over. The old woman looked out the window at the growing dusk, and grasped at the tree, lifting it up, and taking it to the door. The crackle of the small dry branches sounded like screams.

Christmas, she said, was over.

Hatchett hurled it outside and down the front steps, the wood breaking and snapping like brittle bones. Miranda heard it crying, screaming, and didn't know she was screaming, too, until Hatchett slapped her.

The noise woke her father, and he rubbed his eyes, and Hatchett apologized, explaining how naughty Miranda had been, what a fuss she'd made out of a dead Christmas tree. The old woman shoved her toward her father, to give him a curtsy and a kiss for the ice skates.

Miranda refused. All she wanted was the tree.

Her father looked at her, looked at Hatchett, looked at the empty bottle. And did what he always did. He quoted poetry.

Miranda, are you grieving . . .

He laughed, merry mood, funny child, such a strange funny girl, quite entertaining in her eccentricity, if unsteady in her manner. She'd probably grow up to disgrace him, the old woman offered, and he nodded, agreeing that it was very likely, given what her mother had been.

He jumped up, suddenly, full of energy and determination. Come, Miranda, let us skate. There are lights in Central Park.

The skates meant nothing to her without the tree. But she couldn't explain it, not to him.

Over Goldengroves unleaving . . .

Hatchett forced the ice skates on her feet. They were too small, meant for an eight-year-old petite blonde, not the tall auburn girl with freckles and large hands. She tried to stand on them and stumbled, her father clapping and laughing.

On the way out the door she looked for it. Some boys had picked it up and added it to a fort two brownstones down. She was glad to see it again. It was dead now, and at peace.

He took her to Central Park, buying another bottle along the way, just a little for New Year's, we must celebrate, he said to himself, never her.

He shoved her out on the ice, the darkness lifting with the moon and the lights of New York City, and watched her fall, telling her what she needed to do, telling her to start over again. Boys and girls, men and women, danced and glided past her, happy on the evening of Christmas Day, laughter and bells following them.

She learned to skate that evening. And never skated again.

On the way home, after the bottle had been opened for an early New Year,

Miranda felt the trunks of the trees she passed, rubbed her hands over their roughness, feeling their souls. And she cried again, thinking of her own, her very own Christmas tree.

Her father laughed, shaking his head.

It is Miranda you mourn for.

The bells were tolling four o'clock. Teatime at Dianne's, at all the finer establishments of the city.

She raised her head, looked at the empty bottle. Fragile dreams, funhouse glass, shattered, splintered. Over. Opened a desk drawer, searching for a cigarette. Hands shaking. No stick. No luck. No Miranda.

Something inside of her lashed back. Something deep, untouched, sacred. Not her father's daughter. Not awash in the saline pools of self-pity, so plentiful in the swamps of academia. Not overly fond of her own voice, lecturing, lecturing, lecturing.

Miranda felt her face, tracing her cheekbone carefully. Swelling down. She was cold, on the clammy side. But she had a license in her wallet and a dead friend to avenge and a live girl to find, and oh yeah—Eddie Takahashi. He started it.

Her stomach growled with hunger, but she couldn't face a crowd just yet, not tonight, not Valentine's Day. Too many fucking holidays—Rice Bowl Parties, and Chinese New Year and Valentine's Day—blending into one, and San Francisco, gaudy old biddy that she was, loved to celebrate. New Orleans didn't have the corner on the musical funeral—hell, every day was somebody's funeral, and listen to the bells and the cars and the sound of the foghorns. That's a jazz symphony for you.

She stood up, tossed the bottle in the black metal trash can that usually held cigarette wrappers and ashtray contents. Walked to the window, threw it open to the sounds of chaos below.

It hit her with the force of the wind and the fog, left over from yesterday's rain. It always rained in San Francisco. Fog was just rain without determination.

Miranda closed her eyes and breathed in, feeling her head clear, that writhing knot of life and stubbornness growing stronger with every breath.

Allen would be there soon, Allen with information, the privileged kind that belonged to police and Pinkertons. She thought about Gonzales, shoved it aside along with the memory of his lips. No time for cops. And that's what they all were, cops, Gonzales and Phil and Rick, too many goddamn cops.

No. She'd figure it out, find the girl, save Betty's name. Who gave a fuck if it didn't belong to anyone else? It was her name, and it was a good name, and Miranda would make sure that's how the record read. Even if no one was around to read the fucking record.

A loud blaring honk made her jump. Taxi blocked by a White Front. Gotta get home, gotta hurry, flowers will melt and the chocolate will wilt. Hectic, harried, rushing to whoever and whatever they called a lover, throwing themselves into traffic only to be spewed out again, spent, part of the mating ritual, honey, you don't know what I went through to buy you this red rose . . .

She shut the window, drifted back to the desk. Flipped on the radio. Took a solid minute for the vacuum tubes to warm up. Miranda tapped her foot, and then remembered the dress.

She pulled the bag out from under the desk, laid the gown out on top. Evening style, low-cut. Small size, petite. The right size for Betty. She wondered if the maid at the Pickwick would recognize it.

And it was still dirty, smelled of sweat. Whatever Herbert or Robert had done with it, they hadn't cleaned it.

A clarinet squeal from the radio made her turn around, heart pounding. Goddamn Artie Shaw. Shouldn't he be out somewhere banging Lana Turner, child bride? She turned off the radio, not needing it anymore.

Miranda walked slowly around the desk, looking at the dress from every angle. Someone had sent her the receipt. Someone wanted her to have this. She fingered the thickly embroidered material, felt the heft of the skirt and the bodice.

She began from the bottom. Slowly fingering the cloth, inch by inch, methodical and slow. She reached the waistline, turned it inside out, checking the lining for any rips or tears. A seam had been sewn in a different colored thread—but it was an old repair, nothing new, nothing there.

Narrow waist. Not much room. Started up the bodice. Reached the slightly expanded breast cups. Felt something besides fabric.

She quickly turned the dress inside out from the top, flattening the bodice on the desk with both hands. Traveled back to the lining, slightly thicker for better support. And yes, something was there, something small, in the right breast cup.

Miranda opened the desk drawer, grabbed a pair of scissors, looked again.

The lining had been recently stitched in a small location, under where the breast would be positioned.

Cursing the clumsiness of the large blades, she carefully cut the threads. A three-inch line opened and restitched . . . same color thread, just a little brighter than the others.

She set the scissors down, took a deep breath. Wished she had smaller hands. Inserted two fingers into the gap, made contact with something dry and crinkled. Grasped it with her fingers, pulled it smoothly through the opening.

A small brown envelope, folded tight.

She unfolded it, spread it out on top of the dress.

It was addressed to her.

Twenty-six

She sank into the leather chair, holding the thin paper of the envelope in her hands. It shook with the trembling of her fingers.

Someone had written her name in a hurry, scrawling it with no time for the ink to dry. Some of it had soaked into the folds of the envelope. Written, addressed, folded, and hidden. Hidden twice, as the dress was picked up at Cordelia Street and taken to the dry cleaners by Clara, waiting there, while another envelope came to Miranda with the receipt.

She opened the drawer and found the envelope from earlier, studying the writing on each. Both rushed. Same writing.

She needed a cigarette, needed something to still the shaking in her hands. No time now. The letter opener felt heavy, the silver-plated handle awkward to hold. She managed to insert the blade, and tore patiently, a little at a time, wanting to destroy as little of it as possible.

Inside was a thin piece of paper and a storage receipt for the Greyhound lockers.

Greyhound Stage Lines. Formerly the Pickwick Stage Lines. Right next door to the Pickwick Hotel.

She unfolded the letter. Pickwick Hotel stationery.

Found Winters dead. Got there at time Wong set, 4:00 A.M.. Wong working with Winters, get Sammy out. Frame for me I think. Stayed for hour, panic, talked to Eddie. Stored papers at lockers. Eddie wants sister out, Sammy likes her. Eddie took Winters's money, I worry, Sammy and Coppa will know. If they find out about Wong and me God help us both. Going back to house. More if I can.

There was blue ink for the next section.

Eddie killed. Wong wants money, evidence, keep Martini away. But Martini knows something or why kill Winters. Coppa waiting. Coppa left Winters money as bait, find the pigeon. Feel like I killed Eddie. My fault, should not have gave him money. Wong and Charlie argue. Sammy runs Charlie now. Wong worried. Nowhere to go, we give ourselves away. Not sure what to do? The women cry all the time I can't

The ink skittered off the page, interrupted. One more paragraph. Sprawled words, some dripping with ink, some barely scratched.

Miranda—help me. Saw you tonight. Will call tomorrow. Winters try to get out, buy information from Wong. Coppa killed Winters, Eddie took money, Eddie's dead. Sewing this in dress with ticket. Don't trust no one no more.

She stared at the words until they swam around, Treasure Island lights on the Bay waters, kaleidoscope, finally wiping her eyes and reading them again.

Miranda—help me . . . Don't trust no one no more.

Betty Chow had needed her, Betty Chow had been in trouble, deeper than Miranda could have guessed or known. Too late to help Betty now.

Flashbulb scene. Twisted body, dirt and dust and empty bottles. The voice on the phone, crying, trying to reach her, and then the slab, the morgue, dead now, all dead and gone, the bright-eyed girl who laughed shyly, sharing confidences at Dianne's, who wanted to be in show business, because fuck . . . Didn't they all?

Miranda closed her eyes for a moment. Fingernails dug into her palm, the pain an anchor against the wave, lashing her to the mast, Winken, Blinken, and Nod sailing off in a wooden casket.

The creature at the pit of her howled in anger, keeping her on her feet. Read it again, Miranda. Read it again.

Cool, analytical. Like scanning a meter of poetry. Look for the rhythm, look for the truth. This—*Wong working with Winters, get Sammy out.* Then a switch—*Wong and Charlie argue. Sammy runs Charlie now.*

OK. So Filipino Charlie and Wong originally teamed up to smuggle drugs, probably with Winters, probably with outlets in Chinatown. Maybe through Dr. Mike, the Chinese Mr. Lonelyhearts.

Then Martini moved in. Probably part of a new expansion into San Francisco—with Joe Gillio and the International Settlement. Timing was right. But something happened to cool off Charlie and Wong, some part of what Martini did, enough for evidence to be peddled and money to be exchanged, and Wong—and Charlie, at least initially—to want the Italian out.

Papers and money, papers and money. A full suitcase, Winters's dwindling bank account. The NYK man ready to pay for evidence to bring down Sammy Martini, and maybe save his daughter. Lester Winters, respectable Lester Winters of Alameda, giving ammunition to the DA in exchange for getting out and getting a deal. Guilty and not guilty.

Her open hand smacked the desk. Started to pace. Read right so far. Winters was the stoolie, the one who'd go to the cops, turn evidence against Martini, while Charlie and Wong disappeared with the cargo only to reemerge later, go back to small-time numbers and gambling rings.

Desperate trick to turn. They must have wanted Martini out enough to risk almost everything. So they pooled information, warmed up to Winters's money, let him take the heat. What Winters himself had on Martini wasn't enough. Or maybe Winters wasn't guilty of anything except stupidity and bad taste in women. Maybe he didn't know what was going on until his daughter was lost and he was drowning in it.

Wong was the key, the principal agent. Drafted Betty to deliver the evidence, and Eddie to deliver Winters's money back to him and Charlie. Except: *Found Winters dead. . . . Frame for me I think.*

Betty arrived, ready to do business with Winters on behalf of Wong and Charlie. But Needles had been there before her, and Coppa, or maybe Martini himself. He'd caught a change of wind, heard something, sensed Winters's betrayal or desperation despite—or because of—Martini's hold on his daughter. And nobody—not Needles, not Martini or Coppa, his surrogate—took the money in Winters's suitcase. The bastard wanted to trace it, see which of his colleagues was less than collegial.

Fuck. Betty had been on a time clock since the eighth. They let her dangle, let her worry, for four days. Cat and mouse, cat and mouse. No wonder Wong was worried. And that motherfucker Charlie turned again, hedging the bets in his numbers game, making sure if anyone's number came up it was Wong's. Fuck, fuck, fuck . . .

She flung herself into the leather chair, frowning, staring at the letter. *Sammy likes her.* Motivation for Eddie to work with Wong and Charlie and Winters. Sammy "liked" Phyllis—if he liked you enough you'd be sold to a market with a longer life expectancy. Eddie took care of his sister. And Eddie had Winters's money—money he was supposed to give to Wong, money, maybe, that could be used to show Sammy Martini who was with him and who wasn't.

So Wong needed it. Charlie needed it. And Martini sat and waited, cat and mouse again, while they fought, and one of them had Eddie beaten up. And then somebody shot the kid, once they figured out who really had the cash.

Emily. Find Emily, find the money and prove your loyalty. A race to the dough, sugar for Sammy, ticket to survival for Wong or Charlie.

Fuck. No wonder they didn't want her near Eddie Takahashi. The small-time numbers runner in the middle of a statewide gang war. His sister and an undisclosed amount of cash at stake, whatever Winters could dredge up, legally or not. Eddie passed the money to his sister for safekeeping, probably to get her out of town.

Miranda leaned back in the chair, her head throbbing. Fuck. Where the fuck was Emily Takahashi?

She banged open the desk drawer, looking for chewing gum. Found a stale stick of Choward's Violet. Popped it into her mouth, ignoring the lack of elasticity.

There was something she was missing in the sparse, feverish lines, something important. *Going back to the house.* Could only mean Cordelia Street.

Her jaws froze. There it was. Betty's key, the one that turned the lock.

The women cry all the time I can't

Cut off, excised, the phrase isolated, unpunctuated. Coitus fucking interruptus.

Sammy Martini was smuggling more than drugs. He was smuggling women. Not from Mexico, not in San Francisco.

From Japan. NYK Lines. Chinese women. "Comfort" women from the war, prisoners of it.

The fucking Rape of Nanking, over and over and over again.

The sigh spilled out of her, a kind of relief, a recognition of truth. Wong's warnings, why he—and initially Charlie—wanted no part of Martini. Drugs were one thing, but women—women from a country at war, victims and loot, living examples of the superiority of Nippon and the Empire of Japan.

And a Japanese boy named Eddie Takahashi tried to stop it.

Fuck—it all made sense. Dianne's talk about competition, the rumors about something big and dirty on the waterfront. Gillio's complicity, the ex-bootlegger smuggling women into the shiny new Settlement for sin. Even Madame Pengo . . . that Bible quote. Something about a voyage with pain and danger, but not just to a ship—to lives.

Women's lives. A piece of torn brocade by a shipping crate. A little girl, half Chinese, half white, crying in the street. Where's Mommy now?

Miranda stared at the letter. Betty's voice. Parade of people, the dragon dancing for China, fireworks, and the auction. And Sammy Martini with his own celebration, down at the International Settlement. Got a yen for yellow flesh, sir, step right up, they're fresh from market, can't beat the price, imported don't you know. Fresh shipment tonight, fresh from the *Kamakura Maru*.

Welcome to the fucking rice bowl.

She dipped the fountain pen, wrote "Allen" on an envelope, and scratched a note. It read:

> *Martini, Charlie, and Gillio smuggling Chinese women for I. Settlement. House at 110 Cordelia Street. Saw Martini there earlier. Evidence in storage at Greyhound-Pickwick. Going to collect. Meet me back in office.*

She signed it "M," and pushed it to the corner of the desk. Looked at the phone. Debated for a few seconds, then reached for the receiver and dialed.

"Inspector Gonzales, please. No, Gonzales. G-o-n-z-a-l-e-s. He's in homicide. Miranda Corbie."

She waited impatiently, her fingertips drumming the wood, while the operator connected her, first to a bored cop, suffering from barnacles on his ass, and then to someone in robbery. Finally, an Irish voice answered.

"It's over, Corbie. And your boyfriend isn't here. Go back to chasing bigamists."

Phil's speech was slightly slurred. Must have had a long and liquid lunch. She held her temper.

"Nice to hear from you, Phil. I've found more evidence. Mann Act stuff, women smuggled in from occupied China via Japanese shipping. Even saw

Martini in town, not too far from you boys. 110 Cordelia Street. You want to hear it, or do I wait for Gonzales?"

The growl on the other end wasn't listening. "Is he who you're waiting for, Corbie? You like 'em thick and dark, do you? You sure you don't have him in your mouth alread—"

She slammed the receiver, breathing hard. Two fucking drunken bastards in one day was two too many. Oh yes, Mama, they hurt, they hurt, they cry, they feel bad. And only feel better when they hurt back.

Pain begetting pain. Cruelty fucks itself. Maybe that's how the world was born.

It didn't matter. Not now.

She stood up, stretched, her body anxious to move. Greyhound and Pickwick storage. Take the package, throw it in front of the new police chief, and the district attorney and the mayor. Three blind mice. See how the bastards run.

She reached for the Chief pad, leaned on the corner of the desk, and examined the storage ticket. D9830. Date was Thursday, February 8th. The fountain pen still had some ink on it, so she scratched the number on a sheet of paper, redipping it midway, and going over the letters again. Took the .22 out of her purse, picked up the pad and Betty's dress, and opened the safe. The dress she neatly folded, and lay on the shelf inside. The notebook and gun she placed beside it.

Miranda reached to the back of the safe and pulled out what looked like a large cigarette case. Shut the safe door, walked back to the desk, sat down on the edge of the chair. Looked critically at the case, and opened up one side. Picked up the .25 Baby Browning.

She'd bought it in Belgium. Perfect concealed weapon, and one she didn't have a license for. They didn't sell them in America, the cops tended not to like guns they couldn't find on a pat down. And the gangsters liked their substitute manhood big. Cops liked them that way, too.

Miranda didn't take it out for every job. But for close work, for concealed work, it beat the .22 in accuracy and size. The Spanish pistol was just too damn much gun. And she couldn't face the risk of losing it. The Baby Browning fit in her hand. The large Scotch-Irish hands she'd been so embarrassed over.

She checked the magazine, blew into it, and loaded it with the six bullets from the case. Weighed a little over ten ounces, loaded. Lethal as hell. And only four inches long.

The wardrobe smelled a little musty, but the coats were all right. Black one, narrow waist, overlarge pockets. The one on the right was a double pocket. The cigarette case fit snugly inside. Now she just needed cigarettes for the other dummy side, the one she'd open if she needed to.

Next was the storage receipt. Just in case.

She slipped off her left pump, and picked it up. Reached into a desk drawer, pulled out some masking tape. Set the shoe down, tore off a couple of small pieces of tape, and carefully secured the storage ticket to the top of her shoe pump. If they were smart, they searched under the foot pads. But nobody ever thought to search the uppers—at least so far. And she didn't really give a damn what the locker attendant at Greyhound thought of her for taking off a shoe and prying out a receipt.

She slid the shoe back on, put on the coat, buttoned it, and adjusted her hat. Wristwatch said 5:15. Valentine's dinners, the aroma of love drifting through the city like the fog. Gonzales was probably out nursing his nose and extorting sympathy from some simpering fool who didn't know better.

And Rick . . . Rick was working, like he always did, drowned in a pool of ink, buried under a pile of type. Maybe Allen's wife called, and he forgot about Gillio and Martini.

Miranda looked at herself in the mirror, straightening the coat. Cheek was looking almost human again, at least in terms of size.

She stared at herself. She was alone, and that's the way she liked it.

She grabbed her purse and the letter to Allen, shut and locked the office door behind her.

Allen's door was closed, and so was the front office. She knocked on the door, and waited a few moments. Knocked more urgently when no one answered. The third series brought a head of red hair out from a door on the hallway. The office next to Allen's.

"We're closed, lady—oh, Miranda. You want somebody in particular, or just feel like knockin' the door down?"

"I'm looking for Allen. You see him?"

He shook his head, blowing a cloud of blue cigar smoke toward a rumpled matron and bespectacled husband looking for Union Pacific. "Not since lunch. You want me to give him a message?"

His pudgy pink fingers took the letter she extended, and he looked at it curiously. "He doing things he shouldn't be?"

"How the hell should I know? Are you?"

He laughed. "I'll prop it on his desk. See you around, Miranda."

"See you, Bert."

He disappeared and shut the door. Only a few footsteps echoed through the fourth floor, and Miranda rode down in the elevator alone.

The lobby was as crowded as the fourth had been sparse. Men in sweaty-brimmed derbys were buying candy from the lobby girls, the last-ditch panic of Valentine's Day after work, the sun never showing itself, the fog settling into a study in grayish black.

Gladys was busy relieving two business men of guilt and cash, while another woman waited and found nothing to amuse herself. Miranda needed a cigarette, and she lingered between the lobby shop and the doors, trying to catch Gladys's eye.

5:25 already. Traffic would be tough, and so would taxis. Goddamn it, but she needed a Chesterfield.

One of the men wasn't quite done choosing thoughtful gifts for his wife, and an old lady joined the impatient woman. She thought Gladys saw her, but figured she'd survey the traffic scene out on Market for a few minutes, give the girl time to find the promised cigarettes. "They satisfy," all right. Tremors were still coursing through her fingers.

Miranda pushed open the heavy lobby door, and Market Street hit her in the face. Neon was starting to glow in the gray dusk, a sunlight San Francisco could depend upon.

Honks and shrieks from screaming rail tracks, sidewalks packed, people in a hurry. Taxis rode bumpers, weaving in and out with the nerve that only cab drivers possessed. White Fronts and municipals chugged sluggishly, bursting with passengers and no standing room. A man was waiting across the street at Lotta's Fountain with a rose and a smirk on his face, expecting the girl and the Valentine's Day Special.

She turned back toward the doors, the craving driving her forward to Gladys, whoever the hell was in front of her.

A flower seller in a dirty newsboy cap insinuated himself in between Miranda and the door. He held out a white rose and tipped his cap, not looking at her.

"Lady like you should be wearin' flowers."

Surprised, Miranda stopped, smiled, and took it from his rough hands. Still, he wouldn't look at her.

She smelled the rose. A little peaked around the edges, but the perfume was good. She wondered why she'd never seen this vendor before, whether he was selling just for Valentine's Day.

"Thanks, that's very—"

A low voice scratched her ear, and at the same time she felt something in her back. Something hard.

"I ain't happy to see you, lady. So you know what this is."

The flower vendor finally raised his face to Miranda. His eyes said, "Sorry, lady."

Twenty-seven

The barrel in her back prodded her forward. The raspy voice breathed pastrami in her ear, and said: "Natural like. Move to your left. We're around the corner, where you couldn't see us from your window."

Her muscles tensed at the gloating tone, the sense of superiority. And she remembered something Burnett told her once: "Make 'em underestimate you. Let 'em think you're nothing."

So she nodded, letting her arms dangle naturally to the side. She'd play with the boys.

She started to turn toward the left, guided by the pressure on her spine. From the corner of her eye she could see a brown suit, not shabby. From the position of his mouth, he was about six feet, from the voice, between forty and fifty. Breathed a little too hard. Clutched her arm a little too tight. Cheap muscle, not top trigger man.

She walked north down the sidewalk toward the Ferry Building. There were too many people jostling by to hear his footsteps, but she caught sight of his shoes. Cheap, flashy wing tips from Sears. Make that extra-cheap muscle. Probably a local boy, not an L.A. import.

Once they turned the corner, someone else drew up to them on the right, slowly and deliberately. Miranda snuck a glance over, and recognized Bennie,

Wong's gunman. Maybe Wong thought she'd reneged on the deal. Maybe that's what this was about.

Pastrami Man prodded her toward a dark blue Ford, '36 or '37, that waited on the corner. Someone in the driver seat, and one more in the front passenger. A lot of heat for Wong to be burning up. Bennie reached over and opened the car door, no recognition on his face. The gun in her back pushed her forward, and she climbed in, Bennie shoving in next to her on her right, the dime-store torpedo walking around the car and squeezing in from the left.

No one spoke. The driver started the engine. He was wearing a chauffeur's hat and leather gloves, and from the rearview mirror looked Filipino. Probably one of Charlie's boys.

The man in the passenger seat turned around and grinned at Miranda. His silky gray fedora and matching doeskin gloves shone dully in the dusk of the car. Hawklike nose, swarthy face, scar over his left eyebrow. White teeth, most false, a couple of gold molars. Brown eyes, predator eyes, calculating the percentage of profit in any action. White silk scarf around his neck.

An L.A. gangster, style cues from Warners, made and bred on the side streets of Santa Monica, the casting-couch city for trouble boys. Gray fedoras and gold teeth were about as plentiful as buxom blondes on a studio lot.

"Well, ain't she a looker. What a nice mix of business and pleasure . . . or business is pleasure, as the boss likes to say. I'm putting in my claim right now, boys, after he gets through with her."

Miranda stared at him, keeping a bored look on her face. "The boss" couldn't be Wong. That worried her. But they wouldn't see it.

He didn't like her eyes. Mottled color washed over his face, and he barked out to Pastrami Man: "You check for a rod, Malone? Roundheels here's got a ticket, which means she can pack."

Slight hesitation. Sideways glance at Miranda. Then he lied. "She ain't carryin'. Bennie here braced her 'fore we got her in the car."

Bennie sat like a statue, his eyes fixed out the window, his face immovable. Dandy Gun turned around in the seat to look at him.

"That right, Bennie?"

Bennie's idiot voice came out low and a little sad. "What Malone says, boss."

Malone laughed nervously, tugging at his collar. "You know how Bennie is. He don't know his right from his left, but you tell him to do something and he does it. And he's got plenty of swift where it counts."

Dandy Gun smirked at the joke, relaxed, glanced briefly at Miranda, and turned forward again. "Yeah. Only place it does count."

She'd been watching the road, the directions the driver took, though she knew where they were headed. Down the waterfront, a swing around, and back through by Washington Square to Pacific Avenue and 110 Cordelia Street. No one spoke again until they pulled up outside the dilapidated house, the shiny blue Ford as out of place as a Rockefeller in a breadline.

The driver climbed out first, crossed in front, and opened the door for the Italian. Once he stepped out, straightening his gloves, Bennie joined him, while Malone jerked his head at Miranda, and she clambered out on the sidewalk side, directly in front of the house.

Bennie flanked her on the right, Malone on her left, while Little Caesar headed the triumph up the short stairs, kicking off some peeling paint along the way. The chauffeur disappeared with the car, leaving the small driveway empty.

Rap on the doorway, three knocks. Scuffling behind it, answer asked and given. Then the door pushed open, a pool of darkness spilling out over the moving shadows of the porch.

110 Cordelia Street.

Bare lightbulb, old man at the door, wizened face, red eyes, smell of cheap liquor. No rug, rickety staircase swallowed by black. Hallway, doors, basement door by stairway. Odor of sweat and unwashed bodies suffocating, omnipresent.

110 Cordelia Street. The place where they kept the women.

Malone growled "Upstairs" and gestured at her with the gun. She gripped the banister, felt it wobble. Bennie was in front of her, leading the way into the darkness.

On the landing they walked toward the left. Three doors upstairs, some noise behind one of them. Quick sharp groans.

Miranda walked in through an open door into another room with another bare bulb, a table and two mismatched wooden chairs, two cots, and a radio. Malone shoved her toward a chair with the heel of his hand.

"Pat her down, Bennie. Don't want to lie to the boss."

Bennie moved easily behind Miranda, and followed her body with his hands as if he were dressing a wax dummy. No lust, not in Bennie. He stopped at the cigarette case, pried it out of her pocket, and handed it to Malone. Miranda forced herself not to turn around.

"Big case, lady. You must like your smokes."

"Gift from a client—ten carat. I was on my way in for some more Chesterfields when you boys snagged me. Nice work."

The admiring tone deflected his interest, and he tossed the case back on the table, where it landed with a clank next to Miranda. The latch held, and she let out a small breath.

"You must got some choice clients, lady, but like the boss said—you're a looker. Turn around and sit down."

She complied, crossing her legs and leaning back. Malone stared at her, twitching his mouth.

"You really a shamus?"

"Check my pocketbook and see."

"Don't get smart with me, sister. Gimme that purse over there, Bennie."

Bennie had brought up Miranda's bag. Malone opened it, spilling the contents on the table besides the cigarette case. He fumbled through the compact and lipstick, keys and coin purse, opened the pocketbook, shut it again.

"I'll take your word for it. Boss says you are, and the other boys say you are. You may remember 'em—they tried to pick you up the other night."

He laughed, nodding at Bennie to join him, which he did, the gesture automatic and meaningless. Bennie sat in the other chair, staring ahead, laughing for a moment, then blank, utterly blank. She was worried about Bennie. More worried about Wong.

Miranda reached up to rub her cheek ruefully, and Bennie leaned forward, gun in hand. Malone looked over at him, scoffing.

"Relax, jerk. My God, but you're wound up. Fast and slow, fast and slow, like a goddamn watch that never keeps the right time. She ain't got no gun, she's a broad, stupid. We ain't been told to kill her yet."

"Your boss must be a top man."

"Yeah, he looks like one, don't he? I ain't a sap, lady, you ain't gettin' nothin' out of me."

"Oh, I know you boys are smart. I'm not asking for a song. I just figured he rates, the way he looks and all. And the way you boys nailed me, and me not even seein' you coming."

"Smooth work, she says. Y'hear, Bennie? The skirt says we do some smooth work." He picked his teeth with his thumbnail, flicked whatever he caught onto the floor. "The boss rates, all right. But he got a boss higher than he is, and I figure that's who's gonna decide what we do with you."

"You got any ideas what they want with me? Warning didn't take, obviously, but since you boys could've dumped me in the Bay by now I figure they want something."

Malone looked at her, rubbed his heavy chin with a paw, and stuck his hand back in his pocket to feel his gun.

"I don't know what they want you for before, but I figure I know what they want after. What you get depends on cooperation, sister, always does. You in the mood to cooperate? Maybe a little early cooperation with Bennie and me?"

Her stomach clenched at the leer, and the shakes from no cigarettes were getting stronger. She forced herself to sit back, and rested her arm on the table, near the cigarette case.

"You heard what he said. I don't think he'd like it if you and Bennie and I got too friendly."

Bennie made a noise. "Mr. Wong won't like it."

Malone looked over at him, disgust on his face. "You're off the fucking track, moron. Wong's dead, remember? Knocked off, bumped, croaked. He ain't here, ain't gonna be here. Jesus Christ, Bennie, how fucking stupid . . ."

The gun came up in Bennie's hand, pointing at Malone. Bennie's eyes were flat, dull. Animal eyes. Malone choked on the words.

"Jesus Christ, Bennie, put the gat away. I ain't meanin' no disrespect, like I said, you're fast where it counts, and Mr. Wong was a right gee."

Something in the words pacified Bennie, and he lowered the gun. Malone stared at him for a minute, rubbing his chin again.

"You got the twist covered. I'm goin' to find out what they want us to do with her. If you go out to take a piss, tie her up and gag her."

He lumbered toward the door, his skull thick and heavy and shaved close, his brown coat stained with mustard from a pastrami sandwich. Bennie said nothing, just stared straight ahead. Malone shut the door behind him, didn't look back.

Miranda looked over at the short, squat man in the chair.

Wong was dead. Her best chance gone.

And she was alone in the room with Bennie.

————

Not a lot of time. Once Malone came back with a decision, they'd follow it. Whatever it was.

She looked at Bennie, opened softly.

"Mr. Wong was a good man, Bennie."

He grunted, fidgeting with his gun. She tried again.

"Sorry to hear about—"

"—made me kill him. That wasn't right. Wasn't right, was it? Him and his hat and his gloves. Just like the big man."

He was leaning forward, holding the gun out as if he was about to fire it, but not at her. At something she couldn't see. Bennie was shaking a little, focusing on the door. Goddamn it, use it, Miranda . . .

She shifted her weight a bit so that her right hand could pick up the case on the table. Bennie trained the gun on her, his eyes still focused on the past. She ignored the weapon, looked at Bennie, at the brown eyes, puzzled, raging, hurt.

"No, that wasn't right. The man with the gray hat made you kill Mr. Wong?"

He swung his head side to side, like a lion in a zoo cage, and jumped out of the chair. Started to pace.

A shrill scream from one of the other rooms made Miranda jerk her head, made Bennie cock the .38, then safety the hammer again. A few loud thuds and a crash, a male voice, then another, some laughter, a gurgled version of another scream. Then nothing.

Miranda exhaled, started again. "The boss man—"

He pivoted faster than she could follow, gun pointing at her breast, his voice almost hysterical. "He ain't my boss! Wong was my boss! And he made me kill Wong so he could boss me, but he ain't! He ain't!"

Soothing noises. Inarticulate noises he'd understand. He calmed down, sat, his left hand caressing the gun. Her hand was almost touching the case now.

"'Course he isn't, Bennie. Anybody could see that."

"My wife don't like it. Don't like Coppa."

Coppa. The silent partner in the Martini show. Dandy Gun was Coppa, second lieutenant, the Little Caesar to Martini's Nero.

"Your wife's smart."

He slumped over further in the chair, letting the gun dangle between his knees, barrel aimed at the floor. "Yeah. She don't like it. She liked Mr. Wong."

"Mr. Wong was a good man."

"Yeah."

They'd reached the end of the circle. He'd walked the length of the cage, but couldn't figure out how to get out of it. Right back to the doorway, head swinging sideways, an occasional roar. Try again.

She said it softly, cheerily, like an invitation to breakfast. "You don't have to listen to them."

Bennie's brow wrinkled. Couldn't figure out how it would work. She kept going, more urgency in her voice.

"You're your own man, Bennie, just like Mr. Wong treated you. Remember?"

"My wife liked him. She don't like Coppa."

"Right. Maybe she's afraid of him?"

The lion roared again. Miranda was getting used to the gun pointed at her. This time it shook in his hands. Eyes wild.

"I can save her! She don't need to be afraid!"

More soothing noises. But hurried. "Of course she doesn't. She knows you'll protect her from him. Because you know about the women, the women from the ships, don't you, Bennie? You know what they do to them, and so did Mr. Wong, and Mr. Wong didn't like it. He didn't like the ships at all, did he, Bennie?"

More pacing. Around and around Miranda. She didn't move, didn't turn to watch him behind her, kept her voice up. Noises from down the hall. Front door slam. She was running out of time.

"He don't like them. Mr. Wong don't like them. Likes Mary. He likes Mary, bought her presents sometimes. Gave me money for her."

"He didn't like what they do to the ship women. Did Mary come on a ship, Bennie?"

Somewhere behind her, the thud of his footsteps halted suddenly. Effort in thinking, following the tangle. Getting out of the cage.

He slowly said: "Yeah. She come on a ship."

"That's why she doesn't like Coppa. Why she liked Mr. Wong. Mr. Wong was nice. Coppa is very bad to women from ships. Like he was bad to Betty Chow."

Shot in the dark. He took a step toward the door as if he was going to walk through it, hesitated. Turned back to face her, his face contorted with the effort of thought.

"Coppa is bad to Mary, maybe. Mr. Wong was good, that's why Coppa made me kill him."

"That's right, Bennie. He should never have made you do that. Your wife doesn't like him."

"Yeah." His jaw was setting, and he looked at the door again, cocking the gun.

"You can save Mary from Coppa."

Brow wrinkled again. Looked from her back to the door. "How?"

"You can kill Coppa."

He lowered the gun, brought his left thumb up to his mouth. He chewed the nail, rhythmically biting and sucking. Then he walked backward, still facing the door, sitting down again.

More noise below. A couple of loud voices. Door slam, cars outside.

Somebody was climbing the stairs.

The door flung open, and Malone walked in quickly and shut the door, freezing when he saw Bennie standing with his legs apart, his face sweating, his .38 trained squarely on Malone's head. Malone laughed nervously, bringing his hand up to his grimy collar.

"For fuck's sake, Bennie, why you tryin' to scare me? Put that away. I'll cover the broad."

Bennie had seized an idea, and it wrapped him, enveloped him, gave him focus. Drops of sweat tumbled down from his forehead, and his eyes were hurt and raging, like a dog that's been kicked one too many times and figures, What the hell, I'll bite.

"Coppa's got Mary. Where is he?"

Malone blinked several times, and took a step forward. Bennie cocked the gun.

"Jesus H. Christ, what the fuck's got into you? Coppa don't got Mary."

"He told me to kill Mr. Wong. You told me to kill Mr. Wong."

Malone's forehead was starting to bead up. "Wong turned stoolie, Bennie. He was tryin' to send up the boss."

"Mr. Wong's the boss. Coppa ain't got no right to be boss."

Malone shot a look at Miranda, rasped out to Bennie, "This bitch been yankin' your chain or something? You can't go after Coppa, he's the boss!"

The last word was barely out of his lips when Bennie pulled the trigger.

In the flash of the shot, Miranda grabbed the case and palmed the Baby Browning.

Red spread on Malone's shirt, washing over the mustard and pickle from his sandwich. He looked down at it in disbelief, spurts timed to the beat of his heart. His knees went first, and he crumpled, falling to the floor, no strength to look at Bennie, to wonder why and how, wavering, his massive head the last to land, finding a hard place on the floor. Arms splayed, legs crooked. The red was seeping, not spurting anymore.

Pounding feet on stairs, shouts. At least three, maybe more.

Bennie had forgotten about her. He licked his lips, and stared at the doorway. Removed a 9 mm from a shoulder holster, held it out with his left hand. She could hear him whisper "Mary" over and over again. She slowly climbed out of the chair, and knelt behind it.

Door rattled, somebody barked, "Stand back." Another voice yelled, "What the fuck is going on, Malone?"

Bennie didn't answer. His wife's name was a refrain now, a constant hum in his head and down to his hand and trigger finger, to the gun that was a part of his body. Whispered conversation on the other side of the door. Miranda held the Browning, ready to fire.

"Malone?"

The door opened a crack. A gun muzzle peeked in. Followed by a hand, and arm, and a sideways entrance of another Italian boy. Another Dapper Danny. Must be Coppa's or Martini's men.

He was a small man, lithe like a dancer, and he flinched back around the door when he saw Malone's body and Bennie's gun aimed at him.

She caught a few words. "Moron" and "crazy sonofabitch" and "get the boss" and "charge." No volunteers came forward. A few minutes later, more steps, going down, going up. More minutes. Bennie's face was covered in sweat and spattered blood. It fell into his eyes and he didn't stop to wipe it. He didn't need his eyes to see anymore.

Her knees were starting to hurt, and she reshuffled her weight, making herself ready.

Voice behind the door, a purr.

"Bennie? You all right, Bennie? It's Joe, Bennie, Joe Coppa."

Wrong words.

Fusillade. Five shots from the .38, six from the 9 mm. At the sound of the first bullet, something thudded hard against the wood, and bullets fell like yesterday's rain, catching Bennie, shoulder out, blood-spray, thigh and stomach, right arm, but the .38 was already empty, and the left hand kept firing, firing as the elbow got blown off, a bullet finally finding his throat, tearing it open, Bennie falling, weaving to the floor, draping on Malone, brotherly embrace. Eyes glassy. Mouth trying to make the word "Mary."

Silence. Always silence in the aftermath.

Voice muttered, "You OK? Crazy bastard got the boss."

Another one, whiny. "Hurts like fuck. Where the fuck is Needles?"

"It's just your fucking leg, asshole. I'll go get him."

"Somebody's gotta tell Martini. And Charlie."

The other one scoffed. "Charlie don't get told nothin'. He's a big zero. Even Gillio ain't much these days. Fucking San Francisco mutts. Like that hophead Bennie, crazy motherfucker. I'll go get Needles. He's at the Settlement."

Footsteps. Whiny voice. "Wait . . . what if somebody else is in there?"

"You pissin' your pants? I didn't take you for a goddamn pansy, Noldano."

Noldano. One of the drivers. One of the bastards who tried to run her over.

"Fuck you. Just hand me a gun, then. Mine's empty."

"Oh, for Chrissakes. There's no one in the goddamn room. Supposed to be that fucking Corbie broad in there, knows where the Takahashi bitch is. Nutty bastard probably drilled her before she could talk."

"Just give me a goddamn gun."

Heaving sigh. "You're a fuckwad, you know that? I'll go in the door, so you don't have to play with yourself. What a fucking pansy."

He turned the knob and kicked the door open. He stood in the doorway, staring down at Malone and Bennie, shaking his head. His gun was hanging from his right hand, pointed at the floor.

A click. A voice.

"Drop it."

Miranda.

Twenty-eight

S urprise. Anger. Derision.

The 9 mm Luger in his hand came up at the same time his mouth opened.

"Fuck you, bit—"

The last word ended in a gurgle, as the Baby Browning spat, and he jerked backward, staring down in disbelief at the hole in his stomach. He clutched his gut and the Luger fell, skidding across the floor.

Miranda scooped it up with her left hand, dropping it in her other jacket pocket. Kept behind the door. Outside, Noldano was trying to stand up on his one good leg.

"What the fuck—Capella? What the fuck is going on? Throw me a fucking gun!"

His partner backed up against the wall, clutching his stomach with his fingers, fighting for breath. Looked up at Miranda, eyes almost as red as his hands.

"Thought—thought that was a toy."

She stared at him, said nothing.

Noldano was nearly hysterical. "Who you talking to? For Chrissakes, what the fuck is going on?"

She raised her voice. "I just shot your partner in the stomach. You want him to live—you wanna walk again—crawl in here. Or I'll blow off your other kneecap."

Pause. Capella was sweating from the pain. Staring at her gun, trying to figure out how big the bullet was, how long he had left. He braced his back on the wall, slowly slid down it until he was sitting, his legs outstretched, his feet limp.

Noldano tried to put some bluff in his voice.

"You that Corbie broad? Why the fuck should we listen to you? You ain't gonna hurt us. The boys'll be here soon . . . you can kiss your face good-bye, lady, 'cause it won't look the same after—"

"Crawl in here by the time I count to three, Noldano. Or you can kiss your legs good-bye. Who knows? After what you motherfuckers tried to do to me, I might blow out your ankle for the hell of it."

Some shuffling and skidding. A few whimpering noises. He was dragging himself in.

Capella was fighting to stay conscious. Miranda watched his head bob and weave, a boxing match with the wall. Waited behind the door until she could see Noldano on his knuckles scooting painfully across the threshold, his right leg stretched and broken behind him. Like Capella, he was dressed expensively, a pinstripe gray suit, three-piece, with rubber-soled shoes and cashmere socks. The dancer in the doorway.

She waved the Baby Browning at Noldano. "Over there with your partner."

He looked up at the sound of her voice, fear in his face until he saw the gun. Then he stopped crawling, staring first at her, then turning back to Capella.

"A broad with a pop gun? You let a broad with a pop gun get the fucking jump on you?"

She took a step forward. "It's a .25 mm. It might kill you, and then it might not. Ask Capella. Up against the wall."

Noldano managed to park himself next to the bigger man. He nudged his partner with his shoulder, but Capella was almost out.

"When will Martini be here?"

Noldano eyed her and clutched his mangled leg, grimacing, trying to put it back together. Shot-up shin and knee. Dangling, blown apart. Humpty fucking Dumpty.

"Why the fuck—should I—tell you?"

"So you won't get the gas chamber."

He shook his head. "Nuts to you, bitch. Martini'll like doing you."

"Martini. Now. And where the women are."

"Fuck you, lady."

Miranda shrugged, aimed the Browning. Noldano screamed when his left arm hit the wall.

"It could've been your other leg. Next time it will be."

The other gunman was unconscious, splayed sideways against the wall, breathing shallowly. He didn't have much time. Noldano's eyes, large and round, darted back and forth between Capella and Miranda.

"What you wanna know?"

"Martini—he's coming here?"

"For a—for a meeting. Seven o'clock."

She snuck a glance at her watch. Seventeen minutes.

"What's the meeting room—and where is he now?"

"Settlement. Covered Wagon. Upstairs and backrooms. This here's the safe-house. They usually talk downstairs. Dining room."

"Needles with him? And Gillio?"

He shook his head, blood seeping through his fingers where he held the arm above the elbow.

"Needles, yeah. Gillio don't show up except to collect. He and the boss talk by themselves. We never know the cut or nothing."

"What about Charlie?"

"The Flip? He ain't nothing. Still trying to find the money that Jap stole, bendin' over for the boss. We was using his people to take care of the women. After Wong, the boss don't want no slanties around, 'cept for the driver. Willie's OK."

"Where is Charlie?"

"Some Chink joint on Jackson. Little Manila or something."

"And the women?"

He jerked his head toward the floor. "Down in the basement. 'Til they're ready for tryin' out, then Coppa brings 'em upstairs. When they're good enough, they go to the Settlement. This here's a new batch."

Miranda gestured with the small pistol, her voice low.

"When they're not good enough?"

He tried to shrug, groaned, grabbed his arm again. "Mexico. Trade 'em for Mexicans."

If they survived. Shoved into cars and trucks or smuggled into boxcars, down the long road to Los Angeles, and the even longer road to Tijuana, suffocating in the heat. She wondered how many wound up in ditches outside the racetrack, survivors of the Empire of the Sun, small-village women, some girls, some old, some married, watching husbands and fathers and brothers shot and bayoneted, smuggled on a ship, starved, not feeling air or water or sun on skin, then thrown into this house, a basement, a bed, no one to talk to, no one to understand their cries, raped again and again until they were found to be "good enough."

She wiped her brow with her sleeve. Twelve minutes left.

"Betty Chow worked for Wong?"

The fear was wearing off; he was getting numb, going into shock. "Yeah. She could talk to 'em. The boss don't want no Chinks no more, we been short-handed. Lost one of 'em yesterday."

"One of the women?"

"Yeah."

"Noldano—who killed Betty?"

He was leaning against Capella with his right shoulder. The other man looked like he was still breathing, but very shallowly.

"Coppa. Double-crossing Chink bitch. Did her up like the boss likes."

The shot rang through the house, and Noldano started with a jerk. Miranda stood over Coppa's body on the other side of the threshold, the wolfish face drawn back into a smiling rictus, a fresh hole torn out of the back of his skull.

She stepped back in the room, grunting as she heaved Malone and Bennie over, removing guns and pistols from hands and holsters. The spent ones she tossed in the corner; a Smith and Wesson .38 revolver and another 9 mm Luger she stuck in her pockets. Four guns. Seven minutes.

Noldano watched her, sweating, his eyes unfocused.

"Why'd you waste a bullet on Coppa? He's dead, lady. Why'd you waste one?"

Her hand was on the doorknob. She looked down at the body, glanced back briefly at Noldano.

"You wouldn't understand."

She stepped over Coppa's corpse, and hurried down the stairs.

———

She opened the door down the hall.

Small room, bed, closet, lamp. Nobody there. But the sheets were rumpled, dirty. Still some blood on the mattress.

Miranda closed the door softly behind her, listening for any noise from Capella or Noldano. She wanted them to live. Needed them to live.

Find a telephone. Fast.

She started down the stairs. The women would have to wait. She needed the fucking cops, needed them here to catch Martini and Gillio, needed them to see what they refused to see, what they didn't want to see.

She was four steps from the floor when she heard the voices outside. Checked her watch on reflex—two minutes early. Or maybe she was two minutes too late.

Miranda ran down, ran to the right, looking for the kitchen. There. Through the door.

Kitchen was small. Stove with a layer of grease, a stained coffeepot. No place to hide. The door was starting to open in the front.

She grabbed the dirty porcelain knob on the opposite wall, opened the door. Large room with a table, like a boardinghouse. Nothing but a table.

Voices. They were in the house.

Across the floor and around the large square table, toward the door at the other end. Fast, quiet.

The bathroom.

Bathtub, shower. Thin, torn calico curtain. Toilet, sink with a rusty stain.

They were walking into the dining room.

No place left to run.

She sat on the toilet seat, holding the Browning. The other, bigger guns hung heavy in her pocket. If she was going to fire, she wanted it clean. A gun she knew.

The men were filtering in the large room, loud, garrulous voices echoing against the stained wallpaper. If Noldano and Capella were conscious and could hear . . .

Five voices.

One loud, authoritative. Charismatic, even, could have been on the radio.

Martini.

Southern accent. She'd read somewhere that Needles was originally from Arkansas. Check.

Older voice, gravelly. North Beach. Gillio? Maybe a lieutenant.

Two more voices, the subservient braggadocio of the hired thug, yes boss, no boss, anything you want, boss. Like the ones upstairs.

Chairs scraping the floor. Hand slapping the table.

"Where the fuck is Coppa and his boys? Risso, make some fucking coffee. And put some juice in it. This fucking headache of mine—"

"You want me to get you a wet towel, boss?"

Miranda held her breath. One Mississippi, two Mississippi.

"Nix. Coffee. And go upstairs and see if that fucker Coppa is fucking on the job again."

Laughs all around the table.

Deep voice. "I'll go, boss." Heavy footsteps, across to the door and out.

Martini opened in a conversational tone. "So we got the Corbie bitch. Good. Find out where she's got the Jap stashed, then turn her over to Coppa and ice her. She's been a fucking headache, worse than the one I've got. Like finding that little blond cunt I dumped on Coppa."

Laughter again. Then a shout from upstairs.

"Boss! Boss!"

Footsteps, chairs pushed back, Martini irritated. "What the fuck—what is it, Louie?"

More footsteps, agitated. Heavy pair running in, door flung open, banging against the wall. Voice panting.

"Coppa. He's dead, boss. So is Malone and Bennie. Noldano and Capella are almost gone—Capella's got a bad gut shot, he's out. Noldano woke up, said it was that Corbie dame."

Silence.

Hoarse whisper. "What the fuck—I don't fucking believe this shit. Goddamn fucking skirt don't make away with three men and shoot two more. Something's fucking queer. Needles, go upstairs and—"

Slurred drawl. "Already on my way, Sam. Lead the way, Louie."

Footsteps again. Pacing. Silence.

"You still want your coff—"

"Shut the fuck up. I'm thinking." Pause again. Some muffled voices upstairs. Bodies being moved.

"It's gotta be a hit. Somebody's after the goddamn money, stole the Corbie broad. Somebody who don't want us moving in. Charlie ain't got the balls, and the other Chinks in town wouldn't try it after Wong. Some fine fucking criminals, goddamn yellow cowards."

"Yellow—that's funny—"

"Shut up. Ain't been the same out here. They got their own ways, and they've bought and sold and smuggled plenty of their own goddamn pussy, but they ain't touchin' the ones brought in by the Japs. So it ain't Chinatown. So who the fuck is it, Romano? Capone?"

Gravel again. "He's in Alcatraz, Martini. He can't do nothing."

"Maybe he can't and maybe he can. Maybe he's planning his own moves, direct from Cell Block Eight. You need to take this up with Gillio, for Chrissakes. I moved up on the slanties because he said it was clear. Now I'm down a damn good man, and it's going to be up to Gillio to get me a replacement."

The gravelly voice was careful, polite. "I'll talk to Gillio. He knows a lot of people."

Cigarette smoke drifted under the bathroom door to Miranda's nose. Her hands started to shake again.

"I got about thirty Chinks downstairs waiting to be sold. L.A.'s doin' good. I got good business in L.A. Holy Christ, I'm almost fucking respectable. And I come up here—at Gillio's invitation—bring my best man, good boys like Noldano and Capella, and I lose 'em. That ain't right, Romano."

Small pause. Gravelly voice again, considered. "You just need to talk to Joe. He'll sit you square."

"Yeah. And tell him to find somebody who can speak Chink. That moron Bennie has a Chink wife, don't he? Get her down here."

"Bennie's dead, boss."

"So? What the fuck difference does that make? Get her down here."

Pause. Romano clearing his throat. "I'll just go and get Joe now, Sammy, if that's OK."

Pause. "Yeah. You do that."

Footsteps, not heavy. Door open, door shut. One Mississippi, two Mississippi, three Mississippi . . .

Heavy whisper. "Risso—follow that prick. I don't trust that goddamn Gillio, the fucking *culo*. Goddamn snobby-ass bastard. Follow him. But get Louie down here first."

"Sure, boss."

Heavy footsteps. A yawn and a curse from the table.

Then more footsteps, lighter ones.

Walking toward the bathroom.

The bathtub was a small claw-foot, and she crouched down, hiding behind the torn curtain. Trying not to breathe, trying not to shake.

Martini walked in with a cigarette in his mouth, lifted up the toilet seat. Unzipped his pants, groaned a little. The piss came out in a trickle, like it was hard for him to go.

Knock at the door. Miranda jumped, just a little. Martini turned around, saying, "For Chrissakes, what the fuck is it now?"

"Louie. Just wanted to make sure you're there."

Martini turned back around slowly to face the toilet. Too slowly. She felt his eyes on the flimsy curtain. And gripped the Browning tighter.

He shook out a couple of drops, zipped himself up. Dropped the cigarette in the toilet. Raised his voice.

"Stick around, Louie."

"Yeah, boss."

She held her breath. Martini started to whistle. Sounded like "It Had to Be You." Pushed the flush.

Then he spun around and flung the curtain aside, staring down at her, a .45 Colt in his hand.

Miranda stood up slowly, the Browning feeling like a baby's toy next to the .45. Martini looked her over. Said softly, "You the Corbie dame?"

She saw no point in lying, not now.

"Yes."

He looked her over again, taking in the skirt, the shoes, the legs, his eyes on her body the dirtiest thing she'd ever felt.

His voice crooned. "Hey, Louie."

"Yeah?"

"Tell the boys to get down here. I got a surprise."

"OK."

The big man lumbered off, making noise. Martini cocked his head to the side.

"You are a nice piece of tail, lady. Quite a ride. I'm looking forward to you."

Miranda said nothing. Brought the small pistol up to where one shot could do it. He looked down at the tiny gun, lifted his head back up, and laughed.

"Lady, you think that water gun is gonna stop my .45? You might squeeze out a shot, but not before I blow your fucking boobies off. And that, as they say, would be a waste."

He licked his lips, stared at her. "I'll have fun with you, lady. I'll make it last."

"Like you did with Phyllis Winters?"

His face darkened, suffused with color. "Shut your fucking mouth. You been a real headache to me. You owe me, bitch, owe me a plenty good time."

"Try the electric chair, Martini. Maybe then you'll manage to get it up."

He took a step toward her. Voice on the other side of the door.

"Everybody's here, boss, 'cept Noldano and Capella. That leaves Needles and me, and he wants to get back upstairs. He's worried about Capella."

"Fuck Capella." He said it through his teeth, a frozen grimace at Miranda. "I got a surprise for you. Open the goddamn door."

Louie pulled it open. Two shadows fell across the broken tiles on the floor. Martini's grin widened.

"I found the Corbie broad. She was sittin' in here, takin' a bath with her clothes on. That ain't right. Is it, boys?"

"Whaddya gonna do with her?" Needles sounded like he had a professional interest.

Martini unzipped his fly slowly. Reached in, and started jerking at himself, staring at Miranda. She kept her eyes focused on his face, kept aware of Needles and Louie.

Martini spoke thickly, almost in a trance. "First I'm gonna make her pay me off. She's gonna show me a good time, nice and juicy, just look at her. You boys can have her when I'm done. And when we've all been taken care of, she's gonna tell us who killed my boys and where that Jap bitch is. And then maybe I'll let her go to Mexico with me. If I like her enough."

Louie took a step forward. Miranda said, very clearly: "You move again and your boss is dead."

Needles spoke up. "But you'll be dead, too, lady. Look at the size of his gun."

She reached down into the pit of her stomach, fighting, not thinking. No fear, not now. Not to them.

"I've seen the size of his gun. I'm not impressed."

Martini's half a hard-on wilted, trance broken. Zipped himself up, eyes maddened, wild, the .45 shaking in his hand.

"You fucking cunt. You ain't worth my time. No piece of me except a bullet. Talk. Who cut down the boys? Gillio's droppers? Where's the Takahashi tramp? Where's the money? Talk, goddamn you!"

The force of Martini's fury hit her like a wall. Her concentration couldn't hold forever. Hands shaky from no nicotine, her courage dredged up from hard places she'd didn't know she had. But it had to last. Or she'd be dead.

Deep breath. Go out with style, Miranda. Make it mean something. That's what Johnny taught you—

"Fuck you. You're a two-bit Hollywood Capone, Martini. Built your little empire on the backs of women, ones who couldn't fight back."

She held the small pistol with both hands, aiming it squarely at his head. "Go ahead and shoot. I'll take you with me."

Louie looked over at Needles. "She's crazy."

Needles shrugged. "Mexican standoff."

The sound of the front door being thrown open made the other two turn, drawing their guns. Men's voices filled the air. Police whistles.

Footsteps running upstairs, footsteps all over the house.

A voice from the rear, harsh, loud, tough. Behind Louie and Needles.

"Drop the guns. You're under arrest."

Gonzales.

Twenty-nine

The pain and the fear and the ugliness of a thing are always in the aftermath.

Miranda couldn't remember how long it took for someone to find Martini, to coax her out of the bathtub, to take her Browning, to wipe the blood and brains off her face.

All she remembered was Gonzales's voice, and Martini's wildness, his kicking the door shut, and screaming that the next motherfucking cop who came to the door was going home in a body bag. He'd forgotten about her, another caged animal, feral, cornered, baring its teeth. Except the natural world doesn't make animals like Martini, doesn't make wars, doesn't make fascists, doesn't make Martinis. The refrain repeated, her tiny pistol still trained on his skull.

War, Miranda, war. War, Miranda, war. War, Miranda . . .

Ranging, twitching, desperate. Big gun out, small gun from shoulder holster. Then he noticed her. The smile, the big exhale chilled her.

He yelled to the cops outside the small bathroom: "I've got a hostage, motherfuckers!"

And then he started toward her, the .45 on her, the Mauser in his belt.

"You my ticket out, bitch."

He took one step. One more, a foot in the bathtub.

And she fired.

The .25 mm bullet tore through his forehead, a clean shot, spraying blood and brain and bone behind Martini on its exit. Small spatters. Polka dots on the wall.

He fell forward, the force of his momentum landing most of the body in the tub, against the yellow tile, sliding down, red streak, crumpled, rag doll.

Miranda stood, watching the blood seep out on the dirty white of the tub, watching it move slowly toward the drain. Her arms frozen in the firing position.

You OK, Miranda? You OK, Miranda? You OK, Miranda?

Gonzales's voice, over and over.

Echo. Empty. Gone.

Hall of Justice. Nurse was nearby. "She's had a shock" she said. "Give her a couple of hours."

And so she sat, not saying anything, not feeling anything. Alone.

Cops walked by. Once in a while, one would peek in the window. "That's the broad who put Sammy Martini on ice. Yeah, a real bloodbath. Don't know all what happened, not yet, two of 'em in the hospital, the rest won't talk. Bunch of Chinese women in the hospital, too, trying to get someone out to talk to 'em. She was there, cracked the fucking case. Yeah—a broad."

They'd given her a cigarette. Then a pack. Smoke in her lungs made her cough. Then made her still. Shaking less. Just a tremor now and then in her right hand. Shooting hand.

Yeah, a broad. Little bitty gun she had, and all those men . . .

The door opened, finally, a waft of stale air filtering in from the hall. Night air, heavy fog, neon in it.

"Hey, sweetheart—you all right?"

Allen. Pinkerton op. She felt the muscles in her face respond.

"Yeah. I'm OK."

He took his hat off, rubbed a hand on his nearly bald scalp, grabbed a chair, turned it around, straddled it and faced her.

"You look like shit, Miranda. They give you any of this?"

He held out a flask. She took it, gingerly, tilted some into her mouth, felt the heat cascade down her insides like fire.

Wiped her mouth, gave it back.

He said: "Nah, drink it all."

"They gave me a little."

"Not enough, the cheap bastards."

"The nurse said—"

"Fuck the nurse. She ain't an op. We take care of our own."

Words. Whiskey. The frown on Allen's broad face.

"You're startin' to look better now."

"Yeah." She took another pull from the flask. "So where are we?"

"The case? Your case?" He grinned. "You got the new police chief on his ass and on the phone with the dingus in L.A. And the feds are stepping in, hush-hush Q.T. stuff, because of the Jap-China angle. Seems you can't smuggle occupied people out of occupied territory on occupier shipping lines without the occupier knowing a little something about it. Someone worked with Winters and Martini and the rest to set this up, and the state department don't want a ruckus. Not with the war jitters. We keep an eye on Japan, but we don't want to offend anybody."

Another swallow. The flask was almost empty. "They find Gillio?"

Allen shrugged. "They're not telling me. This is just scat I picked up in the hall. But I got a few connections between him and Martini they might wanna look at. The stuff you had me dig up for you this afternoon."

"Anything good?"

"Enough to keep me digging and late on meeting you. Your friend Gladys was the one to tell me you were in trouble. She put in the call to the cops."

"Gladys? Why? Did she—"

"Seems you got a bad habit of running out of Chesterfields. Those sticks saved your life, kid. Gladys was running after you with some decks she found and saw you getting swarmed. She got worried, and followed until she saw you shoved in the car around the corner, grabbed the plate numbers, and called the Hall. Took her longer to get someone to listen to her than it did anything else."

"Yeah. It would. So she found Gonzales?"

"Eventually. And eventually, he found you. Got a message delivered late or something. Lucky thing you left one."

Allen shook out a Lucky Strike, offered one to Miranda. She took it gingerly, and he struck a match on his thumb, lighting both cigarettes.

"I was on my way out. Found your note, figuring you were at the Pickwick picking up the goods. Then I went to buy some candy for the wife, and Gladys told me what happened."

"Shit."

"What's wrong?"

She inhaled the Lucky Strike until it burned back a quarter of an inch, and then tilted the flask, draining the last of the whiskey. And stood up.

"We've gotta go."

"What—why? They're waiting to talk to you about—"

"Yeah, I know. I'll lay it out. But not without the Pickwick evidence."

"Shit, Miranda, you've already been through—"

"You said it yourself. I'm an op. Maybe not a Pinkerton, but I am a detective. So get off your ass and drive me down to Fifth Street."

He grinned up at her, reached over and grabbed his hat. "Glad to see you again, Miranda."

Phil was nowhere to be found. Gonzales came over briefly, eyes worried, bandage still on his nose. He was busy coordinating with the other departments, busy cleaning up the mess Miranda had spilled all over two cities and two countries.

His hand touched her sleeve for a moment, then pulled back.

"We've been waiting for your full statement, Miss Corbie. You're supposed to stay here."

"She hasn't been charged with anything, has she?"

"Not yet. But she admitted she killed Martini—"

"In self-defense."

Gonzales stared at Allen. "You're not her lawyer. Who are you?"

The bald man reached into his back pocket, took out his wallet. "Pinkerton."

Gonzales looked from one to the other, letting his gaze linger on Miranda. She was staring at the smoke from the Lucky Strike.

He said softly: "I'm not supposed to do this. But if you go and get back here in under an hour, I might be able to look the other way."

"Keep lookin', brother. I'll see she gets back here."

Gonzales nodded briefly, still watching Miranda. Then turned abruptly and walked back into the war room, the clatter of voices and phones surrounding him.

She'd forgotten it was night. Valentine's night.

Allen kept sneaking sideways glances at her, dodging the taxis and the streetcars, cursing the pedestrians crossing against the cars on the south-of-Market streets.

"How many were there, Allen?"

"How many what, sweetheart?"

"Women. In the basement."

"Don't know. You make 'em give you that information when you talk. Don't walk away with nothing in your pocket. You want me to call your lawyer?"

She inhaled the third Lucky Strike he'd given her. "Yeah. Meyer Bialik. Guess he should be there, just in case."

"Just in case, sweetheart. Never trust the cops. I don't."

She was quiet again, staring out the window. Yellow, blue, green. Red and pink. Music and noise, neon swirls against the black. Like red on white.

"Miranda."

"Yeah?"

"We're here."

She looked around and saw the Pickwick, its own neon huge and splendid, yellow fireworks in the sky. Wondered how many lovers trysts were being held here, how many dates, how many sweaty embraces, guilty, three-minute climaxes before another evening at home.

Allen climbed out, walked around to her side of the car, opened the door. Held his hand on her elbow, pulled her up.

"You need another drink. C'mon, let's hurry."

They quickly walked to the Greyhound terminal on the Mission Street side. Sleepy time of year for buses. Anybody who had a home or a sweetheart and money enough to get back had already left.

An old man in a Greyhound cap was snoozing at the luggage claim. He wiped his glasses when he saw Miranda. Probably figured the specks were from the glass.

She held out her shoe to Allen, who pried it off her swollen ankle. Then he felt around the top until he found the ticket, and tore it away from the leather. The old man was watching, trying to remember the details.

Allen presented the ticket, and the baggage man cleared his throat, hemming and hawing, then disappeared behind a wall of suitcases, garment bags, and boxes.

Miranda slid her foot back into the shoe with the Pinkerton helping. They waited a few minutes, neither speaking, both smoking. The old man finally emerged, holding a thick file envelope.

He laid it down on the counter, licked his fingers, and started to page back through the list of receipt numbers. Let's see, Friday the ninth? No . . . Thursday the eighth. Nighttime. Let me see, that would be six days, at twenty-five cents a day, that'll be—

Allen had the dollar fifty laid out with a quarter tip. More hemming and hawing while he counted it, and counted it again, hoping for someone to explain what it was all about. Nobody did. He gave up, eventually, turned over the package.

Allen handed it to Miranda, who tucked it under her arm. They walked back to the car, climbed in. And he looked at her.

"That what you want?"

She shrugged. "It's what Winters died to get. And Betty died to deliver. And Wong died to produce."

The car turned over with a slight stutter, then purred back along Mission Street.

"You know, sweetheart, we've got a good fifteen minutes until Gonzales starts to send out a posse. And you need a drink."

"What do you suggest?"

"How about the Rusty Nail? A little dive on Battery."

"Whatever you say, Allen."

The car sped along.

The bourbon was rough around the edges, but hearty and strong. Highball glass, neat, on a scarred wooden counter, a bowl of dice at her elbow, a truck driver on the other side of Allen.

The Rusty Nail gleamed near the waterfront with the twilight of Bayshore neon, softer than downtown. It danced on the water, shimmering on the concrete and steel piers, the small fishing boats just down the way at Fisherman's Wharf. The bar held a crowd that didn't care who you were or what you did, as long as you liked your liquor strong and cheap, and minded the rules of the house.

No rough stuff. No politics. No pickups.

Allen stuffed his thick body into one of the small booths at the back of the room, where they served beefsteak and hamburgers to the dockworkers and the sailors, a bottle of hot sauce next to the salt and pepper. He was calling Meyer.

Miranda gulped the bourbon. Not refined enough to be sipped, the medicinal kind, the stuff that took your bad dreams away and replaced them with courage. The stuff that dreams are made on.

Goddamn it. Quoting Shakespeare like her fucking father. Sure sign of a bankrupt mind.

The cigarette tasted good. She could learn to like Lucky Strikes, but would always prefer Chesterfields, especially now. She'd take Gladys somewhere, do something for her. Not every day when your cigarette girl saves your fucking life. Happy Valentine's, Miranda. Your heart's still beating.

Another gulp. Allen was coming back.

"You feeling better?"

"I'm feeling drunker."

"Drunk is good."

The guttural laughs and higher-pitched chuckles from the single men and married couples around them—the regulars of the Rusty Nail—rose in volume, agreeing with Allen.

Drunk is good.

Miranda drained her glass, almost stumbling when she fell off the stool.

"Whas' in that stuff, Allen?"

His eyes seemed to twinkle at her. Lights in the fog.

"Life, Miri. Life."

Gonzales kept fiddling with his tie. Meyer was there, waiting for them, dressed for the opera.

"My dear girl, is this the man who phoned? Thank you, sir—"

"Don't mention it. Miranda and I are neighbors, I'm a Pinkerton. Allen Jennings."

"I'm glad someone is watching out for our Miranda."

A throat cleared itself from a waiting area across the hall, and footsteps approached. Rick said politely, "Hello, Meyer. Gonzales."

The inspector looked like a man cornered. "If you're here in a professional capacity, Sanders . . ."

"I'm here in a personal capacity, Gonzales. I got the lead, saw Miranda's name, and I've been waiting here to make sure she gets home OK."

Miranda was clutching the package they'd picked up from the Pickwick. "H'lo, Rick."

"Hey, Miranda."

Gonzales threw up his hands, said, "Follow me."

He ushered all of them into another of the small interrogation rooms. Allen looked around. "You're stashing us in the confessional, Inspector?"

"We need to get a full statement from Miss Corbie when she's ready. At that time, you'll all have to leave. With the exception of Mr. Bialik, of course."

Miranda's lawyer drew himself up. "I understand that she has already made a preliminary statement, explaining the outlines of what happened, the names of the persons involved, and the circumstances surrounding the shootings."

"Yes, but—"

"No 'but' about it, Inspector. Unless you're placing Miss Corbie under arrest she should be released immediately. Further questioning can wait until she's had some rest. She is obviously not in any condition to respond."

Gonzales's eyes narrowed at Allen. Miranda was nodding over the Pickwick package, the smell of bourbon wrapping her like a baby blanket.

Bialik expostulated. "For God's sake, man, look what she's been through! Either charge her—and if you do, I'll have her out on a habeas corpus so fast that your ink won't have dried—or let us out of this godforsaken hellhole you mockingly call a Hall of Justice."

Rick pushed his fedora back with a grin and clapped his hands in a slow rhythm.

"Amen, preacher."

Allen leaned over to Miranda, gently nudging her on the shoulder. "Kid— Miranda—wake up, sweetheart. Remember the Pickwick?"

She came to with a start, frightened, breathing hard. Then she focused on the package. Squinted, and saw Gonzales. Stood up, tottering a little— Gonzales and Allen reached out to steady her—and she held the package out to Gonzales with both hands.

She licked her lips, forming her words carefully.

"Winters was buying information from Wong. Information to shut down Martini. He wanted out, wanted his daughter back, needed something to deal with the DA. Betty showed up t' deliver it and collect the money from Winters. Wong was still lookin' for a profit. Still a criminal. But he wanted out of the Chinese slave trade. Betty found him dead. Winters. Figured she was in a frame. Wrote me, tried to call me a couple days later. Meantime, she stashed the evidence 'gainst Martini and NYK at the Pickwick. And gave Winters's money—found it in the room—to Eddie Takahashi. Money disappeared with Eddie's sister. And then Wong and Betty were killed."

Gonzales took the package from her wordlessly. She raised a finger, pointed it at him.

"She's no murderer, goddamn you. Clear her name. Or as God is my witness, I'll spend the rest of my life chasing down every two-bit cop on the take, every third degree behind closed doors, every quickie from a call girl." She turned around, staring at each of the other men. "Y're all my witnesses."

Gonzales said: "Yes, Miss Corbie."

Miranda sank into her chair, suddenly white. Allen jumped up, but by the time he got to her, she'd passed out.

Part Five

Lantern Festival

Thirty

S omething was hurting her eyes.

She tried to move, to block it out. And now someone was shaking her.

Miranda woke to a blurry light, a bright room.

Her room. Her bedroom.

The blurred vision gradually sharpened. Rick was sitting next to her, his hand on her shoulder. She felt her face, her chest. No hat. In a nightgown. Another man was standing at the foot of the bed, mid-fifties, beard, gray hair, narrow face. White coat.

Her tongue was furry, thick, the hand she lifted to her cheek like someone else's.

"Dr. Nielsen? Who called Dr. Nielsen?"

The bearded man smiled beneficently. "Your friend here, Miss Corbie. Seems he found my number in your files, deduced that we've seen each other before, and asked me to come by to look at you. That was last night. I undressed you, cleaned you a bit, and gave you something to help you sleep."

"What time is it?"

Rick answered. "About four o'clock, Miranda."

She tried to sit up, winced at the effort. "Why the hell—why do I hurt so much?"

Nielsen moved around to the other side, placed a dry hand on her forehead. Frowned. "Because you're exhausted. You've also been through a shock."

She tried to shake her head, stopped when it hurt.

"Let me up. I'm fine."

"Miranda, you were almost run over the other night. You've been getting by on no sleep, coffee, bourbon, and cigarettes."

This time, she managed to raise herself up, and glared at them both. Turned to Rick. "And you don't? Just give me some aspirin, for God's sake. I'll be OK."

Nielsen shook his head. His voice that grave tone you heard on radio soap operas. "Miss Corbie—I don't see you as much as I should, undoubtedly. But I believe you trust my opinion. It's been of service to you before."

She looked up at him, her mouth tight.

"Yeah, Doctor. Spit it out."

"You need to rest as much as possible. For at least a week. Give your body—and your mind—time to process what you've been through. If you give me your word that you will rest, perhaps walking a bit every day as you feel stronger—and that you will not drink alcohol, and only one or two cups of coffee—I'll let you recover at home. Otherwise, you give me no choice but to commit you to a hospital."

She could feel the chains snake around from under the bed, manacles closing on her arms and legs. Reminded herself to find another doctor. Rick nodded, looking like Charlie McCarthy with Nielsen taking the Bergen part. Goddamn it, they always thought they knew best . . .

Miranda mustered a trustworthy expression and a small smile. "If that's what you think I need, Doctor."

He nodded, picked up his bag from the foot of the bed.

"At least a week. You should make a full recovery, feel like yourself again."

Miranda thought: "Like the smug bastard would know the difference." She said: "Thank you, Doctor."

He looked at Rick, man-to-man, guardian-to-guardian of that fragile thing called woman.

"Sanders—I rely on you to let me know how Miss Corbie progresses. I'll be by in three days to check on her."

"Certainly, sir."

They walked out of the bedroom together, making lists between them of what she should do and not do. Fuck that. Miranda hadn't lived thirty-three years and survived the last week so that old Dr. Kildare and his assistant could tell her what to do with her life.

She waited until she heard the door shut, and then tried to get her legs to the side of the bed. Groaned, couldn't help it. If only she didn't hurt so goddamn much . . .

"Miranda, what the hell do you think—"

Brown, baleful eyes focused on Rick. "Lay off, Sanders. I appreciate the help, and I heard what that old quack said. I've got his card because he's a friend of my father's—alcohol treatments."

"Then why don't you listen to him, goddamn it?"

She'd manage to drape her legs off the bed, and was trying to prop herself up into a sitting position. Rick watched for a moment, then came over to help her, cursing under his breath.

"You never fucking listen, do you? Gonna kill yourself one of these days, and I won't be around to stop you."

He was sitting beside her. Miranda leaned on him, fighting the nausea. She raised her left hand and touched his cheek, stroked it with the back of her fingers. Her voice was soft.

"Thanks, Sanders. I'll rest. I promise. Right now I need you to help me get down to the Hall of Justice. Gotta make that statement. You call Meyer for me?"

His eyes searched hers. She dropped her hand. He picked it up, held it, rubbing the lines in her palm with his thumb. Stared at it while he spoke.

"I'll call him. And I'll get you there. But for God's sake, Miranda—take care of yourself."

Gonzales had just come on duty. The bags under his eyes made him look older, more like a cop than a matinee idol. His temper was frayed around the edges, and the conversation was kept to a minimum. Still no sign of Phil, though Miranda caught sight of Johnson on the phone pulling overtime, Regan going off duty, Grogan coming on. No one said anything to her except a uniform who came to give Gonzales papers.

"Some prices on those toe tags, lady. You want the reward money?"

Meyer looked at her, Gonzales looked at her. Puff on the cigarette, stamp it out, light another one. "Give it all to Bennie's wife, Mary." She'd made her a widow, after all.

Rick prowled around outside, trying to pick up crumbs for the *News*. Meyer sat next to her, making sure Gonzales's questions were phrased in the right way.

No, she hadn't walked in, broken in, tried to get in. She'd been kidnapped; check Gladys Hillerman's statement.

No, she hadn't shot Malone or Bennie. She knew Bennie was ready to pop; she popped him, he popped the rest. End of story.

Well, not quite. .25 bullet lodged in the wall outside, matching shot in Coppa's skull. Yes, that was her gun. Yes, he was dead. Client was in a state of shock, Inspector, didn't realize she was committing a crime. And technically, as he wasn't interred—quiet, Miranda—yes, she understands. Continue.

Shot Capella. Tried to shoot her, thought her gun was a joke. Type of pistol not sold in America. License to carry conceal? Check. License for that gun? Nix.

But Inspector, that gun saved her life. A woman in her position must protect herself.

What about Noldano?

Yes, she'd shot Noldano in the arm. Client was threatened with bodily harm, Inspector, feared for her life. Thought he had a loaded gun. And still, she didn't fire to kill. Isn't that right, Miranda? Isn't that right?

Whatever you say, Meyer.

Why didn't she go for help? Tried to, ran out of time. Heard them coming in. We've been through this before.

How many times will you ask the same questions, Inspector? Has my client been charged—

Yes, she hid in the bathroom. Martini came in. Pulled a .45. Called the other two down from upstairs.

Threaten her?

You might say that. They were planning to rape her. That's r-a-p-e, Inspector, same thing Coppa did to Betty Chow, same thing Martini did to Phyllis Winters.

Silence. Pen scratching. She shoot him then?

No, she shot him after you arrived, Inspector. Tried to use her as a shield. You heard the gunshot, found her covered in Martini's brains, you make a statement.

Make a statement. Make a statement. Make a statement.

Meyer touched Miranda's arm, while Gonzales kept writing.
It was over. Rick drove her back home.

She crossed the days off on the calendar. Felt stupid, felt indulgent, lounging around in silk pajamas and a bathrobe, working on the crossword puzzle, listening to *One Man's Family*. Slept for hours, sleeping with the sun.

Rick came in every day or evening, every chance he got. She gave him an extra key, sometimes would find him sitting beside her, writing up notes in a tablet. He'd give her the news for the next morning, tell her what the Germans and Russians and Japanese were doing, whether Louis won his latest fight, whether Seabiscuit was going to race again.

Joe Merello sent a huge bouquet of tulips on a rhinestone horseshoe, the ribbon signed by the Moderne staff. Bente came by, sat with her a couple of hours, talked about Spain and the Wobblies and how everything was going to hell and made fun of the Duke and Duchess of Windsor, but life was still good and she'd better damn well pay attention to it.

Edith mailed a get-well card, said she'd read about her in the paper, hoped she was feeling better. Gladys stopped by with two cartons of Chesterfields, personal delivery. Miranda hugged her. Didn't quite have the words, not yet.

Allen stopped by twice during the week, brought her a pint of Old Taylor.

Even Leland Cutler, president of the World's Fair board, sent a telegram, wishing her well. She heard from a few other staff, too, including her federal contacts. Seems the Martini case—and the woman who broke it and was almost broken herself—had been fodder for more newspapers than Rick's.

No word on what would happen to the Chinese women smuggled in. The government had quotas. Mustn't upset the numbers.

As soon as she was well . . .

Nielsen came by to check on her. He seemed gratified. She clenched her teeth in a smile, and reminded herself—again—to find another doctor.

She tried to read *All This and Heaven, Too*, and threw it across the room after thirty pages. Burns and Allen made her laugh occasionally. She walked a little more every day, the weather improving with her stamina, and caught *His Girl Friday* at the Orpheum with a Shadow serial. The salty popcorn tasted as good as anything she could remember. The movie was as good as anything she could remember, even if Rosalind Russell's hats were a little extreme.

She managed to sneak into the office twice. Helen Winters had sent her a check, as predicted, along with a note thanking her profusely for saving Phyllis and stopping the "scourge" of crime that was so endangering the youth of our fair city.

Miranda heard the Supervisor dictating the letter, deposited the Supervisor's money in the bank. Innocence could be traded like any stock—as long as you had the money to play the market. The evidence Betty left at the Pickwick would make Lester a hero, whatever he'd been doing with Filipino Charlie and Wong before Martini entered the picture. Helen's country-club membership was secure.

She walked to Union Square on a day when the sun came out, smelling the pancakes from Sears, smiling at the doormen at the St. Francis and Sir Francis. She admired the saint and preferred to drink with the rogue. She admired the hamburgers at Original Joe's on Taylor Street even more.

City of Paris was offering a hat like Hildy Johnson's from *His Girl Friday*, not quite as extreme. Nice shade of green, went well with auburn hair. Shall I send it to Mademoiselle? No, Mademoiselle will wear it out, thank you. $17.95, in cash. Extravagant, but what the hell. She'd be working again soon.

Almost a week. Rick kidded her that he'd run her at Tanforan, even odds. She smelled salt water on the breeze through the window, and took a walk or three to Chinatown.

The red pagoda architecture curved upward in a smile, warmed by the sun, who'd been making regular appearances. Laundry hanging from the windows of the Chinese newspaper office, the smells from the Far Eastern Bakery, rice and fish and exotic lychee fruit, the small streets humming with people, the ache of the Chinese violin on a street corner. She missed Chinatown.

Quick hike up the hill at Sacramento, no wind, breathing fine. The herb shop shut up and boarded, sign in Chinese. The English below said CLOSED UNTIL FURTHER NOTICE. She wondered what they'd nailed him on. She'd been out of it for too long. Time to call Gonzales.

The Chinese playground was full of black-haired children playing jump rope and hopscotch, boys yelling, girls screaming. Benny Goodman blaring from open doors, the seedy hotels still looking like they were leftovers from the '06 cleanup, but somehow not as seedy as they'd been a couple of weeks before.

Everywhere Miranda went, people smiled at her. Men tipped their hats, women nodded. No-Legs handed her a flower one day, then shoved off on his dirty plywood board. Fong Fong for a quick dessert, on the house for you, Miss, compliments of the management.

The Twin Dragon found her a private booth when she wanted one, served up ten-cent martinis to her and Rick when she convinced him to take her out that night. Sun or moonlight, Chinatown recognized her. And thanked her.

She was nearly well. Memories faded to patterns, chintz or calico. Sometimes red on white, sometimes in her dreams, when she woke up in a sweat, and told herself it was over, over again, except the record was stuck and she couldn't move it forward. *Clack. Clack clack.*

Miranda Corbie, Private Investigator, had offers of employment waiting for her at her office, had money in the bank, her cheek firm and sculpted again, her health restored. It was over.

Except it wasn't.

There was still Emily Takahashi.

22nd of February. Nielsen was as happy as he could be. Miranda was off the leash as of tomorrow. Decided to stretch her legs a little early.

She took the Sutter Street White Front down to Little Osaka, and walked into Matsumara's shoe store to pick up the sunburst pumps.

A young man was at the counter. Mr. Matsumara would be right with her. He disappeared into the back.

She looked around and waited. A few new pairs of pumps, some men's patched work boots. Matsumura, wiping his hands on a leather apron, his broad face beaming at her.

"Miss Corbie—so good to see you! Back for your pumps, are you?"

"Best deal in San Francisco."

His grin grew broader, and he bent down to the shelves inside the counter, pulling out a box with her shoes. "I'll throw in Matsumara's free detection kit. The Japanese Sherlock Holmes."

She laughed. "You been busy?"

"Not so busy as you. I've read about you, young lady. Aren't you supposed to be recuperating up in Calistoga?"

"Is that what they're saying?"

He opened a paper bag with a snap, and laid the box inside. "They say you foiled a human smuggling racket. Not much on the details, though."

She lowered her voice. "You know more than most. What's happened with the Takahashis?"

He shook his head sadly. "They searched the store, closed it down, and now, I think, Hiro is selling it. Or rather, his wife or his sister is selling it. He's in a home. They can't care for him anymore." He looked down at the counter, pretending to examine a pair of shoes, and kept his voice to a whisper. "Or maybe won't care for him. They need money. The milkman tells me they're at each other's throats."

Miranda thought it over, turned it around, trying to get a fresh angle. "Still no word about Emily?"

Small pause while he fiddled with the leather. "Not a thing. Rose has been beside herself, especially when she read the papers, saw a little of what you were involved in. But not even a murmur, Miss Corbie. It's like the girl has vanished."

She frowned. "Eddie gave his sister a lot of money, Mr. Matsumara. Money that no one's found yet. Don't you think if the Takahashis knew where she was, they'd take that money and use it? Especially now?"

He thought it over, his fingers absentmindedly polishing the uppers of the green pumps in front of him.

"It would seem so, Miss Corbie. Japanese people have a great deal of pride. We keep things in the family, and we protect the family. So it would depend . . . if using that money put Emily in jeopardy, then Mrs. Takahashi would never do it. Whatever she knew of Eddie's involvement, whatever other guilt she may have . . . she wouldn't put her daughter in danger."

"But surely—she'll know Emily is safe now?"

He shrugged again, and turned the green shoes over to look at the heels.

"She might not think so. Are all the criminals involved caught? Are they all in prison? Of course not. How safe do you think Emily will be?"

"At this point I think she's safer coming forward. There's risk in hiding, too. Easier to erase someone who won't be missed."

"Maybe. You know they have relatives in Burlingame."

"Rose mentioned that to me. Think that's a good place to start?"

He stared at Miranda for a moment. "You're determined to find her, are you?"

She stared back. "Yes, Mr. Matsumara. I am."

He turned his attention back to the pumps. "Then I think Burlingame would be an excellent place to start."

She nodded. "Thanks. And thanks for the shoes."

He looked up, grinning at her. "Saver of souls and heels, that's what I am, Miss Corbie." He winked, and she smiled. Another woman was walking in the shop holding a pair of rain boots.

Miranda took the bag, threw him a wave, and walked out the door. Past the closed and boarded Takahashi Tailors. Closed and boarded. Just like Ming Chen's.

She stood in front of it, lighting a Chesterfield, inhaled it slowly, savoring the taste.

And wondered how Matsumara knew where Emily Takahashi was, and why he was lying about it.

Thirty-one

The elevator was out at 640 Mason Street.

She was walking up the stairs, the climb feeling good on her calves, when she met a man in a light gabardine coat walking down. She looked up.

Gonzales.

Their eyes met, and she paused, her hand on the banister.

"Inspector."

"Miss Corbie."

He was still wearing a bandage on his nose. Looked ridiculous under the expensive brown fedora.

"Were you trying to see me?"

"Yes, as a matter of fact."

"Would you like to come up?"

"If you're not busy . . ."

"Not at all."

Formalities exchanged, they walked wordlessly up the next two flights together, Miranda breathing only a little harder than normal. He lingered behind her while she walked to number 405, inserted the key, and opened the door. Turned around to Gonzales, said: "Come in, please."

They were both standing in the small entranceway. Awkward, uncomfortable. He was staring at her, intensity in the line of his body.

"Can I take your coat?"

"Thank you."

He stepped out of it. Dressed like an advertisement for the successful young executive in a dark brown suit, white shirt, and rust-colored tie. She hung his coat and hat in the closet with hers. Gestured to the living room, the sofa next to the occasional table with the small Bakelite radio and cigarettes on top. Said: "Have a seat, Inspector."

He took the large wingback chair across from the couch. Sat with his arms on the chair arms, his fingers in a loose, relaxed fist.

"May I get you something? A drink? Coffee?"

"No, thank you."

She sank into the soft pillows of the sofa, leaned back against the green embroidered fabric. Took a Chesterfield out of the table pack. Gonzales jumped up with a match, struck it. She took his hand and held it to her cigarette, puffed, looked up at him briefly, let go. He retreated back to the chair. She crossed her legs, inhaled deeply. Looked at him.

"Thanks."

He cleared his throat. "I would have come to see you sooner, but I didn't want to interfere. With your rest."

"That was considerate of you."

He leaned forward. "Miranda, I—"

"I was going to phone you today."

"About what?"

"Catching up. Had a few questions. D'you mind?"

He stared at her for a moment, then took out his cigarette case, one of his gold-tipped French sticks. Lit it with another match. Exhaled toward the window.

"Ask away."

"I'm curious about the dramatis personae. Gillio, Filipino Charlie, Ming . . . what's the shakedown?"

He looked at his cigarette, inhaled again. "Ming's in jail, waiting trial. Charged with drug smuggling. Not everything in those herbal jars was Chinese medicine, at least of the legal type. He was an outlet for the drugs."

"What happened to his old man?"

Gonzales shrugged slightly. "I don't know, Miss Corbie. He hasn't been charged, if that's what you mean."

"What about Filipino Charlie?"

The inspector shook his head. "The statements, shipping documents, and receipts Wong delivered through Betty left Charlie out of it. Probably part of the Winters deal. And they only dealt with the human trafficking, not the drugs. I think he and Charlie were hoping to resume the opium and cocaine trade—on a smaller scale than when Martini was involved—as soon as Winters got Martini out of the picture."

"So Charlie's free? Even though I've got Betty's own words to implicate him?"

Gonzales stared at the window. "You know how it is, Miranda."

"Yeah. I know how it is."

He took a long drag, looked at her. "I can't help what the system is. The DA thinks it's better not to go after Charlie. He's scared now, knows we're watching him."

"Does the DA plan to charge Gillio, or is he getting free overnights at the Olympic Hotel?"

Gonzales smoked in silence. She watched the blue-gray smoke curl and twist, then vanish through the window. Cars outside, a woman laughing. Rumble of the White Front up the street. No music. Not today.

There was a glass ashtray on the table next to him. He rubbed out the gold tip until it crumbled.

"There's not enough evidence on Gillio."

"How much fucking evidence do you need? I heard Romano talk about him with Martini—Martini thought Gillio had set up a hit. Romano was there, goddamn it!"

"We can't find him, Miranda. He skipped."

More silence. She rose from the sofa, walked to the window looking out over Mason Street.

"Maybe he was warned. You think about that, Gonzales?"

"Yes. I've thought about it."

She flung around, flushed, her eyes sharp. "Then what the hell are you doing about it?"

The sigh rose from his depths, poured itself on the floor. The hand wiping his forehead was trembling.

"Look. I came here to check on you. I was worried. Leave the rest alone."

Miranda watched him, her arms folded. Waited a few seconds. Picked up the deck of Chesterfields, lit another cigarette. This time he didn't stand up.

"What about Noldano and Capella? And the others. They talk?"

"Capella's still in the hospital. The rest aren't talking. At least not yet."

She nodded, walked back to the sofa, sat. "L.A. is cooperating, I expect."

"Better than the federals. They're very nervous about Japan."

"About not offending them, I suppose?"

"Of course."

"Is Betty in the clear?"

"Yes. Officially and publicly."

"I suppose Winters is, too."

His smile was wry. "Publicly, yes. Officially, yes. Unofficially, he was a smuggler, and we're paying some attention to Mrs. Winters's attorney."

She stared at him. He looked at his shoes. She said: "Any ideas about the old man? The one they ran over?"

"Probably Coppa. The car was registered in his name. Martini must have phoned Noldano and Capella, they drove up overnight, and when he found out Eddie Takahashi had died in front of a private detective, he set them on you. Couldn't take a chance—Eddie may've told you something about the money."

He shook his head. "They won't admit to it, of course. Stroke of genius, about the green cars. One hid the other. People remember color more than they remember anything else."

Miranda took a deep drag on the stick. Said it conversationally. "What about Eddie Takahashi?"

Gonzales raised his eyebrows. "We've assumed that one of Martini's men killed him."

"And his sister?"

He leaned forward. "Either she's skipped town or was murdered."

"She hasn't been murdered. At least not by Martini's gang, not by Wong. That leaves Gillio and Charlie. I think she's alive."

He studied at the floor. Neither spoke. Miranda looked at her Chesterfield. Watched the light breeze puff the curtains.

Gonzales's voice was heavy. "Are you going to look for her?"

"Yes."

He nodded, slowly. "I wish you luck."

"Thanks." She studied him, the play of color on his face, the thin film of stubble on his chin and neck.

"You might consider a vacation, Inspector."

"No time. I am temporarily in charge of homicide, until—"

"What happened to Phil?" Her voice was quick, urgent. Guilty.

He looked at her. "I thought you knew. Early retirement."

The smoke blew upward toward the window. A taxi honked outside, two men shouting. Then quiet.

"A little sudden."

"Not really."

More silence. Gonzales tried to smooth his trousers, but they were smooth already. Church bells started to ring the hour, the sound drifting in, the smoke drifting out. One bell, two bell. Her stomach growled.

Gonzales's eyes were on her. Not hiding. He said: "Why do you do it?"

She looked at him. "Is that what you came here to ask me?"

"Yes."

She thought for a minute. Cast around for an explanation, a reason, a defense. Merry-go-round of memory, funhouse follies, step right up, lady, it's your life and for only one thin dime. Incubator babies on a man-made island of make-believe, pickpockets and burlesque queens, Laughing Sal and a firing squad. Bombed-out villages. Kids with no books and no food and no hope. Twisted fields, black with bullets, black with bodies. Dry farms, dusty, dead. Boots, always marching. Always marching.

And Johnny. Always Johnny, the sun in his hair, always in his hair, not needing the sun, he was his own sun, and she was the moon, and together they made the cosmos. Johnny.

Miranda said: "Because I can."

Gonzales rubbed his chin and his cheek as if they were dirty. Reached into his jacket pocket, took out the Baby Browning and her trick cigarette case.

"You might need this. But get a license for it."

She hadn't expected to see it again. Stood up. Took it from his hands. His were trembling again.

"Thank you."

He rose, looking everywhere except her face. "Please let me know if you find the Takahashi girl."

"You know I will." She walked with him toward the doorway. "I want Eddie's name cleared. He gave his life for hers. For those other women."

"That will be more up to the press than to us. But I believe you have connections in that area."

She was taking out his coat, and turned around to a crooked smile that made her stomach tighten. Goddamn it. She handed him the coat and the fedora. And reached a hand out to touch his bandaged nose.

He flinched. She drew her hand back, took a step closer.

"I'm—sorry, Inspector. Mark. Thank you for saving my life."

She held out her hand. Gonzales took it, enveloped it in warmth. "You saved your own, Miranda. You always do."

He held it to his lips. Their eyes locked for a few seconds, until he turned away and walked out the door, closing it softly behind him.

She was hungry. Gonzales bothered her. Too much goddamn rest. She needed to work again.

The weather was still balmy for late February, the Bay wind gentle for a change. Miranda walked to Chinatown, bypassing her usual stroll down Grant for the outskirts on Kearny. Even here, Chinese lanterns hung from windows and doors, more than she'd seen since the Rice Bowl Party. Since Eddie's death.

Even the run-down International Hotel on Kearny and Jackson looked spruced up and ready for a rhumba. Another holiday, maybe. Every day was a holiday in San Francisco, the jewel of the Bay. The City that knew how to do everything but quit.

Little Manila clung to life next to the International, serving Filipino food and American gambling in the back. The small nightclub stayed open all night, and so did the crap games. If Filipino Charlie wasn't hiding in South City, he'd be here, overseeing the numbers game, tightening up his business.

The planted palm trees flanking the doors needed watering. Miranda felt one of the leaves, smelled hamburgers and grilled meat, spices, and Filipino egg rolls, her stomach doing backflips.

She lit a Chesterfield to cut the hunger pains, pushed open the double doors. Little Manila was too cheap to pay a doorman. Dark spilled out on the gum-spotted sidewalk, the inside light lingering in the kitchen but dead before reaching the dining room. Better if you don't see what you're eating. Charlie was known for good food and Mickey Finns, the kind of place where you'd walk in at three in the morning and wake up on a boat to Guam two days later. She wasn't surprised that he was involved in drug smuggling, just that he'd teamed up against Martini to begin with.

Small-timer with big ambition, limited vision, no spine. But an opportunist was Filipino Charlie.

She approached the bar, asked for a bourbon straight up. Straight liquor in a dive, never let them add water. Water could kill you.

The barman looked at her, kept looking at her. There were three other people on stools. Two old Oriental men and another white woman, somewhere in her forties or older. She was throwing back shots like she needed inoculation.

Miranda tossed a couple of quarters on the table. Nodded her head to the bartender.

He arrived with the drink. She let it sit by her elbow, untouched. Said: "Charlie in?"

He wiped the counter down, yelled to the woman at the other end: "Y'want another one?"

She shook her head, her hat with the beaded veil swinging. He turned back to Miranda.

"Who the hell are you, lady?"

So Charlie was home. "Miranda Corbie. He'll know the name."

The confidence shook his resolve. Not much of a bartender, still less of a bouncer. He disappeared into the back, through the kitchen. The old men sucked down their gin, hoping he'd get back before the nipple went dry. The woman was already lost in her own dreams, where she'd always be twenty-five and the men wore mustaches and knew how to treat a lady.

Miranda smelled the bourbon. Maybe she was getting old, maybe her stomach wasn't up to it yet, or maybe that goddamn Nielsen had her scared. She'd save herself for a drink at Twin Dragon or Forbidden City or China Clipper. Chewed on the Chesterfield instead. And took the .22 out of her purse and shoved it in her pocket.

The doors pushed open, sharp light cutting through the darkness. A small figure, man in a fedora, suit too big. A voice she'd heard before.

"Well, well. If it ain't the tomato. You still lonely, lady? Anything I can do?"

She turned around on the stool to face the shiv kid from Fong Fong. The one who knew Eddie—and Eddie's sister.

"Yeah. Tell Charlie I'm here to see him, and I'm a little goddamn tired of waiting around."

He fingered his pencil mustache. Hitched up his baggy pants. Started to say something.

"Listen, sonny. I'm here to see Charlie. It's about Emily Takahashi. Run tell your boss. He knows who I am."

Red face. Angry eyes. "I ain't a kid, lady, don't make no mistakes."

Her mouth twitched. "Make 'em all the time—sonny. Find Charlie before your pants fall down."

He stalked off, muttering to himself, also disappearing into the kitchen. She was through with the games, cut to the end, the happy ending. The final scene. Find Emily Takahashi.

Bartender came back out. Walked to the stool. Said, "This way."

He led her on a circuitous route through back doors, small, dingy rooms half-heartedly decorated, a tiny stage and a bare microphone, and finally down some wooden steps, through another door and into the basement.

Small card table, three men sitting, the shiv kid standing. The man in the middle Filipino Charlie.

He was fat, sweaty, fifty. Wiped his forehead with a dirty yellow hanky. Suit was bright blue, big buttons, white shoes with scuff marks. A cheap, loud lowlife, grubbing along the bottom of the chain until a big fish pulled him up. No wonder he turned on Wong.

He tried to put importance in his voice. Didn't succeed.

"You want to see me?"

She walked to the table, looking at the tired muscle around him. Please, lady, they said with their eyes, don't make us get up from the game.

"How much money did Eddie Takahashi get from Winters?"

Charlie dropped his hand on the table. The thickset man with the mismatched hat sighed, pulled his chair back.

"Who are you?"

The shiv kid piped up, venomous tones. "She's that Corbie broad. Fishing around about Emily Takahashi. I seen her before, at Fong Fong."

Miranda smiled, dropped her cigarette, and stamped it out with two quick motions. "You like your ice cream sundaes, don't you, kid?"

He turned red again, then white, then faded back to the dark. She said to Charlie: "You know who the hell I am. No games. I want to know two things: How much money Eddie gave his sister, and who killed him."

He stared at her, wiped his neck. Sweat was rolling off him. He stank of it.

"Why should I tell you anything?"

"You're not in good shape, Charlie. The cops are pulling the lid off, and they'll look at the bottom and find you. Might think you offed both brother and sister. If I find her—and if I recover the money—no murder case, not for Emily."

He licked his lips. "What about the dough?"

She shrugged. "If she's still got it, I see no problem turning over a little to you. Provided I find her."

"How much?"

She smiled again. "That's what I asked you, Charlie. How much was there?"

He looked hard at Miranda. She looked back. The other two men watched her, bored. No advisers for Charlie. None left. He searched the room for an answer, his fingers drumming on the table. Five card stud. Charlie showed a pair of ducks.

"Ten thousand dollars." The words blurted out of him. The other men woke up a little; the junior gangster gravitated toward the light.

She nodded. "Thanks. What about Eddie?"

He shook his head, an extra chin wobbling. "How much you getting back to us?"

"Two thousand."

"Not enough, lady."

"Three thousand."

"Still not enough."

She looked at her wristwatch. "OK. Five thousand, take it or leave it. I'm in a hurry."

He studied her again, swallowed some beer out of a bottle. "All right. You get the money, we get five thousand dollars."

"Agreed."

"We ain't killed Eddie Takahashi."

"You didn't order it?"

He glanced at the men beside him. "I ordered him to be beat up. An' he was. Up by the playground on Sacramento, an' some more in Ming's place. I ain't crazy, lady. I wanted that money. He knew where his sister was, wouldn't tell. Told us she had it, though. After a while."

He took another sip of beer.

"So Ming shot him?"

"Said he didn't. Don't know, lady, you just asked about us. Remember, we wanted Martini out, too. What he was doin' . . . wasn't right. Japan an' all."

"Yeah. I know all about your patriotism, Charlie."

He looked up at her. "You made a deal. You better stick."

"If I find the money."

He grunted, looked down at the card game. "You find the girl, you find the money."

She left them to finish it. Turned around at the foot of the steps. One of the button men had a pair of jacks. Charlie was watching him pick up the money. The shiv kid was staring at her.

Thirty-two

Chow mein and chop suey at the China Clipper. She used to watch the planes land in the lagoon in the early evening, the silver cigar flashing in the twilight, splashing water on the tourists and fairgoers, mouths open at the beauty man could make.

She asked the waitress about the lanterns. They were everywhere, all different shapes and varieties.

"Lantern Festival, lady. Last day of New Year tomorrow. Full moon. Night for lovers."

She chewed on an egg roll. Night for lovers. How many nights had she seen, had she smelled, had she tasted on her tongue, sweet, bitter, sad?

The food filled the ache in her stomach. Appetite still not exactly right. What she needed was some Old Taylor or Old Crow or old bourbon of any type. What she had was lukewarm tea. She stared into the bottom of the cup.

The leaves wouldn't talk.

No Rick, no Moderne, no club, no bourbon. Radio instead. Merry-go-round of Music. Better than memory, always better. Around and around, music on the radio, big bands, small sets, a tinkling piano from a music store. News, Fulton Lewis. Always a man's voice, a man telling the world to be cautious, to be frightened, to be calm and forget their troubles, to face the music and dance.

Men's voices. Shouting in German. Men's voices. Shouting in Japanese. Men's voices. Dying next to the women. Women left alone, women stranded, women homeless, women with no place to go.

She fell asleep in the chair, the radio on. Woke to a low hum early in the morning, gray and pink light making the apartment glow like a dimly lit circus tent.

Time for the last act.

Roy was downstairs, Adam's apple bobbing, nervously grinning. Hailed a taxi for her to the Hotel Bo-Chow. Eddie's old apartment in South Park.

The district straddled the Southern Pacific depot and the piers, offering short-term and sometimes long-term homes to Japanese and Filipinos, the old Japantown of the prewar, pre-Earthquake days. The driver was a taciturn man, but traffic was light. No time to talk, even if they both felt like it.

Hotel Bo-Chow stood taller than its neighbors, four stories and on a corner, brightly colored signs in Japanese and English. A restaurant and general store waited on the bottom floor, a souvenir shop and Biwako Baths the nearest neighbors. Twenty years ago, it had been a good place to stay for travelers. Now it was just a place to stay.

Miranda rang the bell. A man came out of the general store holding a broom.

"You want something?"

"Young man lived here. Eddie Takahashi. He was killed."

His forehead creased. He said slowly: "You police?"

"No. Private detective."

He looked her up and down, looked up at the windows of the hotel. "Lady, that room is rented."

She was holding a fifty-cent piece. "You sure?"

He looked at the money in her hand, looked at her.

"Rented."

Turned around and went back inside the store.

Miranda stared up at the facade, the arched windows on the second story, the nods to an Italian villa in the detail.

Eddie had lived here, struck out on his own, feeling his independence.

Away from the family, the shop, the mausoleum on Wilmot Street. Slept here, ate here, brought girls here, filled with the noise and the excitement of eighteen, independent, the world his and anything in it. No failure, no worry, no self-doubt in eighteen. No death.

She lit a cigarette, walked farther down South Park, imagining him running the numbers for Charlie, taking crisp dollar bills back home, giving some to his sister. Then more money, less numbers, and drugs. Cocaine, opium, heroin. And maybe Eddie's innocence began to crack open, the ugliness of the world spilling out. Putrid, decaying. And then Martini, and women, women like the ones he'd grown up with in Chinatown, women his sister's age and younger, some almost his mother's age, women he could speak to a little, women his sister could speak to. The filthy animals of his mother's imagination.

And something snapped in Eddie. Snapped decisively, like a soldier at war, faced with the choice, kill or be killed. But he didn't think about it. Still eighteen. Still innocent. Innocent enough.

She stood outside the souvenir shop, looking in the windows. Most of the shops weren't open yet.

Somewhere in the world, his sister was hiding. Alone, mourning, terrified. Cut off. Half alive. Somewhere where Matsumara had discovered her, and decided to keep her secret. Somewhere that wasn't Burlingame.

Miranda inhaled the cigarette, sending a stream toward the souvenir shop window. Her eyes fell to a framed, hand-tinted postcard.

A curved bridge reflected in a still pool filled with goldfish and water lilies. Surrounding it, cherry, plum, and quince trees. Large stones, covered in moss. Bonsai plants. In the distance, a brightly colored, two-story gate.

The bottom of the postcard read, WISHING POOL. JAPANESE TEA GARDEN, GOLDEN GATE PARK.

She was at the gate when they opened at ten. Wandered the paths for a bit, gripping the bamboo rails, marveling at the camellias and Japanese maples. Clean air, fragrant. Peaceful.

Miranda found the bridge in the photo, leaned over it. Watched the large goldfish dart through the water, their black freckles as big as her palm. Some of the cherry trees were in blossom already. One thousand trees, so the pamphlet claimed. All planted by the Hagiwaras, the family who founded and still tended the garden.

The thatched teahouse blended with the trees at the eastern gate. Wisteria clung to a lattice-work arbor on one side, the fragrance still potent in the gray, foggy morning, the smell of green tea mixing with the wisteria and jasmine.

Miranda studied the layout, the tea service. Only three other customers.

She sat near the front. The tables were all made from tree trunks. She felt the wood with both palms, rubbing the surface. Smoothed with time, effort of hands.

Girls in kimonos, neatly sashed, hair sleek and pulled back in buns, approached with trays.

The girl nearest her was tall, graceful for her age, a little younger than the rest. About sixteen or seventeen. She brought a tray to Miranda, setting a small china pot of green tea in front of her, along with a dish of delicate rice cakes. She smiled at Miranda, then faltered.

Miranda said: "It's time to go home, Emily."

The lanterns were lit by five o'clock. Now, in the dark, the narrow streets hummed, throbbed, the full moon yellow and large, wearing a knowing grin on its face. Not competing with Chinatown, not tonight.

Girls of marriageable age giggled in groups. Children read the riddles tacked to the lanterns, brows wrinkled, asking their mothers to help them solve the puzzle. Families headed for dinner out, part of the streets tonight, part of the world.

A party for Chinatown, not in the Hearst papers, not in the Chamber of Commerce. Ancient celebration, tradition, mixed with the ubiquitous jazz music from the juke joints and phonographs, the smell of rice balls and hamburgers mixing in the chilled, moist air of the city.

The Lantern Festival. The night for lovers.

Miranda walked to the door in Salty Fish Alley. The acupuncture shop across the street was closed, the little boy probably forgetting his comic book in the excitement of the festival.

36 Wentworth. She knocked on the door. Nodded to the girl in the cloak and hat beside her.

The door opened after the second time. Frank Lee, his hair pomaded and gelled, dressed for an evening on the saxophone at Forbidden City. He looked at her, about to speak, then saw the girl next to her. He took a step backward, fist to his mouth. Eyes suddenly wet.

Miranda held Emily by the arm. And walked in the door.

She let the reunion play out. Watched them, watched Frank hold her, her young body melting into his. Not the love of friends, lifelong companions, not the lust of blood and youth. This was the shop-worn cliché of love, the catch of the breath, the not having to speak, the constant pleasure of looking, of seeing, of hearing. Of being.

Miranda lit a cigarette. Waited until the tears were wiped, the bodies embraced. And asked: "Where's your father, Frank?"

He looked down at Emily, looked back up at her. "Why—why do you want my father?"

Her eyes were steady. "I think you know why."

Thud on the staircase. Upstairs. Footsteps. Slow, heavy. He'd been listening.

They waited in silence, Chinese boy holding Japanese girl. Miranda inhaled the Chesterfield. Blew a smoke ring toward the staircase.

Feet visible first, traditional shoes, traditional trousers, traditional smock. Old man's face, twisted with traditional hate.

A stream of Mandarin poured out of him. Frank withstood it at first, Emily shrinking into him, both of them diminishing under the onslaught. Finally, he stared at the floor. Then the old man turned to Miranda.

"You there—what are you doing in my home?"

She dropped some ash on the floor. "That depends."

Red-face, full of fury, eyes swallowed in folds of anger. Down the rest of the stairs, flinging himself at her.

"What do you mean, coming in my house—"

"I mean to find out which of you killed Eddie Takahashi."

Silence. Red and white on the old man's face. Red and white. Like Martini. He stumbled backward. Blind.

Frank squeezed Emily's arms, pushed her away. Turned to Miranda.

"I shot him."

"Why?"

"He was—no good. He was smuggling drugs. Women. I wanted to protect Emily."

Miranda stared at Frank until he dropped his eyes.

"It won't do you any good to protect him. Emily already told me the truth. We had a long talk out in front of that giant red-and-black Buddha in the tea garden. Your father shot Eddie. I just wanted to see how much of a bastard he really is."

She turned toward the old man. "I saw you screaming at Ming's father in the herb shop. I figure you were trying to keep him quiet. I don't need your son to testify against you."

He took another step backward, making contact with the banister. Backed up again, not looking at her, and sat down slowly on the second step.

Miranda dropped the cigarette, rubbed it out with her toe, and faced Frank. "Eddie gave his sister the money, went into hiding. Charlie's men found him, beat him, trying to find out where it was. He made it down from the playground to Ming's shop, badly hurt. Ming was part of the smuggling game. Eddie asked him to call you up, figuring his sister was right where she was— with you. You both ran down to the herbalist."

The old man held his head in his hands, starting to whimper. Frank looked over at him, turned back to Miranda.

"Yeah. I did. And I brought a gun and shot Eddie with it."

She shook her head. "No. Your father followed you both. Dishonor, he called it. First your music, your band, and now a Japanese girl. The Rising Sun conquering his own family. He found all three of you, you and Emily making plans to run away with the money. To elope . . . as Eddie intended."

Frank's eyes filled with tears again, his voice hoarse. "No . . . I—I shot him."

"Goddamn it, Frank. It won't do him any good, not now. Look at him."

His father was clutching himself, wrapped tight. Trying not to let it in. Inhuman noises escaped from his lips.

"He cursed all of you, like he always did. And like you always did, you tried to reason, to accommodate, to be the good son. And then he raised the revolver. And fired at you. His own child."

The girl was clutching Frank now, sobs racking her body. He held her, stroking her hair.

"Eddie stepped in front of you. Saved your life, Frank. Japanese for Chinese, in the face of your father's hatred. In the middle of the Rice Bowl Party."

A wail rose from the figure on the steps, a cry for help, for deliverance, escaping to the ceiling, fighting its way out. Nowhere to go. Miranda walked toward him, staring down at the old man.

"Chinese and Japanese. Nanking and Nippon. War, war, always war. Pathetic old bastards. Pathetic old world."

She turned to Frank and the girl. "Emily told me it was your idea to hide her in plain sight with the Hagiwaras, but she didn't tell me what you did with the money. That was ten thousand dollars Eddie gave you. For a wedding present."

The couple looked at each other. Frank said, in a low voice: "It was stupid of me. But I couldn't—I couldn't use the money. That night, I—I threw it in the Rice Bowl flag. All of it, a thousand at a time."

Miranda smiled wryly, lit another cigarette. "What about the gun?"

Emily spoke. "One of the ponds, Miss Corbie. At the garden."

Miranda nodded. "Let's hope it rusts."

The old man was sobbing now. She opened her purse, took out her billfold. Peeled out two hundred dollars. Held it out to Emily.

"Here. Take this, and get the hell out of San Francisco."

"But . . . that's your own money—"

"Not exactly. Extra funds, by way of your brother. Take it, go away. Get married. I'll make sure word gets around that the ten thousand found its way home. Not that they'll believe me. Go on."

He looked over at his father. "What about—are you going to the police? I can't—"

"The police think a gangster killed Eddie. Given a choice between getting justice for his murder and exonerating his reputation—or making sure his sister has a happy life—I think you know which choice Eddie would make. I won't go against it."

They looked at her, the specter of the old man fading away from them, the red lantern light outside playing on their faces. Exquisite ache.

The kind of love buried and born from separation, hurting. Rising again like a Phoenix. Time apart wasn't time, didn't count, didn't matter, impotent to stop them. As impotent as death.

Miranda watched them hold each other, his hand stroking Emi's hair. She thought of Madame Pengo, the strange harsh voice reciting the evil of fathers and sons. But maybe the old lady was right. Maybe there would be some salvation after all.

Emily held out her hand, taking Miranda's. "Miss Corbie—I don't know why you've done what you've done—but I think we can be at peace now. All of us. Thank you."

She patted the girl's shoulder, and opened the door, walking out into the moonlight.

Why did she do it, he asked, and she thought about it, walking home through the lanterns on every door, yellow moon light and red lantern light warming the frigid Bay air, laughter in the streets of Chinatown.

Because of Eddie Takahashi. All the Eddie Takahashis.

She looked up at the moon, hanging in the cloudless, midnight sky. Reflecting the sun, nearly as bright. As bright as red Spanish earth on a summer afternoon.

She did what she did because she could. And that was enough.

Three months later, Miranda got a telegram from Portland, announcing the wedding of Frank Lee and Emily Takahashi. She sent a congratulatory note from Treasure Island. By then she was back on the Gayway, rousing the dips and the hustlers, the grifters who drifted in with the seaweed and foam, working the Magic City on San Francisco Bay.

May of 1940.

Spring before the storm.

Author's Note

The San Francisco of *City of Dragons* was a much different city than what we know today. More working and middle-class, smaller, cozier, slower, it would soon abandon the false optimism of the Golden Gate International Exposition—the San Francisco World's Fair—for the booming economy of world war.

Despite many changes since 1940, some of the places in *City of Dragons* are still with us. Chinatown, in particular, hasn't changed as much as other neighborhoods . . . you can still glimpse the faded neon of the old Golden Star radio sign, and lean against the same wall Miranda does when she first spots the green car. Miranda's apartment building is still there, as is the Monadnock, where she keeps her office. If you travel to San Francisco, you can still stay in The Pickwick Hotel and eat at John's Grill.

When I write about this period, I try my best to construct a time machine. I listen to the music, buy menus and matchbooks on eBay, watch films, listen to radio shows. All of the businesses mentioned were real, and so were the addresses. Even the phone exchanges were the actual phone numbers in 1940, thanks to a copy of a San Francisco AT&T directory I was able to locate.

My hope is that these layers of authenticity will make *City of Dragons* and subsequent novels come alive for you in the same way that they live in my mind . . . fully, richly, with the sounds, smells, sights and aura of the era.

I hope you'll explore the world of *City of Dragons* on my Web site, http://www.kellistanley.com, and in further stories about Miranda Corbie. Thanks for reading . . . and see you in 1940 San Francisco.